FOUR MEALS FROM ANARCHY

DUNCAN ROBB

Believe it or not, this is a work of fiction.
The characters, the things they do,
the places they go, what they think and how they act,
are all a product of the author's overactive imagination.
Any resemblance to real people or events
is pure coincidence,
and quite frankly a minor miracle

To Frances
soul mate, best friend and loving partner

Contents

A Sobering Thought

Julius Weitzdörfe, who studies "Black Spy Hazards" at Cambridge University's Centre for the Study of Existential Risk, said a previous study by MI5 had estimated the country is "four meals away from anarchy" because looting would erupt and civil order would start to break down as soon as people had eaten what they had in their cupboards and fridges. Variations of the quote have been attributed to Lenin and the sci-fi writers Larry Niven and Jerry Pournelle. The original quote seems to have come from Alfred Henry Lewis back in 1896 who wrote "The only barrier between us and anarchy, is the last nine meals we've had" .

PROLOGUE

The cable writhed and twisted like an evil serpent in its death throes. The inner metal wires curled in on each other, and different materials expanded and contracted at different rates, the copper pushing out, the zinc alloy pulling in. Some elements fused together; others pushed apart. Sparks jumped between the strands of wire, the heat grew intense, the metal braiding glowed red hot and the outer PVC casing slowly melted, dissolving into a muddy liquid and evaporating as an acrid black smoke.

Viktor Volkov and Dmitry Egorichev watched in ghoulish fascination from behind the half-inch-thick glass screen. They couldn't smell the smoke or hear the wires popping as the heat eventually caused them to crumble. All they could do was watch. For five minutes, they said nothing, eyes wide, mouths gaping as the scene played out. From the moment Viktor pressed the activation button to the last whisper of smoke being sucked out by the extractor fan, it had only taken three hundred seconds for six feet of data cable to be reduced to a black stain on the white resin floor of the chamber. After months of experiments, after trying hundreds of radical algorithms, after one failure following another, it had worked. They had developed a virus that would hide inside software until activated, then physically destroy the cables connecting computers, processors or whatever they targeted. They turned to each other and high-fived, grinning like a pair of naughty schoolboys.

They were a little older than schoolboys, Viktor 29, Dmitry 28, but they behaved as if they were ten years younger. They'd been hacking into computer systems for over ten years and creating viruses for most of that time, viruses that had already caused damage conservatively estimated in the tens of millions of US dollars. Their notoriety had brought them to the attention, firstly of organised crime leaders, then the SVR, who discovered them while breaking up the gang the two geeks had found themselves working for. Initially, the SVR dismissed Viktor and Dmitry as a couple of computer nerds, clever but ultimately harmless. It was only when the intelligence agency delved deeper into the activities of the two young men that their true genius was realised, and they were put to work on behalf of the State.

To Mecheslav Medvedev, the head of the computer infiltration programme, they were his prize possession, and he guarded them jealously. He handled them like a protective uncle, giving them anything they wanted, denying them nothing and attending to their every need. Not that they required much; neither drank, smoked or took drugs, they ate little and showed no enthusiasm for the women he supplied. He arranged adjoining apartments for them in a brand-new luxury development in the Arbat district, a popular area for government employees. They were chauffeured to the office every day as neither of them drove, and they rarely went out. They had little contact with their families; it was their choice, and they were content, or even thrilled, to spend long days in front of a computer screen or experimenting with specialist equipment, experimental systems and sophisticated instruments. Medvedev was astonished at the speed they acquired new skills The office he assigned to them was more like a laboratory and provided they had a regular supply of fresh coffee, the two of them would work late into the night or the small hours of the next day, making few demands on him or his staff other than a hunger for new challenges or a fresh target. Their brief was simple: develop new ways to attack Western intelligence and create maximum infrastructure damage, with particular emphasis on computer systems and commercial operations.

Dmitry was the first to identify the possibility of creating a computer virus that could do physical damage. Along with Viktor, he had devoted his efforts to software programmes that could be delivered by email to personal computers or direct injection into servers. They had proved highly effective and caused considerable embarrassment to government departments, utility companies and multi-national companies. But Dmitry wanted more. Their victims were fighting back;

security systems were more and more difficult to infiltrate and to make matters worse they were starting to trace the source of the viruses back to Russia. What really concentrated Dmitry's mind was the fact that however much damage he did, however much data his victims lost, they had developed backup systems and could restore the software within a few days. Reputations might suffer, and the Western press loved to highlight the failings of big business to protect the data it held but ultimately, everything was back to normal after a week.

Dmitry wanted more, he wanted to create lasting damage. He and Viktor had been the outstanding students in their class, leagues ahead of the others, they'd seen the disruption that a virus could do and got a vicarious satisfaction from seeing the headlines. It frustrated Dmitry that it was short-lived, and he knew he could do better. The pair recognised the weakness in most viruses. They relied on their victims to take some sort of action for the damage to be done. They needed to find a way to target specific devices at a time of their choosing and then deliver their virus, surgically inject it, in such a way that their victim would know nothing about it until it was activated. A sleeping bug, awaiting the command of its master. It was Viktor who came up with a name for it; it had to have a memorable name, and seeing it come back to life after lying dormant for a six-month trial, he called it Aurora, the sleeping beauty, if the name was good enough for Tchaikovsky it was good enough for him. He conveniently ignored the connection to Disney.

They watched a moment longer as the chamber cleared, three feet long, eighteen inches high and 12 inches deep, it had an hermetically sealed lid with a single outlet at the back connected to a 4-inch wide flexible rubber pipe that sucked the poisonous fumes through a series of filters, before venting them to the outside world. Viktor released the catches on the lid, opening it cautiously before prodding the remains of the cable with a steel ruler. 'We need to call Dracula and let him see this.'

Dmitry was still grinning at the effects of the virus. 'It might even put a smile on his face.' Medvedev rarely smiled, his dour demeanour and dark features made the nickname the two referred to him by almost inevitable.

Viktor made the call and ten minutes later Medvedev appeared in the doorway of the office, having crossed the courtyard from the admin building to their office. He shook the water off a lightweight raincoat and the two computer gurus realised from his appearance it must be raining outside. He threw the coat over the back of a chair and negotiated his way through the discarded boxes, spare chairs, desks and abandoned equipment to where they sat on stools. 'The message said you had something to show me.' He didn't make eye contact but stared at the empty chamber, brows furrowed. 'This had better be good.'

'This is better than good.' Dmitry responded.

'We think you're going to like this.' Viktor added.

Medvedev looked at each of them in turn, then back at the chamber. 'All I see is a pile of black dust, am I missing something?'

Dmitry held up a hand. 'We wanted you to see it from the start.' He nodded to Viktor who opened the lid of the chamber and dropped in another length of data cable, six feet of it tightly coiled and secured with a plastic clip. One end of the cable was plugged into the side of a smooth black box, a little smaller than a pack of cigarettes. Viktor closed the lid and fastened the catches to seal it tight.

Medvedev said nothing, his curiosity piqued and he stood between Dmitry and Viktor arms folded watching intently.

Viktor reached to his right and retrieved a matching black box, this one had a couple of buttons on it, one above the other, and two small LED lights, side by side at the top. Without a word, he held it up to show Medvedev, like a magician trying to convince his audience he had nothing up his sleeve. Dmitry nodded, giving Viktor the go-ahead.

Viktor pressed the uppermost button on the box, and the LED on the left lit up green, he waited a couple of seconds, glancing briefly at Medvedev to make sure his boss was watching. The LED turned red, and Viktor pressed the lower of the two buttons. The second LED illuminated two red lights.

Medvedev's eyes narrowed as he stared at the cable, nothing happened. He angled his head and turned to Viktor, he didn't have to speak, the look said everything.

'Keep watching.' Viktor was untroubled by the look.

There was no noise, the chamber was soundproof. There was no smell, the seal was airtight. It was brightly lit, and Medvedev could see clearly but nothing moved. He inched closer to the chamber and bent forward, his eyes inches from the glass, he thought he saw something. The smallest vibration, as if the cable shuddered. He glanced quickly at his two proteges, the faintest smile played on their faces.

Dmitry almost whispered. 'This is the best bit, watch closely.'

Medvedev was mesmerised, transfixed by the movements of the cable in the chamber. The coils had started to tighten on themselves as if shrinking. The vibration continued, still barely perceptible but constant. The dark blue PVC outer cable appeared to soften and gave off faint whisps of grey smoke.

Suddenly the cable jerked as if in spasm, it took on a life of its own. The coils were wrapped so tight that the cable looked like a rough dark blue ball, the whisps of smoke turned black, more intense, more malevolent.

As with the previous test, the cable went into its death throes, crumbling to dust, the PVC outer melting away like an ice cube in a red-hot frying pan.

Medvedev stood back, unable to take his gaze from the chamber. 'Good god boys.' He closed his eyes and shook his head trying to bring himself back to reality. 'You've done it.'

Dmitry winked at Viktor, who watched Medvedev's reaction with satisfaction, the two of them bumped fists behind their boss's back. They contained their enthusiasm, putting on a show of restrained cool, acting as if they'd done nothing more than learn how to boil the kettle.

Medvedev turned to Dmitry. 'So. Are you going to tell me how you made it work?'

Dmitry opened his mouth, about to answer when Viktor butted in. 'It's all done with ultra-high frequency vibration.'

He paused for breath giving Dmitry an opening. 'We played around with electromagnetic pulses: one on its own had no effect, but when we charged it with two at the same time we set up a resonance, a vibration.'

Viktor continued. 'The complicated bit was getting the pulses to peak at alternate times, if both peaked at the same time, it just vibrated, nothing more, but once we set it up so their wave patterns were opposed to each other, it started to generate heat.'

Dmitry cut across again. 'After that it was just a case of playing with the frequency bands to find the optimum level where the cable became so hot it melted.'

Medvedev was tired of looking left and right as they each spoke; he stood back to get them both in view at the same time. He wasn't sure he fully understood what they had just told him, but he was never going to admit it. His arms were folded across his chest, and he reached up with his left hand and stroked his short black beard thoughtfully. He studied them both without saying a word, eyes narrowed, lips pursed. What they had created could wreak so much damage it almost frightened him. Almost, but not enough for him not to immediately consider how he could use it.

Medvedev addressed his next question at a point halfway between Dmitry and Viktor, his eyes focused on the glass chamber. 'As a virus, it is unique, it has great potential. But......' He paused and looked at them, one at a time. 'But the question is how do we deliver it? How do we get it into the cabling and networks of an organisation we may wish to......' He gestured, hands flapping as if in search of the right word. 'Compromise?'

Dmitry nodded, he gave Viktor a look that said, *I'll handle this*, Viktor kept quiet. 'That was the most difficult bit and that's what we've been working on for most of the last two months.'

'Please tell me you've come up with a solution?'

'You've got people on the inside, haven't you?'

Medvedev squinted at Dmitry. 'That sort of information is classified.'

'Well, let's assume you've got someone on the inside, just for argument's sake.' He got no further comment from his boss, so he continued. 'At first, we scaled down the trigger mechanism.' He nodded to the small black box that Viktor had used to activate the virus. 'That was our original, we just use it for convenience. We created a version about this big.' He held up his right hand, thumb and forefinger about an inch apart to demonstrate. 'The plan was to clip it over a wire or a cable, it would be programmed to activate at a given time.'

Medvedev scratched his temples. 'Hold on, so you're saying that you plan to physically put something in place?'

Viktor couldn't resist taking over again. 'The trouble with every other virus is that it depends on the host clicking on something, usually a link in an email. They have to take some sort of action, open a file or activate a line of code.' He paused while Medvedev listened to the obvious fact and tipped his chin, eyes locked on Viktor, waiting for more. 'You don't need me to tell you that people are a little less gullible than they used to be, virus protection systems are more robust and security protocols prevent links and attachments being delivered or opened.'

Medvedev appeared irritated by this. 'Tell me something I don't know.'

Viktor ignored the question and continued. 'We've always worked on the principle of infiltrating the computer software, and that's where organisations have beefed up their protection.'

'We talked about this months ago. I want to know what you've come up with that's going to make a difference.' Medvedev kept his voice low, but his tone expressed frustration.

'We realised that we could do more damage by looking elsewhere, not so much at the organs of the body, but at the blood supply.' Viktor thought the analogy was self-explanatory.

Medvedev didn't want Viktor to think he didn't follow and turned to Dmitry for further explanation.

'The computer systems process the data that's been transmitted to them but the data, especially financial data is transmitted down phone lines. Financial transactions are the lifeblood of civilisation.' He mocked the last word with air quotes. 'Nine out of ten of those are made by card, and every one of those relies on phone lines.'

Medvedev's eyes widened; he could see where they were going.

Dmitry went on. 'There are only around twenty card processing companies serving the UK, they have hubs and satellites but essentially all card payments go through one of those organisations.'

'So?' Medvedev made hurry-up motions with his hands.

'So, we want to get into the phone lines of those companies. If we destroy those lines...' Dmitry ran his finger across his throat.

'And can you?'

They both nodded.

'How?'

Viktor explained. 'We send Aurora down the phone lines; we've built into the code an algorithm that attaches the virus to the power circuit of the host. The host has no way of knowing it's there. It's a bit like ringing a number and nobody answering, the signal gets to a certain point but no further unless someone picks up the phone. As it's a data line, no one will pick it up. As long as the system is powered up, Aurora will sleep until we wake her up.'

Dmitry could see that Medvedev had identified a potential flaw and jumped in before he could speak.

'I know what you're going to say. How do we target them? The data lines don't have numbers.'

Medvedev nodded.

'They do, but they're not released, they're not publicly available.'

'And that's why you want someone on the inside?' The clouds parted and Medvedev understood Dmitry's earlier question.

'The numbers will appear on the paperwork from the phone companies, they won't be easy to get hold of but if you've got an asset capable of infiltrating the phone companies, they could find them for us. We can take it from there.'

The beard received more stroking as Medvedev considered this. 'Have you investigated how many phone companies there are?'

'Not really, it doesn't matter.'

'I thought it would be vital to know, why have you not done your research?'

'We have, we lost count after thirty, but like I said, it doesn't matter.' Dmitry said.

Medvedev paused; he didn't want to look stupid by missing the obvious answer. After a few seconds, he knew he couldn't maintain the pretence any longer. 'OK, so tell me why not.'

'All the phone lines are installed by the same company. The phone companies just pay to use them. All the lines, the exchanges and the individual distribution cabinets are installed and maintained by a company called Connectivity.'

Viktor smoothly took over. 'You only have to get someone into Connectivity, someone good, someone who can gain access to their internal security, and they'll be able to provide us with the line numbers that each of the card processing companies use.'

'Once we've got those, we send Aurora in.' Dmitry concluded with a flourish.

Medvedev studied the two of them again. He didn't comment. He could see the simplicity of their plan and he liked simplicity. From his experience, the more complicated things became, the more likely it was to go wrong. And from his experience, when things went wrong at this level, people died. He didn't want to be one of those people. He folded his arms and walked slowly around the office, staring at the floor in front of him, deep in thought. Dmitry and Viktor watched, they exchanged glances and shrugged, knowing it was best to say nothing.

Medvedev completed a lap of the office and returned, he pulled up a chair and sat down. He leaned back, legs stretched out in front of him, arms still folded. He raised his eyes and stared at the empty glass chamber as if for reassurance. 'I wish it was that simple.' He said eventually. 'We either have to try and get one of our people into this Connectivity company or turn someone who's already there, someone at a very senior level.' He talked as if mulling the idea over in his mind; he wasn't looking at either Dmitry or Viktor, just letting them know what he was thinking.

'Isn't that what you're good at?' said Viktor.

The faintest of smiles played on Medvedev's lips, a smile that spoke volumes, a smile that acknowledged Viktor's remark but gave nothing away, a smile of inner confidence, knowing it was something he was good at, something he'd done before. Could he do it again? 'Possibly.' He replied.

Dmitry wanted something a little more positive. 'We've worked non-stop for months on this, you told us to do our bit and leave the delivery up to you.'

Medvedev turned. 'You,' His forefinger stabbed at Dmitry, his eyes boring into him. 'Do not tell me what to do.'

Viktor came to the rescue. 'We wouldn't dream of telling you what to do, we just need to know what else we can do to help.'

Medvedev pushed the chair back and stood up. 'Right, I've seen enough. I'm going to arrange a team meeting, and we'll work something out. You two better make sure you're ready to go with this when I give you the word.'

1

Eighteen months later
Friday 22 December

When Christmas Day falls on a Monday, the previous Friday is chaotic, stressful and rushed, the prospect of a four-day holiday induces a siege-like mentality. Supermarket shelves are stripped quicker than they can be re-stocked and overloaded trollies queued at check-outs, while fractious kids test harassed parents to breaking point.

Susie Jones suffered in silence, she tried to shut out the cacophony of noise and consulted her shopping list, checking off the items against the contents of her trolley. Having spent the last hour battling her way around the aisles, she had no wish to go shopping again for at least a week. She joined what she considered the shortest queue and waited patiently while the checkout operator, complete with fluffy reindeer horns and an expression that screamed, how much longer, swiped items past the barcode reader and the machine pinged in response.

The customer in front of Susie started unloading their shopping onto the conveyor belt as the previous shopper's last item registered its details and the bored operator looked up at the screen. 'That's a hundred and seventeen pounds and two pence.' No please, no thank you, just a nod at the card reader.

Susie paid little attention. She was distracted by the behaviour of two children at the next checkout who appeared determined to drive their mother to an early grave with a constant stream of bickering, pushing, pinching, name-calling and face-pulling. There were times when Susie wondered if she'd be a good Mum, right now she knew she wouldn't be.

The customer in the queue ahead of Susie had piled their goods onto the stationary belt, waiting for it to start moving. There was a problem.

'Your card's been declined.' The checkout operator mumbled to the man who had just packed all his Christmas food and drink into bags on his trolley. 'Have you got another one?' He stared at the monitor without making eye contact with the customer.

The man retrieved his card from the reader and examined it, front and back, as if its appearance would explain why it hadn't worked. He wiped the back of the card against his sleeve and re-inserted it. He shook his head, puzzled. 'There's plenty of money in the account, don't know what the problem is.' He tapped in his PIN with a little more care than normal.

Susie watched with interest, trying to decide who was more frustrated, the checkout operator who didn't want to have to call his supervisor, or the customer who was becoming conscious of other shoppers getting impatient with him. She concluded the checkout operator didn't care much either way, but the shopper had started to look agitated and a little flushed as the second attempt failed.

'Have you got another card?' The checkout operator, Susie saw from his badge that his name was Oli, had made the supreme effort to look at the customer, assuming that everyone had more than one means of paying.

'Hang on.' The frustrated shopper fumbled in his wallet and produced another card which he swapped for the rejected one. 'Not sure I can remember the PIN for this one.' He tapped four digits on the keyboard, mentally crossing his fingers. No joy.

Susie watched with increasing irritation. Why did I choose this queue, she asked herself. Her attention shifted to the next queue with the argumentative children. The same thing was happening, the card had been declined and another customer, an already over-stressed mother, was frantically trying an alternative payment method.

At the checkout behind her, Susie turned to see if the scene was being repeated elsewhere but the shopper was peeling off a bundle of notes and handing over the cash. No problem there. Her gaze shifted to checkouts beyond and sure enough, a growing number of customers were struggling to find a card that would be accepted by the system. None worked, and the tension grew.

The supervisor was a woman in her late thirties, with dark hair cropped short, a uniform that was a touch too small and a worried expression. Her badge, a smarter version than Oli's, stated her name was Jeannie. She brushed Oli aside, the message being that he was at fault, and took control of the terminal. She keyed in her admin code to override the automated systems and pressed the reset button to reboot the connection to the card processing company, but the screen went blank. She stabbed at the keys with increasing pressure, aware that a growing crowd of shoppers were watching, waiting for her to find the magic answer to the problem.

Someone behind Susie called out. 'Come on, sort it out, some of us have got better things to do.'

Susie turned to see who had spoken, a bald man about six foot two and big with it some sort of Celtic symbol tattooed on his neck, he looked as if he enjoyed confrontation and was used to getting his own way. He had his arms folded and glared at Jeannie. His partner, a plump woman with bleached blonde hair and too much make-up, stood a foot shorter than him and slightly behind him, she looked embarrassed and dug him in the ribs. 'Shh, Bernie, they're doing their best.'

Bernie was having nothing of it and brushed off her concerns. 'Bollocks, they're bloody clueless, they've crashed the system, it can't cope with the pressure.' He looked around, relishing the attention. He nudged his overloaded shopping trolley, producing a lot of clinking noises. He addressed his next remark directly at Jeannie. 'If ya bloody card machine's packed in, then those of us paying cash should get priority.' He waved a substantial roll of notes at the supervisor to make his point.

Susie watched the reactions of those around her with interest. Human nature was fascinating in circumstances like this, and she noted looks of horror, expectation, and even mild amusement. Some agreed and felt the need to wave their supply of cash. Others looked crestfallen, obviously not in possession of enough of the folding stuff to meet the bill. Her observations were interrupted by her phone, she didn't hear it so much as feel it vibrating in the back pocket of her jeans.

The original customer, the one whose card had broken the system in the eyes of those behind him, was standing beside his trolley, looking forlornly at all the Christmas food he'd painstakingly selected, faithfully following the list his wife had prepared. A bead of sweat slowly slipped down his forehead which had reddened noticeably. Nobody was taking any notice of him.

The red lights above each till, indicating that help was required, lit up at the other 25 checkouts. Jeannie was flustered, and tempers were frayed. She looked around for support, but there was none. All hands were on deck, every available member of staff who could operate one of the checkouts was doing so. She sent Oli to find the store manager.

The manager was in the warehouse attempting to manage the restocking of the shelves, a thankless task made more difficult by late deliveries and the fact that he had no spare staff. He had no idea of the chaos unfolding at the front of the store until Oli pushed his way through the swing doors and called for him.

'Mr Waterford,'

The manager turned to see Oli, standing by the doors looking lost and a little uncertain. 'Jeannie's sent me to ask you to come and help.'

Stuart Waterford gazed at the ceiling in exasperation. 'Like I've got nothing else to do?' He held his arms out, palms up. 'Why does she need me?' He had quite enough on his plate without having to drop what he was doing to help his checkout supervisor. He'd been store manager, a good one, for three years, his staff were well trained, he'd delegated well. Jeannie knew the checkouts better than anyone else. 'What can I do to help, she's the expert.' He glared at Oli

Oli wasn't expecting an interrogation and resented the assumption that he was somehow the cause of the problem. 'There's something wrong with the tills and she can't fix it.'

With a resigned sigh, Waterford retrieved his jacket from the seat of a forklift truck, struggled into it and straightened his tie as he made his way through the doors. Oli gave him a head start, he didn't want to have to talk to the manager, then followed at a distance back to the checkouts.

Jeannie was waiting for Waterford with a group of irate customers clustered about her demanding answers. Several abandoned trollies blocked aisles; the mood was hostile. She extracted herself and caught the manager by the arm, leading him away from the worst of the noise.

Waterford was momentarily confused. 'What the hell's going on Jeannie?'

'The data link's gone down; we can't process card payments.' She watched her manager as he took in the chaotic scene, eyes widening as the full impact took hold.

'Jesus bloody Christ.' Waterford cursed. He turned to Jeannie. 'I'm guessing you've done a full re-boot?'

'Twice,' She nodded. 'Nothing wrong with the system or the terminals. We've got no connection, it's completely dead.'

'Of all the times for it to crash, this is the worst possible.' Waterford was trying to keep calm but failing. He didn't have to be a genius to see where this was going. He became conscious that he had become the centre of attention, all eyes were on him. He was in charge and had to act. 'Are we OK taking cash?' He turned to Jeannie, raising both eyebrows, hopeful.

She nodded in response. 'Yeah, cash is no problem, there's nothing wrong at out end.'

Waterford pursed his lips and studied the shoppers, most of whom were staring back at him. He made a decision, headed for Jeannie's desk, picked up the microphone used for store announcements and keyed the talk switch. 'Ladies and Gentlemen, you may have realised we have a problem at the moment, and I apologise for keeping you waiting at this busy time. I regret that due to circumstances beyond our control, we are unable to accept card payments at the moment. We are working hard to solve this problem and hope to rectify the situation very shortly. In the meantime, any customers who are in a position to pay with cash should make their way to checkouts eight, nine and ten, where we will be happy to serve you.'

He turned to Jeannie who was watching the reaction of the shoppers. 'Get those three cleared of card customers and put your best operators on them.'

'What are we going to tell all the people waiting?' There was a note of panic in her voice.

'Tell them to give us ten minutes. If they can't wait, there's nothing we can do.' He felt as panic-stricken as she was but didn't want her to know. 'I'm going to ring HQ and see if they've got any ideas.'

He was about to walk, or even run, back to his office, when Susie Jones caught up with him. It hadn't taken her long to realise that a, there was a problem and b, it was going to quickly escalate. She was never much of a spectator and her inquisitive nature and professional interest got the better of her. When she spotted Waterford at the microphone she had her target, she pushed her shopping out of the way and elbowed her way through the throng. 'Excuse me, are you the manager?'

'I am, but I'm afraid I'm in a bit of a rush.' Waterford tried to shake her off, but Susie was persistent.

'Just hang on a second, I think this a bigger problem than it appears.'

That stopped the manager in his tracks, he turned and appraised Susie, her mousey brown hair had fallen forward like a fringe and her bright brown eyes drilled into him, she was dressed in jeans and a dark blue microfibre jacket that was zipped up to her neck. He was a few inches taller and looked down at her. 'What are you talking about?'

'It's not just your connection that's gone down.' She'd overheard the conversation he'd had with Jeannie. 'The cash machines outside are off-line as well.'

Waterford absorbed this information for a second or two. 'So, it must be some sort of local thing?'

Susie shook her head. 'I've just spoken to a friend in Oxford, the same thing's happened there.'

'Bloody hell.' The colour drained from his face. 'What am I meant to do?'

'If I was you, I'd get onto your Head Office, but you're going to have to be quick. Another five minutes you'll have a riot in your hands.' Susie had turned away from Waterford and watched angry shoppers jostling for position. Those with cash were already queuing at the three checkouts, they were in the minority, and most had adopted a resigned look, settling in for a long wait while somebody fixed the system. They were going to be sorely disappointed.

When she turned back, Waterford had gone. She hoped he hadn't left the building but felt he must have been tempted. The checkout supervisor, Jeannie, had quickly organised what she could. The three cash tills were doing a brisk trade while the others stood idle. The other operators had left their stations rather than try and make small talk with frustrated customers, they gathered at the checkout furthest from the door. Safety in numbers.

Susie watched and listened as she worked her way through the crowd, returning to her trolley as if it were some sort of refuge. She could feel the tension in the air, like a shaken bottle of fizz, it could pop at any moment. She pulled her phone out and called her husband.

'Hello love, you OK?' Nick sounded cheerful.

Susie had to put her hand over one ear while she held the phone to the other one, the noise level was building steadily and she had trouble hearing what he was saying it didn't help that Nick was speaking from a boisterous bar and the Christmas spirit was flowing freely. 'Are you sober?'

'As a judge my darling girl. I'm on the bike, haven't touched a drop.'

'Can you get outside or go somewhere quiet?'

'That sounds like you've got something serious to say.' The voice became clearer as Nick moved towards a quiet corner.

'Possibly.' Susie had to raise her voice to make herself heard above the cacophony. 'How much money have you got on you?'

'Strange question?' Nick replied. 'You mean cash?'

'Yeah, cash, coins, real money.'

'Why on earth d'you want to know that?"

'I've got a bad feeling Nick.' Susie wanted Nick to hear her but not those around her, she talked in a raised whisper. 'Something is happening that could be serious.'

Nick picked up on his wife's concern. He knew she wasn't one to react without good reason. 'Where are you?' He could the background noises around Susie.

'I'm at Tesco's, the card machines have packed in, nobody can pay for their shopping.' She said, trying to stick to the facts.

'Have you tried the hole in the wall?'

'I haven't, but some other people have, and they say there's no joy there either.'

'Is it a local thing?'

'Don't think so, Anna called me a few minutes ago, she's in Oxford and the same thing's happening there.'

Nick was silent for a moment, thinking. 'Hmm, that might explain why Tim's card was refused when he tried to buy a round five minutes ago. He thought it was funny but just paid with cash.'

'If this is happening all over the place it could get very messy.'

Nick grasped the situation quickly. 'Messy? If they don't sort it out quickly, there'll be a riot.'

'I'm going to have to ring the office.'

'Will there be anyone there? Late Friday afternoon before Christmas, they'll all have gone home.'

'There'll be someone manning the switchboard, they can't all just pack in 'cos it's Christmas.'

Nick agreed. 'Guess so, your gaffer sounds like the sort who's on call 24/7.'

'I'm just worried he'll call me in if he thinks it could escalate.'

Nick had stepped outside; Susie was aware the background noise had receded, and she could hear the occasional car passing. She could hear Nick clearly. 'It's probably just a glitch, a power cut or something, the system might have just cried enough, can't cope with the pressure. They'll be working flat out to get it up and running, they can't afford not to. Think of the money they could be losing.'

While Susie listened to Nick, she looked around the supermarket. The three cash-only checkouts were busy, but not excessively so. The other checkouts stood idle, operators talking to each other in a corner trying to avoid eye contact with disgruntled shoppers. The shoppers were talking to each other, exchanging views, checking watches, making phone calls and in several cases, trying desperately to maintain control of young children who were growing increasingly bored. She noticed a growing number of trollies blocking aisles, where customers had given up waiting and simply walked out of the store, abandoning the essential supplies they'd battled with their fellow shoppers to pick up. Nick was right, each trolley was fully loaded, and the cost of lost sales would be clocking up, thousands of pounds every minute.

She came to a decision. 'OK. Look I'll call the office, at least I won't be accused of doing nothing.' She nodded to herself as if affirming it was the right thing to do. 'In the meantime, don't spend any cash, whatever you've got might be all we have to live on.'

Nick chuckled. 'Well, that gets me out of buying the next round.'

'You can thank me later.' Susie replied. 'I'll call you back when I've got some news from the office.' She ended the call, pushed her trolley even further away from the masses and went outside for better reception. It was dusk and fog had descended adding to the cold and damp. The yellow sodium floodlights were struggling to pierce the gloom and illuminate the car park, people hurried from one pool of light to the next. Susie pulled her jacket collar closer and walked to her Golf, she slowed when she saw a figure unloading his shopping into the rear of a Toyota RAV4, he looked furtive but somehow familiar. She'd seen him before, but it took a few seconds to place him. She walked past, watching from the corner of her eye. It was the man who'd been in the queue in front of her, the one whose card had been declined. Susie did a quick double-take to make sure. He noticed, stopped what he was doing and met Susie's stare.

'Something wrong?' he continued to look at Susie, inviting an answer.

Susie was taken aback, she had him pegged as Mr law-abiding average citizen, not so much as a parking ticket, a family man, sent out to get the supplies for the holiday and too much pride to go home empty-handed. Yet here he was, taking the best part of a hundred and twenty quids worth of groceries without paying. 'I'm saying nothing.' She was momentarily lost for words but checked left and right to make sure nobody was within earshot. 'Can't say I blame you.' She stopped herself, ashamed she was condoning his actions, then added. 'Happy Christmas.' Before walking hurriedly to her car and climbing in.

The switchboard answered after three rings. 'Hello, police, can I help you?'

'It's Susan Jones, can you put me through to Commander Eddington.'

'Commander Eddington has left the office; he'll be back in on Wednesday.' The voice at the other end was firm but polite and efficient.

'I have an ongoing situation, code Nevis, I need to get a message to him.'

The reference to code Nevis had an immediate effect on the switchboard operator and the tone of voice was suddenly business-like and serious. 'One moment please.'

There was silence. The moment lasted thirty seconds, then. 'Eddington here.'

'Sorry to bother you Sir, but I think we may have a problem.'

'If you think it's worth disturbing me, then I have to assume you have good reason for doing so.' Rob Eddington was never off duty, not really, even on holiday his phone was always by his side. 'You used the Nevis code; you're saying there's a situation in progress?'

'I think the data processing lines have been compromised, I don't know how widespread it is, but card payments are being declined.'

'What makes you think the system hasn't crashed temporarily under pressure?'

Susie hesitated. 'I've got no evidence, just a gut feeling. If anyone wanted to do real damage, this would be the perfect time.'

'I agree, but like I say, the system will be stretched to maximum capacity today, if it was going to fail, then you're right, now would be the worst possible time.' Eddington countered without much conviction. 'When did this happen?'

Susie checked her watch; it was just after four. 'About half an hour ago.'

There was silence while the commander of the Cyber Crime Unit digested this. 'Hmmm, three thirty, just as the banks are shutting up shop for four days, sounds like too much of a coincidence for my liking.'

'It may be nothing, it may come back online any minute but I'm sure I've already seen one person walking out of a store without paying in the confusion. He won't be the last.'

'Quite.' Eddington remarked, he considered Susie's report, his brain processing the wider implications. 'I'll need to get on to IT and see what they know.'

'Is there anything I can do in the meantime?' Susie asked.

'Just cross your fingers and hope, we need more intel, find out anything else you can, call me again if anything changes.' He paused. 'If this goes on, your Christmas may not be how you planned it.'

'No Sir, and nor will anyone else's.' The line went dead as Eddington hung up. Susie opened the car door and climbed out, looking around, she could see trollies being wheeled across the car park, a steady flow now, some being pushed in as leisurely manner as it was possible, not wanting to attract attention, and others by shoppers almost jogging behind them, anxious to get to their cars and get away while they could. It was hard to tell which ones had a receipt for the goods they contained. Maybe the system had rectified itself and they were all innocent. She had her doubts.

Susie walked back into the store, ten minutes had passed since she left, and the situation had deteriorated noticeably. The security staff, one man in his late twenties with delusions of importance and power, dressed in black with a peaked cap and a utility belt, was doing his best to contain the growing unrest, trying and failing to stop desperate customers from bypassing the checkouts and heading for the car park. While his attention was taken up remonstrating with one angry shopper, two more would slip around behind him and escape into the darkness. Susie was astonished at how quickly the rule of law was breaking down. How long before the manager saw sense and closed the doors.

She called Nick again. 'Any news?'

'I was going to ask you the same thing.' He didn't sound quite as cheerful as the last time she called. 'Just been to put some fuel in the bike, had to pay cash.'

'Shit.'

'What's happening with you?'

'Not looking good, people are simply walking out, they're not prepared to wait, there's nothing they can do, they're swamped.' She watched the security man wrestling the trolley from a woman half his size. The woman started screaming as if she was being assaulted. While the easy target was being picked on, three others dashed out.

'Did you get hold of the big cheese?'

'Yeah. He knew nothing about it. He's getting on to the tech team to see what they know.' As she spoke, she saw the manager rush to support the security man, he brought three members of staff with him and between them they closed three of the four outer doors, restricting the exit to a single narrow corridor and preventing anyone else from entering the store.

Nick could hear the commotion. 'What's going on? What's all that shouting?'

'It's all getting out of hand.' Susie said. 'They're trying to close the doors and prevent people leaving without paying.'

'Bloody hell love, you'd better get out of there before you get caught up in it all.'

'I know, but I've spent the last hour and a bit, longer actually, getting all our stuff for the next few days. If I leave now, we'll be on bread and water for Christmas.'

Nick was unusually optimistic. 'They'll get it sorted in the next few hours, it'll be business as normal tomorrow, you can go back then. I'll come with you if you want.'

I wish I shared your positive outlook. There's no way I'm coming back, you can come on your own if you think there'll be anything here to buy.'

'So, what you going to do, turn outlaw?'

'I can't, can I?' She replied. 'I am the law; I should be stopping those people stealing but they'd take no notice of me.'

'Rubbish, you can be pretty fearsome when you're riled.'

Susie considered it for a moment, she was torn. 'I don't know Nick, I'm not officially in the Police, I just work for them. I don't have proper ID or anything I could use.'

'Guess so. Just get out love, we'll manage one way or another, it's not worth getting involved and there's not a hell of lot you can do. Leave the shopping and get back home. I'll see you there.'

Reluctantly, Susie agreed, she stuffed the phone back into her pocket and pushed the trolley towards the exit, more out of habit than any intention to steal the contents. A message came over the loudspeakers, it was Jeannie, the checkout supervisor. 'Ladies and Gentlemen, we're sorry that we have been unable to restore our card payment system. We apologise for the inconvenience, but we've been advised that we have to close the store with immediate effect and must therefore ask all shoppers to make their way to the exit and leave their shopping behind. If there are any shoppers who are able to pay with cash, please make your way directly to checkout number ten.'

The effect of the announcement was instantaneous, those who had waited patiently and, in some cases, impatiently, reacted. They had waited long enough, and their patience had expired. Led by a vocal minority, shoppers stampeded towards the exit, they weren't going home empty-handed. Even the mild-mannered, the upright and the god-fearing were caught up in the rush.

The store staff were overwhelmed. The security man gave up his futile attempt to be a one-man army, and after being rammed by a couple of heavily loaded trollies aimed at him with some force, he gave up and scuttled out of the way. The doors that had been closed had not been locked and were re-opened by one man who pulled his trolley while his wife pushed it from behind. Shoppers surged out into the car park and headed for their cars, barging each other angrily in an ultimate display of trolley rage.

Susie found herself swept along, meaning to push her trolley to one side and walk out without it. Once clear of the bottleneck at the store exit, she slowed, unable to comprehend the scene, unable to believe how quickly it had happened and unable to believe that she was as guilty as everyone else. She could of course, leave her shopping, get in the car and drive home. Or she could do what everyone else was doing, load it into the boot and get the hell out of the place before anyone stopped her.

She continued towards her Golf, dodging a speeding pickup, full beam, hazards flashing, engine screaming. The pedestrian traffic was soon outnumbered as cars reversed out of their spaces, horns sounded, tyres squealed, and curses were exchanged as drivers indulged in games of chicken. Who dares wins, Susie thought. She could hear the scraping of metal and tinkle of glass at points around the car park where no one was prepared to play the chicken. She doubted they would be stopping to exchange names and addresses.

By the time she got to her car, there were few others around it. She clicked the remote to unlock it and paused one last time. As far as she was concerned, she hadn't committed any crime so far. The moment she opened the tailgate and transferred her shopping to the car, she was a thief. She looked around in the gloom, who was watching, who would know? Her gaze lifted to the floodlights and the CCTV cameras mounted on them. Real or fake? Were they being monitored or were they just a deterrent? Would they pick anything up in this light, in this fog? She knew the answer, she opened the tailgate and almost threw the contents of the trolley into the back, slammed it shut and jumped into the car. She took a deep breath, started the engine and navigated her way out.

There were still some people emerging from the store, some, Susie noticed, without trollies. "*Bless them*" she thought. She kept her distance from the store entrance and took the long way out of the car park. The exit road joined the main drag out of the retail park where a steady stream of cars were queuing to get out. It looked to Susie as if all the shops had suffered the same fate. She breathed out and relaxed slightly, surely, she was safe now.

2

It took Susie twenty minutes to drive home. The traffic was moving a little faster than normal, people appeared to be rushing, there was little in the way of goodwill to all men, and nobody was going to give way at junctions. The cut and thrust didn't worry Susie, she could handle it, but she couldn't believe common courtesies were so quickly discarded: it was everyone for themselves. There was nothing on the radio about what she had just witnessed. She scanned channels as she drove, just the same old Christmas tunes that get played to death every year. Maybe the news hadn't filtered through yet, maybe someone had been told to suppress the story to avoid panic. It would be on social media by now, it had to be.

She pulled onto the driveway of their house, pleased to see Nick's BMW parked in front of the garage, at least he'd got back safe. She looked around the other ten houses in their close, it all looked so normal. Festive lights on trees, walls and roof edges glowed, blinked, flashed and chased, lighting up the gloom of the fog and creating eerie multi-coloured effects. She was expecting signs of panic, but there were none. Had she just imagined the last couple of hours?

Nick came out of the house to greet her, still wearing his biking gear, he'd only just got back. 'Pretty manic, eh?' He gave Susie a hug, pleased she was home.

'That's putting it mildly.' She said.

'I've never seen anything like it, I saw two fender benders just coming back here from the town centre, no one prepared to back off. Unbelievable.'

Susie popped open the rear hatchback and started passing the shopping to Nick. 'I never had time to put it in bags.' She explained.

Nick grabbed a bag from the assortment in the boot. As he filled it with the items Susie handed to him, he caught her eye, questioning. 'So, you had cash to pay for all this stuff then?'

'Just load up and keep quiet.' She replied, glancing left and right, making sure that nobody was watching them.

Nick got the message, and he shook his head slowly, saying nothing. He filled a second carrier bag and disappeared into the house just as Susie's phone burst into life.

She recognised the number and answered immediately. 'Susan Jones.'

'Susie, it's Yasmin. Sorry to call but the boss has called an emergency meeting, he's told me to contact the team, there's a meeting at Warrenford at six o'clock.'

'Tonight?'

''Fraid so, sorry. '

'It's OK, I'm not surprised Yas, this could get pretty hairy.' Susie checked her watch, 4.45, and she made a quick calculation. The CCU control room was forty minutes away, she had half an hour to spare. 'I've just got back home, been shopping, I'll get sorted then head over. Anything I need to bring?'

'He hasn't said anything, but it might be an idea to pack a bag, it could end up being an all-nighter.'

Susie groaned, the last thing she wanted. She was warned there would be unsociable hours when she was offered the job, but this was taking unsociable to a new level. 'I guess so. OK, I'll see you there.' She clicked the phone off, grabbed the last two bags of shopping, and went inside to tell Nick the news.

'You've got to be joking.' Nick's shoulders sagged in resignation when he heard. He was unpacking the shopping and turned to Susie, a box of mince pies in each hand.

'Sorry love. Nature of the beast and all that.' She shrugged, and turned her palms up in a helpless gesture, her bottom lip pouting like a small child denied a treat.

'Why you?'

'He wants the team in and I'm on the team, simple as that.'

Nick nodded slowly, accepting the fact. 'He must think it's serious if he's pulling you all in at such short notice.'

Susie helped with the unpacking. 'When I spoke to him earlier, he was going to speak to the boffins, they must have told him something that's pressed his buttons.'

'I don't suppose you've been on Facebook?' He asked.

Susie shot a sideways glance at Nick while trying to find space in the fridge for a block of cheese. 'You think I've had time?'

'Didn't think so.' Nick said. 'It's happening all over the country. People are posting videos, it's not quite a riot but it's not far off.'

'There's nothing on the news, I had the radio on in the car but there was no mention. I'm guessing they don't want to escalate it.'

Nick nodded wisely. 'It's too much of a coincidence for it to crash the moment the banks close for four days.'

'That's what Eddington said.'

'Strangely, everything else is still working - phones, internet, mobiles – it's not like there's been a power cut or anything like that.' Nick thought out loud while he found places in the cupboards for the rest of the shopping.

'Can you finish off in here, I need to get a few bits together in case we're kept late.'

'You want me to come with you?' Nick said, concerned, tidying away the last of the bags.

'I'll be OK.' It was a reflex reply, spoken without any real conviction, she was halfway out the door, she paused, considering Nick's offer. The idea appealed. 'Are you sure?'

'Hundred per cent. I'll just sit here otherwise and worry about you.' Nick stood resting against the worktop, arms folded, brow furrowed, eyes locked onto Susie's willing her to say yes. 'I know you're more than capable and I know you can take care of yourself, but it could get tricky if things get any worse.'

'They might not let you in, it's a restricted area.' Susie was warming to the idea, but she could see problems.

'We can worry about that when we get there. Come on, I'll grab some kit as well.' He followed her out of the kitchen.

They arrived at the main gate of Warrenford airfield at 5.50, the forty-minute drive had taken an extra ten minutes due to traffic queues caused by accidents. Minor accidents, but enough to make progress painfully slow. Security on the gate had doubled: Nick, in the passenger seat, spotted the alert status board was black, indicating a threat was imminent. He nudged Susie's arm and with a raised eye-brow, drew her attention to it. Neither of them spoke. Susie stopped at the first barrier, opened her window and held up her security pass for inspection.

Three policemen, dressed in black, wearing ballistic vests and crash helmets approached, they all carried Heckler & Koch MP5 carbines in addition each had a Glock 17 holstered on their right hips. One planted himself in front of the Golf, one came to the passenger window, and the third produced a torch and directed it in Susie's face. She squinted, thrusting the pass forward to try and block the dazzling beam.

'Step out of the car please.'

Susie complied without a word.

'Who is the passenger?' The policeman asked, he studied Susie's pass, his eyes flicking between her and her picture.

'My husband, Nick Cooper.'

'We were told to expect you. No one mentioned him.'

'He offered to come with me, he was worried about the situation.'

The policeman nodded in understanding and leaned into the car, shining the torch in Nick's face. Nick squinted, but kept both hands flat on his thighs, visible and empty. 'Step out of the car please.'

The policeman at Nick's door stood back to let him out. 'Can we see some ID?'

Nick unzipped his jacket, held it open and made a point of slowly reaching inside it, pulling out his wallet between thumb and forefinger. He withdrew his driving licence and his Army reservist warrant card, passing them to the armed officer.

'Army, eh?' The policeman raised an eyebrow after a quick glance at the documents.

'Ex.' Nick replied, he smiled and maintained eye contact. 'Intelligence Corps, eleven years.'

The first policeman, the one standing beside Susie, listened carefully to the exchange. 'You're still subject to the OSA?' It was half statement, half question.

'Absolutely.' Nick replied. 'You know the score, once you've signed, you've signed for good.'

This appeared to satisfy the officer, he nodded, turned and walked out of earshot. He talked quietly into his radio for a minute then returned. 'OK, you can go in.' He tipped his head in the direction of the control tower and stood back from the car as the red and white striped barrier rose. Susie and Nick climbed back in and drove twenty yards to the second barrier.

This time the procedure was quicker. A single armed officer waved them down, flashed his torch into the car, a quick word into the radio on his lapel and without a word he raised the barrier and pointed to the control tower.

Susie exhaled as she slowly drove the 200 yards to the control tower. She glanced across at Nick. 'They're taking this seriously, aren't they?'

Nick nodded slightly in agreement, his attention was elsewhere, trying to spot signs of activity, but there were none. 'This is all very low-key. What else happens here?'

'Nothing much.' Said Susie as she pulled into a parking space between a Range Rover and an Audi estate. 'The runways are de-commissioned, but the buildings are all still working, offices and storage. The comms are state of the art and it's secure.' She got out and waved a hand around the place, the fog was even thicker than earlier and the sodium lights on the sides of the buildings struggled to provide any more than dull yellow pools between the shadows. 'The Police use it for training, I guess that's why they set up the CCU office here.'

There was nothing to indicate the purpose of the place, no signs on doors, no obvious tell-tale indicators of activity, apart from the dozen or so cars parked at the base of the control tower. Nick looked up, the tower disappeared into the gloom of the night sky, he couldn't see the windows at the top. 'You're going to tell me your meeting room is up there, aren't you?'

'Don't worry, they've repaired the lift.' She gave him a half smile, pushed open an unmarked door and led Nick into the brightly lit reception area. Their eyes had grown accustomed to the darkness outside and it took a moment or two to adjust to the glare of the white LED spotlights.

Yasmin sat behind the reception desk and looked up as they entered. 'Hi Susie, sorry about the third degree, everything's been tightened up.' Her attention shifted. 'You must be Nick?'

He nodded.

'Thought so, your name's been mentioned more than once.' She glanced quickly at Susie as if for confirmation.

'We thought we'd both come, just in case.' Susie added, by way of explanation.

'Can't blame you, the boss is worried, he's waiting in the control room, you can go straight up. I'm afraid you'll have to stay down here Nick.'

'That's OK, I didn't think I'd be invited to join the team.'

Susie pressed a button with an up arrow on it and the door slid open immediately, the lift was already on the ground floor. She jammed her foot against the door to prevent it from closing. 'You going to be OK love?'

Nick was casting around for somewhere to sit. 'Don't worry I'll find something to keep me occupied.'

Yasmin reassured Susie. 'I'll keep an eye on him.' She turned to Nick. 'There's a few newish magazines over there and you can make a half-decent coffee in the kitchen if you want.'

Susie seemed pleased with that and she stepped into the lift, letting the door swish closed.

Nick watched as the green indicator light switched from G to 1, there was only one stop.

3

The lift door opened directly into the control room. Even in its heyday, it had never been a hectic environment, aircraft arrivals and departures had been limited and now they were almost non-existent. The general aviation traffic was handled by the airfield manager from her office at ground level, in a building two hundred yards from the control tower.

Susie stepped out and took in the scene. The room was octagonal, with windows leaning out on seven sides, the eighth taken up by the lift. There were no walls on which to mount whiteboards, so two had been set up, free-standing across one side of the room, they looked brand new, nothing had been written on them. Three tables were randomly placed in front of them with about twelve chairs dotted haphazardly. The room was lit by bright downlighters and smelled of electricity.

Opposite the whiteboards, three 50-inch flat-screen monitors, side by side, were mounted on mobile stands. The monitors were on and tuned to CNN, Sky News and the BBC 24-hour news channel. The sound was muted.

There were only six other people in the room, Susie expected more, perhaps they had been delayed in traffic, perhaps they were never going to get here. Eddington had his back to her, talking on the phone, he turned briefly when he heard the lift door open, raised a hand in greeting and resumed his conversation.

Susie recognised the recently appointed admin man, Wade Millard, a short man in his early fifties, halfway between stocky and overweight. He had long unkempt hair and a thick straggly beard, both pale ginger with touches of grey. He had a stumpy nose and hooded eyes, partly hidden by broad-framed glasses. His face, what she could see of it under the beard, had worry written all over it. He worked at his laptop and briefly glanced up at Susie, then resumed whatever he was doing without saying a word.

Two female officers sat side by side at another table. Susie hadn't seen them before, so she assumed they must be analysts, they both looked younger than her, late twenties she thought. They had one laptop between them and an A4 notepad, they were talking quietly to each other when Susie entered and broke off to greet her. 'Hi, you must be Susie?' One of them said.

'I am.' Susie tipped her head in agreement, her eyes darting between the two of them waiting for an introduction.

'Sorry, I'm Grace, this is Ellie.'

'We've been seconded from Corsham.' Ellie added when Susie looked puzzled.

'Commander Eddington asked for two computer experts, and we were all they could find.' Grace explained, she smiled and nudged her colleague.

Susie warmed to them both immediately; she knew they wouldn't be there unless they were at the top of their game, and she liked the self-deprecating attitude. She was pleased they didn't fit the mould of the typical computer nerd. 'Pleased to meet you.' She walked over to them and shook hands. 'This could be a long night.'

Grace shrugged. "That's what we thought, not how we planned to start the weekend.'

Susie glanced over at the other two people in the room, both men wearing jeans and sweatshirts, engrossed with what Susie guessed was some sort of technical device, a black metal box two feet long, three inches high and six inches deep. It had a dozen wires plugged in down one long side, they spread like tentacles over the table and disappeared in different directions.

Ellie followed Susie's gaze. 'The communications guys. They're connecting us up to every security system under the sun by the look of things.'

One of the men, the shorter of the two, caught the end of Ellie's remark and looked across at the three women, he gave a brief thumbs-up and the faintest of smiles.

Eddington finished his call and turned to face his team. 'We happy few.' He remarked with a touch of sarcasm, looking around as if to confirm there was nobody else in the room. 'Sorry to drag you out on such a foul night.'

Not that we had much choice, Susie thought.

'No point beating about the bush, this situation is getting worse by the minute.' Eddington continued. 'I've just been briefing the Home Secretary; we're convinced this is a coordinated cyber-attack.'

Millard looked up from his laptop and cut in. 'This is unlike any previous cyber-attack.' He looked around the room; he had the undivided attention of the other six. 'Whoever is behind this hasn't gone down the usual route of attacking computer systems, they've gone for phone lines and specifically the phone lines of the card processing companies.'

Eddington watched the reaction of his team, furrowed brows, disbelief, questioning. He nodded to Millard and went on. 'We don't know who's behind it or how they've done it, but we've all seen the effects, some of us at first hand.' He addressed the last remark to Susie.

'Any ideas yet about how they've done it?' Susie responded, aware that the others had turned to look at her.

'No, we're stumped. We assume it's an electronic virus of some kind but it's not like anything we've seen before.' He paused, looked at Grace and Ellie, inviting them to speak.

'We've been in touch with four of the companies affected.' said Ellie. 'They're frantic, as you can imagine. There's nothing wrong with their servers, all the systems are online and working properly, it's just the phone lines that have developed a fault. All four said the same thing. They're investigating and promised to get back to us as soon as they find anything.'

'We're trying to get in touch with another five, but they're not answering the secure numbers we have for them, and they're not replying to emails.' Grace gave a helpless gesture.

Eddington absorbed this news, stroking his chin. His attention was diverted by one of the large monitors, the picture showed a crowd of people in a shopping centre, and the ribbon across the bottom of the screen repeated the message, "Shoppers turned away as card payments fail". There was no sound, but the scene left him in no doubt that news had reached mainstream media. He turned to Wade Millard. 'Get on to media control, make sure they play this down, any press coverage is just going to make the situation worse.'

Millard nodded, he picked up a phone and went to one of the windows so he could speak without disturbing the others.

Susie sat next to Grace and Ellie, she rested her chin on her hands, elbows on the table, watching and listening. 'I hate to tell you boss, but it's all over social media, people are posting videos taken in shops, and there's a Twitter hashtag of "*#cashonly*" gaining momentum every minute. The media won't sit on it for long when it's out there already.'

Eddington grimaced. 'Bloody hell.'

'Can I make a suggestion?' Susie sat back and looked up at the Commander.

'Go ahead. Right now, I'll consider anything.'

She pursed her lips, head tilted, eyes fixed on the monitor. 'Can we pre-empt any negative press coverage by putting out a statement, something to the effect that the authorities have traced the source of the problem and are working hard to get everything up and running again as soon as possible.'

'That would make sense,' he nodded. 'Except it's not true. We haven't traced the source of the problem.'

Susie's eyes were still on the TV news feed, she looked sideways at Eddington, eyebrows raised. 'Not yet, but we need to manage this, we need to be seen to be in control of the situation.'

Eddington could see the sense in what she said, he nodded slowly.

Susie took it as a signal to continue. 'It's probably not worth a full-blown press conference at this stage, but if you were prepared to go on camera and make a statement, it would reassure people and prevent the scenes they're showing.' She waved a finger at the three monitors.

'OK, can you draft something for me? Have a word with Wade and see what you can arrange with the press.' Eddington's spirits lifted slightly; he turned to the two men working on the comms network. 'Are we in touch with the military yet?'

The taller of the two men nodded, and he pushed three handsets across the table towards Eddington. 'The grey one's a direct line to the MOD situation room in Whitehall, just press the green button and you're through. The red one goes straight to the Home Office, same procedure. This one.' he held up the third handset, black, slightly smaller than the other two with only a single push-to-talk button on its side. 'is linked to Corsham, press the button, and start speaking, it's wired into their speakerphone, and they'll hear you.

'Is anyone there yet?'

'Commander Martin's asked twenty specialists to come in, only three had arrived when I spoke to him ten minutes ago.'

'Thanks, Raj, that's great. Would you and Danny be able to set up a video link with Corsham, I'd like to be able to see who I'm talking to.'

'Sure Commander shouldn't take us long.' Raj turned to his colleague. 'Is the C200 still here?'

Danny gave a brief nod.

'Give us ten minutes and you'll be good to go.'

'Top man.' Eddington reached for the grey handset. 'I'll have a word with Whitehall while you're doing that.' He turned and walked to the far side of the control room to make the call.

Susie hadn't moved since being instructed to liaise with Millard, she listened to the exchange between Eddington, Raj and Danny, and watched the two comms men with interest. Raj, the taller one, appeared to be the more senior. She was captivated by his intense brown eyes, they were magnetic, almost hypnotic and she had to make a conscious effort to tear her gaze from them. His beard, short and neatly trimmed, set off a handsome face, framed with thick waves of jet-black hair that fell to collar length. He flashed Susie a smile, perfect white teeth. She smiled back, suddenly embarrassed, he'd caught her staring. She made an elaborate show of opening her laptop, aware of the glow in her cheeks and studiously avoided any further eye contact.

Wade Millard returned from his call, he heard Eddington's suggestion and spoke directly to Susie. 'Do you want to put some sort of release together, I've spoken to media control and they're stalling the press, they're going to alert them that the boss making a statement in the next half an hour.'

Susie welcomed his intervention, she looked up as Raj and Danny left the table and headed back to where they had established a base; a haphazard collection of boxes, cables, connectors and assorted technical equipment she didn't recognise. 'No problem Wade. Do we want him to go live with the statement or record it in advance and edit it, cut out any gaffs?

Millard thought about this for a moment, glancing over at Eddington, trying to decide what would be best. 'He's comfortable on camera but it's probably best if we record it first, we need to get it word perfect.'

'Agreed. Can we transmit video, broadcast quality, directly from here?'

Millard turned in his chair. 'Did you catch that, Raj?'

Raj looked up and frowned, a moment of hesitation, Danny jumped in. 'Absolutely, we could do it live, but if you'd prefer to record it we've got the editing software here and satellite links for transmission.'

'What about lights and sound?'

Danny responded again; this was his field of expertise. 'We've got all the kit here.' He waved a hand at the boxes surrounding him.

Susie looked over at the commander, his back to them, engrossed in his phone call. 'Has he brought a uniform?' Eddington was wearing a well-worn Barbour jacket over a red checked lumberjack shirt. 'He can't go on TV looking like that.'

'He'll have something official-looking in his car, always does.' said Millard.

'Thank the lord.' Said Susie. 'Can I suggest we get set up, I'll prepare a script for the boss, and we'll see how he feels about doing it live.'

Millard nodded in agreement. 'I'll let media control know if you chaps get everything ready in the meantime.'

Susie looked over at Grace and Ellie, aware their laptop had pinged several times while she had been discussing plans with the others. 'Any more news I can use in a statement?'

Grace spoke without taking her eyes off the screen. 'We've got through to two more companies both saying the same thing as the other four, but one of the companies we contacted earlier has just come back with an update.' She paused as she checked the details, leaning closer to the screen as if struggling to believe what she was reading.

'What is it?' Susie leaned over trying to see for herself what the message said.

Grace continued slowly, reading the message word by word. "....our technical team have traced the source of the problem to physical damage of the data transmission cables inside our secure terminal cabinets. The cables have been completely destroyed as if burned out..." She broke off and looked at Susie then Millard, her mouth gaping open.

Millard was the first to respond. 'Oh fuck!'

Susie's eyes narrowed; she couldn't understand. 'How is that even possible?'

'Fuck knows.' Millard snapped. 'The fact is, it's happened. This takes it to a whole new level.'

Alerted by Millard's outburst, Eddington ended his call and came over. 'What's happened?"

'This isn't just a virus Rob; we can't just fix the software or re-boot the system.' Millard shook his head, a pained look on his face.

'What have I missed.'

Grace repeated the message she'd just read out.

'Holy Hell.' Eddington's response was slightly more measured than Millard's. He considered the news, thinking quickly. 'Have any of the others reported the same thing?'

'Ellie's emailed all those we're in touch with, asking them to check their cabinets.' Grace glanced at her colleague who was typing furiously.

'We were planning to do a live statement delivered on camera, boss.' Susie said.

'Don't tell me, you want me to do it?'

'Makes sense.'

Eddington nodded ruefully.

'I was all set to write something based on it being a temporary situation, something positive, but this changes things.'

Millard butted in. 'If we say anything about a physical attack it'll create mass panic. You don't have to be a genius to see the implications.'

Eddington folded his arms and stared at the three monitors, all now showing pictures of the unrest, he compressed his lips and narrowed his eyes. 'We're going to have to come up with a sanitised version of what we know, Wade's right, if that message is right, it could take days to replace the wiring, maybe even longer.'

The others in the room said nothing, they watched as Eddington stroked the stubble on the side of his face, they waited for direction.

'We'll have to say that we believe the UK has been hit by a pre-meditated attack.' He looked at Susie as he spoke. 'We also have to make it clear that this is a serious attack and while we investigate the source, we are doing all we can to help the card processing companies get their systems up and running again as soon as possible. I'll leave the wording up to you.'

Susie nodded and scribbled a few notes as he spoke.

'Put in something reassuring. The need to remain calm, the need to be patient, that sort of thing. It might be worthwhile adding something about the need to maintain law and order but try and couch it in words that don't give the impression we're expecting riots. Can you do that?'

'I'm on it.' Susie started on the laptop, ballpoint between teeth.

Eddington turned to Raj and Danny, busy setting up the makeshift studio. 'Can you two make this place look a little more...' He gazed around the control room trying to come up with the right word... a little more business-like?'

Danny, rigging up two large LED light panels, pointed to a spot on the ground. 'If you stand there boss, we'll make sure you fill the screen and the background is out of focus. It'll look busy without distracting from what you say.'

Eddington understood. 'OK, can you manage all this between the two of you?'

'We could do with someone who's a bit more clued up with camera operation.' Raj looked up from the Canon C200 he had mounted to a tripod. He looked puzzled. 'I can sort out all the connectivity and Danny's good with production and editing but neither of us are videographers.'

Eddington looked around the room. Grace and Ellie had their heads down collating data from the card companies, and Susie was concentrating on the statement. 'Wade, you any good with cameras?'

Millard shook his head. 'Strictly point and shoot, holiday snaps are my limit. Why do you ask?'

'Raj and Danny could do with a hand, someone who knows what they're doing with a camera.'

Susie looked up. 'I just caught the end of that, what do you need?'

Eddington repeated the question and then asked. 'Are you volunteering?"

'No, but my other half is down in reception, he's a pro.'

Millard butted in. 'He won't have security clearance.'

'Right now, Wade, that's the least of our worries.' Eddington said.

'He's a reservist, former Military Intelligence, been vetted dozens of times.' Susie added, feeling the need to fight Nick's corner.

That appeared to mollify Millard, he shrugged. 'OK, I suppose, it can't do any harm.'

Eddington made a decision. 'Call Yasmin, get him up here.'

4

The three television screens in the control room all showed the same picture. Rob Eddington speaking directly to the camera. 'Can we switch them off or put something on that's a little more helpful than my tired old face.' He called across to Raj.

Raj broke off from his discussion with Nick about camera lenses, 'Sure boss. Would you prefer live news feeds?'

Eddington nodded in response and turned to Susie, 'I need you to talk to the data processing companies.'

'I thought that's what Grace and Ellie were doing?'

'True, but they're just getting email updates from them.'

'They're getting a lot more than that,' Susie said.

Grace looked up from her screen at Eddington, 'They're giving us all the information we ask for Commander.'

Eddington held up a hand in apology, 'Sorry Grace, I didn't mean to diminish what you and Ellie have achieved so far, it's been invaluable, but we need more detail. What I need is for you,' he locked eyes with Susie 'to go and eyeball one or more of these companies. Investigate how they operate, probe their security arrangements, see if you can find a weak spot.'

'Can't we do that over the phone?'

'You'd get something over the phone, but you can't read body language over the phone, you can't watch their eyes, you can't see what they're not telling us.'

'What about a video call?"

Eddington shook his head, 'Same thing applies, it's just not the same as face-to-face. This is what you're good at, Susie: reading people, investigating, and asking difficult questions. I value your judgement, that's why I got you on the team.'

Susie could see that further protest would be wasted. 'OK,' she said, resigned to a long night ahead. 'When and where?"

Eddington turned back to Grace, 'Which of the companies you've been in touch with has been the most helpful?'

Grace conferred with Ellie, the pair studied their notes for a few moments, 'There's three at the top of our list, we've had messages back and forth, they're keen to help. Actually, I should say they're desperate for us to help.

'Hardly surprising,' Eddington agreed. 'They'll be losing money hand over fist at the moment, and their reputation will be going down the pan.'

'The one that said their wiring had been destroyed, are they one of the three?' Susie asked.

Grace checked the notes again, 'Yes, it's a company called Payline, he's been really helpful.'

'He?' Eddington asked.

'Mr Trent Bracewell, it's his company, he's absolutely frantic.'

'Sounds like a good place to start.' Eddington said. 'Where are they based?'

Another check on the notes, 'Swindon.' Grace said.

Eddington nodded in confirmation and turned to Susie, 'That's not too far away, it'll only take you an hour or two.'

Susie slumped. 'That's going to be a fun drive in the morning.'

'The morning?' Eddington scowled at her.

'What? You want me to go there tonight?'

'This is unravelling by the minute; God knows what will have happened by the morning. The shops are going to open and as things stand, they're not going to be able to take card payments. How's that going to play out the day before Christmas Eve?'

Susie looked defeated.

'You heard what Grace said, the man's frantic, he needs our help.' Eddington continued. 'Get down there, quick as you can, you might be able to uncover something that could save the day.'

'Can my driver come with me?' Susie accepted the inevitable and nodded in Nick's direction.

'Excellent idea. Of course, he can. If he doesn't go with you, we'll run out of biscuits in another hour or two.' Eddington glanced over at Nick and winked at him; Nick pushed the biscuit tin away as if he wasn't interested.

Susie had a sudden thought. 'We'll need cash for fuel.'

'Can you sort Susie out with some cash Wade?' Eddington glanced down at him.

Millard produced a couple of twenties and handed them over to Susie. 'I'll need a receipt.'

'Thanks, Wade.' She pocketed the cash. 'Come along driver.'

Nick got up and said goodnight to Raj and Danny and joined Susie at the lift entrance.

Nick drove. Susie kept him on course with directions Grace had given her. Traffic had dwindled since their arrival at the Control Tower two hours earlier, but the fog was thicker than ever. Its ghostly blanket enveloped them, obscuring everything more than a few metres from them and reflecting the beam from the car's dipped headlights back into Nick's eyes. He squinted against it, avoided using full beam and as a result the speedo rarely indicated more than 40. Nick's attention switched between the white line down the left side of the road and the one marking the centre, he trusted there would be nothing in his way. Their number one priority was fuel; they'd both reached the same conclusion that filling stations would be closing early if they were unable to accept card payments, and the one's advertising 24-hour opening would be hardest hit.

'There's a Shell garage about two miles ahead.' Susie had her iPad open, searching.

'We're OK for another hundred miles.' Nick said, 'I'm more worried about tomorrow. If this doesn't get sorted, we might not be able to get any fuel at all.'

'Are you OK? This is worse than pea-soup.' Susie peered through the gloom and made a vague gesture at the road ahead.

'No kidding, it's going take bloody ages at this speed.' Nick said.

'It'll take as long as it takes.' Susie reassured him. 'Nobody's going anywhere, he'll wait for us if it takes all night.'

'What can you do anyway?' Nick asked, 'I mean, when we get there, what can you do? Your boss doesn't expect you to fix it, does he? And this guy you're meeting must know his stuff. Surely, he'll have done everything he can.'

Susie thought for a moment, 'The boss doesn't expect me to fix it, he's not an idiot. He wants my opinion, he wants me to ask questions, he wants me to see with my own eyes what's happened. He thinks I might have a more objective view than this Bracewell guy as if he's too close to the problem.'

Nick was dubious and made a dismissive noise. He peered into the gloom, not wanting to miss the upcoming garage. He reached over and tapped Susie's iPad. 'Ignore that thing for a moment and keep a look out for this garage, we could drive right past it and never see it.'

'If it's still open.' Susie closed the cover and stared ahead. 'For all we know, they may have given up and gone home. I mean, who pays with cash these days?'

Nick slowed as a faint yellow and red glow appeared out of the gloom, the glow evolved into the familiar Shell logo. 'Well, the lights are on, let's see if anyone's at home.' He pulled off the road and turned onto the forecourt. Seven of the eight pumps had a vehicle alongside: a silver BMW, a black Toyota 4x4, a blue Ford SUV, two small hatchbacks, one white and one red, two vans and a flatbed truck. Nobody was pumping fuel.

'This doesn't look good.' Susie said.

Nick stopped in the space behind the Toyota. He leaned forward and stared into the shop and the cashier's desk. 'That poor guy will be wishing he'd shut up shop before now.'

'I'll go and investigate.' Susie was already halfway out of the car.

'Watch yourself love, don't get involved.'

She nodded and closed the door.

5

What greeted Susie, as she walked into the shop, confirmed Nick's initial thoughts, and it didn't look good.

The seven drivers were confronting the cashier, a young man who in his worst dreams had never expected his Friday night shift at the local garage to turn out like this. He looked lost and appeared to be repeating the same message, no card payments, cash only, payment in advance. The message fell on deaf ears. The glass screen was the cashier's only protection and he needed it. Two of the drivers were banging on the screen with their fists, demanding that the young man switch the pumps on and let them fill up.

One of the men, Susie guessed from his overalls that he was the driver of the flatbed, banged his fists harder than the other man, causing the screen the shudder then crack. The cashier jumped back, visibly terrified, and let out a startled yelp.

'There's nothing I can do,' he pleaded, 'The system's crashed, it's not just here it's everywhere. You can't pay by card.'

'Don't be such a fucking dick, I'm in here three nights a week, you know me.' The man in the overalls shouted, his face red, only inches from the screen, the veins on his forehead standing proud. 'Just put the pump on, I'll fill up and come back tomorrow and pay you when the system's fixed.'

Susie moved closer. She could see that two of the drivers, middle-aged women, showed concern for the young man behind the screen. They tried to appease the man in the overalls, without success. The other drivers watched events unfold in states that varied from anger through frustration to resignation.

The cashier, from behind the screen, wailed in response. 'I can't do that, the regional manager called me an hour ago, and she said I could only accept cash. I'm really, really sorry.'

'Sorry!' The man in the overalls threw his arms in the air and turned to the other drivers to confirm he was speaking on their behalf, two of them gave a half-hearted nod. He turned back suitably bolstered; the screen was now covered in spittle. 'Sorry doesn't cut it, sonny. We've all got to get home and we need fuel.'

'Have you got any cash at all?' the young man asked in hope.

'If I had cash, we wouldn't be having this conversation.' The man banged on the screen again. 'Now put the fucking pump on before I pull this down and do it myself.'

'I'll have to call the Police.' The young man behind the screen feared for his safety as well as his job. He reached behind for the phone.

Susie couldn't stand around watching any longer. She pulled her warrant card from her jacket pocket and pushed between the other drivers. 'I am the Police.' she said, holding the card for the man in the overalls to see.

The effect was immediate, as if she'd popped a balloon. The bluster vanished. The man in the overalls glanced at Susie and then at the card. He was bigger than her, at least a foot taller and probably twice her weight, but there were witnesses and he noticed the CCTV camera. He backed down, harrumphing and muttering.

'It may be frustrating but threatening...' she peered at the young man to read his name badge, 'threatening young Scott here, is going to get you nowhere.'

'Just my bloody luck, a plain-clothes copper when you don't need one.'

'Suck it up, buddy. You can either get going or I can arrest you.'

The man in the overalls looked at the other drivers, their support appeared to have dwindled, and he was on his own. 'So, you're going to slap handcuffs on me and take me in?' He drew himself up to his full height, took a step closer and looked down at Susie.

Susie stood her ground and met his stare; she wasn't going to be intimidated. She glanced out of the window and shook her head. 'Not me, my partner's in the car, he's ex-forces, and he's not in the best of moods tonight. He'd love any excuse to press charges.' She made the last two words sound as ambiguous as she could.

The man's eyes flicked to the view outside then back at Susie. The threat, much to Susie's relief, did the trick and with a final frustrated slap of the screen he left the shop, aiming a kick at a display of Quality Street as he passed.

The other drivers watched him go and looked back at Susie. She held her arms out in a gesture of apology. 'Sorry guys, but you heard what Scott here said, if you don't have cash there's nothing he can do.'

One by one they all left until one of the ladies who'd shown concern for the cashier stood on her own, uncertain of what to do. She fixed Susie with a look of admiration 'That was very brave of you.'

Susie shrugged. 'I'm not so sure brave is the right word, but I can't stand bullying, I had to do something.'

The cashier joined in. 'Yeah, thank you, lady, I thought it was all going to kick off.'

'Can I make a suggestion?' Susie asked.

Scott looked at her, his eyes narrowed.

'Ring your manager and tell her you're closing for the night. Tell them you've been advised by the Police to prevent further trouble.'

He nodded with enthusiasm at the suggestion.

'Before you do that.' Susie checked the cars on the forecourt to make sure they were all leaving. The only car remaining was the red hatchback which assumed belonged to the lady standing next to her. 'Can you switch on pump number eight; I've got forty quid in cash.'

The concerned lady wavered. 'I've got cash as well, I didn't want to say anything and I was hoping to keep it for emergencies, but can I get some fuel?'

Scott nodded again. 'You'll have to pay in advance.'

Susie handed over the cash. 'I need a receipt and when we're done, switch everything off, all the lights, all the signs, then go home. In fact, switch them off now, just keep the pump on. If anyone goes past and sees the lights on, they might be tempted to call in.'

She looked out into the forecourt as the signs went out, and one by one the floodlights were switched off, leaving a solitary light over the pump beside her Golf, she gave Nick the thumbs up, and he jumped out and started refuelling.

The lady with the red hatchback handed over her cash and went out to manoeuvre her car behind the Golf. Susie looked back at Scott. 'Are you OK?'

He looked relieved. 'Yes thanks, I just want to get out of this place.' The printer whirred and ejected the receipt.

'Just remember to ring your boss and explain.' Susie picked up the receipt, left the shop and joined Nick. They urged the fuel into the tank, anxious to get going and watched as the numbers on the pump clicked higher, wishing it would go faster. The pump slowed as it approached 40.00 and shut off automatically when it hit the mark. They couldn't leave fast enough and jumped into the car and drove off without looking back.

The fog was as dense as ever, their speed no higher. 'This is ridiculous.' said Nick, crouching over the steering wheel, his vision straining to follow the road. The glare from the dipped headlights bounced back into his face, he knocked them off and drove using just the fog lights; their wide soft beam was marginally easier on the eye. 'I'm going to pick up the M3.' he spoke without turning to Susie, 'I know it's not the shortest way, but at this rate it's going to take us all night otherwise.'

Susie didn't argue, she trusted Nick's judgement and her eyesight was suffering as much as his.

6

Valley View Cottage lurked at the end of a half-mile track.

Access to the track was a sharp turn off a little used B road that ran from the town below over a depression between two hills. The turn was easy to miss, forty-foot pine trees lined the road and obscured the turn in. There was no sign to the cottage, nothing to give away its presence. For the first hundred yards, the track wound through trees that crowded in and created a tunnel. At the end of the wood, a dry stone wall formed a boundary with the field beyond. Further progress was blocked with a solid five-bar gate, its hinges set into stone gateposts and the latch end securely locked with a heavy-duty chain and padlock. On the other side of the gate, a cattle grid with several missing and broken rails was set into the track. The track across the field was a rough unmade road, deeply rutted with a ridge running down the middle between wheel tracks. It turned and twisted, fell away out of sight and petered out into the field. Even the curious wouldn't think of following the track, it looked impassable. There were no fences, no telegraph poles and no sign of the cottage until the track rose and turned the final corner.

The building itself, a simple two-storey stone-built farm cottage, stood on a rise in the ground and faced south. A low stone wall formed a boundary with the track, extending back to create a small garden on the west side of the cottage. On a good day, it was easy to see how it had acquired its name, the cottage had a commanding view, not just over the valley, but over all the land around it.

At seven in the evening on a cold foggy evening at the end of December, there was no view at all. The darkness was oppressive, the fog rolled in slow waves from west to east. A diesel powered generator hummed quietly in a small outbuilding, it was the only noise, and it was sucked out of the air by a silence that clung to the ground. A twenty-year-old Land Rover Defender stood guard outside the cottage, its paintwork, a colour somewhere between dark green and dark blue was caked in road grime and splattered mud. There were no signs of life from the cottage, no lights could be seen, and no sound could be heard from outside.

There was life of sorts inside the cottage. Harrison Thurlow slouched in his favourite place on the four-person settee with a bottle of Stella and a family-sized bag of tortilla chips. His favourite place took up three of the four places. His head propped up by the armrest at one end, he stretched his length over two more cushions. At five foot five, he could stretch out as much as he liked, there was plenty of room. He wore a pair of desert camouflage combat pants, a matching jacket over an olive green T-shirt and, much to his partner's dismay, a pair of army desert boots, which were still wet with mud from his last excursion to the log shed. His beard, a tangled mess of dirty red whiskers, was ingrained with the evidence of all he had consumed over the previous twelve hours. Crumbs from the tortillas and flecks of foam from the Stella were the most recent additions.

A single lamp perched on a sideboard at the back of the room provided enough light to make out the features of the living room. A door behind the settee led to the kitchen and another in the opposite corner, to the small hallway and the stairs. The only window in the room hid behind a single floor-to-ceiling heavyweight curtain. The walls, painted in a nondescript beige, were home to a bookcase and only two pictures; a mass-produced print of an African sunset and a festival poster from three years earlier. In addition to the lamp, an orange glow flickered from a wood-burning stove that crackled and popped as it consumed a steady supply of seasoned timber. The room was comfortably warm, but no more, Harrison controlled the fire carefully, he didn't want to have to get up every ten minutes to put another log on it.

The main source of light in the room came from a 53-inch flat-screen television that Harrison watched through half-closed eyes. He zapped from channel to channel to find something that would retain his attention for more than a few seconds. More by luck than design, he eventually landed on the BBC news just as video footage of a man in police uniform appeared above a headline that read, "Shoppers urged not to panic after card payments fail.". The caption under the man's picture said, "Commander Rob Eddington, Cyber Crime Unit". Harrison sat up. He put the bottle on the low table between the settee and the television and turned the volume up. As he watched, his face took on a look of satisfaction that bordered on triumph.

He slapped his hand on the table, spilling a handful of tortilla chips. 'Ha!' he shouted and punched the air.

The kitchen door opened and a slight woman in her early thirties peered into the room. 'What's up?'

Harrison didn't take his eyes off the screen. 'It's happening, it's all kicking off.'

The woman walked into the room to see what the fuss was about. She caught the end of Rob Eddington's statement; he was stressing the need not to overreact. 'Where did this happen?'

'It's happening everywhere, all over the country, nobody can use their plastic to pay for anything. Just as planned.' Harrison's tone was gleeful.

Pia Cavell tipped her head to one side, her face screwed up trying to make sense of what Harrison was saying and what the news was reporting. 'I don't understand, how can that happen?'

'It's happened because it's been made to happen. I didn't think it would kick off so quickly, but it has.'

Pia nodded, not wishing to argue.

'They'll be running around like headless chickens if they've got no cash.' Harrison slapped his thigh again and pumped a fist.

'That's a bit cruel, it is Christmas.'

'So bloody what, I bet nobody is better prepared for this than we are.' He turned to look at Pia. 'We can survive for months without ever leaving the house.'

'So you keep telling me.'

'It's true; we've got all we need right here.' He waved his hand to indicate the whole house.

Pia rolled her eyes at this. 'Don't I know it; you've made it like an army storage depot.'

Harrison was having none of it, he tapped the side of his head with an index finger. 'Up here for thinking. Can you think of a single thing we'd have to go out for?'

'Fresh fruit and veg would be nice.'

'What d'you think all those supplements are for? All the vitamins and nutrients you'll ever need, and you don't have to peel them or chop them or cook them.'

Pia wasn't convinced. 'It's not exactly World War Three or the great apocalypse you keep predicting.' She'd had half an eye on the television as they spoke. 'It's only just happened this afternoon, they'll have it fixed by tomorrow and we'll still be holed up here with enough food for six months and sod all excitement.'

'Don't be so sure.' Harrison tapped the side of his nose. 'This is a well planned attack.'

'Why? What did he say?'

'It's not what he said. It's what he didn't say and what I know.'

Pia was a patient woman; she'd lived with Harrison for two years and heard it all before. At first, she loved his rebellious streak, his plans to live off-grid, as he called it. She was impressed with his practical abilities and an almost manic work ethic. They'd bought the cottage as a ruin, and he'd done all the renovation work himself, he wouldn't allow anyone else near the place. The old Land Rover went back and forth to builder's merchants for materials, and every item of equipment they needed was brought in by the same method. She was never sure where the money came from; he changed the subject whenever the topic came up, telling her she didn't need to worry.

The novelty was beginning to wear off. The work was all done, he had built his retreat from the world. They were entirely self-sufficient. From what she could deduce, they didn't exist on any official records. They had no connection to the outside world, no bank account, no bills, no post, no phone. She'd never seen anything relating to taxes, licences or permissions. He was either very good at hiding them or had done a very good job of erasing their presence from the local authority.

It suited Pia. She didn't have a family. She did once, back in Latvia but that was many years ago before she went to the children's home. If they were still alive, she had no idea where they lived. She battled with depression during her teenage years and into her early twenties.

She'd fled to the UK in the hope of a better life but had fallen in with the wrong crowd and experimented with drugs, stumbled from one dead-end job to the next. Her faith in people, the government, the council and officials in general was at rock bottom when she met Harrison. She was living on her own in a stinking bed-sit, having walked out of her last job as a warehouse admin assistant. She fell out with her manager, a woman whose idea of motivation was to scream and shout insults, humiliating staff and reducing them to tears. Harrison had been a delivery driver at the time, and he'd witnessed the abuse. The usual banter had developed into something a little more with each visit, and they'd swapped contact details. When Harrison arrived at the warehouse to find Pia had left, he tracked her down to the bed-sit. At the time, she thought he'd saved her life. She was struggling to find a reason to get out of bed in the morning, she felt unloved and unwanted and since Brexit was terrified she'd be sent back to Latvia. When he turned up at her door, she had never been so pleased to see another human being in her life. He convinced her he could keep her safe from deportation and filled her head with his plans and promised her a life away from all the misery she had suffered. She believed every word and stuck with him through thick and thin.

She looked at him now, gloating over the misfortune of others, and her doubts and frustrations bubbled to the surface. 'So, what didn't he say?'

Harrison reached for another bottle of Stella. 'Nothing about terrorism or organised crime, nothing about the need to stock up or ration what you've got.' He turned away from the screen to look at Pia. 'He didn't once say anything about this being a temporary problem.'

'You're reading too much into it, you've always loved your conspiracy theories.'

'It's not a theory, it's a fact. He knows he can't out and out lie, he can't say it's a technical issue if they know it's deliberate, the truth will come out. All he's saying is that they're on the case, and like all good citizens, we should trust the authorities to sort it out.'

'What else do you expect him to say? Anything else would just incite the sort of panic they want to prevent.' Pia found herself defending the police; it went against all her deeply held beliefs, and it troubled her to think that way, but Harrison's paranoia troubled her more.

'I wouldn't expect him to say anything else, that's the point, every word of that statement will have been chosen carefully. He'll have rehearsed it, done a few takes, they'll have edited out anything they weren't happy with.' He cocked a thumb over his shoulder at the television. 'What we see is a meaningless statement that's designed to give them time and keep us in the dark.'

Pia knew that further discussion was pointless. She had seen Harrison like this before, convinced the system was out to get him. She didn't know what he was hiding or what it was he had to fear, but he always found the negative in whatever he read or watched on television. Pia had her reasons for wanting to avoid people, but he took it to a whole new level. If he went online, it was only ever on the dark web. He avoided anything that involved taking out a subscription or having to make online payments. He had bypassed the mainstream satellite providers and rigged up his own dish that picked up dozens of channels from all across Europe; she was sure it was illegal but knew better than to labour the point.

Once the building work on the house had been finished and they had no further reason to interact with the outside world, Harrison had developed a hermit-like mentality. As far as she could see, he had no family, he said he didn't want to talk about his family, he said they were dead to him. It was another taboo subject. He had no friends; he never talked about anyone else. Once or twice, he had referred to his five-year stint in the army. She suspected he left under a cloud, but when she pried, he'd lost his temper and told her it was none of her business.

She looked at him now, returned to his recumbent position, his mind churning, fuelled by alcohol and paranoid thoughts. He was turning into an outcast; she knew there were those who would label him a weirdo. Not for the first time, she felt trapped. She thought he loved her; he told her repeatedly. She used to love him, she used to feel safe, she used to feel wanted, she used to feel secure, but now she felt trapped. She didn't drive and couldn't remember the last time she had left the cottage and gone anywhere. Harrison provided everything; they had two huge chest freezers and a seemingly limitless supply of food and drink, and if she asked for anything special, he'd always get it for her on one of his monthly supply runs, as he called them. Materially, there was nothing she wanted but she was beginning to feel she was missing out on so much more.

She knew that when he was in this mood and after he'd had a few bottles of beer, further discussion was pointless. 'You want to eat in here?' She gestured at the room.

He had turned back to the television and started flicking through channels, looking for more news. 'Sure, what we having?' He said without looking at her.

'Bangers and mash.' Pia felt she could have said anything she liked and received the same response.

'Sounds great, whenever you're ready.'

Pia rolled her eyes and slowly shook her head, she slipped back into the kitchen and closed the door behind her. Harrison remained focused on the huge TV screen.

7

It was after ten when they arrived at the Payline building, a modern, single-storey building in a business park on the north side of Swindon, all glass and concrete, lights blazing. Nick rubbed his eyes with the back of his hands, squinting to re-focus. 'You want me to come in with you?'

Susie thought for a moment, studying the building. There were four cars lined up outside the entrance and she could see lights behind blinds but no other sign of life. 'Thanks love, god knows what we'll find in there.'

They got out of the car and walked towards the main door, expecting a confrontation with a faceless intercom system. The door swung open when they were a few feet away and a man stepped out to greet them. 'G'day, I'm Trent.' he held out his hand in greeting, 'you must be Jones?'

Susie nodded and shook his hand, Nick measured him up, not what he was expecting. Even in the unflattering light and the fog, Trent looked like a fit outdoors type, bright-eyed and alert with bleached blonde hair, buzz cut short. He was about the same height as Nick, just under six feet and slim. Despite the cold, he was only wearing a sweatshirt, jeans and a pair of Day-Glo running shoes. Nick, wrapped in a thick quilted jacket, guessed he was one of those who didn't feel the cold.

'This way guys, thanks for coming down. Hell of a mess.'

Susie and Nick followed him through two sets of doors into a brightly lit corridor. The offices on either side of the corridor had opaque glass at the windows making it impossible to know if anyone else was in the building.

Susie's curiosity got the better of her. 'Not much sign of life, are you here on your own?'

'Nah, there's four of us, my technical director and two of his staff are at the far end in the server room.'

They arrived at the end of the corridor, the sign on the door said "Strictly No Admittance". Bracewell pushed it open and held it for Susie and Nick.

The room hummed with the sound of electricity, the whir of cooling fans and the buzz computers make when they make and break connections a thousand times a second. Susie detected a faint odour of burning plastic. She sniffed, 'What's that smell?'

Bracewell stopped mid-stride and did a passable imitation of a spaniel catching the scent of a rabbit, nose in the air, eyes closed as he analysed the air. 'You're right, I guess I've got used to it. Come on, I'll show you.' He continued walking past the steel racking that appeared to be alive with red, blue, yellow and green LEDs that blinked off and on. Susie assumed the racking contained the servers Bracewell referred to.

They rounded a corner and found three men with their backs to them, studying the inside of a floor-to-ceiling grey metal cabinet, wide enough for all three to step into. One of them turned when he heard Bracewell arrive. He shook his head slowly, his face a picture of despair.

'Is it as bad as you thought?' Bracewell looked gravely at his technical director.

'It's actually worse. We've got all the protective covers off now. Come and look at this.'

The other two men moved out of the way to let Bracewell examine the wiring. Susie could see the source of the burning smell, a mass of twisted, blackened plastic covered the back of the cabinet.

'Bloody hell.' Nick peered over Susie's shoulder and saw the damage. 'Are those data cables?'

The technical director looked at Nick and then at Bracewell with an expression that said *who's this*?

Bracewell understood. 'Sorry, this is Susan Jones from the Police Cyber Crime Unit, and this is Nick Cooper her...' He paused waiting for Nick to fill the gap.

'Partner.'

'Nick, this is Jay, my technical director.'

The two men nodded acknowledgement.

Suitably assured, Jay answered Nick's question. 'They're phone lines, our connection to the outside world.'

'How many lines?'

'Twenty. Well, there are twenty cables, and each cable has two pairs of wires, so in effect there's 40 lines.'

Susie looked puzzled. 'Doesn't sound like a lot to handle all the incoming calls.'

Bracewell cut in. 'You'd be surprised, each call, each transaction, lasts a matter of seconds. Each line can handle ten to fifteen calls a minute.

'So how come we wait for ages when we come to pay?'

'There's a lag in the software at the retail end, it slows things down. Nothing to do with us.'

Susie nodded, still staring at the burned-out cables, her eyes narrowed.

Nick followed Susie's gaze; he could see what had caught her attention. He pointed at the point where the cables were attached to nine small plastic boxes. 'Are those modems?'

Bracewell and Jay both answered at the same time. 'Yes.'

Susie leaned closer. 'They don't look damaged, it's just the cables.'

'Right again. We assumed the modems must be faulty, but we can't see any damage.' Jay looked more closely and ran a finger over the casing.

Bracewell could see what Susie was getting at. 'So why did the cables burn out if the modems are OK?' He looked sideways at Jay, frowning.

One of the other men who had stepped out of the way reached past Jay, grabbed one of the burned cables and pulled it. It snapped cleanly at the point where it entered the modem, the other end, blackened and distorted, disappeared into a mass of trunking. 'Looks to me like there's been some sort of power surge or something.'

The others made noncommittal noises of agreement.

Bracewell stared at the contents of the cabinet, thinking hard. 'How quickly can you replace the cables?'

Jay looked at his two colleagues. 'What do you think guys?'

The one who had grabbed the burned cable pursed his lips. 'All of them?'

'Just one for now,' Bracewell said, still staring at the damage. 'If it works, we can do the others.'

'We'll have to power down the system, pull out the board, remove the mess, install a new one, assuming we've got enough.' It was the third member of the team who spoke, he looked at Jay for an answer.

'We've got enough for one or two, depending on how far back the damage has spread. We'll have to order more if it works.'

Bracewell turned away from the cabinet. 'That'll have to do, let's see if that solves the problem. If it does, I'll make some phone calls.'

Susie and Nick watched, unsure of what they could do. Bracewell looked at them. 'With a bit of luck, we might have cracked it.' He held up crossed fingers.

Nick glanced at his watch. 'Any idea how long it'll take?'

Jay's eyes flicked between the two technicians. 'Forty minutes?'

The other two gave the smallest of nods.

Bracewell was satisfied. 'OK guys, quick as you can.' He checked his watch. 'Not much we can do here. You want a coffee or something?'

'You haven't got anything to eat, have you?' Nick asked, patting his stomach and looking a little guilty.

Susie shook her head and smiled at Bracewell. 'Sorry, you'll have to forgive Nick, he has a one-track mind.'

Nick was affronted. 'What d'you mean? I've only had a few biscuits since lunchtime and it's almost midnight.'

Bracewell laughed, made a dismissive gesture and ushered Nick and Susie out of the control room. 'I'm sure we've got something to keep the wolf from the door. There's a canteen of sorts at the other end of the building, let's go raid it.'

Nick brightened visibly as they left the server room.

The estimate of forty minutes proved optimistic and after an hour of small talk, two cups of vending machine coffee and what few biscuits remained in the cookie jar, Trent Bracewell could stand it no longer and left the canteen to find out what his technicians had been able to do.

Susie watched him go and her own impatience gnawed at her. She tapped Nick's arm. 'Come on, let's go and see if they've fixed it. We can't sit here all night.'

With a resigned sigh, Nick put down an old bike magazine he'd been idly flipping through. 'Guess so. If I sit here any longer, I'm going to nod off.' He got to his feet and followed Susie.

They arrived back in the server room to be greeted with an anguished cry from one of the technicians. 'I don't believe it.'

Bracewell held his hands to his head. His relaxed demeanour evaporated rapidly.

Susie peered around him and could see whisps of smoke rising from the cable. 'Is that the new one?'

'Yeah. They've just spent an hour putting it in. Nothing happened when they powered up but as soon as we dialled in, poof.' He threw his hands in the air for emphasis.

'Is it the same modem?' Susie asked.

Bracewell appeared surprised by the question. 'Well...yes, we assumed the modem was OK and the problem lay in the cable.'

'And you're sure it's not the modem?'

'It's unlikely; they're all new. Essentially, they're just switches.'

Nick interrupted. 'Have you got a spare modem, a new one?'

Bracewell looked to Jay for an answer. 'We've got one. Remember we bought ten to get the deal they were offering, and we just needed nine for the grid.' The Technical Director waved a hand at the nine white boxes for the avoidance of any doubt.

Susie picked up on Nick's line of thought. 'Is it worth trying a new one?'

Jay gave a deflated sigh. 'Great idea, but that was the last of the CAT6.' He jerked a thumb at the mess of burned-out cable.

Bracewell's gaze fixed on the ceiling, and he shook his head in painful recognition of the situation. 'Bloody Nora, what a total fuck up.'

'Look,' Susie refused to be beaten. 'there's nothing more you can do now, agreed?'

'Agreed.' Bracewell shrugged.

'So, can we take the damaged modem back to HQ? They've got some pretty fancy kit; they can analyse it and see if there's something wrong with it.'

'Yeah, why not, we're all out of options.'

Susie had another thought. 'Where's the other one?' she looked at Bracewell, then Jay, then the other two technicians. They looked blankly at each other for a moment.

It was Jay who caught on first. 'You mean the tenth modem?'

Susie nodded, 'Can we take that as well, it would help to compare them side by side, it might tell us something.'

'Worth a try,' said Bracewell, 'nothing ventured and all that.'

Jay slipped out to get the device in question while one of the other technicians removed the modem connected to the newly burned-out cable. He handed it to Susie.

Bracewell pointed out a couple of details on the modem as they walked back towards the exit and waited for Jay. 'Just keep in touch and let me know as soon as you find anything out.' A note of desperation crept into his voice. 'This is costing us. Big time.'

Susie placed the modem in her messenger bag as Jay appeared with the new one, still in its original packaging. She added it to her bag and held out a hand to Bracewell.

'Stuff that.' He ignored the hand and hugged her. 'Really appreciate what you're doing.' He released her and took a step back looking a little embarrassed. 'Sorry about that, not very PC.'

For a second or two Susie appeared flummoxed, unsure how to react. She glanced at Nick who simply shrugged. 'No worries.' Was the best she could come up with. She took Nick's arm and propelled him towards the door. 'I'll call you tomorrow.'

'It's already tomorrow.' said Nick as he left the building. 'she means later today.'

Nick drove out of the business park three hours after they had arrived. The digital clock on the dashboard ticked over to 01:17.

The fog still weighed oppressively, it swirled and shifted, if anything it had grown even more impenetrable with each passing hour.

'I need to call Eddington and tell him what we've found.' Susie said as she reached for her phone.

'Yeah, see if he can get someone ready to break open those things.' Nick jerked his head to indicate the bag on the back seat.

Susie raised her phone to her lips. 'Hey Siri, call Eddington.' She waited while the device did as instructed.

After four rings a voice answered. 'Commander Eddington's phone.'

Susie's brow creased, she didn't recognise the voice. 'It's Susan Jones, who's that?'

'Oh hi, it's Wade, Wade Millard, the boss is on the other line. Anything I can do?'

'Ah. Okay, hi Wade. Yes, can you let him know we're on our way back. We think we've identified the problem, but we'll need someone who can interrogate a sealed modem, We're bringing two from Payline.'

'That's great, I'll pass the message on. What's your ETA?'

With the speakerphone activated, Nick heard the conversation. Susie looked at him expectantly. Nick didn't take his eyes off the road but pointed at the satnav screen. 'It's set for Warrenford, the ETA's on the screen.'

'According to the magic map, we'll arrive at three minutes past two, but somehow I think we'll be later than that, the fog's even thicker than before.'

'No one's going anywhere, we'll see you when you get here.'

'Thanks, Wade, see you in a bit.' Susie clicked off the phone. She glanced at Nick. 'You all right, love?'

Nick yawned in response, a long, loud and expansive yawn. 'Just keep talking and nudge me if I don't look like I'm not paying attention.'

After negotiating the tight security at Warrenford for the second time that night, Nick parked the Golf under one of the floodlights away from the tower. Susie pushed her door open and stepped out into the cold, misty gloom. 'Bloody hell, this is miserable.' She shivered and pulled her down jacket tight around her. 'At least that place has a decent heating system.' She jutted her chin towards the orange glow emanating from the windows of the control room thirty feet above her.

She walked around the back of the car and joined Nick as they headed for the door. He put an arm around her shoulders and hugged her. She snuggled in close to him, grateful for the extra warmth.

'I'll be interested to see what Eddington says when he sees those two modems.' Susie said as they reached the door, and she activated the intercom. 'It's Susie Jones and Nick Cooper.'

They both looked up at the camera above the door and waited.

A few seconds passed, and then they heard the soft click of the lock. Nick reached for the handle and held the door open. He glanced down at Susie as she walked in. 'Where are they?'

'What?'

'The modems, where've you put them?'

'I thought you had them.'

'No, I thought you had them.'

Susie gave a disbelieving shake of her head. 'Brilliant, what a team.'

'I'll go back for them.' Nick turned to leave.

'No, it's my fault,' Susie held Nick's arm. 'I put them on the back seat. You go on up and I'll join you in a minute.'

'Sure?'

'Yeah, sure. You can get started and tell them what we've found.'

Nick smiled and bent down to kiss his wife. 'Thanks love, anyway, that coffee's gone straight through me, I'd better get up there sharpish.'

Susie watched him enter the lift, then pressed the big green door release button to let herself back out into the night. She jogged across the parking area towards the Golf, aware that her footsteps were the only noise, the oppressive darkness and the clinging fog soaked up all other sounds.

She reached the car and went around to the passenger door, pulled it open and tipped the seat forward to grope for the two modems. Her bag had slid to the right and fallen into the footwell behind the driver's seat.

She grunted with the effort of stretching and had to climb into the back to retrieve what she had come for.

Suddenly the world exploded around her.

A blinding light followed by a deafening crash.

Susie's senses reeled. She lost her footing and sprawled lengthways into the back of the car as chunks of masonry smashed into the side and roof of the Golf. The windscreen shattered as a section of window frame slammed into it as through it had been fired from a cannon.

Susie screamed in terror as more objects rained down. The rear driver's side window exploded into a thousand fragments that covered her from top to toe. She pressed her face into the fabric of the seat and clasped her hands together over her head. She felt needle-like shards digging into her skin.

The roar of the explosion died away to be replaced by the ominous sound of fire and flames, interspersed with the patter of debris falling from above.

After a minute, Susie pushed herself up and peered through what was left of the rear window.

Her insides convulsed.

A scene of complete devastation greeted her. The tower stood like an unfinished folly, flames licked around the top and twisted steel beams indicated where the control room had until moments earlier, had been the safe haven for the staff of the CCU.

Susie stared open-mouthed at the wreckage; at the remains of the building strewn about the parking area, some of it burning, some of it glowing from the heat. Bricks and blocks shattered glass and metal fittings. She saw what was left of the giant TV screens, she saw computer equipment, cables, bits of chairs and tables. Then she saw an arm, dismembered and bloody.

One word escaped her. 'Nick.'

Then she threw up.

8

Saturday 23 December

It took Susie a moment to realise her ears were ringing. She could see but she couldn't hear. The explosion had deafened her temporarily.

She shuffled away from the shattered rear window, her palms pressed down on the fragments of broken glass which cut into her skin. More of the shards fell from her back and from where they had become entangled in her hair.

Her senses battled with each other, she could see the danger outside and terror gripped her at the thought of what she would find if she ventured out.

While the car offered her some protection, Susie knew she had to move; it could catch fire at any time.

She kicked the passenger door open with her foot and reversed her way out on elbows and knees. Her feet made contact with the ground, and she pulled herself upright by clinging to the door frame.

Her body shook, and her heart raced. Vomit still lingered in her mouth, and she reached for the Evian she'd left in the door pocket.

Burning debris lay all around and the air crackled with the noise of electrical connections wrenched apart in the explosion. Rooted to the spot, she stared in horror at the scene. She struggled to take in the devastation, unable to believe what had happened.

Her thoughts remained with Nick. He had to be in the centre of it all. He couldn't possibly survive.

A firm hand shook her shoulder. She turned to find one of the armed policemen from the gate.

'You all right?'

Susie stared at the man. He had run towards the danger and breathed heavily. Concern etched his features.

Her muffled hearing made his words indistinct, but she understood. 'I think so,' she ran her hands over her arms and torso in an exaggerated display of checking, then raised a hand and pointed at the wreckage of the control tower. 'But my husband is in there.'

The policeman's grim face glowed in the reflection of the flames. 'Oh shit.'

'We've got to look for him.' Susie moved from the shelter of the car.

'You can't go there love, the whole thing could collapse at any minute.' He nodded at the decapitated tower and attempted to lead Susie away by taking hold of her elbow. 'There's nothing you can do. We have to wait for help.'

'Sod that.' Susie shook herself free of his grip, driven by the fear of losing Nick. 'You seriously think I'm going to just stand here and do nothing?' She started towards what remained of the entrance door.

The policeman shouted after her. 'You can't. Come back.' He shook his head in frustration as he realised his words fell on deaf ears. If she had regained her hearing, there was no acknowledgement she'd heard him. Resigned to the situation, he shouldered the MP5 and went after her. He activated his lapel mic. '755 to control, I'm going in with the Jones woman, her husband's in there, she won't listen to sense.'

Susie picked her way through the fallen masonry. The acrid smell of burning plastic and rubber assaulted her senses and she pinched her nose in a vain effort to evade it. Then she caught the unmistakable odour of burning flesh. It brought back memories from her time in Afghanistan. She gagged and covered her mouth with her hand in fear of throwing up again. She squinted against the heat and stepped over shattered concrete blocks without looking down, afraid of what she might see.

The policeman followed two steps behind her and held his torch above his head, lighting the way forward. 'I'm sorry love, but if your fella was up there, he wouldn't have stood a chance.'

Susie ignored him again and reached what had once been the door, now just a misshapen frame. The door itself hung at an impossible angle, supported by its lower hinge. Susie pushed it aside and stepped into what remained of the reception area. The desk had been flattened to half its original height, squashed by a massive chunk of the inner wall that appeared to have fallen from high above. A flicker of torchlight caught movement on one side of the desk, a flash of colour fluttered in the swirling eddies of hot air. She recognised it as the bright yellow scarf worn by Jasmin. Susie gasped with shock and the realisation that the receptionist would have been sitting at the desk when the explosion tore the building apart.

The door to the lift stood solidly in place, and Susie beckoned to the policeman to shine his torch on the shaft above. With relief, she saw it appeared to have withstood the blast, but she had no way of knowing where the lift itself was, whether Nick was still in it or if he'd made it to the top and...She shook her head and tried to banish the negative thoughts from her mind. 'I just hope he's in there.' she nodded at the lift. 'It looks like the only thing that's survived.'

The policeman grunted an acknowledgement but said nothing as he studied the area surrounding the lift door.

'Is there a way to open it without any power?' Susie banged a fist against the door in frustration. 'We've got to get it open; he could be in there, he could be injured.'

The policeman placed a hand over Susie's fist and lifted it away from the door. He made eye contact with her and spoke in a low firm tone. 'Hold on love, that's not going to help. We need some tools.'

'Is there no emergency access or something?' A sense of panic crept into Susie's voice.

The policeman held up a hand with his index finger extended. 'Just a minute.' He clicked his mic, '755 to control.'

'What's happening Phil, you OK?' Radio protocols appeared to have been forgotten.

'Yeah, we're OK, we're at the base of the lift shaft, it looks intact, and we need to get in. Can someone bring down the black bag.'

'What's the black bag?' Susie frowned.

Phil the policeman tapped the side of his nose. 'What we need to open this.' He played the light of his torch over the steel door.

While she waited, Susie ran her hands over the door and its surroundings as though she might find a secret button. She grabbed a piece of blockwork and used it to bang against the door. She called Nick's name and placed her ear against the door. There was no response.

Phil the policeman watched in helpless resignation. He glanced up at the remnants of the ceiling, then outside, willing one of his colleagues to appear before the whole edifice crashed down.

Susie saw torchlight outside and shouted for the second officer. 'We're here, hurry.'

Phil turned to see his oppo, who lugged a large black holdall into the place that used to be the reception area. 'Well done mate.' He turned to Susie. 'This is Vince, he's good at this sort of thing.'

Susie glanced up. She thought Phil was big, over six feet, but Vince was huge, at least six six. 'Hi Vince, I'm Susie.' She realised he was the one who'd asked for her ID when they arrived back from Payline. 'How are you going to get this open?'

Like Phil, Vince was clad in black and bulked up by a tactical vest and helmet. He didn't respond initially but handed his torch to Susie and rummaged in the holdall. He found what he was looking for: a three-foot-long crowbar, flattened to a sharp point at one end and curved into a handle at the other. He waved it at Susie and answered her question. 'Brute force and ignorance.'

He approached the door and held the jemmy like a weapon. 'Which way does it slide to open?' He looked at the other two, Phil shrugged, Susie shook her head. 'Great. Just keep that light on the door and out of my eyes.'

Susie watched as Vince ran a gloved hand down the side of the door frame, appeared to settle on a point, then jammed the sharp flat end of the tool into the narrow gap. She could do nothing to help and thought it better to let the man work without distractions. She shone the torch on the business end of the bar and willed it to force the door open.

Vince grunted with the effort of forcing the jemmy further into the gap. The steel under the bar bent under the pressure but the door refused to move. He looked up and winced as more debris fell from above and landed nearby. 'There's another bar in the bag mate, can you grab it and give us a hand.'

Phil did as instructed and followed Vince's instructions. The two policemen heaved on the bars and Susie heard a rending noise as metal tore against metal. The door moved. The movement, small but significant, appeared to breathe new strength into the men and they braced themselves on either side of the door and heaved again.

This time the movement was more pronounced and was accompanied by the sound of a connection being severed. Vince indicated to Phil to stand back, then he wedged the jemmy back into the gap and levered the door sideways. Once big enough, he forced his shoulder into the gap and braced a foot against the door frame. His face contorted with effort, he pushed and with a final crack, the door slid fully open.

Susie gasped.

The light from the torch she held fell on a boot she instantly recognised. Nick's desert boots, he wore them all the time, rain or shine, summer or winter.

The boot poked out from under a mound of smashed plasterboard panels that had fallen in a haphazard heap into the lift.

Susie elbowed past Vince. 'That's Nick.' She fell to her knees and lunged at the debris. In a state of frantic desperation, she pulled at the broken pieces and hurled them behind her.

The two policemen exchanged glances, there was nowhere for them to go and they stood in danger of being hit by the material Susie ejected from the lift. Vince ducked down to avoid a chunk of plaster the size of his head and picked up his torch; Susie had dropped it in her rush to get to her husband. He and Phil shone their beams on the diminishing pile of rubble and dodged the smaller items that flew within inches of them.

With a final effort, Susie pushed aside a short metal beam to reveal Nick's motionless body on the floor of the lift. He lay on his side with his hands over his head, one leg tucked up to his chest, the other extended, pinned down by another beam.

Susie reached for Nick's neck as soon as she cleared enough of the remaining debris. She held two fingers against his skin searching for a pulse. 'Oh, thank God, he's alive.' She brushed plaster from his face and leaned closer. She wanted to hug him, but a sixth sense kicked in, a fear of exacerbating any injuries. 'Nick, it's me, can you hear me?' She got no response.

She turned to face the two policemen and squinted against the two torch beams. 'We need to get him out of here.'

'If he's broken anything, you might make it worse if you move him.' Phil said.

'I know, but he looks OK and if we stay here any longer the whole place could collapse.' Susie looked up. The roof of the lift had fallen in and she could see all the way up the shaft. Jagged pieces of the tower's structure appeared to have dropped down and jammed across the shaft, beyond them she saw flames. 'We need to hurry. Can you help me move this?' She indicated the beam lying across Nick's extended leg.

Vince reached down and grabbed the end of the beam, it must have been heavier than he expected and he grimaced with the effort of lifting it. 'Jeez, it weighs a ton.'

Phil squeezed in beside his colleague and the pair heaved the beam off Nick's leg. Susie recoiled when she saw the damage it had done. Nick's jeans had been ripped where the beam had hit him on the side of his knee, and blood oozed between the torn threads. She ran a hand over the wound. 'It doesn't feel like anything's obviously broken but it's hard to tell.'

With the beam removed, the two policemen helped Susie. They straightened Nick's other leg, then gently pulled and lifted him clear of the rubble and out of the lift. Vince looked around in search of something.

'What is it?' Phil followed his gaze.

'Got it.' Vince left the inert Nick and went straight to the door. It still hung by a single hinge, and with a determined kick with the heel of his boot, Vince smashed it free. He returned with the door. 'Transport.' He said, further explanation considered unnecessary.

Between them, they slid Nick onto the makeshift stretcher and carried him out of the building. Susie walked alongside and held Nick's hand.

As they approached Susie's Golf, the true impact of the explosion hit her. The car had been wrecked. While she lay sprawled out in the back seat and debris had rained down, she'd been aware of objects hitting the vehicle, but she'd never looked at the side that faced the control tower, until now.

Apart from the rear window and the windscreen being smashed, the driver's side of the card been pummelled with masonry. A section of concrete blocks lay on the roof where it had landed. The roof had almost collapsed under the onslaught, distorted in every direction.

Phil, who carried the front end of the stretcher, slowed to a stop as they drew closer to the Golf. 'You have to be kidding.'

Susie's feelings of relief in getting Nick out of the wrecked tower descended into one of complete despair at the realisation of her situation. 'How am I going to get Nick to hospital?'

Phil tipped his head towards Vince. 'Are you going to tell her?'

Vince closed his eyes and shook his head. 'I called the hospital as soon as the explosion occurred. There's no chance tonight, every ambulance in the country is tied up with the rioting.'

Susie suppressed a wail. 'He needs help now; I'd drive him myself if I had a vehicle.' She peered into the gloom surrounding them, most of the overhead floodlights appeared to have survived the explosion and penetrated the fog to create pools of light. She cast about for anything she could use as transport. All the cars parked adjacent to the tower, the ones belonging to those inside, were in an even worse state than her Golf. Some were barely recognisable. 'Are there no other cars I could borrow?'

The two policemen followed her gaze and recognised her dilemma. 'Have we got the keys for the old Volvo at the back of the guardhouse?' Vince asked his colleague.

Phil frowned. 'Guess so, but God knows what state it's in.'

Susie perked up at the suggestion. 'I don't care, so long as it runs.'

'It's not road legal.' Said Phil.

Vince shrugged. 'Minor detail given what's happened.'

'Where is this Volvo?' Susie's anxious stare flipped from one of the policemen to the other, then into the darkness beyond.

'Come on, we'll show you, see if it's any good.' Vince nudged the makeshift stretcher and Phil changed direction and headed towards the guardhouse.

The big estate car sat, lonely and forgotten, in the shadow of a two-storey building behind the guardhouse.

Susie stopped in her tracks when she got closer enough to see it. 'You weren't joking.' A thick film of dust and grime covered the vehicle. The drab green bodywork, indistinguishable from the glass. 'Whose is it?'

'Haven't got a clue,' said Phil, as the two men lowered their burden to the ground, 'it's been here for as long as I can remember.'

'You ever seen it running?'

Phil shook his head and turned to Vince, who did the same.

Susie tried the driver's door and found it unlocked, she pulled the door open, surprised to see the interior light come on. 'Can you find the keys.'

Vince headed to guardhouse, while Susie opened the rear doors and folded the seats down to create space for Nick.

Vince returned and rattled a set of keys in triumph. 'I knew I seen them somewhere.' He jumped into the driver's seat and turned the key. The dashboard lit up and Susie held her breath. Vince turned the key another notch and the engine coughed into life. A cloud of thick black smoke belched out the exhaust pipe, but the engine settled into a steady throb.

Phil opened the tailgate and called for Vince. 'Come on mate, we need to get this fella on board, it's bloody freezing.'

While Vince went to help, Susie found a rag in the passenger footwell and used it to clear the grime from the windscreen, side mirrors and windows. She dropped into the driver's seat and slid it forward until she could reach the pedals.

'Got any gas?' Phil called from the back of the car.

Susie scanned the instruments, 'Half a tank' She turned the temperature control to the max and revved the engine in the hope of generating some heat. 'Thanks guys, I'd have been lost without you.'

'Hang on a minute,' Phil came around to Susie's window. 'don't rush off.' He jogged back to the guardhouse and reappeared a moment later with a bundle in his arms. 'They're a couple of all-weather coats, I'll put them over your old man.'

Susie jumped out of the car and watched the policeman arrange the long woolly coats over Nick. When he emerged from the car's interior and closed the tailgate, Susie reached up and hugged him. 'Seriously, thank you both.' She released Phil and hugged his colleague. 'Is there someone coming to sort this out?' She waved an arm in the direction of the control tower.

Vince stared at the wreckage. 'Yeah, I called it in, but all hell's breaking loose out there, it may take time.' He nodded at the back of the estate car. 'You'd better get going. You know the way?'

9

Wednesday 6 December

Mecheslav Medvedev looked up from his computer screen and appraised the two women who stood in front of him. They both looked fighting fit, toned and focused, both under 30, slim and dressed in jeans and T-shirts. They were of a similar height, a little taller than average, and both had bleached blonde hair, cropped short. One had a narrow face with bright blue eyes and a nose that had healed out of shape after being broken in a training exercise. The other's face was rounder, her eyes hooded and her features cold and hard.

He'd read the notes about them, their service records going back six years and the observations of instructors and coaches who had worked with them over that time. He didn't know which one was which, it didn't matter, they worked as a team. All the reports agreed Ludmila Koshkin and Irina Gubanov were two of the finest operatives the academy had produced. They had proven themselves to be reliable, efficient and above all, ruthless. They were ready for action.

He pushed his chair back and walked to a window at the side of his office. He stood for a minute as if transfixed by something outside, then spoke without turning to look at the two agents. 'You've read the brief, you know what's at stake?' He glanced over his shoulder and fixed the two agents with an intense stare, his eyes narrowed and bushy eyebrows squeezed together as he gauged their reaction.

Both the women gave an almost imperceptible nod in response, neither said a word.

'The key will be to keep the woman under our control. Your actions are pivotal.'

Again, minimal, but positive response. They met his searching gaze.

'You're travelling separately, and you'll meet up at the address you've been given two days after you arrive in the UK, yes?'

Ludmila, the one with the broken nose, replied. 'Yes, I fly tomorrow, Irina goes by train tonight.'

Irina shrugged, 'we tossed a coin.' One side of her mouth curled, a hint of disdain that said, *it sucks, but it's no big deal.*

'OK,' Medvedev returned to his desk and studied his screen, 'you've got plenty of time, we'll make any appointments necessary and let you know. Just be ready to move when you get the green light.' He looked up to see them both acknowledge his instructions. 'Any questions?'

The two women looked at each other as if questioning which one of them would go first. Irina turned back to her controller. 'We have one question.'

'Ask it.' Medvedev made a come-on motion with his hand.

'What backup will we have? Who do we report to and who can we call on for support if we need it?'

Medvedev raised his eyes to the ceiling and folded his arms, he exhaled loudly stifling his exasperation. His focus returned to the two operatives. 'It's all in the brief if you bothered to read it all.'

Ludmila looked affronted. 'We've checked, it just says we have to wait in the safe house until someone gets in touch.'

'That's all you need to know.' Medvedev glowered at her.

Irina flashed a glance at her colleague. 'But...'

'Enough.' Medvedev raised his hand to silence her. 'I thought I made it clear. You stay ready to move when I say so.' He paused; cold grey eyes bore into the two women. 'You'll have everything you need in the house, food, clothing, equipment and if you need anything more, it'll be delivered to you.'

Irina shifted, uneasy and unsure. She tried again. 'But if there's an emergency and we need to contact someone? There's nothing in the brief about any back-up.'

Conscious that he may have omitted a key detail and angry that his two operatives had exposed a potential flaw, Medvedev retaliated through gritted teeth. 'You have phones, you have contact details for

Colonel Kobzar.' He swept his arm around the room as if it encompassed the whole organisation. 'Use your initiative, if you feel it's something worth bothering about, send him a message. If it's something I need to deal with tell Colonel Kobzar and he can contact me.' He relaxed and attempted what he hoped was a look to inspire confidence. 'The whole thing has been carefully planned, rehearsed and resourced, we've left nothing to chance, Is that clear enough?'

Both women gave a brief but emphatic nod.

'Good. That's all then. Close the door on your way out.'

Thursday 7 December

Jacob Crowhurst stared at the year planner with a satisfied look. He tapped a finger on each square in turn, counting silently, mouthing the numbers. The planner lay flat on the table, each corner weighed down by a jar or a bottle. Seventeen days to go until Christmas. The planner was covered in notes scrawled in black felt tip, and small stickers of various shapes and colours were dotted, seemingly at random throughout the year. Each one signified a different club or organisation that used the Community Centre, an event, a group meeting, a social occasion or a booking. Jacob knew what each one meant.

He cast an eye over the food donations on the trestle table in the main hall. All non-perishable items for the Christmas lunch. His appeals had gone well and over the last few days, he'd been gratified by the number of people who had called in with their offerings. He'd had promises and pledges from charities, local companies and even some of the national supermarkets. His cash supplies had never looked healthier with more coming in every day. He felt certain that when the time it came to buy all the produce he needed to feed around 40 people, he'd be able to provide a meal they'd never forget.

'I need to prepare a shopping list your majesty.' He addressed a picture of the Queen hung on the wall opposite. It was an old picture, an official portrait from sometime in the 70s, the colours had faded, the frame was chipped and what was left of the fake gold leaf embossing curled like dead skin. It had hung there for decades, and it was going nowhere. Jacob was on his own in the Community Centre, as usual and he could talk to whoever he wanted, and if he thought a quick word to the former sovereign would help, then that's just what he would do.

He tugged at his beard thoughtfully, twisting the long grey chin whiskers between thumb and forefinger and pulling his head into his chest. He peered over the top of the thick-framed glasses that had slipped down his nose. His face twisted as he wondered where to start.

He glanced at the clock at the back of the hall, and watched it for a moment to check it actually worked, the second hand ticked silently. It was eleven in the morning, a good time to call people. He pulled his trusty mobile from a jacket pocket and stared at it, seeking inspiration. Who to call?

'Morning JC.'

Jacob, lost in his thoughts and oblivious to other noises hadn't heard the door open behind him and didn't see the woman enter the hall. He jerked and almost dropped the phone. He turned to see the smiling face of Wendy Parsons beaming at him.

'Wendy. You'll give me a heart attack sneaking up on me like that.'

'Sorry Jacob, are you all right?'

'I'm fine Wendy. Good morning.' Jacob apologised.

Wendy's concern vanished as she came to stand beside Jacob and survey the contents of the table. Jacob was almost six feet tall, and Wendy had to crane her neck to look up at him. She was wearing an old, thick, woollen coat that had once been dark blue but now just looked dirty, Jacob remembered claiming it from a bag of donated clothing. He couldn't decide if the musty smell came from the coat or Wendy herself, so he shifted slightly away from her. 'Looking good so far, eh?'

She folded her arms and nodded her head rapidly, her unruly mop of bright red hair appeared to shimmy in response to the movement. 'Can't wait for Christmas. What else do you need?'

'That's just what I was thinking when you walked in. I was going to make a list .' He showed her the phone by way of explanation.

•••••

Monday 11 December

Five days after arriving in the UK and after settling into their safe house, Irina Gubanov and Ludmila Koshkin sunk down in the front seats of their rental car, an innocuous white Ford Focus, and watched the dark blue Jaguar pull out of the drive. There was no mistaking it, the registration plate - ABC - was an instant giveaway and the woman behind the wheel matched the description they'd been given. Ludmila started the engine, waited until the Jag was out of sight, then followed. They knew where it was going, they wanted eyes on the passengers.

Irina had her phone in hand, she sent a brief text. Ludmila glanced quickly to her left, seeking confirmation, Irina nodded, neither spoke.

Commuters and school run traffic clogged the road, the pace was painfully slow, it would have been quicker to jog, Ludmila thought. She hung back but kept the Jaguar in sight, always at least four others cars between it and the Focus. It was 8.42 when their target eventually pulled into the kerb, 50 yards short of the main entrance to the school. The three mile journey had taken almost 30 minutes. Ludmila spotted a gap between two cars and pulled in, they watched.

Car doors opened, young people emerged, dressed in grey jackets and trousers or skirts, white shirts, red and grey stripped ties. Doors closed, a brief casual wave and they headed into school.

Up ahead they saw a tall pretty girl with long dark brown hair, jump down from the Jaguar's front passenger seat. They knew she was 14, but she could have easily passed for 18. 'Jenni.' Irina spoke quietly, almost to herself. Ludmila watched in surprise as the driver got out, walked round to the kerb and pulled open the rear passenger door. She had a frustrated look. After what appeared to be a minor dispute involving head shaking and finger pointing, the rear passenger emerged. A stocky boy with a mop of blond hair. He grabbed his bag from the car seat and was about to walk off when his mother put her arm round him, gave him a hug and tried to kiss him goodbye. He shrugged it off, embarrassed. 'That's Noah.' Irina said in the same quiet voice, checking the notes she had on her lap. 'Looks every bit as challenging as any 12 year old.'

The driver turned to her daughter, engrossed with her mobile, she tried again for a hug and was a little more successful, receiving in response, a half-hearted squeeze and a cheek offered for a peck. Jenni spotted one of her mates and dismissed her mum. Mum gave a faint resigned smile and returned to the driving seat.

Ludmila gave the Jaguar a three minute head start before setting off to follow. They were going to the same place and didn't want to arrive at the same time.

•••••

Monday 11 December

The screen of Colonel Rostyslav Kobzar's computer faded to black, then lit up in a pale sky blue with an animated logo emerging from a series of multi-coloured swirls accompanied by an irritating polyphonic ditty, guaranteed to put teeth on edge. The logo, a series of Chinese letters, meant nothing to Kobzar other than a notification that She wanted to speak to him.

He tapped his passcode and the picture flicked briefly then changed to a live feed from the other side of the world.

She sat at her desk, perfectly positioned in the middle of the picture. She gazed into the camera, cold, dark, narrow eyes, unblinking. Her mouth pinched; her lips pressed tight together. Pale, almost translucent skin stretched over hollow cheeks and angular jawline. She stared and didn't say a word. Her hands remained clasped on the desk in front of her. She didn't move and she didn't speak. She simply stared at the camera and waited.

Behind her, the floor-to-ceiling window looked out over Macau from her eyrie on the 20th and top floor of her office building. The sun had set but it was still light enough to differentiate sea from sky and land from water. Lights flickered; streetlights, office and hotel lights, mega casinos and giant shopping malls vied with each other to be the brightest and most glittering. Headlights and taillights, a constant steady stream in all directions. Gaudy or vibrant depending on your point of view.

Kobzar blocked out the distractions behind her and met her penetrating gaze. He waited for her to say something.

She lifted her chin a fraction. 'Are your people ready?' Greetings, pleasantries and small talk rarely featured in her conversations. She spoke in English; she couldn't speak Russian and he couldn't speak Mandarin. Her accent was recognisably oriental but clear, her tone, high-pitched with a vague metallic ring.

Kobzar gave a nod. 'They've been briefed and trained; they have been to their locations and identified their targets. They are just waiting for the equipment to arrive.'

She absorbed this information for a moment. 'Final numbers?'

Kobzar paused, unsure. His head tipped a fraction to one side. 'People, locations or targets?'

'All three.' She snapped back. 'I need details.'

Kobzar winced and glanced away from the screen to consult a notepad. 'I've got 28 people, 16 of those will hit London, the others are spread around the country. They work in pairs and each pair has 4 targets. So that's...'

'56 targets, I'm not stupid.' She butted in. 'I allowed for 80 so you'll have a few spares if you need them.'

'Any update on the planned arrival date?'

'No, the shipment is due into Felixstowe on the 14th as arranged, you have the container details?'

Kobzar gave another brief nod but said nothing.

'When are you seeing the phone woman?'

'In two days. I've got two of my best, Irina and Ludmila, their cover is good, they have made an appointment and...'

The woman lifted a hand and gave an irritated dismissive gesture. 'I'm not interested. As long as they install the device and you're able to monitor the woman, I don't care how they do it.'

Kobzar, usually the one who gave orders and struck fear into those who worked for him, fought the inner demons demanding he retaliate in some form. He tore his eyes away from the woman, nodding sagely and made a show of consulting his notes. He took a moment to compose himself before responding. 'I'll send you an update in the usual way. Was there anything else?' He looked back at the screen and met the woman's intense stare.

'No. Just remember how much is riding on this and remember you get nothing if anything goes wrong.' She glared at him for a few seconds as if daring him to respond. Then, without another word, reached forward and ended the call.

Kobzar continued to stare for a moment, the woman's outline remained, burned into his retina. The animated logo returned, faded and disappeared leaving a blank black screen, then he closed his eyes and shook his head. His mouth twisted into a snarl, and he muttered quietly to himself, an old Russian proverb about greed or avarice, or something similar, he couldn't remember exactly but it felt good to vent his frustration.

Monday 11 December

Alison Burton-Castle parked the Jaguar in her designated spot outside the main office building at the Connectivity headquarters. It was already after nine, she was late, not that it bothered her, she was usually late, but she worked late every day, so she wasn't going to worry about a few minutes lost in the morning.

'Morning Allison.' Her PA, Ruby, was sorting through the morning's post when Alison walked into the office. 'How are you?'

'So far, so good Ruby.' Burton-Castle put the laptop bag on the meeting table in front of her desk. 'Did I imagine it, or did you say something about a nine thirty this morning?'

'Nothing wrong with your imagination, you've got a couple of marketing people coming to see you. Something to do with an overseas infrastructure program. Ring any bells?' Ruby took the laptop bag and extracted the paperwork her boss had worked on the previous evening. She placed the laptop itself on the desk.

Burton-Castle picked up the day's schedule Ruby had printed off and made her way over to the corner of the office, drawn by the aroma of freshly brewed coffee. She poured herself a cup while checking appointments and meetings. 'Are these all confirmed?' She didn't look up from the printed sheet.

'The 11.30 meeting with the training team may have to be cancelled, one of their guys has called in sick. They rang me five minutes ago and said they'd let me know either way by 10.30. Apart from that, it's business as usual.'

Burton-Castle nodded. 'Thanks Ruby.' She took her coffee over to the big picture window that overlooked the manicured gardens, and stood sipping it slowly enjoying a quiet moment. From her position on the fifth floor the view over the gardens and the parkland beyond was one that filled her with a huge sense of wellbeing. She believed in counting her blessings, taking nothing for granted, she'd worked damned hard to get here and loved the rewards that came with it. On a glorious December morning like this, life was good. As Operations Director of the Infrastructure Division she was well paid, very well paid. The job was challenging, at times it was stressful, but it drew on her skills, her analytical brain and her ability to manage people. She gained huge satisfaction seeing the growth in the company and the part she had played implementing more efficient management systems.

'Your nine-thirty appointment is here.' Ruby announced from the outer office. 'They've just checked in at reception.'

Burton-Castle shook herself from her quiet reverie, finished her coffee and sat down at her desk, opened a folder and pulled out the paperwork Ruby had prepared about her visitors. She checked the time, they were a minute early, she approved. 'Have them brought up Ruby.'

She checked through the notes while she waited, some background information and the usual security checks, nothing that raised any flags. Two representatives from a Ukrainian Telecoms company wanting Connectivity to collaborate on a five year development program. It could be interesting.

The noise from the outer office alerted Burton-Castle that her visitors had arrived, Ruby showed them in. 'This is Olga Smiratov and Valentina Borshlov.' She announced.

Olga Smiratov and Valentina Borshlov stood side by side, both dressed in matching dark blue suits, skirts just below knee length, fitted jackets, sensible shoes. They were roughly the same height, about five five, both slim, tanned and toned. Ludmila, the one Ruby introduced as Olga, had shoulder length blond hair, framing a narrow face with sharp eyes behind a pair of designer framed glasses and a warm smile. Irina, aka Valentina, had a rounder face, she didn't smile, maintaining a serious business demeanour as instructed. Her long dark red hair was neatly swept back and tied into a loose pony tail.

They both held slim black folders in their left hands, keeping their right free in case a handshake was in order.

Burton-Castle greeted them and waved them to seats around the meeting table. Ruby closed the office door.

10

It took Ludmila and Irina, posing as Olga and Valentina, thirty minutes to deliver their well-rehearsed presentation. They smoothly outlined a convincing cover story centred on business expansion in and around Kyiv. They produced a glossy brochure with facts and figures to back up the story. They set out a proposal in which Connectivity would part-fund an extensive fibre optic network and set up a training program for their engineers, in return for a fee paid over ten years from the completion of the contract. The numbers involved ran to multiple millions, it was an attractive proposition.

If Burton-Castle checked any of the details, called any of the numbers or emailed any of the personal listed in the brochure, she would have received equally convincing responses, nothing had been left to chance.

'Is there anything else you would like to ask us?' Ludmila asked as they concluded, her voice was slightly accented but otherwise she spoke perfect English .

Burton-Castle studied the brochure and checked the notes she had made while the two women had been speaking. 'I don't think so.' She shook her head slowly in confirmation without looking up. 'You've been very thorough. I've got everything I need here to go to the board.'

'We're in the UK for the next ten days.' Ludmila added. 'If you would like us to come back and talk to your board, we would be happy to do so.'

'I appreciate that, thank you.'

Irina sat up, distracted, and craned her neck to look out of the window.

Burton-Castle turned, following her gaze. 'What is it?'

Without taking her eyes off whatever she had seen, Irina said. 'I'm so sorry, it's very unbusinesslike of me, I hope you don't think I'm rude, but I thought I saw a deer in the grounds, is that possible?'

Burton-Castle was curious, she rose from her chair and went to the window. Irina followed and pointed in the direction of a small ornamental lake two hundred yards from the building, and kept her prospective client's attention focused on the spot. 'Did you see it?' Irina asked with the enthusiasm of a small child.

Burton-Castle squinted against the bright sunlight for a few more moments.

Irina glanced briefly back over her shoulder at Ludmila who had both her hands under Burton-Castle's desk. She caught the faintest of nods and returned to the deer hunt.

'I've been told that we do get deer in the park occasionally but I've never seen one.' Burton-Castle said, she gave a slight shrug and turned away from the window.

Irina looked resigned, took one last look at the park, returned to her chair and collected up her paperwork.

Ludmila stood and extended a hand. 'Thank you for seeing us, Mrs Burton-Castle, we appreciate your time.'

Alison shook hands with them both. 'You're welcome, it's an exciting proposition, I'm sure the board will be interested. I'll get back to you within the week.' She showed them to the door.

Ludmila and Irina had parked the white Focus in a space reserved for visitors. They returned to it maintaining their fake persona, aware they could be seen from the office buildings and CCTV would be following them. Neither of them spoke.

They turned into the multi-story car park of the shopping centre three miles from the Connectivity campus. Ludmila drove to an isolated spot on the fourth floor, away from the lifts, out of sight of more CCTV and away from any prying eyes. She parked and switched the engine off.

Irina exhaled with theatrical emphasis and slumped forward, she turned to look at Ludmila. 'Done?'

Ludmila nodded. 'Phase one done.'

'Come on, let's get out of these.' Irina indicated their suits and pulled a face. 'I'm not comfortable.'

They picked two small tote bags from the rear seat and climbed out of the car, leaving the keys in the ignition. Ludmila wiped the steering wheel, the door handles and anything else they might have touched with a small microfibre cloth she produced from one of the tote bags. Satisfied, they walked towards an access staircase at the rear of the car park, following a pre-planned route that minimised any chance of being seen on camera.

Splitting up on the second floor, Irina headed for the public toilets while Ludmila continued to the ground floor and the slightly more upmarket surroundings of the facilities inside Marks and Spencer.

Fifteen minutes later Ludmila strolled onto the platform at the railway station without a care in the world, wearing faded jeans, trainers, a snug fitting peach T-shirt and a pair of wrap around sunglasses. The blonde wig had been replaced with a dark brown bob. She had a crumpled rucksack slung over one shoulder and carried a cup of coffee picked up from the vending machine at the station entrance. She waited with feigned nonchalance.

Three more minutes passed before Irina arrived having undergone a similar transformation. The suit, and sensible shoes had been replaced with a short cream skirt, a loose fitting pale blue shirt, and strappy sandals with two-inch heels. A wig of short platinum blonde hair had replaced the long dark red one she'd worn for the presentation The whole ensemble was topped with a broad brimmed straw hat. She glanced up and down the platform, spotted Ludmila and walked away from her, a large canvas shopping bag in her right hand.

If Ludmila noticed Irina's arrival, her face and body language gave nothing away. CCTV footage examined at a later date would simply show a mixed collection of mid morning passengers, among them, two unremarkable women travelling alone.

The London bound train arrived on time, Ludmila boarded and sat near the front of the first carriage, Irina selected a window seat near the back of the last. The doors hissed shut. The train departed.

•••••

Saturday 23 December
0400

Susie and Nick had been at the hospital for almost an hour. The journey from Warrenford had been uneventful, despite all the dire predictions. The road conditions were challenging, but they made it safely. Susie had managed to find a porter who helped transfer Nick from the car to a trolley and into the emergency department. Now, she sat by his side, watching the monitor beep and desperately willing him to wake up.

The doctors had performed various tests and seemed optimistic. They assured Susie that Nick would wake up soon and there would be no lasting damage. Holding his hand, she squeezed his fingers, hoping for any sign of response. She had been doing this for over half an hour, repeatedly getting up, bringing her face close to his, and whispering in his ear, urging him to wake up. But she received no response.

When a nurse brought her a cup of coffee, she took a sip while keeping her eyes on Nick. Just as she was about to put the cup down, she heard a strange noise from him – a mix between a mumble and a groan. Setting the coffee aside, she grabbed his hand and leaned closer. 'Can you hear me, Nick?' she asked.

There was another mumble from him. She squeezed his hand tighter and nudged him gently. He mumbled something barely audible. 'Where am I?'

'You're in hospital babe.'

'What the hell?'

'Don't you remember anything?'

'I can't remember... Why am I in hospital?'

'The explosion?'

'Don't remember any explosion,' he said in confusion.

'The control tower at Warrenford blew up while you were in the lift. Do you know what I'm talking about?'

'Where did you go?'

'I... I went back to the car. What's the last thing you do remember?'

'We left... There was an Aussie guy with the modems, I remember that?'

'I went back for the modems, and the whole bloody place exploded.'

'I can't remember a thing. Jesus my leg hurts.'

'I'm not surprised. You were trapped under a pile of rubble.'

'How long have I been here?'

'It's four in the morning now, babe. You've been here for over an hour. It took a long time to get you here.'

'Is it broken?'

'No, you were lucky. Some of the steel beams fell on top of you. The lift protected you from the blast. Everybody else in the control tower has been killed.'

Nick turned to stare at Susie. 'Killed?' he said. 'What, all of them?'

Susie nodded slowly. 'You're the only survivor.'

'Bloody hell.' Nick shook his head, closing his eyes. 'It's all a blank. How did I get out?'

'Two of the police guys from the gate. They came and helped me. We had to remove a whole lot of stuff off you.'

'Did you get me here in an ambulance?'

'No, they're all busy with the rioting.'

'So, what? You put me in the back of the car?'

Susie grimaced. 'Sorry, babe, the car's a write-off.'

'What happened to it?'

'I was inside it when the explosion went off. It protected me the same way the lift protected you, but it took a hell of a beating.'

'So how did you get me here?'

'They had an old Volvo estate they lent me. They helped me put you in the back of it, and I got you here.'

Nick squeezed his wife's hand. 'Thanks, love. Are you okay?'

'I'm a bit shaken, just relieved you're alive. I was so worried when I saw the explosion. I thought I'd never see you again.' She leaned over and gently hugged him.

Nick continued to shake his head in disbelief 'So, who's in charge now, then?' he said, slowly regaining his senses.

Susie looked puzzled. 'I hadn't really thought about it,' she said. 'I've been more concerned about you.'

'Has anybody been in touch with you?'

'I doubt the news even got out yet. There's absolute pandemonium out there because they've all packed in for Christmas. Even this place is working with a skeleton staff. It's a bit of a zombie apocalypse outside.'

Nick adjusted his position and winced as a wave of pain shot through him. 'What did the doctor say about my leg?'

'They've checked it out and examined you. You had a deep cut where the beam landed on you and they've stitched it up, but otherwise, it's cuts and bruises, colourful but superficial. You were dead lucky.'

Nick closed his eyes and shook his head again. 'I can't believe it. I can't believe they've all been killed. This isn't just a cyber-attack. This is something much more serious.'

Susie looked dubious. 'You think it's beyond a police matter?'

'From the sound of things, it's gone way beyond the police.' Nick paused and studied his wife. 'If it's as bad as you say, the counter-terrorist boys will be all over it, probably army as well.'

Susie said nothing. She met Nick's gaze and knew he was right. She glanced at the clock on the wall. 'Not much I can do then.'

'Not until you get some sleep, you can't function properly without it.'

'What about you?'

Nick lifted his hands to his head, deep in thought. 'There's something been troubling me,' he paused and looked up at the ceiling. 'Ever since we were at the control tower last night, one of the guys there... he reminded me of somebody, and I can't think who it was.'

Susie gave him a questioning look. 'Who? Eddington?'

'No, no, the other guy. The one who lent you the money, glasses and big beard.'

Susie tapped her forehead. 'Millard. He was called Wade Millard. He just started last week.'

'That's the guy,' said Nick. 'He reminds me of somebody. There was something about him.'

'What about him?' said Susie.

'He reminds me of somebody. I just can't place him.'

'Don't worry, love. I doubt you can think clearly at the moment either.'

'What time is it?'

Susie nodded at the clock on the wall. 'It's just after 4.'

'Sorry, you've already said. God, I'm tired.'

'After all the meds they've given you, I'm amazed you're making any sense at all,'

'You need to rest,' Nick said. He held her hand and squeezed it. 'It's just a guess, but I think you're going to be busy over the next day or so.'

'Why do you say that?'

'Well, you're the only one left, aren't you?'

'Yeah, but I don't really work for them.'

'You're seconded to them, and you're the only one who knows what's going on.'

Susie laughed. 'I haven't got a clue what's going on.'

'Maybe, but you were there, and you know all the people involved.'

Susie took a deep breath, then exhaled slowly. She gazed out the window into the darkness of the night. 'I may not know what's going on, but I still have those modems. I just don't know what to do with them.'

Nick considered this for a minute. 'Do you know who the boss man reported to?'

Susie thought about this. 'I think it was somebody at Whitehall, the MOD. But I don't know who.'

'Would anyone else know about you?'

Susie shrugged. 'I suppose they must have my details on record somewhere, but if news of the explosion has got out, they may assume everybody has been killed and not even try to contact me.'

'You could always take the proactive approach.' said Nick.

'What? Call them?'

'Yeah, why not?'

'I wouldn't know who to contact.'

'No,' He thought for a moment. 'But Tim would. Give him a call, tell him what's happened. He knows people. Tim was Nick's old army buddy, they'd served together in Afghanistan, he ran an online security business and lived with Susie's friend Anna.

Nick put his head back and squeezed his eyes shut. ‘Bloody hell, my head aches.’ He touched the side of his head where a bandage had been wrapped around it.

Susie reached out and lightly touched the bandage. 'Just take it easy, get some sleep and let the meds do their job. I'll give Tim a call first thing in the morning.' She stood, straightened up and took a deep breath, then exhaled slowly. 'OK, I guess I'm pretty knackered and I could do with getting out of these.' She passed a demonstrative hand over her dust-covered jacket and combat pants and pointed to her scuffed boots with a screwed-up nose.

Nick forced a smile. 'You still look gorgeous love. Give me a kiss and be gone with you.'

‘I'd rather stay here and make sure you're okay.’

‘Appreciated, babe, but there's not much you can do. I'm not going to be much company. Go home, get some rest, eat something, get changed, and come back to pick me up in a few hours. Hopefully, by then, we'll have a better idea of what's going on.’

Susie considered this and nodded. ‘Yeah, you're probably right.’ She stood up on weary legs and leaned in for a kiss.

He squeezed her hand.

She squeezed back. ‘Don't go anywhere. I'll be back.’

11

Saturday 23 December

With Christmas less than 48 hours away, the Saturday morning rush for last-minute food shopping started early. Supermarket doors opened at eight, some even earlier and even then, queues had begun to form as people hoped to avoid the problems of the previous evening, sure in the knowledge that whatever had caused the payment system to crash would have been resolved by now.

Within minutes, they were proved wrong.

Their plastic was no good. The ATMs weren't cooperating. Shops could only accept cash.

The mood grew tense, and tempers flared.

Standing outside Sainsbury's, two men watched as the atmosphere in the shop became heated. They could see staff remonstrating with customers. They could see fingers pointing and wild gesticulations, some pushing and some shoving and eventually a punch being thrown as it all became too much for one of the shoppers.

Both men wore dark hoodies, their faces hidden from security cameras. They both carried black holdalls and, as if they could read each other's minds, turned to each other, nodded and pulled scarves over the lower half of their faces, leaving only their eyes exposed.

They placed their holdalls on the ground and the first man reached into his and extracted three black tubes, about a foot long and an inch in diameter. The other pulled three items, from his holdall, each the size and shape of a beer can with a pull ring at one end.

Without pausing, the first man pulled the top from one of the tubes, turned it through 180 degrees and struck the newly exposed end, like a match. It fizzed like a firework as the 10 second fuse burned through to the main charge. He lobbed it through the main entrance to the store and immediately did the same with the other two tubes.

The second man pulled the pin on the first of his objects and threw it after the tubes, he timed his throw to perfection and as the first of the thunder-flashes exploded with a deafening crash, his smoke grenade erupted, and dense light grey smoke billowed into the store.

As the other two thunder-flashes went off in sequence, two more smoke grenades joined them and within seconds, choking, blinding smoke enveloped the store entrance and drifted along the row of checkouts, down the aisles and across the kiosks and customer service desk.

The effect was almost instantaneous. Customers, already at breaking point, recoiled at the sound of the thunder-flashes and panicked at the sight of the smoke. Some moved further back into the store as if it would offer some protection, others made for the door intent on escaping.

The smoke grenade man reached again into his holdall and withdrew a brick, nothing special, just a common house brick. He checked left and right, hefted the brick in one hand, then hurled it at the plate glass of the shop front. The glass cracked but the brick bounced off and landed at his feet. Frustrated, he retrieved the brick and threw it with renewed vengeance at the star-shaped mark it had left. The glass crack again and the brick fell to the ground.

He tried a third time and the glass gave way with a loud crash and the brick-sized hole was left at head height. The first man pulled the pin from another smoke grenade and dropped it through the hole.

The two men, having previously checked the CCTV camera locations, moved to a blind spot they'd identified. While one of them pulled out his phone, the other removed his hoodie and smeared one side of his face with fake blood from a bottle in his holdall. He dragged his fingers across his cheeks for added effect then jogged into the store.

Once obscured by the smoke, he turned and ran out holding his hands to his head, his face a mixture of terror and pain.

His buddy captured the scene in glorious high definition; a seriously injured shopper escaping a scene of chaos against a background of deadly smoke. Within seconds the video had been pinged to the number they'd been given.

The two men retrieved their holdalls and blended into the crowd of shoppers fleeing the store. A minute later they merged into the queue of traffic in a nondescript grey Peugeot and headed out of the car park.

Rostyslav Kobzar sat at his desk, transfixed by the action he witnessed on his computer screen. The video from the two men at Sainsbury's may only have been ten seconds long, but it was exactly what he'd asked them to do.

Within minutes, similar videos began to arrive from the rest of his team, each slightly different with varying amounts of theatrical interpretation employed by each pair of agents. The orchestrated scenes unfolded exactly as planned and he couldn't resist the faintest of smirks as each played out.

He had his technical team set up more than twenty fake social media accounts and gave them detailed instructions to post each video using a different account initially and then retweet, share and comment at random to spread the word knowing that views would build quickly given the nature of the content.

The tech team had come up with hashtags of #nocards, #cashonly and #systemdown and he had no doubt that as the videos went viral, other more creative tags would be added.

He gave a little fist pump and switched his attention to a second screen set to live TV. As predicted the mainstream news had either not picked up the news, or he felt sure, had been told not to broadcast anything about the unrest for fear of inciting further panic. He checked BBC, ITN, CNN and Channel 4 news, but none of them gave any hint of the scenes gaining traction on Twitter, Facebook and Instagram. He wondered how long they could continue to ignore what was happening.

He turned back to his primary Twitter feed and entered the hashtags into the search bar. He rocked back in his chair as the screen refreshed and he saw the videos dominating the feed with views already into four figures and clicking faster than he could believe.

Jacob Crowhurst had a bounce in his step, a smile on his face and over three hundred and fifty pounds in cash in his pocket. He'd excelled in his efforts to raise funds; the various events, the corporate donations, the outright begging, it had all proved worthwhile, and now he could provide a Christmas Dinner for 38 people who would otherwise be alone and hungry. He felt good and headed for the store entrance.

He glanced up from his shopping list and slowed as he became aware of the disturbance. Grey smoke billowed from the doors and shoppers emerged from the store with hands over their mouths, coughing and spluttering. Confusion and panic filled the air.

Jacob stopped, unable to comprehend. He didn't have a TV; his mobile phone was basic, and he didn't do social media. He had no idea what was unfolding before his eyes. What happened to the Christmas spirit? Tempers appeared frayed, insults flew, and faces were grim. Jacob looked for someone to ask. A woman in her early forties approached, pushing a shopping trolley and wrapped up against the cold. She wore a thick coat, scarf, hat and gloves, but Jacob could see worry on her face. He noticed the meagre quantity of goods in the trolley and raised a friendly hand.

'What's going on?'

The woman stopped, glanced back and shook her head. 'It's chaos in there.'

Jacob followed her gaze, his brow furrowed. 'Why, what's wrong?'

'They haven't sorted the problem out, everyone's going crazy.'

Jacob squinted at the store like someone unable to see the blindingly obvious and not wanting to admit it. 'What problem?'

The woman gave Jacob a pitying look. 'Don't you watch the news? The card payment problem.' She waited to see if her words registered. Jacob continued to look blank. 'It's cash only and nobody has cash.'

Jacob stared at the woman, then cast his eyes around the car park. Instead of leaving the store with overloaded trollies, people heading for their cars, empty-handed, their faces a combination of anger, frustration and worry. 'I had no idea; I don't see the news.'

'Well, save yourself the bother unless you've got cash there's no point in going in there. I'm surprised they're even open. Everybody's going mad.'

Jacob jumped at the sound of shouting from inside the store and saw a man running from the building, chased by the security guard. He watched the pair disappear from view, then turned back to see more people leaving, this time pushing fully laden trollies at pace with their heads down and sense of purpose or was it guilt? Jacob stood transfixed.

'Told you.' The woman waved a dismissive hand at the store, wished Jacob a sarcastic Happy Christmas and headed for her car.

Jacob felt in his pocket for the roll of bank notes. It gave him a sense of reassurance, a sense of righteousness, and he continued on his mission.

Susie woke up bleary-eyed and stared in confusion at the ceiling for a moment. She wondered where she was. Then, memories of the previous 24 hours flooded back.

Closed curtains, dark room. She groaned as she made an effort to get out of bed and did a double take when she realised she was still fully dressed. She had flopped into bed when she got back from the hospital and had only got as far as removing her boots. She reached for her phone to check the time and found it had died overnight.

She padded her way through to the bathroom. Catching her reflection in the mirror, she gasped at her appearance. Her hair stood out at bizarre angles and her makeup was smudged. With the shower running, she quickly peeled off the dust-encrusted clothes and stepped in. She stood almost trance like for a full five minutes and let the warm water revive her.

Wrapped in her dressing gown, she went down to the kitchen to find her laptop and put her phone on charge. With no idea of the time, it came as a shock to see the kitchen clock reading 10.20.

She turned the TV and jumped from channel to channel in the hope of finding some news. The explosion at Warrenford wasn't mentioned by any station and the scenes she'd witnessed the previous evening appeared to have gone unreported. With her phone out of action, she booted up her laptop and opened up her social media pages.

As she expected, the mainstream media were playing down the payment processing failure, but she was surprised there was no news of the explosion. As she scrolled through her Twitter feed, she found numerous videos and posts relating to the payment processing failure #cashonly. She realised she was squinting at the screen through scratchy eyes and with a shake of the head recognised she'd left her contact lenses in overnight.

Over six hours had passed since she left Nick, she was concerned and wanted to get back to the hospital. Her phone pinged to alert her to an incoming message. She jumped at the noise and grabbed it, hoping it would be from someone at the CCU. It was from her friend Anna in reply to the message Susie had sent while sitting at Nick's bedside. Anna's concern was understandable, but Susie was bothered that nobody from the CCU had been in touch. Then again, she thought, they probably assumed she was dead.

Nick's suggestion of calling Tim popped back into her consciousness and she realised she could kill two birds with one stone if she called Anna and put her mind at ease, then got her to put Tim on the phone. Job done.

She debated whether to ring there and then or wait and ring from the car on the way to the hospital. She knew Anna would want to talk so she opted for the second alternative and rushed upstairs to dry her hair and get dressed.

Twenty minutes later, dressed in jeans, jumper, a coat and an old pair of Nikes, she closed the front door behind her and headed for the old Volvo, already missing her Golf. In what passed for daylight, the

Volvo looked no better than it had the previous night. The drab green paintwork did nothing to lighten her spirits. She got in and fired up the engine, grateful it was a reliable old car. She brought a charger from the house, but the lack of a USB port meant she would have to hope there was enough charge to get her through the day or at least until she could find a charging point. She drove with one hand while the other fumbled with the phone.

Anna must have been waiting for the call. She answered on the first ring and Susie clicked the speaker on while she swerved back onto her side of the road, to narrowly avoid a van coming in the opposite direction.

The conversation lasted all the way to the hospital as Susie gave Anna a potted summary of the previous evening's events and then asked to speak to Tim. Tim had listened to the two women talking and didn't need Susie to repeat herself. She told him what Nick had suggested and he promised to make some enquiries and call her back within the hour.

On her way to the hospital, she couldn't believe the difference from the previous day. She sensed a feeling of foreboding, and the Christmas spirit seemed to have disappeared. Drivers and pedestrians appeared determined, and the closer she got to the town centre, the more worrying the atmosphere became. Blue and red lights flashed wherever she looked, and the sound of two-tone sirens provided a disturbing soundtrack to her journey. She couldn't tell which of the emergency services they belonged to, but they heaped tension on top of deep-seated anxiety. To her surprise, she found the car park strangely quiet when she arrived at the hospital, .

The situation inside appeared at first glance to be no different to the scene she'd left in the early hours, but a definite air of panic and trepidation hung over the corridors and waiting areas. The staff looked grim and even more stressed than usual as if expecting a tsunami of casualties at any minute. She just hoped that Nick was still in the same ward she had left him in a few hours earlier and made her way there as unobtrusively as possible.

12

Susie stopped at the entrance to the ward and smiled when she saw Nick.

The ward had six beds and the other five were vacant, he was the only patient, he had the place to himself, and it obviously didn't suit him.

He couldn't help himself. He'd stopped the cleaner from doing her job and appeared to be fascinated by what she was telling him. She leant on the handle of her mop and gazed at the floor as she spoke. Nick listened intently and nodded slowly.

He didn't spot Susie standing in the doorway for over half a minute and almost jumped in surprise when he caught her in the corner of his eye. 'Hello, love.'

'Well, someone's made a speedy recovery.' Susie acknowledged the cleaner with a polite dip of the chin and walked around to the side of the bed and kissed Nick.

The cleaner made brief eye contact and then scurried out of the ward without a word.

'Who's your new friend?' Susie said as she watched the cleaner leave.

'Her name's Heidi.' Nick wriggled in the bed to get comfortable and straightened the sheets. 'I don't think she's used to patients talking to her, she seemed very shy.'

Susie's brow creased. 'What makes you say that? How long have you been chatting to her?'

Nick shrugged. 'Just a few minutes. She's the only person I've seen for the last half an hour.'

'Doctor not been round?'

'She came not long after you left in the wee small hours. Seemed to be happy with me. Leg all bandaged, and meds dished out. Not much else they can do.'

'Uh huh,' Susie studied Nick for a moment, her attention wandered, and she gazed around the almost empty room. 'I guess they want everyone home for Christmas. Makes their lives easier.' Her eyes settled back on Nick. 'What did she say about you coming home?'

Nick gave another shrug and rocked his head side-to-side, he winced and wished he hadn't. 'Depends how I feel, I think. Head still hurts like buggery and whatever they've given me to dull the pain in my leg is going to wear off soon enough.'

Susie pursed her lips and gave a sage nod. 'I don't suppose there's anything they can do for you that I can't do back home. It's not as if you're on a drip or wired up to some expensive bit of kit that beeps every couple of seconds. And you don't want to stay here any longer than you have to, do you?'

Nick kept his head stock still as he replied. 'No. I'll know soon enough; the doc'll be doing her rounds in...' He looked over Susie's shoulder at the clock on the wall. '...Any time now, I guess.' He paused and held his arms out in supplication. 'So, come on then, have you spoken to Tim?'

'Ah yes.' She sat on the end of the bed and composed herself. 'I had a quick word with him after speaking to Anna, he said he'd get back to me with a name or a number, or both.'

'And has he?'

Susie retrieved her phone from her back pocket and checked the screen. 'Not yet. But I've been thinking.'

Nick's eyes rolled. 'Sounds ominous.'

'Don't be mean. I've been thinking about those modems we brought back with us.'

'What about them?'

'Well, what d'you think we should do about them?'

Nick tried a gentle shrug. 'I suppose you need to get them to someone.'

'Any suggestions?'

Nick pulled an I don't know face. 'The cybercrime lot, the police, the army, the government.'

'Maybe, but the CCU has been wiped out and the police are running around like headless chickens trying to control all the who hah. What's left of the army has gone home for Christmas. I just hope Tim knows someone.'

'He will. Give him a few more minutes. He's got fingers in all sorts of pies.'

They both paused. Their combined gaze fell upon Susie's phone, willing it to burst into life.

'So, what's happening out there in the big wide world?' Nick lifted a hand to point at the window and gingerly moved his head in the same direction.

'Well, they haven't solved the problem and it's only going to get worse.'

'What they are saying on the news?'

'That's just it. There's nothing on the news, it's like there's some sort of media blackout.'

'Makes sense.' Nick nodded to himself. 'Big brother doesn't want to create panic among the great unwashed.'

'Yeah, but they can't control social media.' Susie said, her tone a mixture of resignation, concern and a touch of rebellion.

'Oh, really? Come on then, show me.' Nick nodded at Susie's phone.

Susie frowned and peered at the cabinet beside Nick's bed. 'Where's yours?'

'God knows.' Nick tried to shrug again but grimaced at the effort. 'Haven't seen it, must be back there somewhere.' His eyes flicked to the window as though indicating the location.

'Good luck with that.' Susie gave a slow shake of her head. 'If you dropped it in the lift, it's probably buried under a ton of rubble by now.'

Nick's face registered disappointment, but he held out a hand for Susie's phone. 'Let's see then.'

She brought up her Twitter feed and handed him the device. 'Type in the hashtag #cashonly and see what comes up.'

Nick did as instructed and remained silent for a minute while he scrolled through the messages. His eyes tracked across the screen while his expression grew steadily more concerned, eyebrows edging ever closer to each other. 'It's bad, but not as bad as I thought.' He looked up at Susie, in anticipation of some response.

Susie snatched her phone back and checked the screen, puzzled by Nick's reaction. 'It's not so much what they're saying, it's the sheer number of incidents. It's happening all over the country.'

'Hmmm,' Nick stared at the phone in his wife's hand, then he looked up to study her expression. 'So, what are they doing about it?'

'They?' Susie dipped her chin and gave Nick a sideways look. 'I've told you, there is no "they".

Nick closed his eyes and gave a resigned shake of the head. 'Don't tell me. You want to get involved.' It was a statement, not a question. He cautiously opened one eye and met her gaze.

Susie's lips compressed into a tight line. She avoided his questioning look and swiped the screen to update the feed. She said nothing for a few moments while she studied the latest posts, then appeared to come to a decision. 'I'm already involved, I can't sit around and do nothing. Can I?'

Her statement was met with an exaggerated eye roll.

'I mean, some bastard killed everyone I've been working with for the last six months and you're not going to tell me it was just coincidence the place exploded at the very moment we were due to arrive in the control room.'

Nick grunted a reluctant acknowledgement.

'If I hadn't gone back to the car for that bloody modem, we'd...' She tailed off, the full impact of events hitting her hard. She reached out and grabbed Nick's hand. 'Jeez, Nick, we were so lucky, they tried to kill you and me as well. I think it's only right I do something. Those poor guys in the control room, one minute they're hard at work trying to solve a problem, looking forward to Christmas, and then...' She closed her eyes and shook her head.

'It's OK love, you don't have to explain.' Nick gave her hand a responsive squeeze. 'I know you probably feel you owe it to them.'

Susie stirred herself from her reflective stupor. 'Let's hope Tim can help.'

As if on cue, her phone started to ring. She jumped in surprise, then glanced at the screen. 'It's Tim.'

'Well...' Nick prompted her to answer.

Susie tapped the phone and held it to her ear. 'Hi Tim.' She screwed her face up as she struggled to hear a reply. She examined the screen and spoke again. 'Hang on Tim, reception's rubbish in here. Give me a minute and I'll ring you back.' She disconnected and frowned at the p hone.

'No Good?' Nick said.

'Only one bar.' Susie waved the phone around the room in the vain hope of picking up a stronger signal. 'I'll go outside and ring him back.' She stood and turned for the door and almost collided with the doctor.

The doctor, stopped in her tracks and held her hands up to prevent a collision. 'Whoa, almost.' She glanced over Susie's shoulder at her patient. 'Hello Nick, is this your wife?' Her eyes flicked back to Susie.

Susie turned, smiled and offered a hand. 'Hi. Yeah, I'm his better half, Susie. Sorry about that, I didn't hear you.'

'No problem. Pleased to meet you.' She turned to Nick. 'Sorry to disturb you, but I'm off duty in five minutes and I wanted to check up on you before going home for Christmas. I'm guessing you rather be at home than here?' Again, she made eye contact with her patient and his wife.

They both nodded and Susie said. 'That's great, just persuade him to take it easy.' She turned to Nick. 'I'll nip out and try Tim. This is a black hole.' She nodded at her phone. 'Back in a bit.' She left the room in search of a phone signal.

After twenty minutes, Nick began to wonder what had happened to his wife. He assumed she'd speak to Tim and report back. He had no doubts about her capability, but curiosity gnawed at him. Left alone in his room, he blotted out the ambient noises, monitoring machines, ventilation systems and external traffic, and listened out for approaching footsteps. His chin slumped into his chest and his shoulders relaxed.

He didn't hear Susie.

The rubber soles of her Nikes made no noise on the resin floor of the corridor. She appeared at the door to his room, just as his eyes began to droop with the effects of the painkillers.

'Wakey wakey babe, I've got news.'

Nick blinked and shook himself. He glanced at the wall clock. 'You've been ages.'

Susie looked around to check the doctor had left, then continued into the room and sat on the end of Nick's bed. 'What she said then?'

'She wants me to stay in tonight and if everything's OK in the morning, I can go home.'

'Fantastic.' Susie leaned forward and gave Nick a gentle hug.

He hugged Susie cautiously, not wanting to give in to the pain. 'Come on then, what news?'

Susie sat back, her eyes sparkled, and a self-satisfied smirk played across her face. 'I've been busy.'

Nick's eyes narrowed and he pursed his lips as he studied her. 'Was I right? Did Tim know who to contact?'

Susie nodded.

'Don't tell me, he knew someone at Whitehall?'

Susie's head rocked side to side. 'Sort of. He knew which department to contact.'

'And?' Nick made hurry-up signals.

'Well, long story short, I rang one of the numbers he suggested.'

'And?'

'Surprise, surprise, no one answered, not even a voicemail option.'

Nick gave a nod in recognition of the problem.

Susie continued. 'So, I tried a second number, same story. Then...' She held up three fingers with a look of mild triumph. 'Third time lucky, I got hold of someone.'

'Don't keep me in suspense.'

'I think he must have been the only person left at the MOD. He didn't know anything about Warrenford but took my details and promised to get someone to ring me back.'

Nick slumped. 'Is that it?'

'Not much more I could do. Just have to wait for them to call me.'

Nick let out a long, frustrated breath. 'So... you're not rushing off anywhere and can stay with me for a while?'

'Of course, I'll stay as long as they let me.'

'Great. So, you can nip out and get us some food, I'm starving.'

If the remark registered with Susie, she didn't show it. 'Oh, I almost forgot' she did an exaggerated facepalm. 'After Tim gave me the details, he said that he and Anna would come over later this afternoon and visit you.

Nick brightened visibly at this. 'Ah, bless him, better get enough for four.'

Susie rolled her eyes and shook her head slowly. 'I wonder what it would take for you to lose your appetite?'

Wade Millard stared at the face that looked back at him in the mirror. He scraped his fingers through the straggly beard and tugged the lank, long hair. 'Time to say goodbye to you, bad boys.' His thick Norfolk accent emerged from the veneer of the cultivated voice he'd adopted over the last 48 months.

He pulled a set of clippers from the travel bag on the bed and set to work.

Hair fell to the carpet in thick waves. Without any finesse and the blade set to No 1, the resulting DIY buzz cut was a radical departure from the unkempt appearance that had been his disguise since he started work at the CCU.

He tackled the thickest parts of his beard with the clippers, then moved to the bathroom where he finished the job with his razor.

Shawn, and clean-shaven, he emerged with a towel around his neck and patted his face dry. He stared at the mirror again and playfully smacked his cheeks with a self-satisfied smirk. 'You're looking damn fine, my boy. Welcome back to the land of the living.'

His reverie was disturbed by the phone. The new phone he'd picked up two days earlier. He'd only given the number to one person. He'd been expecting the call and picked up with a cheerful 'Hi.' He didn't expect the response he got.

'What the hell do you think you're playing at?'

Millard held the phone away from his ear for a second before replying, 'What do you mean? What's the problem?'

'I thought you were going to ensure that everybody would be in the control tower when your device went off. You assured me there'd be no survivors.'

'I did, there are no survivors. I waited till everybody was there and then left. When I hit the button, all the personnel were inside.'

'Well. They weren't.'

'What are you talking about? I saw it. Nobody could have survived that.'

'Maybe not, but you got out before that journalist arrived back with her husband.'

'No, you're wrong. I waited till they were on their way up in the lift before I got out.'

'Well, in your rush to leave, you didn't stay to wait till they arrived in the control room. They both survived.'

'How the hell?'

'I don't know how the hell, but I've just heard that...' There was a pause, it sounded to Millard like the caller was checking his notes. 'Jones, Susan Jones, was helped by a couple of the security police who helped dig her husband out of the rubble. Her car was written off, so they let her take him to hospital in an old staff car. She told them she's got a couple of modems from one of the processing companies.'

'Yeah, she told me when she called on the way back to Warrenford.'

'Well, it's only a matter of time before she gets them to someone who can hack them and discover what we don't want them to know.'

'Oh, shit.'

'My words exactly. I just heard ten minutes ago. I've sent a message to get our man in Whitehall to call her.'

Millard's face creased at this. 'Hang on, if she takes them to Corsham...'

'She's not going to get to Corsham, is she.' The statement was delivered with menace.

'Oh.' Millard mumbled as the meaning of the words became clear.

'Someone has to finish what you failed to do.'

Millard cringed. 'What d'you want me to do?'

'Nothing. You had your chance; I've got people who can take care of it.'

'I could go to the hospital and get the modems off her.'

'No, keep away. As far as the rest of the world is concerned, you're one of the fatalities. Call me in the morning, I'll have a job for you.'

Millard shrugged. 'OK, you want to give me a clue?'

The voice at the other end gave an irritated sigh. 'It's all going to kick off big time tomorrow, I'll need all the manpower I can get.'

This brought a hint of a smile to Millard's face. 'That sounds a lot more interesting than sitting in that bloody control room.'

13

Nick lay in bed and watched the clock on the wall through half-open eyes. At the stroke of 5.00 pm, Tim and Anna walked in.

He nudged Susie who sat on his bed beside him. She had been scrolling through social media posts, catching up on the latest developments. She jumped in surprise. 'Hi guys.' She eased herself off the bed and hugged the visitors.

Tim had dressed for the cold and wore a multi-layered hard shell technical jacket that wouldn't look out of place on the Matterhorn. He said nothing but gave Nick an appraising look and shook his head. He let Anna do the talking.

'How you doing soldier?'

Nick shrugged gingerly, pointed to his bandaged head and nodded to the injured leg. He looked from Anna to Susie with a raised eyebrow. 'What's she been telling you?'

Anna approached with caution and kissed him on the cheek. 'Just that you're lucky to be alive.'

Nick pulled a face somewhere between a half-smile and a grimace. 'Yeah, I guess so. But the poor buggers in the control tower weren't so lucky.'

'Susie told us what happened but there's been nothing on the news about it.' Tim said, as he moved to the other side of the bed from Anna and offered Nick a hesitant fist pump. 'Bloody hell mate, it sounds horrific.'

Susie stood at the end of the bed; a concerned expression played across her face. 'Thankfully he can't remember anything about it, can you babe?'

Nick avoided another painful shrug and turned his hands palm upwards. 'What can I say, it's a complete blank, you know how the mind blocks out the moments before a trauma.'

Tim nodded sagely at this, his slight limp a lasting testament to an equally traumatic event years earlier.

Nick continued. 'I can vaguely remember arriving back at Warrenford, but I've got no recollection of going into the building or what happened after that.'

Anna looked back at Susie. 'How come there's been nothing on the news about it?'

Susie pursed her lips and frowned. 'There's enough chaos out there without news getting out that the people in charge have all been killed. We're still not sure who's taken control of things.'

The remark puzzled Tim. 'Did you not get through to someone at Whitehall?

'Eventually. I left a message and they promised to get someone to call me tomorrow.'

'So where are they now?' Tim asked.

'They're in the car. Why?'

"I've brought my laptop.' He tapped the bag slung over his shoulder. 'I've got a programme on it that can interrogate the inner workings of a modem. That's what they'll do at Corsham. Might be interesting.' His eyes met those of the other three in the room looking for consent or disapproval.

Nick was the first to respond. 'Go for it Ace, if it wasn't for those things, we'd have both been in that control tower when it blew up.' He fixed Susie with a meaningful stare. 'If you hadn't gone back to the car for them...' His voice faded momentarily. 'Go and get 'em love, let's see what they can tell us.'

'Back in five.' Susie turned and left the room; they heard her footsteps recede as she jogged down the corridor.

Barely out of breath, Susie returned a few minutes later. She reached into the plastic bag she'd brought from the car and extracted the two modems. Tim picked them up, one in each hand and compared them. He turned them over and examined them in detail. 'Which one's which?'

It took Susie a moment to realise what he meant. 'What? Oh, well, in case you hadn't guessed, the one in its original shrink wrap is the new one.' She pointed at the second unit. 'That's the one that was plugged in.'

'They both look the same?" Anna leant across the bed; her gaze flicked from one modem to the other.

Susie tapped the underside of the modem in her hand. 'This one has no sticker.' She nodded at the one in Tim's hand. 'That one's got a sticker on its belly. It's the line ID.'

Tim held the modem closer to his eye and squinted. 'Only just. Has to be the world's smallest sticker.'

'The guy at Payline pointed it out to me, I'd have missed it otherwise.' Susie said.

'OK, so let's see what it can tell us.' Tim opened his laptop on a side table and set to work. The other three set about the goodies Susie had brought back from her earlier shopping expedition. They let Tim get on with it. He powered up the modem then plugged a CAT6 data cable into one of the input sockets and connected the other end into his laptop. He studied the screen in silence.

Susie's curiosity got the better of her and while chewing on a protein bar, she casually sidled over to Tim's side to look at what he had. The screen displayed row after row of letters and numbers, there appeared to be no structure to them, but Tim's eyes scanned down the screen and he nodded slightly as though they made sense to him.

'Well?' he said, unable to come up with anything more insightful.

Without taking his eyes of the screen, Tim replied. 'It all looks fairly normal,' He pointed to a line of numbers, 'it's just booting up and shaking hands with the laptop, but essentially there's nothing wrong with it.'

'So how come all those cables were burned out?' Nick asked from the comfort of his bed.

Tim raised a hand in Nick's direction without looking at him. 'Hang on buddy, I'm about to dial in.' He lifted the modem and checked the number on the sticker, then typed it into the line of text at the bottom of the screen.

At first, nothing happened and the four of them looked at each other, the laptop and the modem, with a sense of expectation.

It was Anna who spotted the first signs. 'Look at that.' Her voice jumped a couple of octaves, and one hand went to her mouth while the other pointed at the cable.

Tim switched his attention from the screen where he assumed he'd see something and saw what had alerted Anna. The data cable had begun to vibrate and twist slowly.

Nick forgot his injuries and sat up to see what the fuss was about.

Susie stared open-mouthed at the cable as the twisting intensified. 'What's happening Tim?'

Tim was momentarily transfixed and didn't reply. The white outer covering of the cable turned dark grey and started to visibly soften. He glanced back at his laptop screen, unable to believe what he was witnessing. 'I don't understand, it's still working normally.' As he spoke, acrid black smoke started to seep from the cable. He reacted quickly and snatched the cable from his laptop and pulled the other end from the modem. He shook his fingers and blew on them. 'Jeez, it's red hot.'

Anna reached for Tim's hand. 'You OK sweetheart?'

Tim appreciated the concern and let Anna stroke his fingers as though it would help. 'Yeah, it's fine, just a shock more than anything.' His eyes remained focused on the screen; his brow furrowed in concentration.

Nick's attention went to the discarded data cable that lay on the floor, still smouldering. 'I recognise that smell.' He wrinkled his nose and looked at Susie, she nodded.

'Good job I've got a bunch of cables in here.' Tim reached into his bag and pulled out a replacement.

'What's your plan? Destroy another cable, set the smoke detectors off?'

Tim glanced back at Nick. 'Funny guy. No, I've got a hunch and I want to test it out.' He turned to Susie. 'Can you pass me that other modem.' He nodded at the unit she'd left on Nick's bed.

The other three, intrigued, watched as Tim ripped the clear plastic wrapping from the new modem and repeated the procedure. With it powered up and plugged in, Tim let the screen populate. He paused; his fingers hovered over the keyboard. 'I need a random phone number, anything, just to configure this one.'

Susie gazed at the ceiling for moment in search of inspiration, then rattled off the landline number for Warrenford.

Tim typed it in. 'Now let's see what happens.' He hit the return key and stood back, eyes focused on the data cable, the others did the same.

None of them spoke. The modem whirred, clicked and buzzed quietly; LEDs flashed. As before, the screen remained unchanged, but so did the cable. Nothing happened.

After a full minute, Tim gingerly reached out and touched the cable with a fingertip, then two, then ran his fingers from end to end. 'As I suspected.' He turned to face a captivated audience. 'It's just normal. That modem's been got at.' He jutted his chin towards the first unit, lying to one side of his impromptu workbench.

'Got at?' Susie repeated.

Tim nodded. 'Yeah, a bug, a virus, malware. It's been sabotaged. Did you say that was one of nine?'

'Uhhuh, we just took that one as it was the easiest to remove.'

'So, it's a safe bet they were all infected.' Tim scratched his chin for a moment, then unplugged the modem and reattached the old one.

Nick didn't follow Tim's actions. 'What's your plan?'

'Just give me a minute.' Tim went back to the laptop and scrolled through lines of code. He paused and tapped a finger against the screen. 'Hmmm.'

Susie leaned in closer and stared at the point he'd highlighted. 'What am I looking at?'

'See that?' His finger underlined a section of text.

Susie nodded but said nothing.

'It's additional code to the other one, it specifies a date and time, twenty-two, twelve, fifteen thirty UTC.' Tim turned to Susie and watched her expression as his words found meaning.

Her eyes opened wide, and she silently mouthed the date and time. The realisation swept over her features. 'Hang on. That's yesterday at 3.30 when the whole thing started.'

'You've got it.' Someone, God knows who, has found a way to inject a virus into the operating system that lies dormant until a specific date and time.'

'And then Kapow!' Nick chimed in.

Tim gave a rueful shake of the head, as much in admiration for whoever had done it, as it was in acknowledgement of Nick's assessment of the problem. 'You said it, mate. it's like a delayed action trigger, when it goes off, it somehow destroys the cables plugged into it .'

'Is that even possible?' asked a puzzled Susie.

'If you'd asked me ten minutes ago, I'd have said no. But there it is.' Tim waved an accusatory finger at the lines of code. 'I've never seen anything like it.'

Anna had listened intently without comment as she processed what Tim had discovered. 'Tell me if I'm wrong, but the only way you could inject a virus into the software is if you knew the line ID.' She gave Tim a questioning look.

Susie picked up Anna's thread and when she saw Tim give a faint nod, she added. 'So, who allocates the line IDs?' She looked at the other three for a response, they looked at each other and shrugged. Susie's face screwed up in thought for a brief moment, then she suddenly smacked her forehead with the tips of her fingers. Her face lit up. 'The guy at Payline, he can tell us.'

Tim glanced at his watch. 'It's after six on a Saturday night. You think you'll get hold of him?'

Susie reached for her phone. 'You bet I will, he's desperate for help.' Her attention switched to the screen in search of a number for Payline. 'Bugger!'

Nick gave an understanding shake of his head. 'No signal?'

Susie nodded in frustration and headed for the door. 'Looks like I'm off outside again.'

***

Ten minutes later and for the second time in an hour, Susie returned to Nick's room, this time she had a look of mild triumph on her features.

'Success?' Asked Nick.

Susie smiled and tapped her temple with an extended finger. 'Up here for thinking babe.'

'Well come on, tell us' Anna said.

'Got hold of Trent straight away. He was so pleased to hear from me. He'd heard on the grapevine about Warrenford and assumed the worst.' She looked at Nick and sighed. Yet again, the reality of their lucky escape hit her hard.

'So, what did he say when you asked him about the line IDs?' Tim asked.

'Connectivity.' Susie said, in a tone that implied, it should have been obvious. The other three said nothing and waited for her to elaborate. 'They manage the entire phone network, voice and data. They might subcontract some of the installations, but for obvious reasons, they are the only ones who can allocate the line numbers.'

'Makes sense.' Said Nick, who by now had eaten an entire pack of Jaffa Cakes and a Mars Bar. His demeanour had improved noticeably.

Tim nodded in agreement and added. 'Could he tell you any more than that?'

Susie paused for a moment while she made herself comfortable on the end of Nick's bed. 'Yeah, he said they guard the numbers like gold dust; again, for obvious reasons.'

Anna considered this; her expression thoughtful. 'If all the payment processing companies are having the same problem, then either someone in the company is on the take or they're being blackmailed.'

'Or someone has hacked into their network.' Tim suggested.

Susie sat with her arms folded. She stared at Tim's laptop through narrowed eyes and pinched the bridge of her nose. 'Anything's possible, I guess. I'm trying to think what's the next step.'

'Not your problem sweetheart.' Nick reached out and rested a hand on Susie's shoulder. 'Just give those bloody things to whoever, tell them what we've discovered and let them get on with it.'

Susie's nose wrinkled at the thought. 'It might not be my problem, but we're involved.' She looked at Nick, searching for support and understanding. 'We owe it to those guys at Warrenford.'

Tim couldn't help but intervene. 'I'm with Susie, we've come this far, it'd be a shame not to do something about it.'

Nick rolled his eyes and saw Anna dithering between him and Susie. 'What do you think? Three against one?'

'Sorry Nick, but I agree with Tim.'

Nick threw his hands up in mock surrender.

Susie suppressed the urge to gloat. 'Thanks, guys, but it doesn't answer the question. What next?'

'You could try Connectivity and see what they say.' Anna suggested.

Nick gave a derisory snort. 'Good luck with that. Saturday night before Christmas. You'd never get through to anyone with any authority at the best of times.'

'We can't be the only ones working on this, I'll bet they've got teams in trying to sort it out.' Susie turned to Tim and indicated his laptop. 'Can you get into their corporate website?'

'I'll have a go.' Tim got to work. 'What you are looking for?'

'See if they list any senior personnel.'

Nick forgot his reservations. 'Forget it, try the Companies House website instead, they have to list the Directors, and it'll show their details.' He met Susie's look of surprise. 'Those people live in fear of trolls, they won't put names and addresses on their website.'

Susie nodded and gave a reluctant shrug. 'Good thinking babe.'

Tim tapped a few keys. 'This might take a minute. I'm on 4G, and it's painfully slow.' He hit the return key and then paused. 'There are four different companies, I'm guessing you want operations?'

Susie nodded.

Tim tapped and scrolled down the screen then gave a triumphant 'Yes.'

Susie rushed to Tim's side and studied the screen. 'Operations Director, that's who we want.' She tapped a finger on the details shown. 'Can you screenshot that and drop it to me.'

'No sooner said than done.' Tim tapped a few keys and a couple of seconds later Susie's phone pinged.

She gave her screen a cursory glance to confirm she'd received what she asked for. 'Thanks, Tim.'

'You realise that address is the company HQ.'

'Yeah, but we've got her full name and date of birth,' Susie gave a little fist pump. 'If that's not enough for me to track her down, then I'm in the wrong job.'

Nick squeezed his eyes shut and shook his head slowly. 'Seriously sweetheart. What are you getting into?'

'I'm doing what I'm good at babe.' She hopped onto Nick's bed and wriggled alongside him. 'We could have been killed last night.' She squeezed his hand.

Nick relented, put his arm around his wife and hugged her tight. 'I get it love, but why not let the proper people deal with it? No one's asked you to do this.'

'True, but this is personal, I want to speak to this woman, this...,' she studied the screenshot Tim had airdropped. '...Alison Burton-Castle.'

14

Sunday 24 December

A cold wind rattled the window and woke Susie from a fitful sleep. She groped for her phone and stared, bleary-eyed, at the screen. Twelve minutes after seven; she groaned and longed for a Sunday morning lie-in. The events of the previous 36 hours had caught up with her and despite her tiredness, thoughts of the explosion, Nick's injuries and Tim's revelations with the modems, she felt she'd been awake half the night. A sense of foreboding hung over her and she knew she had to get moving. With extreme reluctance, she pushed the covers off and forced herself to move.

She planned to pick Nick up at lunchtime, assuming he'd been passed fit enough to go home. She had a few hours to kill and the urge to track down the Operations Director at Connectivity nagged at her. The fact that nobody in authority had been in touch, helped convince her that she had to act. Tim's concerns about red tape and layers of bureaucracy bounced around her thoughts and buoyed her resolve to take matters into her own hands.

She dressed quickly and, once in the kitchen, opened her laptop and went in search of Alison Burton-Castle. The search didn't prove to be much of a challenge. The name was unusual enough to avoid too many matches, and Susie's investigative skills quickly narrowed the few possibilities to just one. It appeared the woman avoided social media, a fact that didn't surprise Susie, but she had other tricks up her sleeve in the shape of the electoral register, media archives and trade publications. The fact that Burton-Castle had a high-profile role in a major company made it almost impossible for her to stay under the radar, and within thirty minutes, Susie had an address. She had no phone number or email, but she had pinpointed her location, and it was less than an hour away.

She sat back, stared at the displayed information and contemplated her next move while munching a hastily prepared breakfast of mashed banana on toast. Should she go with her gut instinct and visit the woman, or go through official channels and let them tackle her? She knew what she should do, but pride, stubbornness or sheer bloody-mindedness pulled her in a different direction.

Her face set in a mask of determination, Susie closed the laptop after committing the address to her phone and hurriedly tidied the kitchen. A quick trip upstairs for more appropriate clothing revealed presents hidden at the bottom of her wardrobe and the realisation that it was Christmas Eve made her pause. With everything that had happened since 3.30 on Friday, the festive spirit had somehow escaped her consciousness. She'd walked past the tree in the hallway and hadn't given it a thought.

She resolved to confront Alison Burton-Castle, contact Whitehall again then pick Nick up. While she packed everything, she thought she might need, she came up with what she considered a realistic timetable and was about to send Nick a text, then remembered he no longer had a phone. She decided to ring the ward when she had a minute spare.

As predicted the journey to the address she'd found for Burton-Castle, took just under an hour. It was around 9.30 as she entered Radmore Road, in the affluent Jericho region of Oxford and she drove slowly enough past the three-storey properties to note the numbers, odd ones on the left, even numbers on the right. She wanted number 23 but pulled over when she reached 19. She planned to continue on foot.

Like the other houses on the road, number 23 was constructed in pale Cotswold stone with a wide, imposing front door, a double garage and a gravelled in-and-out driveway. Susie sat in the old Volvo, engine running, heater blowing and studied the house with a critical eye. There was only one vehicle on the drive, a dark blue Jaguar SUV with a private plate beginning ABC; this had to be the right place. She got out and shivered as the cold wind hit her. She raised the collar of her coat and set off towards the front door, unsure what to expect.

A holly wreath hung on the door, the only visible concession to Christmas. A doorbell with a built-in camera sat to the side of the door, and Susie made a conscious effort to smile at it as she pressed the buzzer. She could hear the chimes inside the house, almost drowned out by the sound of a blender. She waited for the blender to stop, then pressed the bell again. This time, she heard voices arguing: a woman and a boy. The argument persisted for a full minute before she heard soft footsteps approaching and then a key turning. Eventually, the door swung partially open to reveal a stocky boy of about 12 in his pyjamas and slippers, a tousled mop of blonde hair and an orange-tinted upper lip. He held a slice of toast in one hand and a paperback in the other held open with his thumb where he'd been interrupted. He looked expectantly at the visitor while he chewed on the mouthful he'd just taken.

'Hello.' said Susie.

This received a non-committal grunt by way of reply.

Susie tried again. 'Is your Mum in?'

She heard a woman's voice shout from further back in the house. 'Who is it Noah?"

The boy turned away from the door and shouted back down the hallway. 'It's a woman asking for you.' With that, he left Susie standing at the half open door and padded back to the kitchen.

Unsure whether she was expected to follow Noah or stay put, she thought it best to wait and avoid getting off on the wrong foot. Her patience was rewarded a few seconds later when she heard more footsteps and Alison Burton-Castle fully opened the door. Susie was in no doubt it was her, after her online research. The woman looked different from the glossy media images Susie had seen. Catching her off guard on a Sunday morning; no make up, dressed in yoga pants, sweatshirt and trainers. If being caught off guard bothered her, it didn't show.

She smiled and quickly looked Susie up and down. 'Hello, can I help you?' No trace of an accent, friendly tone. She was a few inches taller than Susie and held her chin high enough to project just a hint of superiority.

'Mrs Burton-Castle?' Susie checked.

'Yes, and you are?'

'My name is Jones, I'm from the Cyber Crime Unit.' she held out her police ID for inspection.

Burton-Castle peered at the credentials and gave a small shudder. 'If this is about the payment processing issue, my team are working on it? What's so important you have to bother me on a Sunday morning.'

'I'm sorry, but we've discovered something you may be able to help us with.'

'I'd be very surprised.' She looked past Susie as if checking to see if anyone else was in sight. 'Look, this is obviously important. Come inside and close the door, it's freezing out there.'

Susie walked into the expansive open-plan hall. A huge Christmas tree stood at the foot of a staircase that wound its way around three sides of a square. The stack of presents surrounding the tree's base reminded Susie of the interiors staged for a photoshoot Nick had been commissioned to take a few months back. Burton-Castle walked towards the kitchen and beckoned her visitor to follow.

The kitchen was equally magazine worthy. Grey units, black worktop and gold door handles, it featured a large island unit at which Noah sat, re-engaged with his paperback, the glass of orange juice stood in front of him explained the top lip. He didn't look up as his mother and Susie entered the room.

Susie felt as if she had entered an inner sanctum and looked around to see who else was in the room. A large canvas print dominated one wall, a family portrait with Noah, an older girl, Alison Burton-Castle and a man Susie assumed must be her husband. There was no sight or sound of anyone else in the room.

Burton-Castle perched on a stool at the island and poured a green smoothie from a blender into a tall glass. It appeared to have the consistency of sludge and left her with a green moustache to rival her son's orange one. From the look on her face, after she'd taken a couple of gulps, she was determined to force it down despite its taste. While digesting the potion, she flapped a hand at another stool and made signals Susie took to mean, grab a seat and tell me what you want to know.

Susie took a seat on the opposite side of the island. 'We've had a specialist look at a couple of modems we took from one of the processing companies.' she began. This was met with a nod from her host, while one hand clasped her chest in an effort to suppress the urge to gag. Susie pushed on. 'We took one of the modems that had failed and one brand new one to compare it with.' The hand moved from chest to mouth as if she was going to vomit. Susie hesitated but more hand signals prompted her to continue. 'Well the specialist, identified a virus in the failed modem, it had been set to activate on Friday at 3.3 0.'

At this, Burton-Castle swallowed and shook herself as if to clear her head. She wiped her mouth with the back of her hand. 'Sorry about that, this stuff tastes vile but it's supposed to do me some good.' She pushed the half-drunk glass slowly away with a single rigid finger as if it might explode at any moment. She turned her attention to Susie. 'That would make sense, my people have confirmed there's nothing wrong with our systems, we're not to blame for any of this.'

Susie nodded in agreement. 'Absolutely. We're pretty sure this is some sort of terrorist cyber-attack, possibly state-sponsored to be on such a wide scale.' She had no evidence, just a gut feeling, but thought if she wanted the woman's cooperation, a little exaggeration wouldn't go amiss.

Burton-Castle closed her eyes and lowered her head. 'Bloody brilliant, but ingenious. If you're going to disrupt the system, why not do it on the busiest day of the year?'

'The thing is,' Susie continued, 'we worked out the only way the modem could have been infected by the virus, is via the phone line which would mean whoever did this would have to know the line IDs for all the processing companies.' Susie stopped in expectation of the reaction. She wasn't disappointed.

'No way.' Burton-Castle blurted out, she sat up suddenly, her digestive issues forgotten. 'No way in hell. Those numbers are highly confidential, only four people have access to them. Me, and three members of my team, all of whom I'd trust with my life.' She looked indignant at the very thought.

Susie held out a calming hand. 'Please, nobody's pointing the finger. If this is state sponsored then we can't rule out sophisticated levels of clandestine operations, hacking, blackmail, high-tech industrial espionage.'

Burton-Castle frowned and jumped down from the stool. She paced the kitchen floor, arms folded across her chest as if protecting herself from an unseen threat. She shook her head repeatedly unable to believe what she was being told. 'It's impossible, the files are encrypted at the highest level and if anyone one of us accesses them, the other three are notified.' She stopped at looked at her visitor seeking confirmation.

'We've got every faith in your security, but external forces are constantly coming up with ways to outwit the most advanced countermeasures.' Susie gave a helpless resigned shrug. 'We try to stay one step ahead, but as the old saying goes, we have to eliminate every threat, the bad guys only have to succeed once.'

'I thought that just applied to terrorist attacks.'

'Sadly, that's exactly what this is. They've already destroyed the CCU headquarters and killed the core personnel. I only just escaped. My other half is in hospital.'

'Oh God, I'm sorry, I had no idea, there's been nothing on the news.' Burton-Castle looked genuinely shocked.

Susie pulled her phone from her jacket pocket and brought up the BBC News. 'You're right. There's no mention of it, mainly because of all the unrest breaking out.'

Burton-Castle peered over Susie's shoulder at the screen. 'OK, I get it, but you said, you thought I could help. What can I do?'

'We'll go on investigating and we'll track down whoever is behind the attack later, but right now our priority is to get the system up and running again before total anarchy breaks out.' Susie put her phone away and stared intently at Burton-Castle almost daring her to argue.

'Fair enough, but like I said, our system is not the problem.'

'No, but it could be the solution.' Susie said.

'I'm not following.'

'Can you issue new numbers to the processing companies?' Susie gave a look somewhere between a question and a request.

Burton-Castle didn't respond immediately. She stopped pacing, ran a hand across her face then pinched her top lip between thumb and forefinger. She returned to her stool, deep in thought. 'Would that work?'

Susie nodded. 'We tried it with the failed modem. Allocated a random new number and it was fine. There's nothing actually wrong with the modems, it's the numbers that trigger the virus.'

The Connectivity woman considered Susie's words. She reached for the glass of green sludge to buy herself more time. Her eyes narrowed as the implications of the task hit home. 'It's not as simple as that.' She focused on the contents of the glass, her nose wrinkled in disdain. 'Do you know how many numbers we're talking about?'

Susie shook her head.

'I don't know the exact figure but it's several hundred, could be over a thousand.' She paused and turned slowly towards Susie, a look of horror on her face. 'What am I talking about.' She tapped the side of her head with a forefinger. 'It could be several thousand, some of the bigger companies have multiple sub lines on top of their main numbers.' She grimaced as the scale of the problem hit home.

'I wish there was another way, but if they keep their existing numbers, chances are, the system will crash again.' Susie knew she was asking a lot, but added constructively. 'How big a job is it?'

Burton-Castle exhaled loudly spread her arms wide then slumped. 'It's a nightmare. We've got to create the numbers, test them, then allocate them while keeping the details totally secret. We'd normally send them by secure post but in an emergency I daresay we could use some form of encrypted email.'

'When could you start?' Susie subconsciously glanced at the kitchen clock as she spoke. It was after 10.00.

Her host noted the look. 'I suppose you want me to start today?'

Susie pulled an apologetic face. 'Sorry to do this to you, I know it's Christmas Eve, but we don't have a choice.'

Burton-Castle held a hand up, struck by a thought. 'Hang on, I've got an idea.' She jumped off her stool again and headed out of the kitchen. leaving Susie with Noah who was still engrossed in his book.

She returned within a minute holding a laptop. 'I can log into the main computer from here.' She opened the computer and followed what appeared to Susie to be a complicated login procedure. 'I can't do much from here, but I can set wheels in motion.'

'That's great.' Susie said as she watched the other woman focus on her keyboard. 'I really appreciate it. Can I leave you my contact details, I have to go, I'm supposed to be picking up my other half from hospital and I'm already running late.'

'Sure, I'll call you with an update as soon as I can.' Burton-Castle looked up and nodded at Susie. 'Can you see yourself out?'

'Yeah, thanks, and...' Susie gave an apologetic shrug, 'Sorry about all this.'

The other woman gave a dismissive wave, her eyes never left the screen.

Susie headed for the door and out into the cold. Once outside, she pulled her phone out and dialled a number as she walked back to the old Volvo.

15

Susie settled into the musty interior of the old Volvo, started the engine and let it warm up while she considered her next move.

She resisted the urge to call the hospital again and trusted Nick had got the message. She assumed someone would ring her if, for any reason, they were planning to keep him in any later than they told her last night. She stared at her phone as if it would give her an answer when it suddenly burst into life. She almost dropped it in surprise but regained her composure and frowned at the screen, number withheld.

Curious, but feeling it could be important, she tapped the screen and the speaker function. Holding the phone at arm's length she answered with a dubious 'Hello.'

'Is that Susan Jones?' The voice belonged to a young woman, she sounded unsure and a little nervous.

'Who's calling?' Susie's eyes narrowed as she failed to recognise the voice.

'I'm calling from the Ministry of Defence in Whitehall, my name is Millie Peterson, I'm an analyst here, I've been tasked with following up on the Warrenford explosion.'

'Uh-huh.' Susie remained sceptical.

'You are Susan Jones?' The voice gained a little confidence.

Susie could see no reason not to drop her guarded attitude. 'Yes. And it's Susie.'

'OK, that's great, thank you, Susie. Are you all right? The security guys at Warrenford told us about you. They said they'd helped get your husband out of the building and into a car.'

'That's right. I got him to hospital in their old Volvo.'

'Oh God, I'm so sorry, is he OK?'

'Yeah, he's a bit battered and bruised, but he'll live. Not like the guys in the control room.' Susie squeezed her eyes shut as she spoke, and another wave of relief mixed with grief washed over her.

'It's such a shock, it must have been terrible for you.'

Susie nodded. 'To put it mildly.' She shook herself and sat up straighter. 'I'm glad you've called. I didn't know who to get in touch w ith.'

'Sorry it's taken so long. Everything's a mess, all the records have been hard to access, and you're not listed in the personnel files.'

'I know, I'm a bit of an oddity. Commander Eddington head-hunted me after I exposed an organisation marketing unlicensed meds. That was six months ago and I've kind of...' Susie gazed out as a runner went past, a yellow Labrador trotting happily alongside. She envied him. '...I suppose I've become part of the team by default.'

Peterson confirmed. 'That would make sense. I found your details eventually, ex Military Police?'

'Yeah. That was a few years ago but I must have bypassed the usual vetting procedures.'

'Well, anyway, my orders were to track you down and get you to call the Cyber Security Operations Centre at Corsham and speak to the boss, name of Matthews.'

'No problem.' said Susie. 'Text me the number, I'll call him now.'

'Will do. And take care, Susie.' Peterson clicked off.

With a mild sense of relief, Susie exhaled and sank back in her seat. Ten seconds later, her phone pinged with the arrival of the text. She called the number immediately. It was answered before it had rung once.

'Matthews speaking.'

Taken aback by the abruptness of the response, it took Susie a moment to compose herself. 'Er, hello, it's Susie Jones, I've been asked to call you.'

'Jones. Jones, ah yes. Are you the one who was at Warrenford?' Matthews sounded impatient and irritated.

'Yes, I work there, or at least I did. I just got back with my other half when it exploded.'

'Hmmm, back from where?'

Susie noted the complete lack of concern for either her or Nick but replied anyway. 'We'd been down to one of the payment processing companies and brought back a couple of modems for analysis.'

This resulted in an audible sharp intake of breath and a moment of silence, Matthews said. 'I see, and what have you done with them?'

Susie recounted what had happened at the hospital the previous evening. Matthews made the occasional comment but otherwise, let her continue. She concluded with. 'So, I traced the Operations Director of Connectivity and went to see her this morning.'

At this, Matthews burst out. 'You did what!'

Stunned by his reaction Susie paused for a moment, but before she could respond, Matthews continued in a more restrained voice. 'Sorry about that. I'm just astonished you've been able to do so much.'

Susie frowned at her phone, puzzled by the sudden change in attitude. 'Er, that's OK, it's what I do.'

Matthews made a few vague noises as if he was conflicted. 'Yes, well, very good. And what did this woman do.'

'At first, she said there was nothing she could do, but when I told her about the line IDs and asked her to issue new ones, she understood and promised to get onto it straight away.'

This was met with silence. She could hear laboured breathing. After what felt like an age, Susie spoke. 'Hello. Are you still there?'

'Yes. Sorry. This is a little tricky.'

'How come?'

'We're trying to keep a lid on this. We don't want rumours getting out.'

'You've lost me. I thought you'd want to sort the situation out as soon as possible.'

'Absolutely. But we need to make sure we know what caused the problem so we can take steps to prevent it from happening again. I applaud your initiative, but this must go through the right channels.'

This response resulted in more frowning and Susie hesitated before replying. 'Forgive me for being a cynic, but, the right channels, means it'll get bogged down in a load of red tape.'

'Not at all. My technical team are working on this as I speak. If you can get those modems to me, they'll start work immediately.'

Susie remained unconvinced. 'Hang on. I told you we've figured out what was wrong. What else are you going to do?'

Matthews' tone changed. 'Ms Jones, this is a National Emergency. You must leave this in the hands of the authorities.'

'But...'

'Sorry.' Matthews talked over her. His voice had an edge to it. 'I need to make a phone call. Don't go anywhere, I'll ring you back in five minutes.'

He ended the call. Susie stared at her phone, her frown lines growing. 'Yeah, that's OK, I'll just sit here and wait.' She mumbled to herself before starting the engine to generate a little warmth. The sun may have broken through the clouds but according to the temperature gauge, it was still below freezing.

Rostyslav Kobzar paced back and forth in his office. He smoked with determination, cigarette pinched between thumb and forefinger. He took huge drags, inhaled deeply, flicked ash on the carpet and exhaled through his nose as he scrutinised the news on his iPad. He'd left his phone on his desk and when it rang, he glared at it, as if outraged it should interrupt his thoughts.

He strode over to his desk and gazed at the number on the screen. He shook his head in mild despair and ground the remains of his cigarette into an ashtray. He tapped the phone to accept the call then tapped the speaker icon. He left the device on his desk, folded his arms and looked down at it through narrowed eyes as if the sight of it caused offence. 'Yes.'

'I've had some alarming news, I thought I should call you.' Matthew's voice sounded hesitant.

Kobzar's gaze shifted to the ceiling, he closed his eyes and let out a long slow breath. 'Tell me.'

'I've had a woman on the phone who worked at Warrenford, she escaped.'

'So, what's the problem?' Kobzar's frustration grew.

'She's got a couple of modems from one of the processing companies and she's had someone look at them.' Matthews rushed the words out as if he feared the reaction.

Kobzar's face twisted at this. 'Keep going.'

'They discovered the virus and how it was delivered.'

'Yebat' Kobzar snarled.

Matthews continued. 'And she's been to see you-know-who to ask her to issue new numbers.'

'Who the fuck is she?' Kobzar's voice grew in volume.

'She's a journalist, name of Jones.'

'What the fuck was she doing at Warrenford?'

'I'm not sure exactly, but she's ex-forces.'

Kobzar said nothing but grunted in acknowledgement while he lit another cigarette. He took a long drag and stared at the screen on his phone through eyes narrowed to tiny slits.

'Hello?' Matthews asked after thirty seconds had passed.

'Quiet, I'm thinking.' Kobzar's face twisted. He paused for a few beats. 'Two things.' He stated eventually.

Matthews gave a noncommittal. 'Uh-huh.'

'First, we've got to prevent new numbers being issued.' His gaze wandered around the office as his thoughts took shape. 'We need another couple of days.'

'Ooookay.' Said a plainly uncertain Matthews.

'Grab the kids, use them as leverage.' Kobzar nodded to himself as his plan formulated. 'I know just where to hold them, I'll send you details.'

'But...' Matthews started.

'And secondly,' Kobzar cut across him. 'The modems and this Jones women. What's she doing now?'

'She's waiting for me to call her back.'

Kobzar took another drag and studied the glowing ash as if seeking enlightenment. 'Tell her bring the modems to you.'

'What? Where? I mean...'

'Shut up and listen.' Kobzar's irritation now turned up to maximum. 'I don't care about the modems, they're just a means to an end.

What bothers me is an unknown sticking their bloody nose in and fucking up the plan.'

Matthews gave another 'Uh huh.'

'Hold on a minute.' Kobzar sat at his desk and brought up a map on his laptop. 'Where is she now?'

'Oxford.'

Kobzar zoomed and scrolled until he had Oxford on the right-hand edge of his screen and Bristol on the left. He ran a finger from right to left, then stopped and tapped. 'Got it.' He took another drag and brushed ash onto the floor with the back of his hand.

'What?' Matthews said,

'Tell her to meet you at Corsham, that's your place, isn't it?'

'Yes, but...'

'Just tell her. It sounds official. She'll believe you.'

'But what then?' Matthews sounded alarmed.

'She's not going to arrive. Just tell her to go there. Once she's on her way, you're going to ring her with a change of plan.' Kobzar's brain worked overtime as he plotted times and distances. 'Do it now.' He stabbed the phone to end the call with more than a little aggression.

Halfway through composing a text to Nick, Susie's phone rang again. After waiting ten minutes for Matthews to call back, she had almost given up. She fumbled it for a couple of seconds before answering. 'Hello.'

'I've checked with my team.' Matthews didn't waste time with apologies or greetings. 'I need you to bring the modems to the Cyber Security Operations Centre at MOD Corsham.'

'That's bloody miles away.' Susie reacted impulsively, she had been to CSOC twice during her initial training for the Cyber Crime Unit and knew it was at least an hour's drive. 'Can't somebody come and pick it up?'

'Impossible, you'll have to deliver them.' said Matthews bluntly.

'I can't. I'm not being difficult,' Susie started 'but I've got no way of getting fuel, and this thing,' She waved a hand around the Volvo's interior as if Matthews would understand. 'Is an absolute gas guzzler and I'm almost down to the fumes as it is.'

She heard an exaggerated sigh, a pause, then. 'This is most irregular.' More laboured breathing followed, and she imagined Matthews grinding his teeth in frustration. 'Give me another minute, I'll have to see what I can do.' The line went dead.

Susie rolled her eyes, sank back into her seat and pulled her coat around her. The engine may have warmed up, but she still felt cold. 'How much longer?' She mumbled.

She returned to her phone and looked at the half-finished text. She read what she'd written before she stopped, smacked her forehead with her palm, and remembered Nick's phone was somewhere in the rubble of the control tower. It took her a moment to find the number for Nick's ward, and she was about to ring it when her phone chimed into life for the third time.

Matthews wasn't joking when he said he'd call back in a minute.

'Change of plan.' he stated without any preamble. 'There's a Starbucks just off the roundabout on the A420 at Kingston Bagpuize. It's only a few miles away from Oxford. Somebody can meet you there and take the modems off you.'

'Er, OK.' Susie said, taken aback by the man's bluntness or any attempt to check the arrangement was convenient for her.

'Good. Can you be there for 11.30?'

Susie checked the time; it was just before 11.00. 'I guess so.' Her thoughts whirred. 'Who's meeting me? How will I know who they a re?'

'Not finalised yet, but they'll recognise you.' Without another word, Matthews ended the call.

The old Volvo predated built-in Satnav, so Susie used her phone to locate the rendezvous and check the mileage and ETA. She had five minutes to spare, so she called the hospital and left a message with the duty nurse to tell Nick she'd be calling to pick him up before 12:30.

——••●••——

Susie rolled into the Starbucks car park and glanced at the dashboard clock, exactly 11.30. The satnav had been bang on with its ETA. Being Christmas Eve and a Sunday, the place was busy but she found a space in the car park and debated her next move. Stay in the car and wait, or go in and get a drink. The idea of a hot chocolate won the argument.

She left the two modems in the car and entered the building, scanning the restaurant for anyone who might look "official". She didn't know what that meant and didn't know whether to expect a man or a woman, one person or two. The fact that none of the dozen or so customers even appeared to notice her led her to believe that whoever was supposed to be meeting her hadn't arrived yet.

She took her hot chocolate, topped with several inches of squirty cream, to a corner table where she could sit with her back to the wall and watch the door.

She waited.

Five minutes passed. Nobody entered the place, and nobody approached her. She told herself to be patient, not something she classified as a strength of hers, but she'd done as asked and resigned herself to wait another ten minutes while she absentmindedly stirred her drink with the extra-long teaspoon, slurping large mouthfuls of cream as she did so.

After another five minutes, she'd finished the hot chocolate and pulled her phone out to pass the time. She was about to go down the rabbit hole of social media when she heard the door open, and two women walked in.

Susie resisted the urge to look up and eyed them carefully through her fringe while making a show of looking down at her phone. They both looked to be in their late 20s, slim, athletic, taller than her, casually dressed in tight jeans, dark sweatshirts and military-style black boots. They were striking as opposed to pretty and carried themselves with a confidence that bordered on arrogance.

Neither of the women approached the counter, they stood near the door and surveyed the room. Susie noticed one of them nudge the other and nod in Susie's direction. Susie kept her head down, but out of the corner of her eye saw them both walk in her direction.

'Are you Jones?'

Susie looked up in feigned surprise to see one of the women standing over her, arms crossed, penetrating ice-blue eyes boring into her. She couldn't help but notice the high cheekbones, the broken nose and a round face she could only describe as Slavic. Susie gave a brief nod. 'And you are?'

'We have come to collect the equipment.' The woman's penetrating stare never flinched.

Susie looked around the restaurant, several people had stopped mid-sentence or mid-sip and turned to see what the two women wanted. Something about them gave Susie a feeling she couldn't name; uncertainty or suspicion. Why would Matthews send two women, and if they were sent by him, why didn't they produce some sort of ID? An uneasy sixth sense bolstered her resolve. She tested the woman. 'What equipment is that?'

The second woman stepped forward and leaned closer to Susie. 'We have come to meet a woman named Jones and pick up equipment. That is all you need to know.'

Susie glanced around and noticed more people had stopped what they were doing and appeared to be enthralled by the developing encounter. She refused to be intimidated. 'That's not all I need to know.' She glared at the two women. 'You've shown me no ID and haven't told me who sent you.' She sat back, folded her arms and continued to stare from one of the women to the other. 'You don't even know what you've come to collect.'

'Just give us the equipment.' Broken nose's voice grew in volume. 'Our names not important, you were sent to hand over equipment.' As the volume increased her accent slipped.

Her colleague tapped her on the shoulder, pointed at the area around Susie, the fact there were no bags or packages, and gave a small shake of her head.

Susie's suspicions grew, the accent confirming her initial thoughts. 'Ladies...' she paused and stood up in the hope of conveying a little more gravitas, The two women didn't appear troubled by her actions but took a step back. They still had a few inches on her. Susie continued. 'Ladies, if you think I would hand anything over to you without any authority, then you're sadly mistaken. I'm not some wet-behind-the-ears junior clerk. Learn some manners and tell whoever sent you to get in touch with me when they've got someone who knows what they're doing.' She didn't wait for a response and shouldered between the two women and headed straight for the exit.

Once outside she didn't look back and jogged quickly to the Volvo, jumped in, slammed the door, started the engine and headed out the car park as the two women emerged, a look of cold fury on their faces.

As she accelerated away, Susie reached for her phone to call Matthews and tell him what had happened, but in the process glanced in the rear-view mirror and saw a silver BMW pulling out of the Starbucks car park. It wasn't there when she arrived, and she realised it had to be the two women. They were bad news. She forgot the phone, dropped a gear and floored the throttle. 'If you want to play silly buggers, then you'd better know what you're doing.'

The old Volvo's engine had plenty of grunt despite its age and mileage. Somebody had obviously taken care of it. The same couldn't be said for its suspension or the tyres. Susie had set off on the back rounds and after a few twisty corners began to wish she'd returned to the dual carriageway where she might have been able to outrun the nimbler BMW.

It gained on her with every bend.

Despite all the training she'd had in defensive driving, there were limits with an old heavy estate car on well-worn rubber that slewed and squealed every time Susie changed direction. The silver BMW loomed ever larger in her mirrors, she had to keep going.

While the countryside was flat, the road twisted and turned for mile after mile, following what Susie could only imagine were ancient farm tracks going back centuries. It gave her no respite, no junctions, no buildings, no safe haven. All the while the two women hounded her. They could keep pace easily, but they couldn't pass her.

She rounded a tight bend in third gear with the rev counter nudging the red line. With a long straight road ahead, she kept her left foot pressed hard on the accelerator, changed to fourth and repeated the process. The car leapt forward, the speedo climbing rapidly, up to fifth gear and with the engine howling and the landscape a blur, she caught a glimpse of the railway on her left that ran parallel to the road. Up ahead she spotted a goods train, dozens of wagons trundling slowly towards Oxford, she gained on it quickly. She'd cycled the road often, knew it was the regional line, and the road continued straight for another two miles. At over 100mph with the car lurching over the uneven surface, she struggled to keep it between the impossibly narrow verges but she quickly pulled in front of the train.

She risked a glance in her rear view and in horror realised the two women were upon her, inches off her rear bumper. She contemplated stamping on the brakes knowing that the heavier Volvo would come off best, but the chances of getting away without suffering made her hesitate. As if they could read her mind the driver of the BMW pulled out in an attempt to pass her. Susie jinked the steering wheel and veered across the front of the German car forcing it to back off for a moment. The narrow back road was barely wide enough for two cars and getting a wheel on the wet grass verges would almost certainly lead to instant carnage. She took her foot off the throttle and allowed the Volvo to slow without touching the brakes. She positioned the car in the centre of the road and started to weave from side to side. She knew her pursuers couldn't risk trying to pass her, their only option was to ram her, and she almost wished they would, she had faith in the old car.

She hadn't anticipated their next move.

With her speed down to an almost pedestrian 45mph, Susie could see the two women in the car behind and reacted in horror when the one in the passenger seat leaned out the window with a gun in her hand. This time, she didn't hesitate. She braced herself against the steering wheel, then jammed her foot on the brake and clutch pedals. The ABS prevented the wheels from locking, but the move achieved the effect Susie hoped for, and the BMW, taken by surprise, crashed into the back of her car. The woman leaning out the window was almost flung clear; she dropped her gun with the effort of hanging on.

Without pause, Susie selected first gear, gave it a boot load of throttle and released the clutch. The Volvo took off while the stalled BMW and its stunned occupants floundered. The passenger jumped out to retrieve the fallen firearm, then leapt back into the car. By the time they got going, Susie had pulled out a 100-yard advantage.

As she accelerated away, Susie checked her mirrors and realised the BMW hadn't sustained enough damage to stop it and they were back in pursuit. She passed a sign indicating a turn off to the left and she had an idea. She slowed slightly and looked over her left shoulder to check the progress of the goods train. A smile played across her face, and she waited for the BMW to close on her as she approached the junction.

With the BM almost upon her again, and without any indication, Susie spun the wheel hard left. The Volvo's tyres squealed in protest with the sudden change in direction, the rear end of the car skidded, and smoke billowed from the spinning back wheels as Susie changed down and hit the throttle. The car charged towards the level crossing where flashing red lights indicated the barriers were about to close.

Susie had time to check her rear-view mirror and see the BMW miss the turn-off, its ABS working overtime. She thumped over the railway lines and the barriers closed behind her.

She eased off and took a few calming breaths. The train would take a few minutes to pass and there was nothing they could do about it. It would give her time to regroup. She roads were familiar to her from her triathlon training, she cycled them throughout the summer and she plotted a course that she knew would leave her pursuers baffled and she hoped, lost. A circuitous route taking in back roads, through hamlets, and over main roads, brought her back to Oxford. She kept an eye on her rear-view, just in case, and another on the fuel gauge, the needle barely registering and a red light warning her as if she didn't already know.

16

As much as she wanted to get back to the hospital as quickly as possible to pick Nick up, Susie forced herself to drive as economically as she could. After she'd thrashed the old Volvo in her bid to escape the two women, she feathered the throttle and freewheeled down what few inclines there were. All the time, the fuel gauge refused to indicate the presence of anything in the tank. More alarmingly, even if she was prepared to part with the little cash she had, she passed petrol station after petrol station with cones blocking the forecourt and no sign of life within.

She arrived at the hospital just after 3.00 and for once, found the car park almost empty. Some kind soul, given the ongoing payment issues, had had the decency to waive the usual fee, the barriers were open, and she parked as close to the main entrance as she could.

Despite the commotion on the streets, the hospital remained calm, with little to indicate any sort of emergency was going on outside its walls. Susie imagined any non-essential staff had gone home for Christmas and those left on duty had either drawn the short straw, or the prospect of spending time with family was enough reason to volunteer for work.

Her message to the hospital must have done the trick. When she entered Nick's room he looked ready to go, apart from the fact he was still in the hospital gown. With nothing in the way of personal possessions, the only thing he had to carry was a bag containing his meds. It sat on the bed next to him like an unwelcome, but necessary reminder.

He greeted Susie with a smile. 'Darling girl. Am I pleased to see you.'

Susie reached his bedside and without saying a word, threw her arms around him, burying her head in his chest.

'Steady on sweetheart, what's up?' Nick winced under the force of the hug.

Without looking up and with her voice muffled Susie said. 'God. I never thought I'd make it.'

Nick gently pushed Susie up. He met her gaze as she looked up at him and he frowned. 'What's happened?'

'I'm beginning to wonder who we're dealing with.' Susie shook her head as if trying to shake off the memory of the last hour.

Nick studied her for a moment, his brow furrowed. 'Go on.'

Susie released her grip on Nick and sat back. She closed her eyes and took a deep breath. 'Did you get my message?'

Nick nodded. 'Yeah, they said you were delayed and wouldn't be here till after 2.00.'

'They didn't tell you I'd been asked to deliver those modems?'

Nick's eyes narrowed and he gave a slight shake of the head.

Susie rolled her eyes in a why do bother way. 'Doesn't matter. I got a call back from Whitehall eventually.' Her gaze wandered to the window. 'They put me on to some big cheese who got really agitated when I told him what Tim had discovered last night. He asked me, or rather, he ordered me to deliver the modems to CSOC.'

'What's sea sock got to do with anything?'

Susie waved away his question. 'Not important, I told him there was no way, he wasn't pleased, and he dithered about then said someone would meet me at a Starbucks about half an hour away.'

'So, is that where you've been?'

'I went and waited, then these two women arrived.' Susie stopped when she saw Nick about to speak, a puzzled look on his face. She held up a hand to stop him. 'Hang on. There was something about them that just wasn't right. They didn't know what they were supposed to be picking up. They had no ID, wouldn't tell me their names or who had sent them, and...' She paused again. Nick had sat up and leaned forward, concern etched over his face. '...and their accents were...' She jiggled her head looking for the right description. '...suspicious.'

'Suspicious?'

'Hmmm, yes. I couldn't swear to it, but at a guess, I'd say Russian or Ukrainian, something like that. Their English was good, but it started to slip when I wouldn't play ball.'

'Don't tell me.' Nick gave his wife a rueful smile and shook his head. 'You refused to give them the modems?'

'Damn right. Anyway, I'd left them in the car as a precaution.'

'So, what did they do?'

'Nothing. I left them standing there, jumped in the car and bugged out.'

Nick dropped his head into his hands. 'Jeez babe, why?'

'Call it a sixth sense or whatever. They were dodgy.'

'So...' Nick paused, hardly daring to ask. '...what happened? Did they follow you?'

Susie gave him a sideways look and a hint of a smile crept over her face. 'Hmmm. Chased me, would be a better description.'

Nick closed his eyes and slowly shook his head. 'Don't. I don't I want to know.'

'It's OK. I'm OK, thanks for asking. I got away.' She gave him a playful punch on the shoulder.

Nick opened his eyes and gave her a resigned look. 'I'm glad you're OK love, but...' He exhaled in mock desperation. 'Have you called the guy who sent you there and told him?'

'I've tried three or four times on the way here. He's not picking up, and there's no voicemail option.'

'What do you mean, escaped!' Rostyslav Kobzar roared at the phone on his desk.

'There was nothing we could do.' The hesitant female voice responded. 'We couldn't take any action in Starbucks, there were too many people, and some had their phones out taking pictures.'

'Do you think I give a flying fuck about that?' Kobzar slammed his fist on the desk causing the phone to jump. 'I was told you two were highly trained, capable of problem-solving and responding to situations to get results.' He paused and glared at the phone as if his fury would somehow reach the two women. 'You could have followed her outside and stopped her.'

'She was very quick.'

'And you're not?'

'She surprised us, she was in her car before we could stop her.' The hesitancy now replaced by resentment at having their abilities brought into question.

Kobzar's face twisted in frustration. 'So? You've got a fast car, you know what to do, how come you didn't drive her off the road?'

There was an audible sigh at the other end. 'She knew what she was doing, she was very good.'

This produced more exasperation, clenched fists and silence for half a minute. Eventually, he replied. 'You're supposed to be better.'

His tone had struck home, his reply produced no response. He paced back and forth waiting for some reaction. He stopped pacing and returned to stud his mobile, wondering if was still working. 'Are you still there?'

A tentative voice answered. 'Yes. We are waiting for your orders.'

Kobzar shook his head in despair. 'Orders.' He paused and looked around seeking some sort of divine intervention. 'Right, forget the modems, get back to the farm. That woman already knows too much and you two have just added fuel to the fire. She'll have to be eliminated.' He picked up the phone and walked over to the only window in his office. He rubbed his chin, fingers scraping through three days' growth of stubble. 'When I know where and when I'll call you. Copy?'

'Yes Colonel, we understand.' The women responded in unison.

Kobzar continued to stare out the window as he killed the call. He muttered obscenities as he stuffed the phone into his back pocket and considered his next move.

Alison Burton-Castle arrived at her office at 3:00 pm in complete panic.

Going to the office on a Sunday was bad enough but on Christmas Eve? As if she didn't have better things to do.

She'd changed from her workout gear into jeans, jumper and trainers and felt self-conscious entering the building without her usual corporate wear. She hadn't had time to do anything with her hair and resorted to tying it up as best she could. Needs must, she thought, at least there'd be nobody around to see her.

Last-minute calls to her trusted team had required every persuasive trick in the book to get them to come in and help her sort the problem out, and even then, two key members were away and unable to make it.

Harassed didn't cover it. Ever since her morning visitor had left, Burton-Castle's brain had whirred as she made plans and tried to remember what was involved in issuing new numbers to all the payment processing companies. As she dropped into her office chair and fired up her desktop, Chris Durham arrived, her second-in-command. He looked annoyingly relaxed. 'Hell of a way to spend Christmas Eve Ally.' He peeled off a wax jacket and unwrapped a thick scarf.

'Tell me about it.' the Operations Director said without taking her eyes off the screen.

'How did you find out?' Durham asked as he walked around the desk to see what had captured his boss's attention.

Burton-Castle dismissed his question with a wave of her hand, moved her mouse a fraction, and clicked, her eyes glued to the results. 'Just give me a minute, Chris.' She clicked again and gave a slow shake of her head as the screen refreshed to tell her what she didn't want to see. 'Oh God.'

Durham leaned closer. 'Is that all the companies you mentioned when you called?'

'Yeah, but that's not the problem.' She turned to look at him for the first time, then her attention reverted to the screen, and she tapped a column on the displayed spreadsheet. 'That's how many lines each of those companies has.'

'Shit, I had no idea there were so many.' Durham linked his hands behind his head and stared at the numbers while he performed some quick mental arithmetic. 'It's going to take hours to archive the old numbers and issue replacements.'

'Hours.' His boss snorted. 'More like days. We're going to need more people.'

As if on cue, the third team member stepped into the office. Holly Holding looked as stressed as her boss. Dressed for the cold with a down jacket over a maroon polo-necked jumper and dark blue jeans, her long jet-black hair scrunched into a loose ponytail. At twenty-nine, she was the youngest of the team and, Burton-Castle thought, probably the brightest. Her pale features looked flushed as if she'd run the last mile to the office.

'You all right, H?' Durham asked.

She nodded. 'Not really, but it sounds like we don't have a choice.' She tipped her head towards Burton-Castle. 'You sounded worried when you called, I couldn't let you down.'

'Appreciated Holly. Hopefully, we won't be too long. Any sign of Gareth?

"I think I saw his car coming into the carpark as I came up.'

'Great. I'm afraid it's just the four of us. Malc's somewhere near Aberdeen with his family. He said he'd come down, but I told him we'd try and manage without him.' Burton-Castle glanced at her two team members, who nodded in understanding. She continued. 'And obviously, Beth's not going to leave Sharm El-Sheikh after just one day on the beach.'

'Can't blame her.' Holly said as she shrugged off her jacket. 'We'll just have to manage, won't we.' She raised an eyebrow at Durham, who gave a brief nod.

'So, are you going to tell us how you found out about the problem with the numbers, or is it a state secret?' Chris Durham levelled his gaze at the boss.

'Just hang on till Gareth gets himself here. I don't want to have to go over the whole thing twice.' All three turned to look at the door. Holly had left it ajar, and they could hear footsteps heading in their direction.

Gareth Evans walked into the office and stopped dead in his tracks when he saw the welcoming committee staring at him. 'Hi guys, sorry I'm late. Had to arrange cover for the kids.' He gave an apologetic shrug. Like the others, he was well wrapped up. He shed his outer layer of a red all-weather jacket and draped it over the back of one of the chairs.

'Nothing to apologise for, Gareth. I'm just sorry to drag you in, today of all days.' Burton-Castle pushed her chair back and stood. 'We can use that.' She indicated a small conference table at the far side of her office and ushered her team towards it. 'Grab a seat; I'll put the kettle on.'

After hot drinks had been prepared, the team settled into business mode. The Operations Director recounted the events from earlier in the day when the woman from the police Cyber Crime Unit had come to visit her in person. She'd made some notes after Susie had left and went through the details, leaving no one in any doubt about the seriousness or the scale of the problem. When she'd finished, she gazed at the three faces staring back at her. 'I don't think we can do much today, but I wanted to get you in so we could decide between us how best to proceed and what to prioritise.' She paused to allow questions or comments; there were none, just concerned looks. 'I thought we could have done this on screen from home, but...' She pulled a face. 'Too many interruptions, and I know we work best when we're all together.' This met with more nods of approval.

Holly Holding raised a hand. 'From what you've said, we're going to need more people. We'll be on all week if we try to do this on our o wn.'

'Absolutely. The trouble is, given the nature of the problem and the need to keep new line numbers totally secure, we can't just bring in agency staff. Even if any were prepared to work on Christmas day.'

Evans tapped his pen on the pad he'd been writing on, and without looking up, he asked. 'Has anyone asked how the hell anyone got hold of the line IDs in the first place?'

Durham echoed his concern. 'It shouldn't be possible. We're the only ones with access to the data, and the computer logs all sign-ins and changes.'

Evans looked up from his notes and met Burton-Castle's troubled look. 'That info isn't kept anywhere other than the main computer, is i t?'

The Operations Director pursed her lips, her brow furrowed, and she shook her head. 'I have a backup on my laptop, but nobody else has access to it, and anyway, it's password protected and encrypted, so I think we can rule that out.'

'What's done is done.' Holding said. 'We can track down the source of the leak once we get the system up and running.' She glanced at her boss for confirmation.

'Absolutely.' Burton-Castle said. 'Holly's right. Our focus has to be issuing new line IDs and getting them to the payment companies as soon as we can.'

This remark drew looks of agreement from the other three, and for the next ninety minutes, they dissected the problem and broke it down into bite-sized chunks, which they allocated to one or the other of them. As 5:00 pm approached, Alison Burton-Castle stretched and yawned. 'OK, guys, I think we've got a workable plan. There's not a lot more we can do tonight, so I suggest we all go home and prepare for Santa Claus and hope we wake up in the morning and discover this was all a terrible dream.'

'More like a nightmare.' Durham quipped as he stood and went to retrieve his jacket.

'My other half is going to kill me.' Evans groaned as he got to his feet. 'She's out tonight and has no idea about any of this.'

'Just blame me.' Said his boss. 'I don't think tomorrow is going to be much fun for anyone this year.' She walked with them to the door and wished them a merry Christmas as they left. Then she turned back to her desk, an uneasy feeling nagging at her.

17

Rostyslav Kobzar slouched in what he called his thinking chair – a deeply padded recliner, complete with footrest, finished in a deep dark red leather – his Macbook rested on his lap. He stared at the screen through narrowed eyes as it displayed social media videos of numerous civil disorder incidents breaking out all over the country. He sat back with arms folded and let the images scroll, prompted by the occasional finger prod to select another platform or advance the feed.

It was a procrastination, pure and simple. He had to ring the woman and wasn't looking forward to it. He knew how she would react. She demanded a sitrep at 8:00 am every morning, her time, which meant calling her from the UK at midnight. He closed the windows he'd been watching and clicked to activate his preferred video feed. Her name appeared at the top of a list of contacts and his finger hovered over it for a second before he realised where he was sitting and how he would appear. He scrambled to his feet and took the laptop over to his desk where he felt the background would give her less to comment or complain about. He had no wish to provide her with any unnecessary ammunition.

He studied the thumbnail image of himself in the corner of the screen and self-consciously straightened himself up and brushed his hair back. It'll have to do, he thought. He took a deep breath and clicked the red button to initiate the call.

She must have been sitting at her computer waiting. Her image filled the screen, the morning sunshine in Macau, bright over her shoulder. 'You're late.' The usual cold eyes bore into him.

Kobzar glanced at the screen's menu bar, 12:02, two minutes behind schedule. It took an effort to restrain himself from comment. Instead, he nodded and adopted what he hoped was a suitably contrite attitude. 'My apologies.'

She waved his words away. 'Update.'

'Everything is going ahead as planned. My people did an excellent job this morning. You will have seen the videos?'

This produced a dip of her chin in acknowledgement. If he expected praise, he'd be waiting a long time. 'Have they identified the cause yet?'

Now for the difficult bit, he thought. He'd considered various approaches, but in the end, decided there was no point in sugarcoating it, she'd find out sooner or later. 'We've identified a woman who worked at the Cyber Crime place. She got hold of one of the infected modems and she's had someone look at it. They've worked out how the virus was delivered, and she's been to see the Connectivity woman and told her to issue new line IDs.' He stopped and braced himself for her reaction as if she could physically assault him from the other side of the globe.

As expected, the woman's features creased. Her mouth twisted and her eyes narrowed to dark slits. 'You cannot let that happen.' She leaned closer to the camera. Her words came out slowly, almost a whisper. 'We need at least another 48 hours before we put phase two in operation.'

Kobzar nodded, partly in agreement, but mainly in relief that she hadn't unleashed her vicious temper. Not that he was scared of her. The pair stared at each other, and neither spoke. She remained inscrutable, he watched, waited and kept his mouth shut. He knew how she operated.

'The woman has children?'

Kobzar tipped his head to one side at the unexpected twist, unsure if it was a statement or a question. 'Yes. Two, a boy and a girl. they're...'

The woman silenced him with a dismissive wave. 'Spare me. We need leverage to stop her.'

With wide open eyes he gaped at the woman's image on his screen. 'What are you...'

She held up a hand to silence him again. 'You know what you need to do. You don't have to harm them, just hold them. Let her know if she issues new numbers, she'll never see them again.'

'That takes things to a whole new level.'

'You've already destroyed the Cyber Crime HQ, snatching a couple of kids shouldn't be a problem.'

Kobzar let his eyes leave the screen and he scanned the room while he considered the implications. Capturing the kids wasn't the problem, it was looking after them. Where could he keep them and who would look after them? He didn't want to tie up resources on babysitting duties. He returned to the screen and met her gaze. 'OK. First thing in the morning after she leaves the house I'll get my people to do i t.'

'Good. Make it happen. And.' She paused and waited until she had his full attention.

'Yes.'

'The woman who went to see her.'

'Yes.'

'Get rid of her. I don't like people who get in the way.'

If only you knew, thought Kobzar, thankful she knew nothing of events earlier in the day. 'Consider it done.'

'I'll consider it done when it's done and not before.' Her face deadpan. she reached forward and killed the connection.

Kobzar continued to stare at the blank screen for a moment, before dropping his chin to his chest, closing his eyes and muttering. 'You just sit there in the sunshine giving orders, while I put up with the cold and dark and do whatever you say.' He snapped the Macbook closed and got to his feet. His two highly trained agents had just been selected for a new assignment. It was time to let them know.

Alison Burton-Castle surveyed the team. Ten of them assembled around the conference table, and another 6 squeezed into gaps. None looked happy to be there, they looked like she felt. Coming into work on Christmas day and leaving family behind. In her case, she managed a brief hour of present opening with Noah and Jenny, before leaving the house just after 9:00. She'd left Don to look after the kids and had to trust they would behave. She'd left strict instructions not to bother her unless it was an emergency. She didn't want anything to distract her from the job in hand and she owed it to the team to be 100% in the room.

Chris, Holly and Gareth had each left the night before with a list of names to call with instructions to do whatever they could to induce experienced clerical staff to give up their Christmas morning. She'd given them the authority to offer a selection of incentives to sweeten the deal, including triple pay, extra holidays and even concert tickets and hospitality at one of the events Connectivity sponsored throughout the year. The bribes must have worked; she had what she wanted, and while she wished it wasn't necessary, she was grateful to every one of them for being there.

She got to her feet and tapped her coffee mug on the table. All eyes turned to her. She'd spent a sleepless night planning what she had to say and what she wanted them to do. She launched into her spiel, thanked them for coming and outlined their roles over the next few hours. She had no idea how quickly they'd get through the process. If things went to plan and the work was divided equally among them all, it might only be a few hours. If anything went wrong or if they discovered something unexpected, they could be here all day. She shuddered at the thought.

Her phone lay face up in front of her. She'd set it to silent and when it lit up, it caught her eye and knocked her off her stride. She paused mid-sentence and glanced down at the screen. A text from Noah. Unlike Jenny, who spent far too long on her phone for her mother's liking, Noah only sent messages if he felt it was important, and this one had an image attached.

The assembled staff gazed at their boss, then at each other, as they wondered why she stopped speaking.

Burton-Castle apologised for the interruption, reached down for her phone and tapped the screen to open the message. Her hand shot to her mouth, too late to stifle the sudden audible intake of breath as she read what had been sent.

DO NOT ISSUE NEW NUMBERS IF YOU WANT TO SEE YOUR CHILDREN AGAIN - STOP WHAT YOU ARE DOING NOW

She scrolled down to the image. This time the noise that escaped could not be silenced. A keening cry, almost a wail. She stared at the picture of her two children. They were each tied to chairs with their hands behind their backs and gags around their mouths. They stared into the camera with terrified eyes. She dropped the phone as though it were red hot.

Holly Holding sat at her boss's right hand, she was the first to speak. 'What is it, Alison?' Concern etched into her face.

Burton-Castle squeezed her eyes shut and clasped her hands to her face. She felt the room spin and her stomach turn. She opened her eyes when she heard the phone vibrate, it lit up again. She grabbed it. Another text.

SAY NOTHING DO NOTHING AND DO NOT TELL ANYONE. IF THE POLICE ARE INVOLVED THE KIDS WILL DIE.

Holding reached out, but her boss gripped the phone with both hands and held it to her chest. She shook her head. 'I can't.'

'Can't what?'

'Sorry Holly, I can't tell you.' Her voice little more than a whisper.

Chris Durham spoke from the far end of the table. 'Is there anything we can help with Ally?' He scanned the room. All eyes were on the Operations Director, no one else said a word.

Burton-Castle held up a hand. 'You'll have to excuse me for a minute.' She got to her feet, her legs wobbled, and she held the table for support. Holly Holding pushed her seat back, ready to join her. 'No. Thanks, Holly, but I need to take of this on my own.' She turned and left the room.

Out in the corridor, Burton-Castle struggled to hold herself together. She didn't want her team to see her falling apart, but she could feel tears welling up and her mind losing focus. She went into one of the empty offices, stared at her phone and re-read the two texts from Noah's phone. Whoever had sent the message would only have to search for "Mum" in his contacts and they would know she'd get it. She winced when she thought what they must have done to him to reveal his passcode, she knew he'd never let the facial recognition software get a clear shot of him.

She started to type a reply, then stopped as she remembered she had the Find My feature enabled on Noah's phone. She tapped the icon and waited impatiently for it to load. A map appeared on the screen with a large circle that quickly reduced to a smaller one with Noah's image in it. The location clearly shown. She took a screenshot of it. They hadn't switched his phone off. Must be waiting for a reply.

She typed quickly:

RECEIVED UNDERSTOOD PLEASE DO NOT HARM THEM

She went back to the map and tapped on Noah's image to refresh the location. Whoever had Noah's phone must have guessed what she was doing. The screen reloaded, and Noah had vanished. She cursed and stared at the phone, willing it to tell her what to do next. If she sent them another text, would they get it? What would she say? What could she say? The message was clear. She couldn't take the risk of issuing new numbers.

Holly Holding opened the door. 'Sorry boss. I know you wanted to be alone, but I couldn't just sit in there.' She jerked her head in the direction of the conference room. 'Whatever was in that message, it must have been beyond serious, judging by your reaction. There's got to be something I can do to help.'

Burton-Castle felt conflicted. Part of her wanted to show the message to someone she trusted. The other part of her was terrified of risking her children's lives. She'd always preached the old proverb about a problem shared being a problem halved, but in this situation, she wasn't so sure. 'Thanks, Holly, just give me a few minutes. Bottom line is, we've got to stop what we're doing. Can you go back in there and pass that message on and tell them I'm sorry to have dragged them in, but they can all go back home.'

'But how are we going to get the system up and running again? I thought you said this was a national emergency?' Holding looked at her boss with hands spread, unable to make sense of what she'd been told to do.

'I know. It is an emergency, but...' her voice tailed off and Burton-Castle looked at the clouds beyond the office window desperate for an answer, for guidance, for the ability to think clearly. 'Get them all gone, then come back here and I'll try to explain.'

Holding considered saying more, she opened her mouth to speak, then thought better of it, there was nothing to be gained, she knew her boss well enough. She left the room.

Burton-Castle held her phone and stared at the map image. She didn't recognise the place, even when she zoomed out, it took her a moment to get her bearings and estimate how far away it was from home. At the thought of home, she was struck by another worry. What happened to Ed? He was looking after the kids. She called him. It rang. It continued to ring. 'For God's sake pick up.' Her voice raised in frustration. The call went to voicemail. 'Ring me let me know you're OK. I've had a message from someone with Noah's phone, they've got the kids and told me not to issue new numbers. I'm sick with worry. Please love, call me back when you get this.' She ended the call and turned to see Holly Holding standing at the door. She'd heard every w ord.

'Jesus, Ally, why didn't you say something?'

'I, I can't. They said...They said not to tell anyone.' Burton-Castle gave a hopeless gesture. 'They said if I went to the police the kids would die.' The tears started, her head flopped, and her shoulders slumped.

Holding rushed to catch her before she collapsed. She hugged her. 'Come on, sit down. Tell me what you know, we can sort this. Show me what they sent.' She reached for a box of tissue on a nearby desk.

Burton-Castle handed her the phone.

Holding read the texts and looked at the image of the kids, all the while shaking her head in disbelief. 'Bloody hell, what are we supposed to do?'

Her boss dabbed at her eyes with one of the tissues. 'I don't know Holly, there's no operating manual for when your children are kidnapped.'

'There must be someone you can speak to, off the record.'

'What, do you mean, like a private detective?'

Holding shrugged. 'Sort of. Some sort of investigator.'

'Trouble is, they wouldn't have any resources and if they went to the police...' Burton-Castle shuddered. 'I don't want to think what would happen.'

Holding brightened suddenly. 'What about that woman who came to see you yesterday, the one who said you needed to issue new line IDs? Where was she from?'

'She said she was police at first...' Burton-Castle paused and thought for a moment. 'But, later said she was attached to the Cyber Crime Unit which had been blown up on Friday night.'

'Have you got her contact details?'

'Yeah, she gave me a card. It's in my bag, in the conference room.'

'What did you make of her?'

'She was good. She had initiative. I thought I kept a low profile, but she found me and came to see me in person. If it wasn't for her, we wouldn't be here now. Having said that, if it wasn't for her, I would be at home with the family enjoying Christmas.'

'So, she must be connected to all this.' Holding pointed at her boss's phone as if it explained everything.

'Hmmm, hopefully in a good way.'

18

Monday 25 December

Christmas Day had lost its sparkle, Susie struggled to get excited and after she and Nick had agreed to postpone the big day until the "situation" was sorted, they both felt lacklustre.

Susie stomped about the house like a bear with a sore head. She couldn't raise the enthusiasm to cook, she opened cupboards, peered at the contents of the fridge and rummaged in the freezer in the hope of finding a quick fix. When Nick suggested she went for a run to clear her head, she initially, and uncharacteristically, made lame excuses. He persisted, knowing what made her tick, and she grudgingly agreed.

Wearing several layers of warm running gear, Susie headed out and promised to be back in half an hour.

'Take as long as you like babe, I'm going nowhere.' Nick was secretly pleased to have time to himself, without his wife fussing about unable to settle. He hobbled back to the sofa he'd been resting on and was dozing off when he heard the familiar ringtone of Susie's phone. For once she'd left it behind. He hauled himself back on his feet and made it to the kitchen before it rang off. The number was withheld. He'd normally not bother answering if it wasn't someone saved in contacts but given the ongoing situation and Susie's penchant for leaving her number with people and asking them to call her back, he relented.

'Hi.' Nick Cooper, a man a few words.

'Err, I'm trying to contact Susan Jones, is this the right number?'

'It is. She's out at the moment. Who's calling?'

'It's Alison Burton-Castle, Miss Jones came to see me yesterday.'

'Ah yes, she mentioned you. Can I help?'

'Thanks, but I really need to speak to her. It's very urgent.'

'She won't be long, she's gone for a run, should be back in 20 minutes or so.'

'Can you ask her to call me as soon as she can? It really is very urgent.'

Nick noticed the desperation in the voice. 'Of course, does she have your number?'

'No, can you make a note?'

'Hang on.' Nick grabbed a pen and a scrap of paper. 'OK.' He wrote the number she gave him and repeated it back to her. 'I'll make sure she calls as soon as she's back.'

'Thank you. Sorry, I didn't get your name.'

'It's Nick.'

'Oh, hi Nick. Susie mentioned you, she said you'd been injured. Are you OK?'

'I'm fine, thanks for asking.'

'What a relief. I'll look forward to Susie's call.' She ended the call.

Nick studied the number and added the caller's name under it. He glanced out the window in the off-chance Susie was approaching. She wasn't. He placed the scrap of paper on the kitchen table with the pen on top, pointing to the number. He filled his mug from the coffee machine and limped back to the sofa. He wondered what was so urgent to make the woman call on Christmas morning.

When he heard the back door open ten minutes later, the thought still whirred around in his mind. He called out. 'You OK love?'

'Yeah, much better.'

He heard her kicking off her running shoes and she appeared in the living room a moment later, her face flushed, a film of sweat on her brow, her breathing elevated. She glowed.

'Thanks for giving me the push to do that.' She peeled off her hi-viz running jacket, rolled it up and tucked it into the bag she'd brought from the kitchen. 'Best cure in the world.' She came over to Nick. 'How's the injured hero? Been having a little snooze while I've been ou t?'

Nick smiled. 'If only. No, you had a call from the woman you went to see yesterday. She sounded really desperate; she wants you to ring her back ASAP.'

Susie looked surprised. 'The Burton-Castle woman?'

Nick nodded. 'Her number's on the kitchen table.'

'Can't think why she's calling me. I thought she'd be up to her eyes issuing new numbers to all the payment processing companies.' Susie shrugged. 'Better see what's bugging her.'

Nick watched her turn back to the kitchen and heard her pull a chair out to sit down. He listened as she called, he couldn't hear the other end of the conversation but gathered from what little Susie said that whatever was troubling the woman must have been serious. He heard several 'Oh Gods' and various sympathetic sounds from his wife but struggled to catch any meaning. He heard Susie asking questions and then finish the call asking the woman to forward texts and images to her. Susie repeated a few reassuring words, then ended the call. She reappeared in the living room, a look of concern on her face.

Nick knew better than to speak while Susie processed. He tipped his head and looked at her with eyebrows raised. He waited.

Susie shook her head as if unable to believe what the woman had told her. 'Her children have been kidnapped.' She paced around the living room, her head still shaking. Her focus on her phone.

Unsure how best to react to this, Nick held his hands out, palms up, waiting for Susie to elaborate.

'She got a text telling her not to issue new line IDs otherwise she wouldn't see her kids again.'

'Bloody hell.' Nick sat up. 'How come she's calling you?'

'The message told her not to speak to anyone and they warned her if she went to the police, the kids would die.' Susie paused as her phone pinged to announce an incoming text. She read it, open-mouthed. 'Jeez, this is terrible. Whoever is behind this...' She passed her phone to Nick.

Nick read the message without saying a word. He scrolled down to the image of the two Burton-Castle kids, gagged and bound. Horrified, he passed the phone back to Susie. 'Has she sent that to anyone else.'

'No. She doesn't dare ring the police. When I saw her yesterday, I told her to call me if she had any problems, I guess she thought she was safe to ring me.'

'What does she expect you to do?'

'She thinks I'll know who to contact without the people behind this, finding out.' Susie wiped her brow with the back of her hand.

Nick considered this. 'Trouble is, you don't know who to trust.' He rubbed his injured leg as though the action would inspire a moment of clarity. 'We could ask Tim again. He knows people.' Nick wrapped the last word in air quotes.

Susie gave a reluctant nod and pursed her lips. 'No harm is asking. Anna's going to love me calling him on Christmas day.'

'Just do it, he's always willing to help, bless him.'

'S'pose so. Anna knows what he's like.' Susie retreated to the kitchen, better phone signal. This time, Nick got to his feet again and followed her.

Tim and Anna were walking their new puppy in the fields behind their house when Susie called. They'd stopped walking much to the dog's frustration, and while Anna did her best to control the excited animal, Tim held his phone to his ear and concentrated. It took him a moment to grasp the full implications of what Susie was telling him. He got her to send the messages and read them as Susie gave him a little more background to her meeting earlier the previous day. She also mentioned her and Nick's fears about who to trust.

'So, we're looking for someone who's not police but has the resources of the police. Correct?' He summarised when Susie finished.

'That's about it. Do you know anyone or anything like that? This crisis is only going to get worse if we can't restore the system.'

'There might be someone I can think of.'

'Who?'

'Someone I've known for many years. I'll have to call him and see if he's still operational.'

'Oh, come on Tim, can't you tell me more than that.'

'I haven't spoken to him for ages, he heads up a covert Government organisation.'

'It all sounds very cloak and dagger, what's his name?'

'I'm not saying until I've called him. Give me ten minutes, we're out with the pup and I don't have his number on my phone. I'll give him a bell and call you back. Promise.'

True to his word, Tim called Susie ten minutes later.

Susie answered on the first ring. 'Any joy?'

'Better than expected.' Tim sounded upbeat. 'I got him straight away, he's alone for Christmas and seemed pleased to hear from me.'

'And? Can he help?' Susie's impatience was barely under control.

'Well, I gave him a quick summary of what you told me. He said it wasn't strictly what his group was set up for, but he said, absolutely, he could help.'

'Brilliant Tim, thank you. Are you allowed to tell me his name now?'

'His name's Alex. Commander Alexander Hawke.' Tim announced with a degree of reverence.

Susie didn't reply immediately as she pondered the name and tried to see if it rang any bells. All the bells remained silent. 'Sorry Tim, should the name mean something to me?'

'It shouldn't really, he's operated in the shadows most of his career, what he doesn't know about covert operations, isn't worth knowing.'

'So, what's this new outfit he's joined?' Susie pressed on with her questions.

'You won't have heard of it, all very hush-hush.'

'It must have a name?'

'It's the Tactical Intelligence Group for Emergency Response.'

For a moment Susie remained silent, then burst out. 'You're kidding.'

'No. Why?'

'Did someone come up with a catchy acronym and then think of some words to fit?

Tim chuckled. 'Yeah, I guess so, Alex admitted his call sign was Tiger One, I hadn't really thought about it.'

Susie stifled a chuckle. 'I love it, Tiger One, whatever next.'

Tim turned serious. 'Don't underestimate him, Susie. Alex is the real deal. He can draw on any resources he needs: Police, Army, SIS, GCHQ, Home Office, Foreign Office, Treasury, and even private contractors. You name it; if he thinks it will solve a problem he can get it.'

Suddenly sober, Susie responded. 'He sounds incredible Tim how much were you able to tell him?'

'Well, obviously I've only had a couple of minutes talking to him, but he was already all over this thing. I should have thought about him when we discovered the virus, but I didn't know what you'd managed with the Connectivity woman, and to be honest, my mind was elsewhere with the puppy and Christmas.'

'Don't beat yourself up about it, we're all in the dark. Do you say anything about meeting up?'

'Yes, that's how I left it. I said I'd get back to him after speaking to you and see if we could get together as soon as possible.'

'Where's he based?'

'His HQ is just off the M25 near Maple Cross, less than an hour away.'

'Hang on Tim.' Susie paused a beat. 'I need to speak to Burton-Castle, make sure she's happy about this. She sent me those messages in good faith and it's her kids' lives on the line.'

Tim agreed. 'Give her a call. I'll ring Alex back and give him more details. Let me know what she says.'

Alison Burton-Castle shouldn't have been driving. She was in no fit state, and she knew it. She had no choice, she had to get home and find Don. With her vision blurred by tears, her hands shaking, and her concentration shattered, she drove as if on autopilot and when she pulled into the drive, she had no idea how she'd got there. She jumped out of the Jag and ran to the front door. It stood wide open. She stepped into the hall and almost collapsed when she saw a pool of blood on the laminate floor and marks where something had been dragged through it. Her head swam and she felt faint. She lurched for the stairs and grabbed the bannister before lowering herself onto the third step. She sat staring at the mess, her breath coming in rapid gulps. Where was Don? She called for him, her voice hoarse.

With supreme effort, she pulled herself to her feet and went in search of him. She saw signs of a struggle, a mobile phone smashed on the floor and dirty footprints leading from the front door into the house. She followed the footprints and called Don's name again, this time a little louder. There was no response. She dreaded what she might find and gasped when she entered the kitchen.

Don lay sprawled, face down, motionless.

Burton-Castle ran to him on wobbly legs and fell to the floor beside him. 'Don, Don, can you hear me?' She placed a hand on his shoulder and shook him gently. She could feel him breathing and allowed herself to relax a fraction. At least he was alive.

He stirred. He groaned. 'What happened?' His voice thick. He moved a hand to his temple. 'My head.'

'Shhh, it's OK. Can you move?' Burton-Castle had spent three hours doing workplace first-aid training, several years ago. Most of what she'd learned had long since been lost in the mist of time and she'd never had to put any of it into practice. She was sure you weren't meant to move an unconscious patient, but Don wasn't unconscious so it must be OK. She helped him roll onto his back and immediately noticed the gash on the side of his head. The obvious source of the blood. 'Can you speak?'

He blinked his eyes open and immediately squeezed them tight shut as a fresh wave of pain hit him. 'Where are the kids?'

'They've been taken. I got a message and tried to ring you, and when I got no reply, I came straight here.' She tried to wipe the blood from his head, but he put his hand out to stop her. 'What can you remember? Who did this?'

'I can't, I can't remember much. Two or three of them, they had ski masks on. I tried to stop them but...' His eyes remained closed, his voice faint. He appeared on the verge of losing consciousness.

She studied him, her face puzzled. she looked back at the front door. 'How did they get in?'

He mumbled incoherently.

'Didn't you see them on the camera?' Did you let them in?' An irritated tone crept into her voice. She wanted to shake him awake but leaned closer to catch anything he said.

He turned away from her as if he couldn't look her in the eye. 'Noah. Noah opened the door.'

Burton-Castle frowned at this. 'He wouldn't do that, he's mister super cautious. Are you sure?'

No reply. Her partner's head had lolled back, his eyes closed, his mouth fell open. She reached for a tea towel on the nearby island unit and folded it into a temporary pillow for him. She got to her feet and stood for a moment, unsure. She went into the living room and returned with a lambswool blanket from the back of the sofa and wrapped it around Ed. She considered calling an ambulance but dismissed the idea when she recalled the chaos she'd witnessed on her way back from the office. There was little chance of any emergency services responding to anything other than immediate threats to life. Besides, she thought, it looked like his injuries were relatively minor and she could cope. The whereabouts and safety of her two children was her sole focus. Don would be OK. She'd clean up his wound and get him comfortable when he came around.

Her phone rang. It took her a few seconds to dig it out from the bottom of her bag. When she looked at the screen, a wave a relief washed over her. It was the Jones woman. 'Please tell me you've got some good news.'

'Hi Alison, how are you doing?'

'I'm a total mess, Miss Jones. Thank you for asking, but I've just got back home and found Don. It looks like he was attacked by whoever's taken the kids.'

'Is he all right? And please, it's Susie.'

'I think so, I hope so Susie. He's got a cut on his head, he must have been hit by something, he's slipping in and out of consciousness.'

'Have you called an ambulance?'

'I thought about it, but no, I don't think it's that bad.' Burton-Castle gave the man lying on the floor a pitying look then turned away. 'Have you managed to find someone to help? Please say yes.'

Susie paused before replying, she did have good news and wanted to choose her words carefully. 'Yes, I have. Thanks to a friend, I've found what I hope is the perfect person. He wanted to talk to you, but I said I'd speak to you first, make sure you're happy for me to put you in touch.'

'Of course. That's amazing, thank you. Who is it?'

'He runs an organisation that I'd never heard of until a few minutes ago. He can tell you more when he meets you.'

'Oh, right. Is he coming here, or do I have to go to him?'

'Whatever works for you. It might be best if he came to you, given the fact your other half's been injured. Would that be OK?'

'More than OK. I can't thank you enough Susie, I feel like my world is falling apart.'

'You can thank me when Noah and Jenni are back home safe and sound. I'll give this guy a call. It's 11:35 now. Can we say, an hour from now?'

Burton-Castle instinctively glanced at the kitchen clock. 'That's great. Will you come too?'

'If that's OK with you. It would be good to meet him. I can make introductions and bring him up to speed with what we know.' Susie paused; a thought occurred to her. 'Would you mind if I brought my other half, Nick, you talked to him earlier. He's a problem solver, good in a crisis. I value his input.'

'Of course. You said he'd been injured. How's he doing?'

'He's frustrated, more than anything. He's been home for less than two days and he's already sick of being cooped up. It'll do him good to get out of the house.'

'That's great, I look forward to meeting him and seeing you again, and of course, meeting this mystery man.' Burton-Castle ended the call and looked down at Don. She could have sworn she saw him close his eyes. Had he been listening to her?

She knelt beside him and studied his face closely, looking for any reaction. 'Come on Don we need to get you up before these people come. It's not going to look good if you're still lying here.' She nudged him gently, and then more forcefully. Her hand rocked his shoulder.

He recoiled from her touch and moaned. 'Don't. I can't move.'

Burton-Castle looked dubious. 'You're going to have to Don. That cut's not too bad. Come on, let's get you up.' She manoeuvred behind him, put her hands under his shoulders and lifted.

'Don't Ally, you're making it worse.' He remained limp, a dead weight.

'For God's sake Don make a bloody effort. The kids have been taken, there's a national emergency, people are coming to help us and you're doing nothing to help.' Her patience wearing thin, Burton-Castle ditched the gentle approach and heaved. She dragged her partner into a sitting position. 'Right, we're halfway there. Let's get you to your feet.' She squatted down beside him and draped his arm over her shoulder.

The move appeared to inject some life into the injured man. 'Jesus, Alison, have you no sympathy? I could have concussion or broken bones. Pushing me about like a sack of spuds could make it worse.'

Burton-Castle's eyebrows jumped in surprise, and she gave him a sideways look. 'Well, you seem to have found your voice all of a sudden. Just find the strength in your legs to stand up and walk with me to the living room.' She pushed herself to her feet, grateful for once that Don was on the skinny side and grateful also for those painful gym sessions that gave her just enough strength to lift him to his feet. Her words appeared to have the desired effect, and Don took his own weight, albeit still leaning on his partner for support. She encouraged him to keep going. 'Attaboy, one step at a time, you can get comfortable on the sofa, and I'll clean you up and bandage your head. She got no thanks as the pair of them made slow progress to the living room.

19

Susie pulled into the drive in front of the Burton-Castle home. Two cars were parked neatly in front of the double garage, they both had private plates. There was ample room for turning and at least four more cars. She parked the old Volvo facing the house and turned to Nick. 'Looks like he's not here yet.'

Nick glanced about. 'No sign of Tim either.'

Susie checked the time. 'We're a few minutes early. Tiger One said he'd be here for 12:35, so he's not late.'

Nick chuckled. 'Tiger One. You love it don't you.'

Susie had to smile. 'All right. But, you've got to admit it's a catchy callsign. What do you want me to call him, Commander Hawke? Boss?'

'Tim just calls him Alex.'

'Yeah, well, Tim's known him for years. They've got history. I'll stick with Tiger One unless he tells me otherwise.'

'Speak of the devil.' Nick peered over Susie's shoulder. 'There's an orange and black striped Land Rover coming down the road.'

Susie spun around to look. Then slumped down as she realised her other half was up to his usual tricks. 'Sometimes, Mr Cooper, you are a fool.'

Nick fended off the fingers about to jab him in the ribs and pointed. 'Actually, I think this is your man now. It is a Land Rover, but it's black.'

'Don't take me for an idiot, I'm not falling for it again.' Susie refused to turn and look.

'Seriously. He's turning in now. A big black Discovery, fully tricked out with tinted windows and a bunch of aerials.'

Her resistance weakened, Susie followed the direction of Nick gaze. 'Oh, yeah, I think you could be right. We'd better say hello.'

Susie jumped out and went around to help Nick to his feet. He tried to brush her off, but she insisted on fussing over him.

He had dispensed with the crutch the hospital had given him and rescued an old walking stick he'd had in the garage for more years than he could remember. He felt the stick might generate a little respect, rather than the sympathy he'd get with the crutch. He also liked the fact that he could prod people with it, or use it to point. He pointed at the Discovery. 'You lead, I'll hobble along behind you.'

The Discovery had stopped facing away from them and as they approached, they saw a man climb out the driver's door. He wore a lightweight ballistic vest over a utility jacket, combat pants and boots, all black. One hand held a thick zipped document folder to his chest, the other hung by his side. His eyes swept the house, the parking area and the road beyond as if assessing risk. He turned briefly to the passenger and gave an almost imperceptible nod.

Susie and Nick stopped as instructed. Nick leaned closer and whispered in Susie's ear. 'Does that bring back happy memories?'

She whispered back without taking her eyes off the man. 'At least when I did CQP we were armed. He's got nothing on him.'

'Not that you can see,' confided Nick 'but who knows what he's got under that jacket.'

Their hushed conversation stopped when they saw the passenger emerge. Susie didn't know what to expect, but after Tim's effusive description of the Commander, she imagined someone impressive. He didn't disappoint. At least six feet tall, broad shoulders, lean and toned. He had a presence about him, a confidence and self assuredness, with a strong jawline, high cheekbones and a slightly crooked nose. Susie noticed dark eyes scanning his surroundings, left, right, up and down, committing it all to some inner database. He was dressed like his driver, but somehow made the clothes look like they had been designed to fit him. He ran a hand over a silvery grey buzz cut and after a few seconds, he appeared satisfied. His attention settled on her. He tipped his head in her direction. 'Susie Jones?'

Susie continued to stare at the man, she didn't speak, Nick nudged her, and while supposedly scratching his nose, said, *sotto voce*. 'Close your mouth and speak to the man.'

'Err Yes, I'm Susie, you must be Tiger Hawke, I mean Commander Alex, sorry, I mean Commander Hawke.' She felt her cheeks redden.

He strode forward with a hand outstretched. 'It's Alex.'

They shook hands. 'Thanks, Alex. Sorry, I'm not usually...err, thank you for coming.'

Hawke dismissed Susie's clumsy apology with a flick of his fingers. 'Just hope I can help, Tim's briefed me as far as he can, sounds like time's pressing. Should we go inside and meet Mrs Burton-Castle?' He nodded at the front door and headed towards it.

Susie fell in beside him. 'I've spoken to Tim, he should be here any minute.'

'Excellent.' He reached the door, pressed the bell, then posed for the camera. 'I gather from Tim you're ex forces, RMP right?' He turned to look at her while they waited for some reaction.

'That's right, we both are.' She tilted her head in Nick's direction. 'Still reservists.'

'Good to know.' Hawke stared at the camera and pressed the doorbell again. 'She's taking a long time, I thought she was expecting us.' He turned to Nick who had caught them up. 'I'm guessing you must be Susie's other half?'

Nick did a quick stick shuffle in order to shake hands. 'Yeah, Hi, I'm Nick.'

'Good to meet you Nick. How's the leg? Tim told me what happened to you on Friday night.'

'It's a bit bruised, but I'm not complaining. I got off lightly. Those poor guys in the tower didn't stand a chance.'

Hawke looked sombre. 'Terrible business. Tragic. They were good people. Rob Eddington was an old mate of mine.'

Susie and Nick exchanged glances. Susie shook her head. 'You knew Commander Eddington. Tim never said. I'm so sorry.'

'Appreciated. I was supposed to retire last Friday, but when I heard about Rob, I decided retirement could wait, especially the way everything's gone since then.' He was about the press the bell again, when the front door burst open and a flustered Burton-Castle greeted them.

'Hello. Sorry to keep you waiting, I was upstairs. Please come in.' She held the door open, stood aside and waved them into the hall.

Hawke paused to introduce himself, then pointed to the driver who had followed Nick into the house. 'This is Mitchel, my ADC.' The younger man said nothing, but gave the others a polite nod.

Burton-Castle closed the front door and stood with her hands clasped to her chest, unsure. 'Thank you for coming.' She turned to Susie. 'Thank you for what you've done. I. I'm not sure...what to do. I'm normally good at dealing with emergencies, but this...' Tears started to well up.

Susie touched her lightly on the arm. 'It's OK Alison, You've done everything right. Commander Hawke and his team are the best in the business. We'll have Noah and Jenni back as soon as possible.' She indicated Nick who stood to one side, leaning on his stick. 'This is Nick, you spoke to him earlier.' Nick responded with a casual wave.

'Can we get round a table and make a start.' Hawke's tone made it clear, it wasn't a question.

'Is the kitchen table all right for you?' Burton-Castle pointed at a half open door near the back of the hall.

'That would be ideal.' Hawke took the initiative and lead the way.

After a little shuffling of chairs and stools, all five were sat at the table. Hawke at one end with his ADC on his right and Susie on his left. He asked Burton-Castle to sit at the other end and Nick sat next to Susie. 'Can we start by going over the events of the last couple of days to avoid any confusion and make sure we're all up to speed. Susie started the process with the visit to Payline and went through the sequence of events and what she had learned or suspected since then.

Hawke concentrated on everything she said. He took no notes, leaving that to Mitchel. He interrupted her whenever a point needed clarification, or he wanted her to expand on something she had remembered. It took Susie almost twenty minutes to bring him up to date. It was then Burton-Castle's turn. Her account started with Susie's visit the previous morning, and ended when she came home to find Don lying on the kitchen floor. She pointed to the spot where she had found him.

'Where is he now?' Hawke asked, while he gazed at the indicated location. 'Did you say he was bleeding? There's no marks.'

'He's upstairs in bed. I cleaned him up and bandaged his wound, then I mopped the floor in here and the hall. I'd just gone back up to check on him when you rang the doorbell.'

'We needs to speak to him. Is he in a fit state?'

'I'll go and ask him.' Burton-Castle rose from the table.

'Sorry Alison. In the circumstances, he has no choice in the matter. If he's conscious he can speak to us. Please ask him to join us.' Hawke fixed her with a look that made it clear, this wasn't a polite invitation.

She bobbed her head and hurried out of the room. They heard her climb the stairs and all listened carefully to catch any conversation from upstairs. The doorbell chimed. They jumped in surprise and all eyes turned to the small monitor screen. Nick was the first to recognise Tim staring fixedly at the camera. He was about to get up when Hawke nudged Mitchel. The message was clear and the ADC, jumped to his feet and went to let Tim in.

They made space for Tim alongside Mitchel and waited for Burton-Castle to return. In the silence they heard raised voices, the words were indistinct but the tone was argumentative. A minute later Burton-Castle returned on her own. 'He won't come down. He's says he's too weak.' She gave an embarrassed look and shrugged her shoulders. 'Sorry, I did my best.'

'Would you mind if I went up and had a word with him?' Hawke asked.

'You're welcome to try. Straight up the stairs, turn left, it's the second door on the right. and sorry about the mess.'

Hawke didn't reply. He left the kitchen and took the stairs two at a time.

Tim watched him leave and said. 'What am I missing? Who's he gone to see?'

Burton-Castle hadn't returned to her seat. She'd put the kettle on and was getting mugs ready. She replied without looking back at the table. 'My partner, Don. He was knocked out when the kids were taken. I didn't think it looked that bad, but I think he's milking it for all he's worth.'

Susie butted in. 'Alison, this is Tim.'

The other woman turned. She'd walked past the assembled team, without realising someone new had joined them. She stopped what she was doing, came over to Tim and shook his hand. 'You must be the genius that discovered the virus. Susie told me about what you did.'

Tim gave her an appreciative smile. 'It's kind of you to say so, I'm sure one of your people would have found it if they had one of the modems.'

'Maybe. But they didn't, and you did. We're all grateful.'

They were interrupted by the sound of Commander Hawke coming downstairs. He entered the kitchen with a look of thunder on his face. 'Bloody useless. I apologise Alison, but I've never come across anyone so utterly hopeless.' He sat back down at the table. The others looked at each other, unwilling to be the first to speak. He continued his rant. 'He appears to have very little interest in rescuing his kids?'

Burton-Castle piped up from the other side of the kitchen. 'That's half the problem, they're not his kids. Their father died five years ago. They've never got on with Don since we've been together.'

Hawke shook his head in disgust and disbelief. 'Whether they're his kids or not, they are young people who've been taken against their will. They're in danger and he doesn't seem to care.'

Nick observed the reaction of those around the table. 'Sounds like you're not going to get much help from him.' Nobody disagreed. He turned to look at Burton-Castle who stood behind him making hot drinks. 'How far did you get with issuing new line IDs before you got that first message?'

She appeared taken aback by the change in direction and it took her a moment to gather her thoughts. 'Not far at all. We had assigned tasks the previous day. When we got together this morning we were looking at ways to retire the old numbers and then speed up the process of issuing new ones. It's always taken time in the past as we send them out in the post for security reasons. Given the situation, we were going to send them by encrypted email but that's as far as we got before the messages arrived.'

Hawke understood the thinking behind Nick's question. 'The message told you not to issue new numbers, correct?'

Burton-Castle nodded.

'So, there's nothing to stop you doing everything you need to do, short of actually sending the emails out?'

'I don't suppose so.' She looked worried.

Susie recognised the woman's concern. 'Whoever has taken Noah and Jenny won't know what you're doing. You won't be doing anything they told you not to, so you wouldn't be putting your children at risk. If all the prep work is done, you can send those emails out the moment we rescue them. You could even send the companies an email and tell them what to expect.'

This appeared to mollify the Operations Director and she nodded slowly as she handed drinks around. 'So, you want me to get the team back in again?'

Hawke took his mug of coffee from her. 'Absolutely. I know it's Christmas Day and you've already dragged them in once, but it has to be done.' He took a sip of his drink then put the mug down. 'Susie mentioned rescuing the kids, that's our priority. I understand you took a screenshot of the location the message was sent from?'

'Yes, it came from Noah's phone, I use the Find My app to check where he is.'

Hawke pursed his lips. 'Good move. And I'm guessing the phone was switched off after that?'

'Not straight away. They sent a second message, then they switched it off.'

'Can I see the screenshot?' He held a hand out for the phone.

She brought up the image and handed the device to him.

Hawke examined the screenshot and zoomed in. 'These things are usually fairly accurate, but they're not completely reliable.' He squinted at the screen as if confused by what he saw. He glanced sideways at his ADC. 'Dig the iPad out and bring up an OS map of North Oxfordshire.'

Mitchel did as instructed and held the screen adjacent to Burton-Castle's phone.

'See there,' Hawke pointed to the thumbnail image of Noah on the screenshot. 'Zoom in on your map and see if there's a building of any sort. If there's one here, it's hidden by the thumbnail and the address is too vague.'

Susie, Nick and Tim craned their necks to see what the two men were looking at.

'It looks like a single dwelling on the edge of Wychwood Forest, just off that yellow road from Finstock.' Mitchel spoke quietly, but loud enough for Susie to detect a faint Scottish burr in his accent.

'Hmmm,' Hawke contemplated both images.' I can't think whoever is behind this would be stupid enough to let us know where they sent the messages from by accident. It's either a serious mistake on their part or...'

'...Or it's a trap.' Finished Susie.

Nick scratched his ear and frowned. 'Maybe it's neither. What time did you get the first message Alison?'

'Around 10:30, it'll say exactly when, on the app.'

'OK. And what time did you leave the house?'

Burton-Castle shrugged. 'Must have been after 9:00, maybe 9:15. Why?'

Nick folded his arms across his chest and indicated the iPad with a jutting chin. 'Wychwood Forest is what, half an hour away from here? If they were waiting for you to leave before taking the kids, they could have been in and out and up there by around 10:00. If they'd prepared a place in advance, they could have tied and bound the kids, taken a photo and be out of it before anyone took any notice.'

'That makes more sense than it being a mistake.' Hawke concurred.

Susie cocked her head at Nick. 'So you don't think anyone would be there if we went and had a look.'

'Nah, they'll be well out of it. Too obvious.'

Susie persisted. 'Nothing to lose by looking. Even if they're not there, we might find something that would give us a clue.'

Hawke drained his coffee and made a decision. 'We need action. Alison, can you round up your team and get cracking with the prep work.'

'Certainly, I'll get onto it now.'

'And Susie, I think you're right. We need to follow whatever breadcrumbs they may have left. Can you guys follow me to that location.' Hawke got to his feet.

Susie hesitated. 'No problem, only...'

Hawke gave her a querying look.

'Well, we're running on fumes and even if we had cash, the garages are all closed.'

'Fair point.' Hawke conceded. He turned to his ADC. 'Give them one of the fuel cans from the truck.'

20

Half an hour later, Susie followed the black Discovery down a single track lane running alongside Wychwood Forest. 'It's got to be here somewhere.' She said to no one in particular. Nick sat in the passenger seat. Tim was in the back having left his car at the Burton-Castle's house.

They approached a cottage on the right hand side of the road and the Discovery stopped. Susie pulled in behind it and got out as Hawke emerged from the passenger side of the big Land Rover.

He stood on the verge with hands on hips and surveyed the building 'It has to be here.' He glanced at Susie. 'There's nothing else on this road and we're at the centre of the screenshot Alison took.' He pointed at the grass verge. 'And these wheel tracks look very fresh. I'm no expert, but they can't be more than a few hours old.'

Susie stepped forward for a closer look. 'Any sign of footprints?'

They both bent down and examined the ground. 'There's loads, it's a complete jumble, nothing that makes any sense. Different shoes, different directions. Again, they look recent.' Hawke stood up and looked around.

Susie stared at the cottage. 'It doesn't look as if anyone's lived in it for a while.' she walked towards the gate in the paling fence.

'Hang on Susie, we need to check they haven't left us any surprises. I doubt it, but let's just play it safe.' He turned towards his vehicle. 'Mitchel, can you bring the sniffer out.'

His ADC jumped down from the drivers seat and hit a button on the remote control to open the rear door. It swung upwards to reveal a purpose built, high-tech compartment, bristling with securely stowed hardware. Nick and Tim gazed in wonder at what, to them, looked like the ultimate collection of gadgets for grown-ups. Mitchel pulled out something that could have been the bi-product of an encounter between a metal detector and a hand-held vacuum cleaner. He turned a handle and half a dozen stiff metal rods, each about six inches long, pinged into position, some sort of sensing array. He hit a switch and the device hummed into life.

Tim looked enviously at the machine and turned to Nick. 'Never seen one of those before.'

Hawke heard him. 'That's 'cos it's the only one. It was made by one of the tech teams. They claim it can detect explosives, like a sniffer dog, and pick up electrical impulses that might be used to trigger an IED.' He took the machine from Mitchel, and then, casting it in front of him like a blind man with a white stick, he advanced towards the gate, pushed it open and entered the narrow garden in front of the cottage. Susie, Nick, Tim and Mitchel, stayed on the road, watched and waited for the all clear.

Hawke cautiously wanded the windows, then walked to one corner of the building and back to the other, before returning to the front door. 'OK so far. Mitchel, get round the back. There's no sign of anyone, but just in case, be ready.' His ADC jogged out of sight behind the cottage. Hawke gave him a few seconds to get into position then turned the door handle.

The door wasn't locked. It had warped in the damp and took a firm kick to free it from the frame. It swung open on squeaky hinges straight into a living room, no hallway. The only furniture being two kitchen chairs, in the middle of the room, both lying on their sides. Hawke continue to use his "sniffer", but appeared more confident. A door in the back wall of the living room led into the kitchen where he found the staircase and a back door. He called Mitchel in. The back door opened without fuss and on Hawke's direction the pair climbed the stairs, Hawke led the way holding the machine in front of him like a modern day broadsword. He appeared at an upstairs window a couple of minutes later and called down to Susie, Nick and Tim, and gave them the thumbs up.

Susie entered the living room at the same time as Hawke returned from his first floor inspection. She stared at one wall. 'This is the place, no doubt about it.' She pulled out her phone and opened the image Burton-Castle had forwarded to her. She showed Hawke. 'Same wallpaper and see that dark mark running down the wall.' She pointed to both the wall and the screen.

Hawke nodded at the two chairs. 'They're a bit of a giveaway as well.'

Nick and Tim stepped into the room. Nick's nose wrinkled. 'This place should be condemned.'

'Oh, I don't know, a little TLC, a lick of paint. Could be nice.' Tim winked at Susie who tried hard to suppress a smirk.

Hawke ignored the interaction, his focus on the floor around the chairs. Scuff marks where they had been dragged across the floor and an assortment of footprints in the dust. 'They haven't exactly cleaned up, but they've left nothing behind to help us. Just a convenient place to grab a quick picture and waste our time. If we had more time, I could get some SOCOs up here, but I doubt they'd be able to tell us anything.' He rubbed the back of his neck and frowned.

Susie shared his frustration. She scowled at the chairs, willing them to tell her something. They remained where they were, mute.

Nick stood in the doorway facing out and stared at the road and two vehicles parked on the grass verge. He turned to face them, his expression thoughtful. 'What about traffic cameras? I don't mean the ANPR stuff, just the ones you use for traffic management.'

Hawke's eyebrows jumped at this and he gave Nick a considered look. 'It's worth considering, but...'

Before he could continue Tim jumped in. 'I know what you're going to say – without a number plate to follow, it would require actual human beings to try and spot something.'

'Yes. But if you only select any camera's near Alison's place, and only the timeframe when we estimate they took the kids, say, between 9:30 and 10:00, it would make the job manageable. And with it being Christmas day, there wouldn't be much traffic, so that should make it easier.' Nick paused waiting for a reaction.

Hawke followed his thinking. 'You're right, it would have to be a decent sized vehicle, and if we isolated any likely suspects and noted their reg numbers, the automated systems would kick in and be able to track them.'

'And,' Susie added. 'The DVLA system would identify them and you could eliminate the genuine ones. What you'd be left with has to be the one we're after, especially if it tracks in this direction.'

For the first time since they had met Commander Hawke, they saw a hint of a smile. 'Good thinking team.' He turned to his ADC who'd been listening to the conversation. 'Mitchel, get on to HQ and tell them to make it happen. And tell them we'll be back there in an hour; that'll motivate them.'

Susie, Nick and Tim drove back into Oxford to collect Tim's Audi. They noticed Burton-Castle's car was no longer at the house and assumed she'd done as requested and gone back to the Connectivity HQ. Tim headed home, anxious to see Anna, and their new puppy and Susie and Nick set off for their place.

It was already dusk by the time they arrived home. Street lights were on, and festive lights flashed and chased in windows along the street. Nick gave an expansive yawn as they pulled into their drive. 'Hell of way to spend Christmas day.'

'Yeah, we're not going to forget this one in a hurry.' Susie flopped back in the Volvo's comfy seats, and with the engine still running, luxuriated in the warm air from the blower. 'It seems wrong just to go home and do nothing while Alison's team are working and the TIGER people are burning the midnight oil.'

'Not a lot we can do love.' Nick gave Susie's hand a gentle squeeze. 'Alex said he'd be in touch the moment they get a lead of any sort.'

Susie wasn't so sure. 'I know that's what he said, but he's got all the resources he needs. Does he really need us?'

'According to Tim, he does. His "team"' Nick did the air quotes thing again. 'Is just a handful of people, he's more of a co-ordinator, with the power to draw on whoever and whatever as required. Like it or not, you're at the centre of all this, and he needs you, front and centre.'

'Maybe, but all the same...' She gazed off into space and noticed a giant inflatable snowman in the garden a few houses away. She gave it a pitying look, shook her head and closed her eyes. 'You know what I'm like. I need to keep busy. Do something. If he doesn't need me at the moment, there must be something else I can do.' She gave Nick a sideways look, eyebrows raised.

Nick pondered a moment. 'We've had nothing to eat for hours and I don't think either of us is in the mood to cook.' He returned Susie's questioning look.

'What are you suggesting? There's nothing open.'

'What about Jacob?'

Susie considered this. 'I thought you said he was doing a Christmas lunch for anyone on their own.'

'I did.'

'Well it's gone four in the afternoon, you think he'll have anything left?'

'Can't say for sure, but I saw him a few days ago, he's had loads of donations, I doubt it's all gone. Besides, I did say we might pop in and give him a hand.'

Susie tipped her head side to side. 'Not a bad idea. At least the community centre will be warm and it might be a welcome distraction from everything that's going on.' She thumped the palm of her hand on the steering wheel, decision made. 'C'mon then, let's go.' She reversed out the drive and headed back into town.

The community centre appeared to be buzzing. The tree outside was lit up, like a Christmas tree, and festive lights hung around the door and all the windows. As Susie and Nick got out of the Volvo, they could hear Roy Wood wishing it was Christmas every day, they exchanged glances and eye-rolls, then headed inside.

Jacob Crowhurst saw the pair enter the building and shuffled over to them as fast as he could. He looked stressed.

'What's up JC, looks like a hell of a party.' Nick gave the old man a hug.

The room buzzed with activity, twenty or more people sat at tables around the edge watching another dozen or so dancing. Disco lights flashed and speakers boomed.

Crowhurst shook his head. 'It's been chaos, it's quiet now, you should have seen it a few hours ago. I had thirty-eight booked in for lunch and was all prepared for them, we had turkey and all the trimmings, even enough wine for everyone to have a glass or two. Some of the donors have been ever so generous.' He looked around the room, his face fell.

Susie followed his gaze and saw his reaction. 'It sounds great Jacob, what's the problem?'

He waved a hand at the trestle table arranged down one side of the hall. They were covered in empty dishes, discarded plates and assorted left-overs. 'There must have been over a hundred people turned up. They just descended on the place. None of them had booked. None of them had been here before. Word had got out, free food, and they came like locusts. They filled doggy bags, grabbed bottles and left without doing anything to help or offering to contribute.'

Nick's mouth fell open; partly as he realised that his generous offer to help would not be met with a selection of tasty treats, but mainly in horror at the way some people's greed and selfishness made them resort to the behaviour his old friend had described. Anger stirred inside him. 'What is wrong with people? They can't last more than a couple of days before animal instincts take over.'

Susie mused. 'I think you're being unfair to animals.'

Nick looked at the remaining people in the hall, the dancers and the watchers. He noticed for the first time, that none of them had a drink or any food in front of them. 'Are these the ones who booked?'

Jacob nodded sadly. 'Bless them. They didn't get half of what they should have done, they all mucked in and volunteered to get everything ready, then they and had to put up with the mob that turned up and took what should have been theirs. But, I think they'd rather be here than go home alone.'

'Is there anything we can do to help Jacob?' Susie took Jacob's arm and met his sad gaze.

'I wish there was. It's kind of you to offer, but there's nothing open and from what I've heard, anywhere that is, is suffering the same treatment as here.'

'We can at least help you tidy up.' She peeled her coat off and draped it over a nearby chair.

Nick was about to do the same when the double doors flew open and three young men strolled into the hall, arrogant and hostile. They were no older than late teens, dressed in dark hoodies and baggy jeans. They appeared high on something, drink, drugs, adrenalin or a combination of all three. They looked wild-eyed and ready for trouble. One of them brandished a shiny new baseball bat, the other two had fists balled. They saw Jacob and headed for him.

'Right Grandad, where's the cash?' Baseball bat sneered.

Jacob glared back at the boy. 'Cash? The cash was spent providing food for these people. Your friends have taken everything we have, there's nothing left. See for yourself.' He spread his arms and turned his back to them to face the empty tables.

'Bollocks.' The boy shouted. He raised the bat, his intention obvious.

He hadn't noticed Nick and Susie standing beside Jacob, if he had, he saw them as no threat. A mistake he'd soon regret.

As the boy swung the bat behind him ready to strike, Nick shifted his weight and flicked his walking stick up with an explosive energy that caught the would-be assailant's fingers. The crack of solid aged oak against soft flesh and brittle bone, could be heard above the sound of Jona Lewie wishing he was at home for Christmas. The boy screamed and released the bat. Susie stepped forward in the same instant, scooped it up and swung it forcefully into the side of the second boy's knee. The boy who'd lost his weapon was doubled over clutching his broken fingers. The second boy fell to the ground crying in pain with both hands wrapped around a knee that would take weeks to recover. The third boy hesitated a moment too long. He stood unsure whether to help his fallen buddies, or make a run for it. Susie didn't hesitate. She held the bat in two hands and jabbed him in the balls. Three down.

'All right love?' Nick glanced at his wife as he took a step towards the one who had planned to hit Jacob.

'Never better.' Said Susie. 'Nice work with the stick.'

'Told you it was more useful than a crutch.' Nick leaned over the boy who lay on the ground, cowering. He prodded him in the chest with his stick. 'Get up, get out, and never come here again, you worthless little shit. I'm here every day, and if I see you again, I'll break more than your other hand. Understand?'

The boy whimpered and struggled to his feet, his two compadres did the same. They headed for the door. Susie blocked their exit and stood smacking the baseball bat into the palm of her hand. All three were taller than her, but they recoiled and stopped in the tracks. 'You've forgotten something.'

They looked at her and each other, blank faces. The one who'd brought the bat considered asking for it back and then thought better of it. 'What?' The second boy asked.

'Apologise to Mr Crowhurst for your behaviour.'

Incredulity spread across their faces and almost masked the pain all three were in. They exchanged glances again, noted the look on Susie's face, and, as one, they faced Jacob and mumbled. 'Sorry.'

'You will be, if you ever show your faces again.' She stood to one side and swung the baseball bat up and onto her shoulder. 'Now go.'

Jacob Crowhurst watched them leave with a sad shake of his head. 'Thank you both, that was so brave.'

'Nonsense Jacob, we needed a little exercise.' Susie walked back to him. 'Now where were we? About to help with cleaning up.'

One of the people sat at the tables, started to clap, others joined in and within seconds everyone in the hall was applauding the pair.

Nick gave a self-conscious bow, Susie looked embarrassed, Jacob joined in with the display of gratitude.

21

Harrison Thurlow lay on the sofa, mesmerised by the TV. He'd had two or three beers and was drifting in and out of a pleasant stupor. An alarm pinged on the wall behind him and stirred him. He'd set up an infrared beam across the track, adjacent to the cattle grid. When broken, it sent a signal to the house. It triggered the alarm to tell him something was approaching the cottage. He'd had to experiment with the sensitivity to avoid the alarm being set off by the assorted wildlife in the area, but he knew he had it right and he knew who and what was on its way. He paused the film he'd been half watching and dropped his feet to the floor, groaned with the effort of standing, yawned and stretched, his hands almost touching the low beams.

'You there Pia?' He called towards the kitchen.

No response.

He shouted louder. 'Pia, where the hell are you, they're here.'

Pia appeared in the doorway, her arm cradled a ceramic mixing bowl, she held a tea towel in her free hand. 'Yes.'

'Go and let them in, and make sure the light's off in the hall'

She said nothing, turned her back to him and disappeared from view.

'Did you hear what I said?' This time he yelled.

From the kitchen he heard a faint reply. 'Yes, I'm doing it.'

Harrison sneered in the direction of the kitchen and backed towards the open fire, the flames radiating warmth. He held his hands behind his backside, palms out, soaking up the heat. He listened and heard his girlfriend click the light switch, then pull the front door open. He waited.

A figure emerged from the darkness of the hall and walked into the living room. Miles Wilson, stopped a few paces in, folded his arms across his chest and studied Harrison. He broke into a smile. 'How's my boy then? Happy Christmas.'

'Hello Dad, how's it going?' Harrison didn't move, his features remained stony.

Wilson spread his arms and walked closer. 'What's up? Got a hug for your old man.'

Harrison recoiled and sunk his hands into the pockets of the camo pants he wore. 'Don't think so. I never wanted this. It's been forced on m e.'

'Ah. Don't be such a grouch. Nobody will find us here. It's only for a few days, then you can get your life back.'

'Huh. You'd better be right. It's taken two years to get this place the way I want it. If you fuck it up...'

'Nobody's going to fuck anything up and just remember who coughed for all this.' Wilson waved an expansive arm around the room. 'We made a plan. We keep the kids here for three days, as agreed, four at the most, then we drop them off miles from here. They never see our faces; they have no clue where they've been. You're in the clear.'

Harrison sighed knowing he couldn't argue. 'Let's get on with it then. Where are they?'

'That's more like it, I'll tell the girls to bring them in.'

'What girls?'

'Kobzar's girls, Irina and Ludmila.'

'You never said anything about two girls.'

'What? You thought I could manage all this on my own?'

Harrison shifted uncomfortably. 'No, but...'

'Don't worry. They're good, they're both highly trained operators and more than capable.'

'Whatever Dad, just get on with it.'

Wilson returned to the front door and made 'bring them in' signals. A minute later Irina entered the living room holding Noah. She pinned the boy against her side by one arm, the other trying to restrain his head away from hers. He writhed and struggled with his arms tied behind his back. She held him off the ground and had to contend with his flailing feet and his every effort to kick her as hard as he could. He had a gag in his mouth, but still managed to make enough noise to make conversation difficult.

'For God's sake Dad, I thought you said these were well behaved kids and they'd be no trouble.' Harrison had to raise his voice to be heard.

'Yeah, that one's a bit lively, the girl's not so bad. Show Irina how to get to the basement.'

Harrison took a couple of steps towards a narrow bookcase on his left. He reached for the book nearest him on the top shelf and tipped it away from the wall. There was a soft metallic click, and he swung a section of wall open, complete with the bookcase, revealing steps that lead down to the basement. He turned back to Irina, tipped his head and swept his hand towards them. 'Take him down.'

As Irina descended, Ludmila arrived with Jenny. Wilson had been right. The girl walked meekly in front of her captor; tears ran down her face. She looked to have given up, resigned to her fate. She was bound and gagged, like her little brother, but made no noise. Her eyes dark and red from crying, smudged mascara and tear stains down her cheeks. She glanced nervously around the room. Ludmila prodded her in the back and told her to go down the steps. Jenny obeyed without a sound.

Ludmila stayed at the top of the steps, she and Harrison could hear shouting and sobs as gags were removed. More scuffling noises as Noah tried to make a run for it, then a cry of pain as he was stopped. A door at the bottom of the steps slammed shut and they heard locking bolts engaged. Irina appeared at the top of the steps, slightly breathless, a cut, or possibly a bite mark on one arm and a murderous expression on her face. 'Little bastard.' She muttered. Harrison swung the bookcase-cum-hidden-door, closed.

Wilson had returned to the room by the time Irina emerged from the basement. 'Safely locked up?'

Irina grunted an acknowledgement.

Pia stood at the doorway into the kitchen. She watched the two children being taken to the basement and her face was etched with concern. 'Are they going to be all right down there?'

Harrison snapped at her. 'Of course they are. They've got food, drink, beds, a toilet, they'll be fine. You just leave them alone. Understand?'

His remarks did nothing to lessen Pia's concern, but she knew there was nothing she could do.

She was on the point of turning back to the kitchen when Wilson called to her. 'Be a love and get us a drink, a beer, a decent one, not that fizzy cat's piss he drinks.' He jerked his head in Harrison's direction.

Harrison didn't rise to the insult. 'Yeah, and I'll have the usual.'

Wilson shot a glance at the two Russian women. 'You want a drink?'

They looked at each other, tempted by the offer. Ludmila shook her head. 'Just Coke, we've got to drive later.'

Wilson called after Pia, who had left the room. 'And two Cokes.'

Harrison threw a couple of logs on the fire, returned to his sofa and grabbed the remote. He hit play and his film resumed. 'Is the food ready yet.' He shouted, his attention on the TV.

Wilson gave Irina and Ludmila two hours to rest and have something to eat, then stirred them into action. 'OK ladies, I reckon it's time. Have you sorted out who's doing what?'

Irina gave him a withering look. 'I'm taking the van; she's taking the BMW.'

'You've got the directions?'

The withering look descended into one of contempt.

'And you remember what I told you about setting the charges.'

Ludmila stood up and glared at Wilson. 'We know what we're doing, you just sit there and drink more beer. Let us get on with what we're good at.'

The two women picked up their coats and left.

Harrison watched them leave, saw his father's expression, and smirked.

Susie snatched her phone up as soon as she saw the caller ID. 'You got news?'

'Hi Susie,' Commander Hawke responded. 'You must have been waiting for the call.'

'Kind of, I can't settle.' She checked the time. 'It's been almost five hours, I guess you've had no luck?'

'To be honest, we could do with a lucky break.'

'Does that mean you've drawn a blank?'

'Not exactly. It's proved difficult to get people to come in. They're all willing but, like you, they need fuel, and not many can get it.' Hawke's tone was matter of fact, nothing he could do about it.

'So...' Susie started.

'So, it took us a while to get going. We concentrated on the nearest cameras to Radmore Road. There are three, and anyone going in or coming out would have to pass at least one of them.'

'And did you see anything?' Susie stopped pacing and sat on a stool at the breakfast bar.

'Yes, we did. Didn't take us long in fact. It helps that today is one of the quietest day of the year on the roads, that, and the narrow timeframe made it relatively easy.'

'Come on Alex, don't string me along. What did you see?'

'We spotted a dark blue or dark grey van passing one of the cameras at 09:21 and leaving past another camera at 09:49. It was the only vehicle that could have carried five people.'

'Could you see who was in it?'

'Sadly not, the image isn't that great, but we could make out the reg number.'

'Brilliant. Does that mean the ANPR system could track it?' Susie sat up, energised.

'Don't' get too excited.' Hawke cautioned her. 'Not all cameras have the technology, but..."

'But enough of them do?'

'Well. You mentioned luck. We had a little luck, a couple of hits heading out of Oxford towards Finstock.'

'That's got to be it, surely?'

'That's what we thought. We ran the number through the DVLA database, and it came up as stolen a week ago.'

'Are you still able to track it.'

'We can, and we did.'

'What do you mean, did?'

'We've got the number flagged, if it passes any cameras, we'll know immediately. So far it hasn't.'

Susie took a moment to think. 'What does that tell you?'

'We've been running through the options. Either they've just been dead lucky and somehow managed to escape detection. If they stuck to the back roads and avoided built up areas, it wouldn't be that difficult to fly under the radar. Or they know where all the cameras are, and they've planned a route to avoid them. Possible but unlikely. Or, they've gone to ground somewhere near to that abandoned cottage. Of the three, I think that's the least likely.'

'So. Other than knowing what vehicle they're in, we're no further forward.'

'That's about the size of it. There are more cameras out there, but they're not all linked up to the network. And then there's all the private CCTV systems; business parks, industrial estates, forecourts, retail parks, that kind of thing. The people who monitor them are probably having a day off. If they come into work tomorrow and spot anything, we may be able to find them.'

'Is there nothing else we can do?' A hint of desperation crept into Susie's voice. 'Can't you track things by satellite or drones or something?'

'If only the real world worked like Hollywood.' Hawke's tone implied he'd heard the remark more than once. 'Sadly not. It looks great in the movies but I'm afraid Jason Bourne is a fictional character, and we don't have anything like the resources people think we do.'

'Hmmm.' Susie struggled for something positive to say. 'I promised Alison I'd get back to her tonight with news.'

'I understand. I wish I was in a better position, but as it stands, we just have to wait and trust the technology. If you speak to her, make sure she knows there's a team of specialists working through the night to find her children. I'll call you in the morning with an update.'

'Just call me anytime, I doubt I'll sleep much. Goodnight Alex.' Susie ended the call and looked around the kitchen. It was after midnight; Christmas Day was over. She wandered through into the living room, Nick had dozed off in front of the TV and the tree still had unopened presents at its base. They would have to wait. She decided against ringing Burton-Castle and instead composed a brief text to reassure her as best she could.

Woken by the sound of the phone sending the message, Nick rubbed his eyes and looked up at his wife. 'Bedtime?' He croaked.

'Come on then handsome, what girl could resist an offer like that.'

Tuesday 26 December

She woke with a start just before 7:00 am when her phone buzzed into life. Alison Burton-Castle had replied to Susie's text, thanking her for bringing her up to date and urging Susie to let her know the moment she had any news.

She sat up in bed, switched her bedside light on and sent her a thumbs-up emoji. Nick lay on his side, his back towards her. She gave him a gentle nudge. 'You awake?'

He groaned. 'Urghh. No. I'm sound asleep you swine. What ungodly hour is it?'

'Just after seven, I thought I might go for a run.'

'What?' Nick rolled onto his back, lifted his head off the pillow and propped himself up on his elbows to stare at the window. 'You must be joking. It's pitch black outside and it's Boxing day. Why not give yourself a day off and come back here and snuggle up.' He patted the bed beside him.

Susie smiled at him. 'A tempting offer, and almost impossible to resist. But I'll have to take a rain check, you know what I'm like once I'm awake. Besides I'm waiting for a call from Tiger One. I doubt he'd be impressed to find us behaving like a couple of lazy articles when we're in the middle of a national emergency.'

Nick lolled back, unimpressed. 'Go on then if you must. Any chance of a cup of tea for the poorly patient before you go?'

'I daresay, although I think you've made a remarkable recovery, judging by your performance at Jacob's place.' She gave him a playful punch on the shoulder and slid out of bed.

She re-appeared in the bedroom ten minutes later wearing a hi-viz running jacket, day-glo hat and gloves and reflective running tights, with a head torch strapped to her forehead.

'Steady on, you'll blind me.' Nick held up a hand to shield hie eyes. 'How long you going for?'

She handed him a mug of tea. '30, 40 minutes, I'll see how I feel. Depends if I get a call.' She tapped the phone in its holder on her upper arm.

'Thanks for the tea love. Watch how you go out there. Do I get a kiss before you vanish into the dark?'

Susie leaned over the bed, hugged him and gave him a kiss. 'Back soon.'

Nick watched her leave, considered having an extra 30 minutes in bed, then, overcome by the prospect of a guilty conscience. threw the covers off and headed for the shower.

Thirty-five minutes later, Susie entered the kitchen from the back door at the same time as Nick, showered, shaved and dressed, entered the room from the hall. 'Well, someone's determined to impress.' She said, as she peeled off her jacket and checked her Garmin.

'Good run?' Nick poured his half-drunk mug of tea down the sink and put the kettle on for a new brew.

Susie studied the data on the watch. 'Not bad, almost five miles. It's cold out there, but at least it's dry.'

'You've been a bit longer than I thought, I'm guessing Alex hasn't called you?'

Susie twisted her face in concern and checked her phone in case she'd missed anything. 'No, nothing. I guess it means they've had no more hits on that car.'

'Either that, or he felt you needed a lie-in and didn't want to disturb you.'

'Nice thought, but I doubt it. I told him to ring at any time, and he doesn't strike me as the sort who'd be too bothered about waking anyone in the middle of the night if necessary.'

'You want one?' Nick waved a mug in her direction.

'Thanks, but not now. I'll have my shake and cool down. I'll ring Alex after I've showered and dressed. Can you make a pot of coffee?'

It was almost 8:30 when Susie returned to the kitchen and called Commander Hawke. It rang and rang, she waited and waited, sure his voicemail would cut in any moment.

'Hawke.' He sounded breathless.

Susie assumed her name hadn't shown up on his screen. 'It's Susie Jones. Good morning.'

'Morning Susie. Sorry about that. One of the analysts had called me over to the other side of the ops room and I left my phone behind.'

'I'm guessing you've had no hits; you'd have called me otherwise.'

'Well, until two minutes ago that was true. That's what the analyst called me about.'

'Sounds encouraging, what had they seen?' Susie poured herself a mug of coffee and resumed her position at the breakfast bar.

'It's a bit of an odd one. We, or more accurately, I, thought if they had headed West out of Oxford, they'd continue in that direction.

'Is that where you've been looking?'

'Kind of. The ANPR network is Nationwide, so you can imagine it's processing thousands of plates every second. Even with the fastest computers it could take a while for a flagged number to set bells ringing.'

'Can't you break it down and search by region or something?' Susie asked.

'No flies on you.' Hawke said. 'It's a grid system and I prioritised the search in the grids North and West of Finstock.'

'So, what makes this one odd?'

'It's the number we're after, but it's 40 miles in the other direction, not in any of target grids, and it's from a private contractor, so it didn't get prioritised. It only came through to us a few minutes ago.'

'So it has to be the one we're looking for?'

'I agree, but there's something strange, it was recorded entering an industrial site, South of Bicester, loads of warehouses and factory units.'

'What's strange about it.'

'There's only one way in and one way out, and it hasn't left.'

'So, it's still there?'

'Has to be.'

'What time did it enter the site?'

'Hang on, I made a note.' Susie heard the rustling of paper. 'Three minutes after two this morning.'

'So, it's been there over six hours. And where is this place?'

'It's called Boarstall Park on the edge of a village called Arncott, more of a small town really. Odd location for an industrial site, the analyst said it was an old MOD depot.'

'It has to be worth investigating.'

Hawke hesitated. 'Agreed.'

'You don't sound so sure.'

'Sorry. You're absolutely right, but you won't believe this, I've got a real issue with getting people in. Even tactical units geared up for rapid response. Whoever is behind this mess, knew what they were doing. We're supposed to have people ready to go anytime, day or night, rain or shine, even if it's Christmas, but somewhere in the planning stages, nobody considered what would happen if the very people we need, can't get fuel to report for duty.'

Susie frowned at this and took a swig of coffee. 'How long will it take to get anyone over there?'

'It's going to be a least a couple of hours. I want an armed unit with backup, transport and coms.'

While Hawke spoke, Susie opened Google Maps on her phone, she located Ancott, zoomed in on the location, then tapped the directions button. 'I can be there in less than 30 minutes. I could do a quick drive-by and save your guys time when they get there.'

'Hmmm, I appreciate the offer, but I'm not sure that's such a great idea, I don't want you putting yourself at risk.'

'Understood. It's just that it looks like a big site, it might take a while to find out where they are. If I drive around, I'm not going to raise any suspicion or take any risks, and I can report back and tell you where the van is. Your guys will know what they're dealing with then.'

'OK, but strictly on the understanding that you don't try any heroics.'

'Of course. I'll wait for your guys to arrive and stay close by. If the kids are there, they'll need to see a friendly face.'

'OK, Susie, take care and keep in touch.'

22

Tuesday 26 December

The drive to Boarstall Park took less time than Susie had estimated. The fact she was on a mission spurred her on and with quiet roads and an enthusiastic right foot, she arrived shortly after 9:15 am. The cloudless sky brightened her mood, and she drove slowly down the park's main drag, noting the layout of the place and the way the roads had been set out in a grid formation.

Neglect hung over the park. Signs were faded, some units looked abandoned, there were gaps in fences, potholes in the roads, and discarded broken pallets piled haphazardly at the entrances to some of the units. There were signs of life, but nothing looked new or cared for.

She turned left at the end of the main drag, onto what she assumed must be a perimeter track that ran round the outer edge of the park. She followed the road for less than 100 yards, then turned left back into the grid. She spotted a grimy sign announcing this was Avenue 2 and marvelled at the thought and imagination that had gone into the naming process. She reached the intersection where roads crossed, left back to the main drag, and right towards what she assumed would be Avenue 3. There were intersections roughly every fifty yards. Avenue 2 had some bigger units, mostly single storey, but some two and three storeys high. None of them had any vehicles parked outside and she continued to the end. This time she turned right, then right again down Avenue 3.

After ten minutes, Susie was convinced she had driven down all six Avenues and along all five crossroads, which she discovered had been designated as lanes and named, bizarrely, after wildflowers. Convinced she must have missed something, Susie re joined the perimeter track briefly, then criss-crossed the grid, her head on a swivel, looking for the grey van. She almost missed it and rather than reverse back and attract attention, she went around the block again to make sure it was what she thought it was.

On the corner of Avenue 4 and Buttercup Lane, the two storey building stood on its own, the plots on either side had been bulldozed. The van had been reversed in and parked under a covered area near the main entrance. It was in shadow and as a result, difficult to spot. A sign to one side of the entrance read "Festive Mouldings" with the catchy strapline underneath proclaiming, *"you think it, we make it"*. There were no other vehicles parked anywhere near the building and a noticeable absence of any activity on Buttercup Lane or Avenue 4.

She continued driving, turned a corner, made sure she was out of sight of "Festive Mouldings", and stopped. She called Tiger One.

'You on location?'

'Yeah, found the van, no sign of life.'

'What can you tell me?'

'Check out Festive Mouldings.' She gave him the address and heard him repeat it to someone in the operations room.

'Give us a second.' Hawke went quiet and Susie could hear chatter in the background. 'OK, got it. According to our data, they went out of business last year.'

'Can't say I'm surprised, this place is a dump. The building looks deserted.'

'Just stay put. I've got an armed response unit on its way to you. Their ETA is 1014.'

Susie checked the time, 25 minutes to wait. 'OK, copy that. Tell them to come up Avenue 3 from the bottom end and look for me, I'm parked out of the sight.

'Don't worry, these guys are the best, you can trust them.' Hawke clicked off.

Susie sat in the car and looked around. When she told Hawke there were no signs of life, she wasn't exaggerating. She hadn't seen another human being for twenty minutes and the only animal life was a flock of crows scavenging in bins next to a unit that promoted itself as the home of "*authentic Indian samosas*". She'd assured Hawke she wouldn't interfere and promised Nick, she would stay in the car and not go nosing around. Having seen the van and the abandoned unit where it was parked, she told herself it would do no harm just to walk past the place and see if she could identify any vulnerable areas that might help the ARU. Nobody would know, it looked safe enough. She zipped up her jacket, pulled on a beanie hat and stuffed her hair into it, then wrapped a scarf around her neck. Feeling a little self-conscious, she opened the door of the Volvo as quietly as she could and stepped out into the cold wind.

The whiff of samosas caught her senses, (not entirely unpleasant), mixed with the less appealing smell of a waste incinerator on the other side of the park. The only discernible sound came from a car wash, she'd passed about half a mile before the entrance. She locked the Volvo, more out of habit than any fear someone might steal it and headed back towards Festive Mouldings. She kept her pace slow and began to wish she had a dog to walk, convinced it might legitimise her presence. She felt out of place, the only person for miles, ambling through a run-down business park on a quiet Boxing Day. It only took her a minute to draw level with the van and she slowed to a geriatric shuffle as she passed it. She cast surreptitious glances in its direction. There was no doubt, the number plate confirmed it was the one they had been tracking. She carried on past the building until it was out of sight, then she stopped, acted as if she'd just forgotten something and turned to retrace her steps.

This time she couldn't resist stopping in front of Festive Mouldings. She took a few steps towards the van and peered around it to see the main entrance door. The glass in the door was smashed and it stood ajar, only by an inch, but defiantly open. She quickly checked up and down the road, still nobody in sight, and crept closer to the door. This brought her under the covered area and once behind the van, she was out of sight from any passing people.

Susie leant forward closer to the door and listened. No voices, no sound at all. She gave the door a gentle push and discovered why the wind hadn't blown it fully open. The floor behind it was covered in junk mail, envelopes marked "final notice" and assorted other mail, piled so high she had to give the door a firm shove to open it wide enough for her to squeeze through.

A year's worth of dust covered every surface and the smell of damp hung in the air. She switched her phone's torch on and inched her way down a corridor, watching out for hazards that could cause her to trip or alert anyone to her presence. She stopped every few paces and listened, still nothing. She began to wonder if this was a wasted trip. Had they been fooled? The corridor opened into a hallway with a reception desk. She found it strange that the receptionist would be located this far into the premises and not at the front door, but dismissed it as irrelevant. A staircase led from the hall. Susie cast her light around and could see no reason not to go up to the next floor. If they had brought the kids here, it would make sense to get them away from the ground floor. The stairs creaked as she climbed, and Susie winced at the noise. If there was anyone in the building, they couldn't fail to hear her.

As she climbed, her focus was on her feet, making sure she didn't trip. She didn't look up and when her hat caught on something, she assumed it must have been something dangling from the ceiling. She reached up and flailed at the object, it felt like an electrical cable, probably from a disconnected light fitting. She grabbed at it pushed it out of the way. She heard a click.

The boom that followed deafened her for the second time in three days and she reeled backwards. A frantic grab for the banister prevented her from falling down the stairs. The noise reverberated around the building; the shock reverberated around her body. She cowered on the stairs, her eyes tight shut, waiting for the blast wave and the impact of debris. Her ears rang and she covered them with her hands, at the same time realising she'd dropped her phone. After a couple of seconds, she opened her eyes and squinted around her, afraid of what she might see. There was no dust, no debris. Her phone lay on the floor, the torch still shining. She picked it up, got to her feet and shook her head. She thought she could hear voices, but the noise was distant and muffled, she dismissed it.

A thunder-flash and a tripwire, whoever had taken the kids wanted to make a point, or they wanted to waste her time.

Realising there was no point in going further, Susie stepped cautiously back down to the hall. She heard the voices again, this time a little clearer. They sounded like men shouting, her hearing was returning slowly, but she couldn't make out what they were saying. She headed down the corridor towards the front door and daylight, and then she saw them. Two figures walking towards her, they were silhouetted, she couldn't see their faces, but she could see they held carbines at the ready.

'Armed police, stay where you are.' She heard one of the men shout. Her ears still buzzed; it sounded as if he was speaking from underwater.

She held her hands above her head. 'Don't shoot guys. It's Susie Jones, I'm the one who called this in.'

'Hands on the wall, now.' The first man reached her, ignored her comment and spun her against the wall. 'Where's your ID?'

Susie pressed her hands on the wall at shoulder height. She turned to face the man. 'It's in my inside jacket pocket. I can't get it out unless you let me, and no, you're not going to rummage around in there looking for it.' She met his gaze, both eyebrows raised and waited for a response.

The two men exchanged glances, the second one shrugged at his mate. 'She fits the description. I'll keep her covered.'

The first man, Susie reckoned he must be the team leader nodded. 'Go on then. Slowly.'

She took her right hand off the wall and with exaggerated care, unzipped her jacket and reached into the left inside pocket. She withdrew her warrant card between thumb and forefinger and handed it over.

After studying the ID as if it were a valuable artefact, he passed it back to her. 'OK, you can drop your hands. Sorry, but we don't take chances.'

'No need to apologise, I've been in your shoes, I'd have done the same. You must be the team Hawke sent.

'Hawke?' The man looked blank.

'Tiger One.'

'Oh, right, yeah. He told us you'd be waiting in that old Volvo parked around the corner.' He jerked his thumb over his shoulder.

Susie looked suitably chastened. 'Hmm, sorry about that. Couldn't resist a quick peak. Got carried away.'

'You had us worried. When we found the car empty, we were revising options when we heard that detonation. We decided we had to go in. What the hell was it? A thunder-flash?'

'Yeah, trip wire at the top of the stairs, head height. Didn't see it.' Susie shook her head. 'Rookie error.'

The second man turned towards the exit. 'Come on, let's get you out of here. We'll get the other two in and do a full sweep of the place.'

As they headed for daylight, she turned to him. 'I'm pretty sure there's no-one here. Someone's pulling our chain. Wasting time and resources.' Susie huffed in frustration. Once outside the other two men joined them. Susie gave the four of them her most engaging smile. 'Can I ask you guys a small favour?'

They looked at her and at each other. 'Depends what it is.' The team leader said.

She looked a little embarrassed. 'If you have to report back to the boss, can you skip the bit about finding me in there. He told me not to go in, and I don't want to fall out with him.'

One of the other team members chuckled. 'I reckon he'd let you get away with murder darling. If it was one of us, he'd tear us to shreds.' The others nodded in agreement.

'I'm not so sure, but thanks guys. I'll call him now; tell him you're checking the place out and you'll report back when you're done.' She walked back to the Volvo and let the men get on with the search.

Nick was waiting in the kitchen for Susie when she arrived back. He hugged her. 'Got your message, there's a fresh pot waiting for you.'

'Thanks love, you're an angel.' She reached up and kissed him.

'What happened then?' Nick handed her a mug of coffee. 'No sign of anyone being there?'

Susie had a rueful look. 'Someone must have been. The glass in the front door had been smashed, forced entry, and the armed response team found evidence of booby traps.' She figured she wasn't lying to Nick, just skirted around a full explanation of her involvement. She hoped her guilty conscience didn't show.

'They obviously knew the van would be found eventually.' Nick took his mug and came and sat next to her.

'That's what I thought. I told Alex the same thing when I called him.'

Nick blew on his coffee and stared into it; his lips pursed. 'She where does that leave us, or you, or Alison?'

'Screwed.' Susie said, exasperated. She slumped on the breakfast bar and used her folded arms as a headrest.

'What did Alex say when you spoke to him?'

'He's just as frustrated and pissed off as I am. More so, probably. He's had to deploy resources and got nothing back that might be called a positive outcome.'

'Don't beat yourself up love, you've done all you can.'

Susie tilted her head to look at him. 'Just wish I could do more. I feel bad because I promised Alison I'd get kids back, and I haven't.'

Nick put a hand on Susie's shoulder and gave her a gentle squeeze. 'Sweetheart, you've already done more than anyone else, it's not your responsibility.'

'Maybe, but...it's like I said a couple of days ago, I feel I owe it to the CCU team. They deserve justice, or vengeance, or revenge, or whatever you want to call it. And anyone who's prepared to blow up a government installation, killing everyone inside, won't think twice about harming two kids.'

'You're right.' Nick said. 'But, it looks like they're holding the kids as leverage to prevent the payment system from functioning again. If any harm came to them, they'd lose their bargaining chip.'

'Poor Alison, she must be under so much stress.'

'Have you spoken to her since the van was located?'

'No. When I spoke to Alex, he said he'd do it. He thought it would be best coming from him.' Susie sat up and reached for her coffee, took a swig and scowled at nothing in particular.

'We're just going to have to sit tight and wait. Either they'll get in touch again, or you'll get lucky.'

'You know I'm useless at waiting. I think I prefer that old golf maxim. *"The more I practice, the luckier I get"*, something that implies you make your own luck.' She slid off the stool, gave a bemused Nick another kiss and headed towards the living room.

'What are you going to do?' He called after her.

'I'm going online. Do some digging, see if I can create some luck.'

Nick checked the clock. 'Fancy some soup for lunch?'

'Yeah, great, give me a shout when it's ready.'

He limped into the living room two hours after they'd eaten to find Susie crouched over her laptop on the sofa. 'Any joy?'

'Bugger all.' Came the blunt reply. 'I don't know what I expected, but I've gone down too many rabbit holes and too many blind alleys, to think I might ever find something helpful.'

Nick saw the look on her face, he wanted to help. 'You need a break love, a change of scenery. You'll go nuts staring at that screen for so long.'

Susie sat back, closed her eyes and dug her fists into the small of her back. 'Any bright ideas?'

'Why not have a trip into town?' Nick joked, 'I've heard it's quite lively.'

'What? Go and see Jacob again, are you itching for another fight?'

Nick gave a dismissive snort. 'No. I was thinking more about the Boxing Day sales, all those bargains.'

'Yeah, and nobody able to buy them.'

'Except those with cash.' Nick gave her a cheeky wink.

Susie turned slowly in his direction. 'What are you hiding Mr Cooper?'

'Well,' He had his hands behind his back and with as much drama as he could manage, slowly brought them forward, face down, then flipped them over with a triumphant. 'Ta-da.' He held a wad of notes in each hand. 'Remember that job I did a couple of weeks ago for the guy who sold fireplaces.'

Susie peered at him suspiciously. 'The one near Abingdon?

Nick nodded, beaming.

'What about it?'

'He wanted me to do him a deal and we haggled a bit. He offered to pay me in cash, and I thought, why not? Probably a bit dodgy but given the circumstances.' Nick shrugged.

'And you've been hiding it from me since then?'

'Certainly have. I wanted to surprise you for Christmas, but you look like you need something to take your mind off things for a bit. I know how much you love a bit of a spree, and now seems as good a time as any.'

'You're a dark horse sometimes babe.' Susie perked up, frowned at the laptop screen and theatrically closed it, as if not to disturb its contents. 'You think anything will be open? It's after three.'

'Only one way to find out, Come on.'

23

Fifteen minutes later, after a quick change into something a little more weatherproof, the pair headed back into town. Despite claiming he was fit enough to drive, Susie insisted Nick ride shotgun. She said she was worried his leg might cause a problem if they ran into any sort of trouble. He was going to argue but could see her mind was made up. Besides, he freely acknowledged she was more than capable behind the wheel and had been trained in handling tricky situations.

They arrived at the car park behind the high street, puzzled by the light in the sky. Dusk was approaching and the light fading, but the area above the shops appeared to be glowing. They'd found an old Fleetwood Mac CD under the seat; the car was old enough to have a CD player. They had the music playing loud enough to prevent the outside world from reaching them, and it wasn't until they opened the car doors that they heard it.

The sound of breaking glass, the crash of masonry, the aggressive shouts of angry people, and the wail of sirens.

They got out of the Volvo and stood in awe of the spectacle. The reflection of blue and red strobe lights bounced off rooftops, a counterpoint to the yellow and orange flames that appeared as a backdrop to the scene.

Nick leaned his elbows on the roof of the car, spellbound.

Susie had her back to the car. She leaned against it and held a hand up to shield her eyes. 'Shit, this looks nasty. I need to see what's happening.'

'You've got to be joking love. It sounds like all hell's broken loose.'

'Don't worry, I'll just take a quick look. Mainstream media isn't reporting this. Alex needs to know.'

Nick shook his head; he knew how stubborn she could be. He tried to discourage her. 'Seriously Susie. You've got no idea what you're walking into.'

'True, but if it looks too dangerous, I'll turn around and come back. There could be people in trouble, people who need help.'

'But...'

'It's OK Nick.' She turned and held a reassuring hand up. 'Don't worry, I'm just going through that alley.' She tipped her head in the direction of a gap between two buildings. 'I'll make an assessment and be back in a couple of minutes.' She didn't wait for his reaction and jogged towards the alley.

The alley opened onto the high street between a betting shop and an amusement arcade. Susie stopped, stunned by the sight that greeted her. The term *"like a war zone"* came to mind. Journalists love to use it when trying to describe a scene of devastation. Having been in an actual war zone, Susie was a little more circumspect. As far as she could see, there were no bodies strewn across the street, no gunfire or explosions, no bullets ricocheting off walls, no buildings collapsed or on the point of collapse; but there was everything else. She saw at least two cars burning furiously, debris from shops lying everywhere, broken glass, bricks and concrete blocks were scattered in random heaps. There were planks of wood, some on them fire and torn sheets of shuttering board, undoubtedly ripped from the windows of shops whose owners had tried to prevent the looting.

The looting was widespread. Some people stood around watching, while others had brazenly smashed their way into shops and taken whatever they wanted. The police were fighting a losing battle. Outnumbered and dangerously ill-equipped for civil unrest on such a scale, the four officers she saw, were struggling to simply hold their ground, or prevent their cars being set alight. She could do nothing to help them. A fire engine at the bottom end of the high street, sat with its lights flashing, unable to deal with the two cars already burning because of the blockade created by looters to prevent access.

Susie wanted to see more and set off down the street. She jogged past damaged buildings and dodged lumps of masonry and metalwork. Nobody appeared to take any notice of her, but she felt threatened all the same. Surrounded by the crackling of flaming timber, the acrid smell of smouldering plastic, the shouts and screams of a lawless mob and the heat and light from fires all around. After fifty yards, she'd seen enough and ducked back through another alleyway to escape the madness. She stopped and glanced back. She found it hard to believe, only a few yards separated her from the mayhem, it was so contained, like an arena or a movie set. In comparison, where she stood, it was dark, quiet and safe. She turned and started to walk back to Nick when a noise behind her made her jump.

Two men, their faces covered by scarves, their heads hidden under hoodies, staggered along the alley towards her carrying a large white cardboard box. She saw the SHARP name and logo on one end of the box and caught a glimpse of the number 72 along its front. She didn't have to be a genius to work out what they were looting and stepped smartly out of their way to let them pass her. 'Happy Christmas darling.' One of the men called, slightly out of breath, his voice muffled by the scarf.

Slightly stunned by how blatant they were, Susie was lost for words and watched in disbelief as the men bundled the giant TV into the back of a pickup truck, and then calmly drove off.

The Volvo had been parked facing away from her and as she walked back to it, she saw Nick sitting in the passenger seat. He looked to his right, almost transfixed, towards the alley where he'd watched her disappear onto the high street. He hadn't seen her approach from the other end of the car park. She tapped on his window, and he jumped.

She pulled his door open and gave him a playful jab on the shoulder. 'You'd make a useless sentry.'

Nick sank back in his seat and placed a hand on his chest. 'Do you really want to give me heart failure?'

'Sorry love, couldn't resist it.' She closed his door, went around to the the driver's side and climbed in.

'Am I pleased to see you or what?' Nick reached over and hugged her. 'You had me worried, there's been at least half a dozen people coming back here with stuff they've taken. the Boxing Day sales have taken on a whole new meaning.'

Relieved to be back in the car, she hugged him back a little harder. 'Thanks sweetheart, I'll admit I was a little worried too. It's madness, they're destroying the place.'

Nick released her, sat back and looked her up and down as if checking she was uninjured. He gave her enquiring stare. 'What's happened to the cops?'

'There's just four of them, they look terrified for their lives.'

'Can't they call in backup or something?'

Susie shook her head. 'I bet they've been screaming for backup. If this is happening on every high street, where's the backup going to come from?' She returned Nick's questioning look and shrugged. 'I just hope the poor buggers get out of there before any of them get attacked.'

Nick winced at the sound of more masonry crashing to the ground. 'Let's get out of here love, this was a bad idea.'

Susie didn't argue and headed home as fast as she dared.

•••••

The last of the daylight had slipped over the Western horizon by the time Susie and Nick arrived home. They both felt defeated, even the festive lights and the giant inflatable snowman couldn't lift their spirits.

Once inside, Susie shrugged off her coat and made for the kitchen. 'I'll put the kettle on and ring Alex, tell him what I saw.'

'You think he doesn't already know?'

'I'm sure he does, he'll have people reporting back to him, I just thought I should give him a first-hand account.'

Nick jerked a shoulder in a "suppose so" sort of way. 'If you're making a brew, can I have a mince pie with mine?'

'Good thinking, just what's needed.'

•••••

Wednesday 27 December

sStill in her running kit from her morning workout, Susie stood in the kitchen drinking her protein shake and wondered where they could go next. Her conversation with Commander Hawke the previous evening had done nothing to make her feel positive. Between them, they thought they had exhausted all options and just had to wait until the people who had abducted the Burton-Castle children got in touch again. Meanwhile, the problems caused by the card processing network crash continued to escalate.

Nick wandered into the kitchen, his limp noticeably better. He saw the look on her face. 'You all right love? I thought a run would have cheered you up.'

'So did I.' She huffed and gave him a resigned smile. 'This is so frustrating. If Alex can't do anything with all his connections and authority,' She threw her hands in the air, 'what chance has anyone got to fix this?'

'At least the banks will be open today. I know it's not going to solve the online problem, but at least people will be able to get their hands on some cash and buy stuff.'

Susie shook her head. 'Haven't you seen the news?'

'No. Why? What have I missed?'

'All the high street banks have issued a joint statement to say they will not be opening today.'

Nick looked stunned. 'You have to be joking.'

'I'm serious. It's just been announced.' She nodded at her phone by way of explanation.

'Bloody hell, what excuse have they given?

Susie gave a derisive snort. 'Their official line is that people with cash on them will be vulnerable. She picked up her phone and opened the news app. They say, and I quote, *"Given the current level of unrest, anyone seen buying something will be a target for opportunist thieves or muggers."*

Nick frowned at this. 'I can see their point, but they can't stop people taking their own money out. Jesus: talk about nanny state, surely, we don't have to rely on the banks telling us how much cash we can carry around.'

'It's just a semi-plausible line to feed to the media isn't it.' Susie finished her shake and gazed into the empty glass. She studied the dregs as if they could offer some solace.

Nick said nothing, he tipped his head in her direction, waiting for her to finish.

'It's pretty obvious to anyone with half a brain, they're shit scared of a run on the banks.'

'Understandable.' Nick said. 'Banks are about as risk averse as it's possible to be. Spineless tossers.'

Susie couldn't help but smile at his outburst. She shared his view. 'I wouldn't mind, but when did you or I last go into a bank? There used to be four of five in every town, now you're lucky to find one, and that's only if it's a big town.'

Nick gave a sage nod. 'The price you pay for a cashless society. Whatever genius created that virus, they knew exactly what sort of havoc they could wreak. Just a bloody shame, none of the bean counters did anything to prepare for it.'

'Well, whoever they are, they must be rubbing their hands in delight and laughing at the bean counters.'

Nick was about to get up from the breakfast bar, when he stopped as if Susie's words had sparked a thought. 'Beans. Random thought. Coffee beans.'

'What are you talking about? Have you...' Susie asked.

Nick held a hand up to stop her and give his thoughts time to process. 'Coffee beans. Starbucks.'

'I'll never understand the way your brain works but go on.'

'When you went to Starbucks the other day and those two women chased after you.' He paused to make sure Susie was following.

She nodded, confused.

'They have to be part of all this; the virus, the modems, abducting the kids. Agreed?'

'I think we can safely assume so.'

Nick paused again and fixed Susie with a serious look. 'The car they chased you in, a beemer right?

'Yeah, 3 series, silver.'

'What can you remember about its reg number?'

Susie's shoulders fell. She stared at the ceiling and shook her head. 'Nothing, I can't even remember seeing it, let alone remember any letters or numbers. I was more bothered about getting away from it.'

'It's OK, I didn't think you would. You'd have said so if you had.'

'So why bring it up?'

'Just bear with me here, I'm thinking out loud, what are the chances that Starbucks have a camera covering their parking area?'

Susie stared at Nick with curious interest. 'I didn't see any, but these days they're fairly discreet, it's perfectly possible.'

'If they do, it's unlikely they'll be the sort that can recognise a number plate automatically, so no help to your Tiger, but if he could access their feed for when you were there, they might have a shot of it and he might be able to trace it.'

'There are times Mr Cooper when you amaze me.' Susie looked suitably impressed. 'I thought about the BMW and the idea of tracing it, but without a reg number...' She turned her hands palms up. 'Nothing. I've been beating myself up about it. Never even considered the idea of Starbucks having a camera.'

'It's worth a try isn't it, what have you got to lose?'

Susie reached for her phone. 'I'll call him now.'

The phone was answered on the first ring. 'Tactical Intelligence Group.'

Susie recognised the accent. 'It's Susie Jones. Is that Mitchel?'

'It is. How can I help?'

'I need to speak to Commander Hawke, is he available?'

'He's on another call, can I ask him to call you back, or do you want to wait?'

'I'll wait, it's important.' She heard Mitchel put the phone down. She did the same and put the speaker on.

Nick opened his mouth to speak, and she put a finger to her lips then pointed at the phone. He got the message and walked around Susie to put her between him and her phone. He leaned in close and whispered in her ear, 'If he asks, you came up with the idea. It'll earn you a few extra brownie points.'

Susie turned to face him, their noses almost touching. 'Thanks love, but credit where it's due, he needs to know you're not just a pretty face.' She cupped his cheeks in her hands and planted a warm kiss on his lips.

'Mmmm more ple...'

'Susie, you there?' Hawke's voice cut through the moment and they both reacted like a couple of teenagers caught in the act. They jumped apart self-consciously.

'Yes Alex.' Susie felt her face redden. She took a deep breath to compose herself. 'Good morning.'

'Yes, morning. Sorry to keep you hanging on, I was on to the Home Office about this morning's situation. I don't know if you've heard but the banks are refusing to open.'

'I saw it on the news feed, Nick and I were just talking about it.'

'It's ratcheted up the violence to another level. The police are past breaking point, they can't cope. It's worse than what you saw last night.'

'What can you do? Is the army an option?'

'That's what I was talking to the Home Sec about, trouble is, the army is stretched, it's half the size it used to be and we simply don't have enough people. On top of that, the rioting is so widespread we wouldn't know where to deploy them. Our only hope is to get the payment processing system up and running as soon as possible and doing that means we have to get those two kids back. I'm assuming that's what you called about?'

'It is. We, Nick and I, have been thinking about what else we can do to rescue Alison's kids, and Nick's come up with an idea that might help.

'I'm willing to consider anything at the moment Susie, we're fresh out of suggestions.'

'It's a bit of a long shot, but...' She summarised Nick's suggestion. 'What do you think?'

'It's definitely got legs, Say thanks to Nick from me.' He paused to consider the next step. 'I'll get someone to call them. We need to know if they've got any cameras and if they have, do they record the feeds and if so, how it's stored and how long they keep the recordings. Some people erase them after a few days to save storage.'

'Yeah, we thought that too. Is there anything else I can do to help?'

'No, sit tight. I'll call you as soon as I've got answers to those questions.' He ended the call.

Susie gave Nick another kiss. 'I think you've gone right up in his estimation.'

•••●•••

After fifteen minutes, which felt to Susie like two hours, Hawke called back. 'Well, I think we might be in luck.'

'Go on.' Susie got Nick's attention and held up a hand, fingers crossed.

'Mitchel spoke to their duty manager who confirmed they have four cameras, none of them have ANPR technology, but we never thought they would. However, they do record the feeds from all four onto a solid-state hard drive and swap them over every Monday morning. And better still, the videos are time and date stamped, so it'll mean we can go straight to when you arrived and left on Sunday morning.'

'That's got to be good, right?' Susie hesitated, suspecting there was going to be a catch.

'What the duty manager couldn't tell us, was what area of the car park the cameras covered. She was very helpful but said she'd didn't have much to do with them and she would have to get her boss to authorise us seeing the footage.'

'They don't really have much choice, do they?'

'There's probably some data protection laws we'd have to promise to observe, but at the end of the day, no. If we want them, we can force them to hand them over. And that's the next minor issue.'

'Don't tell me you have to wait for her boss to come back from holiday or something stupid?'

'No, it's much simpler than that. They can't send us the video we want over the internet and obviously the post isn't an option. I could search around for a courier, but it would make more sense if you could go there and bring it down to us. Also, it would be helpful to have you with us when we're looking at the footage, you'll be able to tell us what we're looking at'

'Of course. I'll need to scrounge some more fuel from you, but I'd be happy to. If you call them back, say I'll be there in half an hour.' She ended the call and put her phone down. 'Get your coat Mr Cooper, we've got another mission.'

24

Alison Burton-Castle didn't chew her nails when stressed. If she did, she would have been down to the quick by Wednesday lunchtime.

After five hours of frantic activity, she allowed herself time to relax. She sat at the conference table, breathed out and drained her mug of coffee. She'd been on her feet the whole time, pacing from one member of her team to the next as they worked through the list of companies and allocated new identification numbers to all their lines. The process had proved more complicated than she'd imagined, and thrown up issues the team hadn't bargained for, but they had found solutions and were confident they were ready to go as soon as they got the green light.

Burton-Castle tapped her empty mug on the table to silence the hubbub, all eyes turned to her. 'It looks like we've done all we can, I can't thank you all enough. You've gone above and beyond what anyone could expect of you.' She looked at the faces staring back at her, they looked exhausted. 'Just to confirm, all the companies have had an email to let them know new numbers are on their way?' She paused and waited. Nobody said otherwise. She nodded her approval. 'Great, and have any of them come back to you?'

A woman at the far end of the table raised a tentative hand.

'What is it, err...'

'It's Carol.'

'Of course. sorry Carol, what is it?

'I've had a message from one of the companies asking about hard-ware. They're worried about replacement problems.'

Burton-Castle frowned. 'It's OK, they don't have to replace their modems. The tech guys have checked, and the virus is only activated when the original line number is live. Once they have the new numbers, the virus will lie dormant. Their modems are fine.'

Carol nodded and looked at the laptop screen in front of her. She appeared confused and worried.

'You look concerned, doesn't that answer their query?'

'Apparently, it's not the modems they're worried about, it's the data cables.'

It was Burton-Castle's turn to look confused. 'The data cables. Why are they asking about cables?'

'They are all burned out. They all need replacing.'

'Surely that's just a minor issue, isn't it? They just need to run new cables to the modems.'

Carol flushed; she felt the eyes of all those around the table burning into her. She wondered if she had misread the email or if she hadn't understood the problem. 'That's not the problem. Apparently, they don't have enough stock and when they contacted their supplier, there was nothing available.'

The Operations Director said nothing as the implications of Carol's message hit home. 'I can see that would present a problem.' She turned to Holly Holding sat on her right. 'Can you call a few suppliers for me Holly, just see what options are out there.' She paused and addressed the rest of the team. 'We'd better check with all the companies. If they all have to replace the cables, it would be good to know how much stock they have. Meet back here at two.'

Burton-Castle watched her team return to their workstations and offices. She wondered how many more curve balls she would have to deal with.

After grabbing what they could from the in-house cafe, the team returned to the conference table forty minutes later. Their faces told a story and having heard snatches of conversation as she walked around the office, Burton-Castle had an uneasy feeling as she took her seat. 'Who wants to start?'

Chris Durham spoke first. 'My sub-team.' He gestured at the three people sitting next to him. 'Have spoken to seven companies. We asked each of them to check their stock and had to wait for them to call back.'

'And have they all come back to you.'

Durham pulled a face. 'They have, and it's not good news. None of them have got enough cable. They buy it in 100-metre reels, which is fine for any modifications or new lines. They have no reason to keep any more than one reel at a time. To replace the burned-out cables, which is literally all of them, it will take hundreds of metres, and they don't have it.'

Gareth Evans echoed Durham's findings. 'Same here. My lot spoke to six of the bigger companies. It took a couple of them a while to get back to us, but they all admitted they just had bits and bobs, whatever was left on a reel. They only order in when stocks are low, and it's never been a problem.'

Burton-Castle turned to Holly Holding. 'Please tell me you've got some better news from the suppliers.'

Holly shook her head. 'I spoke to five of the big players. Their websites all offer a full range of cables, but when I got through to an actual human, they were all quoting two to three weeks delivery. Their stock comes from the far East.'

'You mean they don't have anything in stock now?'

'A couple of them had some old CAT5 cables, but everyone wants CAT6 or even CAT7. All the good stuff is made in China, probably all in the same factory and they've been unable to get deliveries.'

Burton-Castle fought the overwhelming urge to put her head in her hands and weep. She took a deep breath to calm herself. 'So, even if we could issue new line numbers right now, the system can't return to normal because they can't replace the cables.' She tried to make eye contact with her key team members, but they appeared engrossed in their notes and couldn't meet her gaze. 'This puts a whole new perspective on things. All your hard work in getting numbers ready to go out will be worthless if the companies are unable to go back online.' She leaned forward, elbows on the table, her chin resting on her hands. 'The priority has to be finding supplies of data cables. Can you all get back on the phone, try Amazon, Google, any website you can think of, even eBay, and see what you can find. I can't believe a single manufacturer has got us over a barrel. I'll get in touch with the people who are trying to find my kids and see if they can offer any help.' She gave them all a sympathetic look. 'Sorry to do this to you, but you've seen what's going on out there. We have to do this.'

After an uneventful trip to Starbucks, Susie and Nick headed down to London on the M40. The SSD with the video recordings had been safely tucked into a padded messenger bag on the back seat. Susie kept the speed to a legal 70, partly to avoid the embarrassment of being pulled over and partly to save fuel. Even with a cloudless sky, dusk was upon them by the time they reached the TIGER headquarters, located at the centre of a former military training camp a couple of miles off the M25. Getting to it required passing through no less than three control barriers and going through the same security procedure every time.

'Not taking any chances, are they.' Nick commented as they cleared the final barrier and were pointed in the direction of an unimposing single-storey building.

Susie nodded. 'Probably on high alert after Warrenford, can't blame them.'

At the mention of Warrenford, Nick said. 'That's been bugging me. With all the security and the vetting, how did anyone get in there with whatever they used to blow the place up? And how come nobody noticed any suspicious packages?'

Susie pulled into the parking area in front of the TIGER building and killed the engine. 'I was thinking the same thing, and the only answer I could come up with...'

'Inside job.' Finished Nick.

'You think the same?' Susie unclipped her seat belt and reached for the door handle.

'Absolutely. It would have to be one of the people in that control room.' Nick opened his door, stepped out then reached back inside the car for his stick.

Susie watched him limp around to join her. 'I thought your leg was better, you'd done away with the stick earlier.'

'Ahhah.' Said Nick with a flourish and waved the stick in the air. 'I may not need it, but you have to admit, it adds a certain air of authority.' He pulled a few fencing moves, thrusts and parries. 'And it came in very useful the other night.'

Susie gave him a dubious look.

'Anyway,' Nick continued as the pair approached the entrance to the building. 'I was going to ask how well did you know the rest of the team?'

Susie shrugged. 'Not that well. It's not like we went socialising. The girls and I would have a little banter, but Rob Eddington and Wade Millard were, work, work, work – there was no chit-chat or small talk with them.'

'What about the two tech guys? Don't think I didn't notice you flirting with one of them.' He nudged Susie with his elbow.

'Later.' Susie hushed him as the pair entered the building and were greeted by more security. They were asked the same questions they'd already been asked multiple times, then had to empty their pockets and pass through an airport-style scanner. Susie explained about the SSD and insisted it wasn't subjected to the X-Ray machine. This caused a short stand-off until she invoked Commander Hawke's name and suddenly, they were cleared.

One of the security staff escorted them along a corridor until they reached a set of doors. He pressed a button on the wall and the doors slid open to reveal a lift.

Nick was taken aback. 'Hang on, this is a single-storey building, there's no first floor.'

The security guard tapped the side of his nose. 'You're not going up mate. You're going down.' He emphasised the last word and pointed at the floor with a mischievous grin.

Susie and Nick were ushered into the lift without their escort. The door closed, the lift dropped for a few seconds, the door opened, and they found themselves in another dimension. At least that's how it felt.

It was what Susie imagined a Tactical Intelligence operations room would look and feel like. Subdued dark green lighting, a wall on one side made up of ten huge monitors, two rows of four workstations – more like booths- all facing the TV wall, each with two or three regular-sized monitors, more red and green LEDs flashing and blinking, and everywhere the quiet hum of cooling fans and air conditioning and the ever-present buzz of electrical current. Six or seven people were quietly getting on with their work, none of them turned to look at the new arrivals. The place screamed high-tech and top secret. Susie was awestruck.

Commander Hawke appeared out of the shadows. 'Hello, you two. Glad you've made it.' He spotted the bag Nick was carrying. 'Is that it?'

Nick nodded.

'Great. Follow me, we're all ready for you.' He led them to the far end of the room where one of his technical team sat waiting. 'This is Oliver, he's my number one tech guy. If you give him the drive, he'll run from here and project it on that screen.' Hawke pointed at the leftmost screen on the top row of the wall, it currently displayed its screensaver, the TIGER logo.

Oliver acknowledged Hawke's introduction and without a word took the drive Nick handed to him.

Hawke let Oliver do what he needed to do and indicated to Susie and Nick to step away from the workstation and join him out of earshot. 'I've had a call from Alison, not good news.'

Susie's hand shot to her mouth. 'Not the kids?'

'No, nothing like that.' He held up a placating hand. 'It's a more practical problem.' He took a couple of minutes to summarise the issue with the data cables. 'It looks to me as if the people who instigated this mess, have either bought out all the available stock, or the manufacturers are linked to it, either directly or indirectly.'

Susie's head shook from side to side. 'As if we haven't got enough to deal with. Have you had a chance to make any enquiries?'

'Not yet. She called just before you arrived. I'll get someone on to it in a minute. I want to see what's on that drive. See if it gives us any clues about where they might be holding the kids.' He led them back to Oliver. 'Are we good to go Olly?'

Oliver's eyes never left his monitor. 'All sorted.' He pressed a few keys and clicked his mouse and the Starbucks logo appeared on the big screen. He looked up at Susie who stood beside him. 'The boss told me what we're looking for. What's the date and time of your arrival?'

Susie squinted as she recalled events from Sunday lunchtime. 'It's the 24th and I think it was about 12:30 when I got there.'

'OK.' Oliver clicked the mouse and the images from the cameras came up as a four-square grid. Using a trackball, he scrubbed the slider at the bottom of the screen to the right, and the pictures blurred as he raced through the previous six days to arrive at Sunday. He adjusted the sensitivity of the slider and moved it in increments until the time stamp showed 12:30.

All of their attention switched to the big screen.

The images showed four different angles of the car park, including one covering the drive-thru, all black and white, all frozen in time. Oliver pressed the play icon, and the images moved. The quality was sub-standard but good enough to make out the registration numbers of the parked cars. They watched for a full minute, and nothing happened. They could see the trees in the background swaying in the breeze, so they knew the video was still playing. Just as their patience was about to expire, Susie made them all jump. 'Look, that's me.' She pointed to the bottom right-hand image. They watched as the old Volvo reversed into a parking space. The front of the Volvo was visible in one of the other images, and they could follow Susie as she left the car and walked into the building.

Hawke interrupted. 'How long did you have to wait until the two women arrived?'

'It felt like ages. I'd finished my drink by the time they showed up.'

Oliver said. 'OK, I'll scrub it forward 15 minutes.'

The images blurred again as Oliver's fingers moved the controller, they watched the timestamp advance, then stop at 1247. Four pairs of eyes scanned the images, no sign of the BMW in any of them.

'How well can you recall the layout of the car park in relation to those camera angles?' Hawke didn't take his eyes off the screen.

Nick understood the question. 'You're thinking about blind spots?'

'I am. Did you notice we didn't see Susie drive into the car park? It looks like none of the cameras cover the entrance.'

Susie cocked her head as she looked at the four images and tried to picture the layout. 'Have you got a piece of paper? I'll draw a rough sketch, then we can plot the camera angles.'

Oliver produced a sheet of A4 and handed Susie a pencil. She studied the four images for a moment then found a flat surface to rest on, she drew lines to represent the edges of the car park, an oblong box to represent the building, an arrow to indicate the position of the main entrance and another arrow to show the entrance to the car park from the main road.

She laid the sketch on the end of Oliver's desk and all four looked from the images on the screen to her plan. They quickly worked out where each of the camera were sited and what areas they covered. By the time they'd finished, camera angles were denoted by dotted lines and hatched areas showed the blind spots.

The screen still showed the images at 12:47.

Hawke tapped Oliver on the shoulder. 'Scrub it as slow as you can.'

The images jerked. It wasn't a fluid video, it looked like one frame every couple of seconds instead of the more usual 24 frames per second. When played at normal speed, it would have resembled an old-fashioned silent movie, with figures walking too fast. Oliver rotated the trackball a couple of degrees and the action, or lack of it, moved forward a few seconds at a time.

'Stop.' Susie made them jump again.

The images froze. Nick glanced sideways at Susie. 'What?'

Susie pointed at the bottom left-hand image. 'See there?' She pointed at a pale shape on the very edge of the picture.

Hawke swapped his attention from the screen to Susie's sketch. 'That's camera 3' he placed his finger on the plan and ran it along the angle they'd marked until it came to one of the hatched areas. He tapped it and spoke. 'If that is the BMW, those women were either very well trained in counter-surveillance, or they were dead lucky.'

Nick stared at the screen. 'I know we couldn't see it enter the car park, but you'd think it would cross in front of...' He looked down at the plan. 'In front of camera 4 to get there.'

'Olly, just back it up a couple of frames, we may have missed it.' Hawke said.

The previous frames showed no sign of the BMW.

Susie frowned. 'They must have driven in at a hell of a speed and gone straight there. If that is them?'

'We might have more luck when they leave and set off after you.' Hawke tapped Oliver's shoulder again. 'Move it forward another five minutes.'

Oliver did as instructed until they saw camera 2 capturing Susie as she jogged back to the Volvo.

'Right,' Susie said. 'They came out of the building a few seconds after me and went straight to their car.'

They watched as the Volvo accelerated out of its parking bay and waited for a glimpse of the BMW. 'If they parked nose in, they'll have to reverse out and turn. We should be able to see them properly.' Hawke leaned forward and watched all four images with the focus of a cat stalking its prey.

The BMW appeared in the camera 4 image, sideways on, travelling backwards at speed. It flashed across the screen. Oliver paused the image and then advanced the video frame by frame. They could clearly see the tyre smoke from a rear wheel as the driver floored the accelerator to chase after Susie. The car turned right to head for the exit, and they caught a flash of the rear number plate. Oliver rocked the trackball backwards and forwards to find the clearest image. He settled on the best one and froze the screen again.

All four peered at the plate. 'Is it just my eyesight, or is that blurred beyond recognition?' Nick squinted at the image.

'Can you zoom in on the plate Olly.' Hawke, like Nick, could make no sense of the numbers and letters.

Even when the number plate filled the screen, none of them were confident about what they saw. 'Is it possible to enhance it all?" Susie asked.

Oliver shook his head. 'Sorry, the quality isn't there. It pre-dates 4K. There's just not enough resolution in the image to do anything with i t.'

'The back end of the car must have been moving sideways when the image was taken.' Nick rubbed his chin and tipped his head to one side. 'First letter looks like an F or an E, second one could be an M or an N or maybe a W.'

Susie copied Nicks head tilt. 'That's actually a little clearer, the two numbers look like 16 or 18, the first one's definitely a 1.'

Hawke copied them both. 'I think your eyesight's better than mine, it's all a blur to me.'

'The last three letters are even more indistinct.' Nick continued to study the screen. 'If I had to guess, it could be something like SGP, then again it could be ZCB or something like that.' He straightened up and turned to Hawke. 'Is that enough for your database to search?'

Hawke folded his arms and pursed his lips. He asked Susie. 'You're sure it was a 3 series?'

'Absolutely, no doubt at all.'

'It's not the most common car, and it's a popular colour. We can narrow the search down to just silver BM 3 series and if you're right about the year, 16 or 18, that'll narrow it down further.

'Even then you're going to be looking at what? Hundreds? Thousands?' Susie grasped the size of the problem.

'Probably hundreds. If we select only those registered within say, 100 miles, then we might get down to less than a hundred. The tricky bit is the letters.'

Oliver chipped in. 'I can run a program that will run random permutations of suggested letters. It wouldn't take long. I'm not making any promises, but I'd be surprised if we can't get it down to less than a dozen.'

Hawke brightened visibly. 'Excellent Olly, get onto it. We'll be in the bunker if you need us.' He signalled for Susie and Nick to follow him.

25

Noah Burton-Castle didn't sleep. Not because he was worried, but because his mind was too active. He hated being held captive, but he wasn't going to let his situation get to him. Quite the opposite; he used the pressure to come up with schemes, to plot a way out, to find a way to get a message to his Mum. The fact that he hadn't thought of anything, didn't worry him, it simply meant he hadn't come up with the right solution, yet. He loved his spy novels and was sure the heroes and heroines of his stories would find a way to escape.

Without a phone, a watch, or even a clock on the wall, Noah had no idea of the time, or exactly how long he and his sister had been down in the basement. He could only assume that they were being fed when their captors ate, and by his reckoning, they'd been there for two and a half days. The routine was predictable and hadn't varied since they had first been led down the steps. Every morning, noon and night, the woman who had carried him down to the basement, would enter the room and hold Noah and Jenny at the far side of the room while another woman who looked like she lived at the house, brought a tray in, placed it on an upturned box in the centre of the room and took away the leftovers from the previous offering. Neither of the women said a word and never responded when Noah asked them a question. They never said hello or returned his greeting. He was grateful, at least, that the food was edible, not much in the way of fresh veg, but he could survive on pizza and chips for a few days without complaint. He knew it could be a lot worse.

Without windows, he had no way of knowing for certain if it was night or day. His body clock told him it was time to sleep, but he remained alert and occupied himself reading old survival magazines he'd found piled in one corner of the basement. He found them interesting but sadly not much help in his present circumstances. They had a camp bed each, the only furniture in the room, excluding the upturned box that doubled as a table, and he sat on his bed and tried to think. He looked across at his sister and wondered if she was asleep.

Jenny lay on her camp bed. he couldn't tell if she was awake or not. He knew she was bored and miserable. Deprived of her mobile phone for the first time in years, she didn't know what to do with herself. She'd screamed, she'd cried, she'd banged on the door until her hands bled. She complained about privacy and hygiene; the toilet was a simple affair behind a curtain in one corner, and it had been over 48 hours since she'd had a shower. On top of that, she'd been wearing the same clothes all that time.

Noah wanted to protect his big sister. She made fun of his flights of fancy, the books he read, and his dreams of being a secret agent. This was his chance to prove himself.

Their evening meal had been delivered hours ago and he didn't expect anyone to come down to the basement until the morning, so when he heard footsteps, he was immediately wary. The footsteps stopped when they reached the door and he waited for it to open. Nothing happened.

He tiptoed across the room to the door and placed his ear against it. He listened. He couldn't be sure, but it sounded like breathing.

With a single knuckle, he tapped quietly on the door next to his ear and whispered. 'Hello. Anyone there?'

He heard a faint response. 'It's Pia, stand back from the door.'

Noah knew who Pia was, did what she asked and took a few steps back. He waited and watched. He wondered if this was his chance to escape.

The door opened slowly and quietly; Pia poked her head around to see where he stood. She put a finger to her lips.

Noah stood still and nodded; he saw no threat.

Pia entered the room, still holding the door. She pushed it almost shut, leaving a one-inch gap, just big enough for her fingers.

'What do you want?' Noah whispered as she came closer.

'I want to help you.'

'Help us escape?'

'I wish I could, but they will find out.' She pointed to the ceiling by way of explanation.

Noah looked confused. 'But how can you help?'

She pulled a mobile phone from her back pocket. 'You can send a message to your Mum. Tell her you're all right.'

'OK.' He held his hand out for the phone.

'Be quick, it's not my phone, if they wake up and find me down here, I'll be in big trouble.'

Noah typed quickly. 'I want to tell her where we are, but I don't know.'

They heard movement in the room above them. Pia grabbed the phone back. 'Don't worry, I'll send this. Don't say anything.' She put a finger to her lips again, slipped out and locked the door behind her.

Jenni stirred and turned to Noah bleary-eyed 'Who was that?'

'It was Pia, she's trying to help us.'

When her phone pinged with the arrival of a text message, Alison Burton-Castle stirred from a fitful sleep.

Half-awake, she reached for the device, its screen still illuminated, and stared, uncomprehending, at the time: 03:32 a.m. Without lifting her head from the pillow, she squinted at the notification. She didn't recognise the sender's number, but the first few words of the message made her sit up with a sharp intake of breath.

mum its noah me an jen are...

With trembling fingers, she tapped the message to open it fully.

mum its noah me an jen are ok in a basement dont no where send help

She read the message twice more, Noah's punctuation had never been his strong point but for once she didn't care and promised herself, she'd never mention it again. She was about to reply when the phone pinged again.

pleese no reply they will find out

Burton-Castle threw the covers off, reached for her dressing gown and headed for the spare bedroom, her tiredness forgotten. She heard Don before entering the room, his snoring reverberated off the walls. She sat on the edge of his bed and shook him. 'Don, Don, I've had a message from Noah. Wake up Don.'

Her partner groaned. 'What is it? What have you woken me for? What time is it?'

She repeated herself. 'Noah's sent a message, he and Jenni are all right.' She held the phone in front of his face.

He blinked the sleep from his eyes and tried to focus on the screen. He gave up and reached for his reading glasses. 'Oh, thank God.' He murmured after a moment.

'Aren't you pleased?' She looked at him suspiciously.

'Of course, I am. It's just a bit of a shock to be woken in the middle of the night with news like that.' He made no attempt to lift his head off the pillow.

She stood up and read the messages again. 'I'm going to send this to Commander Hawke and Susie, it's the breakthrough they've been waiting for.'

Don rubbed his eyes and muttered. 'It's not much help to them, he hasn't said where he is.'

'I'm sure they'll have whatever it takes to find them. At least we've got the sender's number, they'll be able to trace it from that.' She gave him a withering look and left the room.

26

'Have you got the message from Alison?' Susie's voice conveyed the excitement she felt.

Hawke responded in a more measured tone. 'Affirmative. It arrived at about four this morning. I didn't see it until five thirty.'

'You did better than me, it was after seven when I woke up. We didn't get in until after midnight.'

'Not a problem. You were late leaving here. I thought I'd better give you time to surface before I called. If the message is genuine, it makes the search for the BMW almost irrelevant.'

'Is there any doubt about it?'

'Alison knows how the boy texts. She's 100% convinced it's the real deal.'

'Any idea how he did it?'

'Not a clue. I guess we'll have to wait until we find him.'

'Are you able to locate where the message came from?' Susie sounded anxious.

'They're working on it now; the network provider is triangulating the call. They won't be able to pinpoint the exact location, but they said they can narrow it down to about a square mile. After that, it's up to us to search.'

'Just have to hope it's not the middle of a town.'

'Precisely.' Hawke said.

'Will you let me know when you get a result?'

'Of course. And by the way. In case you're interested. Oliver's software did the trick, we found that BMW. All those miles you and Nick put in yesterday weren't wasted.'

'Well, that's something at least. What did you discover?'

'Bit of a long story. The plates belonged to a Renault stolen in Staines a week ago. The BMW was stolen in Watford around the same time. It took a bit of detective work to put it together but, like I said, this message changes everything.'

Susie pondered the information. 'Someone's going to a lot of effort here to make sure we can't find them.'

Hawke continued. 'They are, but we'll get them in the end. I've got one more update for you.'

'Data cables?'

'You're one step ahead of me. Alison forwarded the list of suppliers they had contacted, and we put a bit of pressure on them. We've discovered over the last month that they've all had orders far in excess of normal. As we suspected, someone's been buying up data cables as if they were going out of fashion.'

'Could they tell you who the buyers were?'

'They weren't keen, but really, they had no choice. We got five names, all fake companies, addresses all over the home counties, all either empty or convenience offices. We also checked with some of the big retail chains, and they've done a roaring over-the-counter cash trade no paper trail. Somebody somewhere has got deep pockets and must have container loads of cables.

'Bloody hell. This gets worse everyday Alex.'

'Not necessarily, there's a team from the fraud office doing what they can to identify the buyers. I think we're making progress. I'll call you when we've got a better idea where those two kids are being held.'

The phone clicked off and for the first time in four days, Susie felt as if there was light at the end of the tunnel.

The lights on the drone flickered and four propellors whirred into action. Sounding like a swarm of angry bees, the machine rocketed skyward and within seconds had virtually disappeared. Unless you knew where to look it was almost impossible to see it, and at 300 feet, it was inaudible.

Susie craned her neck to look over the operator's shoulder. 'What's its range?'

'About 3 miles, 4 miles with clear line of sight.' The pilot, as he liked to be called, concentrated on the control console and its monitor. He didn't turn to look at Susie. 'It can stay up for about 45 minutes before it has to come back to base for new batteries.' He sat on a folding chair twenty yards from the others and held the console between his hands, its weight taken by a strap around his neck. The forefinger and thumb of each hand rested lightly on a left and right joystick. The monitor showed a live view from the drone's forward camera, angled down, showing the terrain below.

Susie turned to Nick who stood a few yards away talking to Commander Hawke. 'It's like that one of yours, except it's bigger and got a few more controls.'

'And a few more noughts on the price.' Nick replied.

The phone company had worked fast and within three hours had sent a map outlining the area the message had been sent from. They were all relieved to find it looked to be fairly unpopulated with only 15 dwellings within its boundary. Hawke's team checked out each of the dwellings through online records, electoral rolls and any other official channels they could access. They all checked out as innocent and were ruled out as the source of the text. The drone – or the UAV as the pilot insisted it should be called - was the final part of the process, searching the more inaccessible places, even though nothing was indicated on the map. They didn't discount the possibility of a caravan, a mobile home or even a disused cottage, anywhere that might harbour hostages and their captors.

The pilot, stuck to an agreed search pattern, and flew the drone South to North and back again, each track 400 yards further East. The image on his control screen repeated on a monitor in the back of Hawke's Land Rover. They had parked on the edge of a field just off a quiet lane to one side of the search area and had a printed copy of the map alongside the screen. As the drone turned at the end of each track, Mitchel drew a line with a red marker pen, to signify nothing of interest.

Susie walked back to join Nick, Commander Hawke and Mitchel, and the four of them focused on the screen, each determined to be the one to spot what they were looking for.

Hawke spoke quietly to Mitchel. 'What's his name?' He jerked his head in the direction of the pilot.

'Jake'

Hawke turned to the pilot. 'Jake, how much lower can you go without being noticed?'

'I could drop to 250 feet, but the air's fairly still, so if anyone's outside and they're quiet, there's a chance they could hear something.'

'Understood.' Hawke stepped back and looked at the sky, he could see little movement in the few grey clouds but estimated there was still enough light for the drone's camera to pick out potential targets, even at 300 feet. 'Keep it at 300 for the last four passes. If we don't see anything, we'll have to go lower.'

The pilot responded. 'Copy that. I'm going to have to return to base for new batteries in ten minutes anyway.'

After another minute, Nick spotted it first. Either his photographer's eye or his sense of perspective, but he stabbed at the monitor. 'There, what's that?'

The other three leaned closer to the screen.

'Hold up, Jake.' Hawke called to the pilot. 'Can you come back a bit and zoom in on that light coloured shape, it looks out of place.'

They watched the monitor as the drone reversed its path then went into hover mode. The camera rotated down a few more degrees and refocused on the object Nick had seen. The image enlarged as the telephone lens did its job. 'It's a house.' Susie exclaimed.

'I don't bloody believe it.' Hawke stared at the image. 'Someone was paying attention in class when they taught effective camouflage. You can see the outline of the building now, but they've disguised the straight edges with netting or tarps.'

Nick added. 'That light-coloured shape is the roof, reflecting the low sunlight. Blink and you'd miss it.'

Hawke called to the pilot again. 'I don't suppose you've got thermal imaging on that machine?'

'Certainly do, Commander. Two seconds.'

The image changed from full colour to shades or red, yellow and orange, the warmer areas showed brighter, and the colder areas darker.

'Good grief. There's two vehicles there.' Mitchel couldn't help but comment. The camouflage netting was no barrier to the infrared camera and a saloon car, and a van were clearly visible as bright white objects.

Nick peered closer. 'I'm trying to see a track, a way in and out. Nothing is showing on the map.'

Susie tapped the monitor. 'There's no lights showing, but there must be people in there if there are cars. And the cars wouldn't show up so bright unless they were still warm from recent use. So...that has to be the place, they are doing everything to remain undetected.'

Hawke nodded in agreement and turned back to the pilot. 'Can you give us a 360-degree look at it, Jake, but from a lower angle?'

'No problem.' Jake appeared to relish the fact that his skills were being recognised.

The image changed as the drone descended, the camera rotated up slightly to keep the property in the centre, and then, as the drone flew in a wide circle, they could see all the elevations and details they had missed from the steeper perspective.

'I'm going to have to return to base, Commander. Batteries are running low.' Jake called after two minutes of orbiting the cottage.

'Go ahead Jake, bring it home. Excellent work. I take it you've marked the location on the map.' His last comment directed at Mitchel.

Mitchel nodded; he tapped the marker pen on the map where he'd circled the location of the cottage.

Hawke checked his watch and then switched his attention to the western sky. 'It's 1548 now, sunset in, what 40 minutes? Susie, Nick and Mitchel shrugged or nodded and waited. 'We need a team up here to go in. And I don't mean storm the place. If those two kids are in there, which I think we can agree has to be the case, we can't do anything to put them at risk.'

'You're assuming they're armed, and they'll put up a fight.' Susie said, more a statement than a question.

'I think we can take that as read. If these are the people behind the Warrenford explosion, I'm taking no chances.'

Nick considered the problem. 'Have you got anything between an assault team and a hostage negotiator?'

'I'm thinking of one unit in particular, they're special forces with all the skills you'd expect, but they take stealth to the next level. They're trained for just this sort of situation, this is right up their street.'

He was interrupted by the incessant buzz of the drone returning to base. They watched as it swooped in, its automatic guidance system stopped it in a hover for a moment then it slowly settled onto a six-foot square target, Jake had pinned to the ground a few yards from his chair. Safely landed, the motors stopped, and silence returned.

'They've found the kids.' Alison Burton-Castle burst into the living room where Don had moved to. He lay on the sofa, "resting". The bandage on his head had been replaced by a sticking plaster. He appeared to be engrossed in one of the Indiana Jones films, he must have seen a dozen times before. He didn't take his eyes off the TV. 'That's great Ally. Where are they?'

Burton-Castle, stopped in her tracks, stunned by his response. 'Is that all you've got to say?'

Without turning to see her reaction, he replied. 'What else can I say, it's great news, you must be relieved.'

'Relieved?' she shouted. 'I don't believe you sometimes.' She stepped forward to block Don's view, snatched the remote from the coffee table and clicked the TV off.

'Hey, what d'you do that for, I was watching that, it's just getting to the best bit.' His tone had echoes of a whinging child.

She resisted the urge to throw the remote, or something heavier, at him. 'For God's sake, it's on every bloody Christmas, you must know the script inside and out. How about taking the same level of interest in the welfare of Jenni and Noah. They've been held prisoner for almost four days. I hate to think what they've gone through.

'Yeah. OK. Sorry. It's been tough for you too Ally.' Don adopted a more conciliatory tone.

'Jesus Don. Tough? Is that what you think?' She folded her arms and stared at him. 'As if having your kids abducted wasn't bad enough, the whole online payment system in the country has been held to ransom and I'm the one responsible for sorting it out.' She paused and gave him a withering look. 'And how much support have you been?'

'Hang on a minute.' Don raised a hand to the side of his head. 'I was assaulted. At any other time, I'd have been in hospital.'

'Oh, spare me the dramatics. You've got a bit of a cut. There's nothing wrong with you. You need to man up.'

Don's face twisted at the reprimand. He changed tack. 'So, where did they find the kids?'

Burton-Castle was about to leave the room. She slowed and looked back at him. 'Apparently, they've been held in some place in the middle of nowhere.'

'And are they OK?'

'Well. Thanks for your concern.' She said, mollified. 'I don't know yet. Susie Jones has just been on the phone. They located the place the text message came from, and they are preparing a specialist team to raid the place. They plan to go in at two in the morning to rescue them.'

Don reacted to this news with shock. 'I don't like the sound of raid.'

'What? Would you rather they walked up to the front door, knock politely and said, "Excuse me, have you got two children held hostage and if so can we have them back."'

'Of course not, I just don't like the idea of a firefight and them getting caught in the crossfire.'

'Nor do I, but Susie assured me that the people going in, are the best in the business, and the kids' safety is their priority.' She shuddered momentarily and checked her watch. 'We just have to wait seven hours and trust they'll be OK.' She left Don looking worried and left the room.

27

The credits rolled at the end of "Indiana Jones and the Last Crusade". Miles Wilson nudged Harrison Thurlow who sat next to him on the sofa. He'd fallen asleep watching the film and reacted to the nudge by lashing out as if woken from a bad dream.

'Whoa. Steady on there boy, you'll do yourself an injury.' Wilson ducked to avoid being hit.

Harrison shook himself awake. The effect of six cans of strong lager, still lingered, his eyes swam as he tried to focus. 'You could have just left me. Why did you do that?'

'It's getting late and some of us have had a busy day and would like some shut-eye.'

'I'm not stopping you.' Harrison gave a half shrug; it was as much effort as he could manage.

'Maybe not, but there's things to do and you need to lock up and set the alarm.'

'What's the bloody point, nobody knows about this place, they'd never find it. You're the one who wanted to fit alarms, why don't you go and set them.'

Wilson got to his feet. 'I would if I could, but you've never shared the codes, so you'll have to do it.'

Harrison groaned with the effort of getting off the sofa. He muttered and mumbled and looked at where he'd been lying, a confused look on his face.

'You lost something?' His dad asked.

'My phone.' He patted his pockets in case it was there and he couldn't feel it. 'I thought I had it on me.'

Wilson scanned the room, his head on a swivel. "When did you last have it?'

'Dunno, before the film started.' With an effort, Harrison lowered himself to the floor, peered under the sofa and reached into the dark, his hand sweeping back and forth. 'Got it.' He proclaimed with a mild sense of triumph. He struggled back to his feet, gave the phone a cursory glance and jammed it into the back pocket of his combat pants.

A phone rang, and the pair looked at each other unsure whose it was as they both had the same ringtone. They both reached for their phones and gave a self-conscious chuckle when they realised how they looked.

Wilson held his up. 'It's me.' He accepted the call and listened. The smile on his face vanished immediately to be replaced by concern, then alarm. 'Oh shit.' He looked over at Harrison as he continued to listen and started to shake his head. 'How the hell?' One exclamation followed another. 'Yes. Understood. Will do.' The call ended, and Wilson slumped, his face drained of colour.

Harrison frowned. 'Who the hell was that?'

'Our Russian friend. He's had a message to say they've found this place.'

'No way.' Harrison shouted. 'There's no way they could find us nobody knows about it apart from us.'

'I don't know how they did it, but they are planning to raid us at two in the morning.'

'Fuck. I bloody knew this would happen. I've kept off grid and undetected all this time, then you come along with this crazy scheme and within a couple of days...' Harrison stomped around the room as he ranted. When he paused, he confronted his father. 'What am I supposed to do now then?'

Wilson couldn't meet his son's accusing stare. He looked down at the floor. 'He wants us to set fire to all the merchandise and get out of here before they raid the place.'

Harrison clenched his fists in front of his chest, they shook with rage. 'No fucking way. There's tens of thousands of pounds worth in those containers, we stand to make an absolute killing in a few days.'

'Sorry son. but we have to do as he says.'

'You might have to. I've never met him; he doesn't know me. You can fuck off with those two girls but I'm not leaving this place.'

'You're forgetting the two kids.' Wilson jerked a thumb at the bookcase as if he needed to explain. 'That's what they're coming for. Anything that gets in the way will just be collateral damage.'

'Bollocks. They can take the kids, they've served their purpose, you said so yourself. They don't know about the containers.'

'Don't be so naive. If you're here when they come knocking, and they find the kids, you're going to get arrested. Even if they don't find the containers, you'll still be in a shit load of trouble.'

Harrison considered this briefly. 'OK then, you take the kids. The worst they could charge me with is violation of planning regs. All those cables were bought legally. I'm not going to prison just for that.'

Wilson scoffed. 'I'm not taking the kids. If they've got this place under surveillance they'll know if we take the kids out. And besides, I've got work to do, I can't be nannying a couple of bloody kids.'

'They won't see you leave if you use the tunnel, just release them in the woods and let them get on with it.'

'Brilliant. So, the kids wander off, bump into whoever is supposed to be rescuing them, point them at this place and tell them about you. Any more bright ideas?'

Harrison opened his mouth to reply, gave a resigned sigh, turned and took a couple of steps towards the kitchen. He stopped and glanced back at the bookcase that hid the door to the basement. 'You'd never guess that was there, would you?'

'The door?'

'Yeah, the door. Unless you knew it existed, you'd never find it.' Harrison rubbed the side of his face, an idea forming.

Wilson stood back from the bookcase and studied the wall around it. 'True enough. You've done a damn fine job of blending it in, you can't see the join.' He paused and turned to Harrison. 'Are you thinking what I think you're thinking?'

Harrison held a hand out towards the bookcase, palm up, as if he were a salesman trying to convince a potential buyer about the value of this wonderful piece of furniture. 'They can shout and scream as much as they like down there. It's soundproof, the door has got four inches of insulation behind it.'

'So, we leave the kids in there and get out through the tunnel?'

'No, you leave. I'm staying here with Pia. Besides someone has to stay behind to close up the tunnel entrance after you get out and also stop the kids getting out. Also, someone needs to close up the door to the basement.'

'You're taking a hell of a risk son.'

'It's better than giving up and losing everything. I can let whoever it is come in and search the place, act all innocent and offended. They apologise for the inconvenience and leave us alone. Next day I blindfold the kids, take them a few miles away and drop them off. Job done.'

Wilson jiggled his head from side to side. 'If it works, it's a win, win. It's a big if, but it's probably the best idea if you're happy with it.'

'I'm not happy, but there's no better option.' Harrison pulled his phone out and checked the time. 'You've only got a couple of hours you'd better start getting your kit together.'

Nick saw the lights coming up the road and tapped Susie on the shoulder. 'This must be them.'

They sat in the old Volvo, parked alongside Hawke's Discovery, wrapped in the sleeping bags and blankets they'd brought with them in the event of a stakeout.

Susie didn't need to see where Nick was looking, the beams of light from the approaching vehicle lit up the countryside, and she couldn't miss it. Their vision, attuned to the darkness, was abruptly shot to pieces. She shielded her eyes from the glare. 'I thought Alex said these guys were masters of stealth.'

'Give 'em a break love, they've scooted over here from Hereford in the middle of the night and that cottage is well over a mile away.'

Susie conceded the point. 'Guess so, I was enjoying seeing so many stars. Doesn't happen very often.'

They watched as the vehicle slowed, then turned into the field and came to a stop beside the Discovery. Susie's brow furrowed. 'What sort of machine is that?'

Nick studied it. 'It's a new one on me. Looks like a cross between a minibus and an armoured car. Those guys always have something special, prototypes, one-offs and pre-production models they test out. I suppose they're used to jumping out of aeroplanes or being dropped off by helicopter. Must really nark them having to go by road.'

They stayed in the Volvo and watched as three pairs of doors opened, and eight men climbed out. Hawke approached the men and shook hands with the one Susie assumed must be the one in charge. Hawke looked towards them and made come and join us signals. Susie and Nick shrugged off their warm blankets and went to meet the team they'd heard so much about.

'Susie, Nick, this is Matt. Matt these guys have been involved in this from the start. They're civilians, but both are ex-army and are still reservists and they were both almost blown up on Friday night.'

Matt acknowledged them both with a polite nod. 'Pleased to meet you.'

Hawke continued. 'These lads,' He swept his hand through an arc. 'Are the rest of SU6, Shadow Unit 6, also known as the Ghostwalkers .
'

The men chatted amongst themselves as Susie, without making it too obvious, cast a surreptitious eye over them. Even in the little light from the back of Hawke's Discovery, none of them were overly large, but they all looked lean and deadly serious. As she expected they wore black combat clothing, she assumed they'd left body armour, helmets and weapons in their vehicle.

Mitchel, with the help of Jake, the drone pilot, had erected a pop-up gazebo to act as the command centre. They had sited it about twenty yards away from the vehicles and equipped it with a table and a couple of battery powered lights. The roof and walls of the gazebo were made of light-absorbing blackout material, preventing internal light from escaping and making it virtually invisible in the dark. Mitchel had outlined the location of the cottage on a large-scale plan and annotated it with what details they'd been able to ascertain from the drone's camera feed. Jake had flown the drone back to the cottage and got as close as he dared. As a result, they'd been able to plot the track that led into the property and identify doors and windows.

Hawke led the way to the ad-hoc command centre and waited until everyone had found space around the table before he started. 'We're here,' He tapped a spot on the plan with his finger. 'The target is here.' His finger moved to the top end of the plan and tapped an area circled by a red marker pen. 'That's just short of three thousand metres.' He looked up. He had the undivided attention of everyone around the table. 'The target is a two-storey building, it's not shown on any maps, so we have to assume it's been built recently and illegally. There are no plans registered with the local authority.'

'Structure and entry points, what do we know?' One of the SU6 men asked.

'Not a great deal.' Hawke confessed. 'You can see what we've been able to deduce from the notes. It's been well disguised, doesn't show up on Google Earth, it took eagle eyes here,' Hawke indicated Nick with a flick of his thumb, 'to spot it. The thermal imaging camera on the drone was able to identify the location of the doors and windows. The drone also identified spoil heaps that would indicate there's been a fair amount of digging, but we've been unable to figure out what they've done. They get top marks for concealment.

The Ghostwalkers studied the plan and conferred among themselves. One of them asked, 'What is there in the way of cover?'

Hawke turned to Mitchel with a raised eyebrow.

'There's woodland about thirty metres to the East.' Mitchel reached under the table for a spare tent pole and used it to point out each area as he spoke. 'There are gullies running North, South, here and here. And there are the remains of three outbuildings, here. They're little more than a pile of stones but they will provide cover.'

Hawke added. 'We'll show you the drone footage in a minute. You'll see for yourselves.'

Matt shifted his attention from the plan to his team. 'Thoughts so far?'

'The cover isn't a problem, 'One of the men commented, he checked with his buddies on either side of him, who both nodded. 'but what do we know about the layout inside?'

Matt turned to Hawke. 'I think we need to see that footage before we can make a plan.'

Mitchel, at a signal from his boss, opened his laptop and played the edited and enhanced footage taken by the drone. The SU6 men crowded around, watched and commented as the building and its surroundings were shown from all angles. They watched it through twice and paused it whenever they identified anything of note, either a potential source of danger or something they could use to their advantage. The process took over half an hour. Hawke stayed with them but left it to the team to work out their tactics.

They pushed the laptop aside and concentrated on the plan. Matt produced a black marker pen and, with input from the rest of his team, added arrows to indicate the routes each pair of men would follow as they approached the property. Susie could see they would have the place surrounded by the time they were all in position. Matt tapped the end of the marker pen on the plan, he appeared to be searching for a solution.

'What's up?' Susie couldn't help but ask.

'They don't know you found them, right?'

Susie nodded.

'So, obviously, they're not expecting us?'

More nods.

'So, we can assume they'll all be tucked up in bed, sleeping in blissful ignorance of what is about to happen.'

Hawke listened to the to and fro. 'I'd put money on them posting a lookout. I would.'

Matt considered this and nodded his agreement. 'It would make sense. In normal circumstance, if they were expecting us, we'd blow the windows and go in that way. But if do that here we could get spotted by a lookout before we get to the building, and that would put the kids at risk. If they are as tactically aware as they are at concealment, then it's not a risk worth taking.'

'So...what are you thinking?' Susie, ever inquisitive.

'I'm thinking we need to draw them out, make them show their hand.' Matt folded his arms and focused on the plan. 'If we're in position where I've indicated, nobody can get out without us seeing them. If there is someone on stag, we need to know.' He checked with his team, and no one disagreed.

'If we created some sort of diversion without giving away our positions...'

'...They'd blow their cover if they responded in any way.' One of the team finished.

'Exactly.'

'If we're approaching the place under cover, we don't want to be compromised by looking out for the stag.' The same guy added. 'We need someone in a forward OP on the comms network.'

Susie jumped in. 'I can do that; I've done observation duty before.'

'Hang on a sec.' Nick intervened. 'You can't go out putting yourself in danger.'

'I'd just be observing, where's the danger?'

Hawke agreed with Nick. 'He's right Susie, I can't put you at risk if it turns into a firefight.'

'Seriously, I know what's involved, I get up there ahead of these guys and lie low in the woods with a set of night vision optics and a headset. I can provide a running commentary if required, and when the kids are rescued, I'd be on hand to look after them. They'll be traumatised and in need of a friendly face.' Susie pointed at her face and gave her most endearing smile.'

Hawke and Nick exchanged glances and both shrugged. 'There's no point trying to argue with her.' Nick shook his head.

Matt noted the exchange. 'Works for me guys. If Susie sees nothing, we can go in with the soft surprise. If she does, we go in with the not-so-soft surprise. Either way, she's not in any danger.'

Hawke checked the time. 'It's 01:30. I suggest you guys get your gear ready, it'll take 15 minutes to advance on the target and take up positions. We agreed to go at 03:00, but I suggest you go as soon as you're in position.'

Susie said, 'I'll need to go a bit sooner to find a suitable OP, so, as soon as you can kit me out, I'll get going.' She was about to leave the gazebo when a thought hit her. 'Oh, by the way, what's the diversion?'

Matt tapped his nose. 'Wait and see, you won't be disappointed.'

28

'How much time have we got?' Wilson called from the bedroom he'd slept in for the last two nights.

'Why ask me? Where's your watch? 'Harrison shouted back up the stairs.

'I must have packed it, just tell me the time'

'It's 1:47, you've got over an hour. What's taking you so long?

'Nearly done, just trying to zip everything into the bag.'

'You've got more kit than those two women combined. Get a bloody move on. I want you out of here so I can sort the place out, I don't want a trace of you left.'

Wilson appeared in the living room a few minutes later and dumped an overstuffed rucksack on the floor. Ludmila and Irina gave him a pitying look. They stood side by side in front of the fire with small backpacks over their shoulders. 'How far is it to the van?'

The two women exchanged eye-rolls. Irina said. 'It's 20 minutes through the woods.'

'Bloody Hell. This thing weighs a ton, you expect me to lug it through the trees in the dark for 20 minutes.'

They both shrugged, it wasn't their problem.

Harrison reached for the hidden switch on the bookcase and let it swing open. 'I'll have to get Pia to come down and stop the kids getting out while I close up the tunnel, hang on.' He shouted for Pia and told her what he wanted her to do. Ludmila went down the steps first and unbolted the bottom door. It swung out into the basement. She checked the kids were in their beds then called the others to follow. Harrison was the last to arrive, he closed the door behind him and told Pia to stay and guard it.

A single bulb provided the only light in the basement, and they all kept quiet assuming the kids were asleep. Harrison moved to the East wall of the basement where a floor-to-ceiling whiteboard covered most of the wall. He released a catch high up on one side and held it steady as in swung down, hinged at floor level. The wall behind the whiteboard had a low door in it. no more than five feet high. He turned a catch in the door and lifted it to one side. They all felt the draft of cold air rush from the tunnel. Harrison reached inside and clicked a switch, the tunnel lit up with small white LEDs strung along its roof.

Ludmila looked sceptical. 'Is it safe?'

'Safe as houses. Just keep your head down, it's only about 40 metres, lit all the way.' Harrison ushered her in without smiling.

Irina shared her Ludmila's concern. 'What's at the end?'

'There's a ladder up to ground level, then there's a board over the entrance, you'll have to heave it aside, it might weigh a bit with branches and stuff, but you'll be OK.'

Irina ducked down and followed her comrade.

Harrison turned to his father. 'Your turn old man.'

'You've still got time if you want to get out.' Wilson grabbed his son's hand, suddenly desperate.

'I've told you what I'm going to do. I'll see you in a couple of days. Don't worry.' He pulled his hand free and stood aside to let Wilson drag his rucksack behind him down the tunnel. He waited until he was out of sight, then picked the door up and placed it back in its mount with a click.

Harrison turned back ready to lift the whiteboard back into position when he saw Pia kneeling beside one of the kids, she had her back to him and appeared to be talking to the boy. He frowned, heaved the whiteboard up until he heard the catch engage, and then walked closer to catch what she was saying.

'It's OK, your Mum must have got the message. There's some people coming to rescue you, I heard them talking about it.'

He heard the whisper and a rage erupted inside him. He stepped closer until he was leaning over her and raised his fist.

The boy's attention suddenly shifted from Pia to the man about to strike her. He recoiled.

Pia reacted to the boy's gaze and felt the shadow looming over her. She jumped to her feet. The top of her head smashed into Harrison's jaw. He fell back stunned, blood dripping from his mouth where he'd bitten his tongue.

Pia ran for the door, pulled it open a ran up the steps as fast as she could. She heard Harrison scream her name and race up to the living room behind her. She backed towards the wall desperate for sanctuary. She knew what his temper was like and knew this time she had crossed a line and he'd feel no remorse.

Harrison advanced on her, fists clenched, fury in his face. 'You fucking bitch. You betrayed me. I'm going to lose everything because of you.' The words came out as a guttural noise from deep within him.

Pia held her arms over her face in anticipation of the blows that were sure to come. She closed her eyes, turned away from him, fell to the floor and cowered.

Harrison let out a yell of pure hatred and swung his boot into the small of Pia's back with all the force he could generate. The kick sent her sprawling full length on the living room floor. She curled into the fetal position and whimpered.

Harrison snarled and looked around. He wasn't finished and wanted something he could use to do more damage. He spotted a holdall on the floor next to the kitchen door, and he knew the solution lay in its contents.

Pia peered through the gap between her arms and saw what Harrison was going for. She knew what was in the holdall. It galvanised her. She jumped to her feet and raced him to it.

He got there first, snatched the bag, inches from her clutching fingertips, stepped out of her way while his hand dived into it and came out with the handgun it contained. The gun might not have been a fashionable Sig Sauer or a Glock, but the Beretta APX was just as lethal.

Pia saw the weapon and knew she had no choice. She had to tackle him, or he would shoot her. She could see it in his eyes, all reason had left him.

Harrison took a second to work the action, chamber a round and aim between Pia's eyes. The second was all Pia needed. She lunged for his wrist with both hands and forced his arm sideways and away from her. His finger must have already taken up the initial pressure on the trigger. The blow to his wrist was all it took to complete the action.

With a deafening crack, the gunshot reverberated around the room.

'Fuck you.' Harrison cursed and tried to bring the gun to bear. Pia tightened her grip on the wrist of his gun hand with one hand. She kept up the pressure to prevent him from turning the gun on her and released her other arm to wrap around him and pull him in tight. It gave him no room to manoeuvre and trapped his free arm.

With their faces inches apart, Harrison yelled at her. 'Let go of me bitc.' Blood and spittle flew from his mouth. He fired again; the bullet smashed through one of the windows.

Pia fought back with a strength she didn't know she had, knowing anything else could only end with her death. 'Not this time, you selfish piece of shit.' Despite her determination and desperation, she couldn't hold him. She felt her grip on his wrist weakening. His arm moved closer to her; the barrel of the gun slowly being forced in her direction.

With a final do-or-die effort, Pia took a step back, pulled Harrison towards her and fell. She twisted to one side as she fell, knowing he would have to put a hand out to break his fall. She braced herself for the impact but found they'd rotated enough for him to take the brunt of the fall. She still clung to him. He had landed on his right side, his gun arm pinned under his body and his left arm pinned to his side by her. He cursed and twisted, as he tried to throw her off.

His grip on the Beretta never slackened, even with it jammed under the small of his back at an awkward angle, he kept his finger on the trigger.

They were both hyperventilating with the effort, their hearts beating at their maximum. Harrison wriggled his body to one side and released his elbow. The wrist, the hand and the gun would follow. Pia could see what he was trying to do and with her last ounce of strength, slammed the edge of her free hand down on his elbow.

She felt the shot more than heard it. For a moment she thought she'd been hit, then realised the fight had left Harrison. He groaned and swore at her and went limp. She let him go and got to her knees. His eyes fluttered then closed.

For a brief moment she wanted to help him, then reality struck home and hardened her heart. He would have killed her. He had made her life a misery for the last two years, treating her like an unpaid slave. She pulled herself to her feet and leaned against the wall for support as she let her breathing slow and her heartbeat return to normal. She looked down at him, not knowing if he was alive or dead and realised, she didn't care.

She checked the time, 2:15 am. Not long to go. She went around the house and switched on every light in the place, then propped the front door open. They were coming for the kids, and she headed back to the basement. Noah and Jenni were both awake.

'Who was shooting?' Noah asked, more excited than frightened. 'Is it the people who've come to rescue us?'

'No, but they'll be here soon.' Pia had a sudden thought. She didn't want them to see Harrison lying on the floor. 'You'd better stay here until they arrive, I'll leave the door open, but don't come up. OK?'

Jenni gave Pia a curious look. 'Are you all right? You look like you've been in a fight.'

'Don't worry about me, I'm fine. In fact, I've never felt better.'

Susie lay prone in a shallow depression. She had found the spot a few yards in from the edge of the wood, it gave her an unobstructed view of the cottage and kept her profile low. She'd brought a groundsheet to prevent the dampness in the undergrowth from getting through to her and arranged a few fallen branches over herself to complete her cover. As far as she was concerned, she was invisible.

She propped herself up on her elbows and studied the cottage through the night vision binoculars Matt had given her on the understanding they were just on loan. She would have liked to have kept them. They transformed her view. Everything appeared in shades of green, the binos hummed quietly as the technology enhanced what little light there was.

She could monitor the progress of the Ghostwalkers via two wireless earbuds that kept her in the comms loop. She reported back through a miniature microphone positioned millimetres from her mouth. Her whispered updates inaudible to anyone more than a few feet away. Her attention focused on the cottage. The rest of the world ceased to exist.

'Spectre 9, any sign of movement?' Hawke's voice was crystal clear in her ears.

She liked the call sign. 'Nothing here at all.'

The open channel network meant she could hear any and all communications between the eight members of the team and Hawke.

'Spectre 1 to control. All Spectres in position, ready to go.'

'Copy. Stand by.'

Susie felt her pulse quicken in anticipation. She waited for the promised diversion and focused on the cottage with renewed intensity.

The first gunshot made her jump. Something was happening. 'Shot fired.' She whispered into her mic, barely able to keep her voice under control. 'Was that you guys?' In the excitement, she forgot radio protocol.

'Negative.' She recognised Matt's voice.

The second shot came a few seconds later and seemed louder. She couldn't hear the glass breaking but noticed a chink of light at one of the ground-floor windows. 'Another shot, internal like the first.'

Hawke's voice came over the network. 'All Spectres. Go, go, go.'

Susie shifted her gaze to watch the SU6 men approach. She swept the area around the cottage but saw nothing. She heard a third shot, this time muted but still obvious. 'Another shot, again internal, no sign of movement outside.'

'Copy that.' Matt's voice again, calm and in control.

The green of the night vision optics suddenly glared as the front door opened and light spilled out. Susie saw a figure stand in the doorway briefly before returning into the cottage. She listened intently to the back and forth between the Ghostwalkers as they evaluated their strategy in line of what could be either a trap or surrender.

She wasn't aware of the two figures advancing on her from behind. She saw nothing and heard nothing until a boot slammed into her back between her shoulder blades and pinned her to the ground. She felt hands rip the comms pack from her and before she could move, another pair of hands jammed a rag into her mouth and tied it in place with a gag around her neck. She tried to move but one of her assailants grabbed her wrists, held them behind her back and the other tied them with a length of cloth.

She still had the earbuds in her ears and could hear Matt's voice. 'Going in now, no resistance.' A pause. 'There's a body on the floor and an unarmed woman. Checking...' She never heard the rest of his transmission as the earbuds were ripped out and she was lifted to her fe et.

The woman stood at the glass wall of her office on the 20th floor and gazed out as the sun climbed over the Macau marina. She could taste revenge; she could sense victory. Only three days to go.

Her reverie was broken by an alert from her computer. A couple of repeating notes to let her know someone was calling her. She checked the time. She assumed it was Kobzar and if so, why was he ringing now? He'd reported in on schedule two hours ago. What could have changed?

She strolled, unhurried, back to her desk. One glance at the screen confirmed the identity of the caller. She remained standing, leant over the desk and moved the mouse to accept the call. She stood up straight, took a step back and folded her arms. She waited for his image to appear.

'I assume you must have news to call again so soon.' She looked down her bony nose at the screen.

Kobzar remained unruffled. He looked forward to her reaction when he told her why he'd called. 'You are correct.'

'Well, out with it. Don't sit there looking smug, I don't have time for it.'

'As planned, my two agents got out of the place, with the explosives expert, before the soldiers arrived.'

'And the two children?'

'They were left with the couple who live there. They're hidden and will be released tomorrow.'

'They served their purpose. What about the merchandise?'

'We don't know if they have found it or not, we'll have to wait and see.'

The woman waved the matter away. 'Even if they find it, it will take days to distribute. More than enough time. Is that it?'

'No there's more.' Kobzar paused, he wanted to relish this. 'Irina and Ludmila captured the woman who's been causing all the trouble.'

At this news, the woman sat down at her desk, her interest suddenly piqued. 'How? When? Where? What have they done with her?'

'She was in the woods acting as an observer for the soldiers. They found her after they'd got out through the tunnel. I've told them to take her to the farm.'

'That is good news.' The woman paused and looked off, deep in thought. 'I want to put pressure on the UK Government. She'll be ideal' She scratched her nose as an idea came to her. 'Tell your people not to harm her. I want you to record her making a statement. Give me a couple of hours to prepare something.'

Kobzar checked the time. 'It's almost three in the morning. I'll call again at nine. That's...'

'That's five o'clock this afternoon.' The woman snapped. 'I can work it out myself.' She didn't wait for Kobzar to reply and ended the ca ll.

29

Friday 29 December

'Susie, can you hear me? Come in spectre 9.' Hawke's tone grew more agitated as the lack of response grew to over two minutes.

Nick stood beside him and listened for a reply. 'Could her comms have failed?' The look of concern on his face belied his confidence.

'Doesn't sound like it.' Said Hawke. 'I can still hear static,'

'It's not like her.' Nick frowned. 'She's good at this stuff.'

'Control, this is Spectre One, we've found the two kids, they're both OK.' Matt's radio message interrupted the two men.

Hawke responded. 'Good news. Keep them there. We'll come and get them.'

'Copy that, commander. We've also got a casualty. Gunshot wound, looks serious and there's a woman here who says the casualty is her partner. She says she's the one who sent the message to the kids' mother. Make any sense?'

'Understood, Spectre One. Can you take care of the casualty until we get there?

'Will do. Spectre five is the team medic, he's already working on him.'

'One more thing. Can you get two of your guys to find Spectre nine's OP. We're getting radio silence at this end. Make sure she's OK.'

'On it.'

Hawke grabbed a mobile headset and beckoned Nick to follow him out of the command centre. He called to Mitchel. 'The area's secured,

I'm going to pick those kids up and Nick's coming with me to find Susie.'

Mitchel nodded. 'I'll keep the comms up and running until you get back.'

Hawke started the Discovery, donned the headset and plugged it into the vehicle's own communication system. He waited while Nick climbed into the passenger seat, his leg still slowing him down.

Hawke tapped a button on the side of his headset. 'Tiger One to control, comms test.'

'Control to Tiger One, 5 and 5.' Mitchel's voice came over the car's speakers.

Nick looked at the navigation screen in the centre console and turned to Hawke. 'Are we going route one?'

Hawke half smiled. 'Only way togo.' He tapped the screen and it changed to a topographical image showing their location and the location of the cottage. 'I can't go through stone walls, but this thing will go everywhere else. Buckle up.' He selected drive, hit the throttle and the big Land Rover lurched forward.

True to his word, Hawke's route followed a straight line to the cottage, The Discovery making light work of the boggy grass and muddy fields. Once or twice, they had to deviate slightly to avoid the occasional tree and the powerful headlights warned them of any suspicious terrain. After five minutes they pulled up at their destination.

Nick's only concern was for Susie. He jumped out of the car and looked around, hoping she'd be there to welcome him. All he saw was four of the Unit 6 team, searching the area around the cottage, they carried xenon Maglites, their weapons slung. He called after them. 'Anyone seen Susie?'

'You'd better come with us, mate.' A voice from behind called out.

Nick spun to see two more of the team. 'What have you found.' He suddenly felt sick with worry.

'Come on. You'll see.' One of the men said, before he turned back towards the woods.

It took a couple of minutes of clambering over fallen branches and rough ground before they reached the spot Susie had chosen as her Observation Post. The two soldiers played their Maglites over the area. One of them said. 'This is how we found it.' He pointed to the groundsheet and the comms pack. 'There's footsteps leading over that soft ground. It looks like two people walking and one being dragged. See here.' He shone the torch at the ground and Nick knew they were right.

Nick had his hand over his mouth, not wanting to believe what he was looking at. He dropped his hands to his sides in despair. 'How far have you followed those footprints?'

'This is as far as we can follow. Once they go over all those branches, you'd have to be one of those specialist trackers to follow.'

Nick studied the footprints in the soft ground. He placed his boot alongside one of the prints. 'These are small, say a 6 or a 7, I'm no expert, but Susie's a 6 and they look similar, they must be female.'

The two soldiers exchanged glances. 'Never noticed mate, I think you're right.' One of them said.

'I think I know who they are.' Nick turned back to the cottage. 'I need to speak to Commander Hawke.' His limp had disappeared.

By 5.00 a.m. the Ghostwalkers had finished checking the cottage and the land around it. They found two shipping containers dug into the ground and concealed with camouflage netting. They were both packed with boxes of data cables. Hawke instructed Mitchel to organise a logistics company to move all the cables to a distribution centre. He called Alison Burton-Castle to let her know her children were safe and well. She thanked him through tears of relief and drove out immediately to pick them up.

Because Noah had watched Harrison open the entrance to the tunnel, the Ghostwalkers were able to get in and follow it to its exit in the woods. Footprints around the exit showed the direction the two women had gone and explained how they had come across Susie. A third set of prints, larger and more pronounced, they deduced, must have been made by a man. They were able to track the man's footprint for about a mile through the woods until they came to a narrow lane where they found fresh tyre tracks.

Nick did his best to stay calm and keep his faith in Susie. He told himself she was resilient. He reminded himself she was more than capable of dealing with difficult situations. He may have looked calm on the outside, his insides were churning.

Pia explained what had happened to her, and how Harrison's had shot himself. She told Hawke about Harrison's father and the two Russian agents who had abducted the children. She couldn't supply any more details as she'd been kept in the dark, but she'd been bringing the two kids their food and had built a bond between them. Hawke didn't see her as a threat, and she waited with Noah and Jenni until their mother arrived. He wanted to talk to them but given the time and how long they'd been held captive, he thought if best for them to go home, get some sleep, get freshened up, and then they might be able to help him.

Hawke consoled Nick as best he could. 'They need a hostage. They'll use her as leverage. If they meant her harm, well...' He spread his hands. 'You don't want me to spell it out.'

Nick had to agree. 'Yeah, I know. It has to be the two women who chased her on Sunday. If she was no use to them, they wouldn't have taken her. And she said they were armed, so if they didn't want her...' He closed his eyes, not wanting to dwell on the possibilities.

'Come on, we need to get the word out. Hawke put a supportive hand on Nick's shoulder. 'I can get Mitchel to drive your car if you want.'

'Thanks. I think I'll be OK. Got to get back on the horse sometime.' Nick shrugged and followed Hawke back to the Discovery.

The drive back to the command centre took longer than the outbound trip. Nick felt as if he was leaving Susie behind, and while Hawke couldn't have shared the same depth of emotion, he was empathetic enough to say the right things and assure Nick he'd draw on every resource he could to find her.

Nick shook hands with Hawke and left him in the command centre. He approached the old Volvo and dug into his pockets for the car keys. He stopped in his tracks when he remembered Susie had them. Without thinking, he reached for his phone, he'd give her a call. Reality hit him hard. His phone was somewhere in the rubble of the control tower and Susie was missing. He could feel his head spinning. This couldn't be happening.

He staggered to the Volvo and leaned on it for support. His legs had turned to jelly. He was in the middle of nowhere, the cold had become numbing, and the oppressive darkness showed no sign of lifting. He had no phone, no keys, no cash and no idea what to do next.

'You don't look too good Nick.' Hawke's voice came out of the dark. 'Why not come back here and take a minute.'

Nick turned to see Hawke silhouetted against the light from the open curtain of the gazebo. He gave a dismissive wave. 'I'm OK, just getting my act together.'

'Pull the other one.' Hawke replied. 'You shouldn't be on your own. Come and sit down for a few minutes.'

'Sorry.' Nick confessed. 'I'm all over the place. Just realised I can't drive the car.'

'Don't worry. I said I'll get Mitchel to drive you.' Hawke strolled over to Nick.

Nick managed a little chuckle. 'I appreciate that Alex, it's not that I can't drive. The problem is, Susie has the keys.'

'Ah, I see. That does kind of bugger up the plans, doesn't it. Look, forget the car. We'll get you back to your place. We can worry about the car another time.'

Nick heaved himself off the Volvo and followed Hawke back to the command centre. It may have been just a tent in the middle of the field, but it somehow offered a degree of sanctuary that calmed his shattered mind.

Nick tried to settle.

Mitchel had dropped him off at 6:30 and he promised he'd be OK. But instead, he paced around the house. He went into every room, just checking. He knew Susie wasn't there, but he couldn't help himself. Without a phone, he felt cut off from the world, he wanted to try calling Susie's phone, even though Hawke tried it earlier and got no reply. He felt certain that whoever had taken her, would have taken her phone. Despite that, he still wanted to call her. The need to speak to someone, anyone, filled his conscious mind. He wanted reassurance, he wanted to tell someone how he felt, and he wanted to blow off steam and rage at the world. Most of all he wanted Susie back home.

He couldn't do any of those things without a phone.

The kitchen had always been their thinking and talking space, they lived in it, more than the living room. He made a pot of coffee, sat on a stool at the breakfast bar and gave himself what he called "*a damn good talking to.*". He wasn't a pessimist, he didn't do morose, and he wouldn't let himself fall into a state of despair. He had to remain positive, be active, and keep telling himself how resourceful she was. But there had to be something he could do.

Being a photographer, he worked visually. He liked to see work-flows, processes and systems set out on paper. Squares, circles, triangles and arrows. He thought of the incident boards they showed on police crime dramas. Pictures of suspects, victims and witnesses with lines connecting them and notes alongside that might trigger a moment of clarity or lead to a breakthrough. He slid off the stool and fetched a few blank sheets of paper and some coloured pens from his study. He spread them out on the breakfast bar and set to work.

He drew a timeline running left to right, starting at 3.30 p.m. a week earlier and divided it into seven equal portions for the days between then and now. On each day he noted what had happened and who was involved. Without photos, he drew a simple smiley face to indicate each person that either of them had mentioned or interacted with.

He drew faces of all the people in the control tower and to the best of his memory, wrote names under each face. He'd voiced his doubts about one of the people at Warrenford to Susie. Something niggled him; as if one of them was familiar, but he couldn't put his finger on what it was. He remembered that he'd never brought the matter up again and added a question mark over the faces. The fact there were no survivors from the explosion, led him to question who or what he had doubts about. None of them struck him as a suicide bomber. But, if it wasn't one of them, how could anyone have got past the security with enough explosives to do so much damage?

He drew faces for the team at Payline, then moved to Saturday and drew nothing at first. He remembered Tim and Anna and added them to his timeline with the flourish of a little tick mark beside their names to indicate they were above suspicion. On Sunday he added Alison Burton-Castle with two smaller faces for her children. He remembered Susie saying she'd had a call from Whitehall, he didn't know who called her, but she'd been asked to call Matthews. So, he drew a face for him and added him to the plan. The two women who had chased Susie from Starbucks were portrayed with evil faces and he added a question mark beside them with a red pen. He was about to tackle Monday when he recalled Susie had been unable to reach Matthews ever since then. He added a question mark beside his name.

Tempted to draw a tiger to depict Commander Hawke, Nick relented, but added the tick of approval beside his name, he did the same for Mitchel. He'd never met Alison Burton-Castle's partner, Ed, but added him to the timeline as he'd been a victim of the abduction. He noted on the timeline when the text messages had been sent, and who knew about them. He added Burton-Castle's office meetings and drew arrows to indicate the wasted visit to the abandoned cottage near Wychwood. He thought of doing the same for the community centre but didn't see it as relevant and left it off. Susie's trip to the Industrial Park filled Tuesday morning and their trip into town where they'd witnessed the rioting, completed Tuesday.

After half an hour's writing and doodling, Nick sat back and tried to make some sense of what he'd drawn. Nothing jumped out at him, so he continued with Wednesday and the mission to Starbucks, followed by their drive down to TIGER HQ. Yet again, he saw no clues or potential suspects.

That brought him to Thursday and rescue of the kids. Somebody had tipped off the people holding them. More question marks. Who knew the location had been found and who knew when the special forces team were going in? He drew lines and arrows connecting those in the loop. The lines lead to Alison Burton-Castle, she was the only one outside of the operational team who had been told.

Nick tapped the end of the pen on her name and pondered. The only names connected to her, apart from the team, were her kids, her partner Don and her staff. He discounted her kids and Don Burton-Castle and thought about her team. She'd told Susie she trusted her team, but someone had the inside knowledge about the confidential line IDs and any one of them could have been persuaded or blackmailed into giving the details to whoever had created the virus.

He concentrated on the red question marks. Who had passed on the line numbers? Who had planted the explosives and who the hell was Matthews? He missed Susie's input. She excelled at this sort of thing. She could see a connection or come up with an idea and see where it led. He checked the time again and urged the clock to move faster. He wanted to go into town and buy a new phone. He still had an hour to wait.

Taking a leaf out of Susie's playbook, Nick left the kitchen, grabbed a coat and headed out for some fresh air and exercise to clear his head. The clear sky meant cold air, and at as brisk a pace as he could see his breath on every exhale. After ten minutes, he could feel the tension building in his leg, so he turned for home and slowed a little, breathed deeply and forced himself to think. By the time he got back home, he had a plan.

He headed straight for the spare room that doubled as his office, opened his email account and sent a message to `Tim`:

`Hi mate, Susie's been abducted, no idea where she is. I've got no phone. Any chance you can come over?`

Tim had a reputation for responding quickly, and sure enough, two minutes later his reply arrived:

`Jesus Nick, WTF, I'll be there in 15 minutes.`

Nick breathed a sigh of relief and kicked himself for not emailing Tim sooner. It was almost 9.00 a.m., the shops would be open soon.

30

Susie tripped and staggered to stay on her feet as one of the women pushed her. She guessed she had crossed a threshold. The echo of her footsteps and the metallic reverberation of the space she'd entered had a familiar ring. With her hands tied behind her back and a thick black cloth bag over her head, she felt disoriented. The one-hour journey to wherever they had brought her had tested her resolve. She was grateful for the warm clothing she'd worn for the surveillance, but the back of the van, with its lack of any heating or padding, had left her numb. Along with the anger she felt at being captured, the frustration at not knowing where she was amplified her helplessness.

The woman who had pushed her told her to stand still. Not knowing what was around her and what she might crash into, Susie did as instructed. She heard the woman talking quietly to her colleague. The language was alien to Susie, and she had no idea what they were talking about. After half a minute of back and forth, a decision appeared to have been reached, and Susie sensed one of them step closer to her. She felt what she assumed was the barrel of a gun pressed against the base of her neck. She closed her eyes and braced herself for what was to come. But nothing happened—no gunshot, no blow. "Don't turn around," one of the women ordered, and with that, the bag was unceremoniously yanked off her head.

Susie blinked repeatedly. She had expected to be blinded by light, but instead, pitch blackness greeted her. With a repeated "Don't turn around," the gun was withdrawn, and she heard the woman back off. With her hands still securely bound, Susie was in no position to fight back. She fought the temptation to turn around as she heard metal grind against metal. It rekindled memories from her RMP days when her team investigated a smuggling operation and she recognised the closing mechanism of a shipping container. She gave way to temptation as she heard a final crash and turned to see the last chink of light extinguished.

She turned slowly through 360 degrees, her feet gingerly reaching out for objects on the floor. In the absolute darkness, she felt vulnerable and squeezed her eyes tight shut for a second, then opened them in the hope her senses would have readjusted. She stared into the nothingness as she turned, seeking out the faintest pinprick of light. Containers were designed to be watertight, and if water couldn't get in, there was little chance of any light making its way through the steel shell. Susie walked forward with small, tentative steps, her feet probing ahead. She reached a wall. Unsure if it was the side or the end of the container, she turned her back to the wall and slowly headed back the way she had come, counting her steps as she went. She recalled dimensions of 8 feet by 20 feet, and it didn't take her long to figure out she had walked from one side of the container to the other.

Keeping the wall on her right shoulder, she walked the length of the container again, counting her steps and feeling in front of her with her feet in case she tripped over anything on the floor. The binding on her wrists dug into her skin, and she fought the urge to tug at it, knowing she would only tighten the knot. Her left boot struck something hard and unyielding. She froze.

She tapped the object with the toe of her boot and felt it move; it gave a hollow clang as it rolled against another object. The fact it rolled, Susie assumed, meant it had to be a pipe of some sort—a tube, a cylinder. Whatever it was, it was heavy, judging by the noise it made as it rolled. She tapped her foot in an arc, hoping to detect whatever the object had rolled into. She didn't dare move further forward in case she fell. From the outline of the object, she estimated it had to be a couple of inches in diameter, but she had no idea of its length. She had to get her hands free. It was bad enough not being able to see, but not being able to touch just added to her frustration. She ignored the objects on the floor and, with her back to the wall, slid down to a sitting position with her legs tucked, her chin resting on her knees. Susie prided herself on her flexibility and suppleness and knew she could get her hands free if she could get them in front of her. She'd seen it done but never tried it herself. The bulky combat jacket didn't help, but she wriggled and twisted and forced her bound hands down her back.

She shifted from side to side and strained every sinew in her shoulders and arms. Through gritted teeth, she pushed harder and fought the pain of the bindings digging deeper into her wrists. She rolled onto her side. The move trapped one arm under her body but gave her the freedom to squeeze her backside over the knot that held her. She paused for breath. Almost there—one more effort and she would be free. She felt beads of sweat dripping from her forehead. One way to keep warm. With a restrained grunt and a final push, her hands slipped around her bottom. She sat up, tucked her legs in, pushed them between her arms, and exhaled loudly. First part of the exercise complete.

It took her a minute for her heart rate to slow and her breathing to return to something approaching normal. She sat with her back against the wall of the container and brought her hands up to her face. Her nose wrinkled at the smell. Not clean. It felt like a rag or a piece of cloth, and against all her better instincts, she touched it to her lips. Without sight and without her fingertips, it was the only way to work out the location of the knot, and she knew her teeth would have to do the hard work. They had tied her hands together palm to palm and tightly enough to prevent her from twisting her wrists and loosening the knot. With her thumbs towards her, Susie figured whatever it was had been tied in the most difficult place for her to reach: the side of her hands facing away from her. It meant twisting both hands for her teeth to get any purchase on the fabric. Her teeth found the knot. If the smell was bad, the taste confirmed the rag must have been whatever was lying on the floor of the van when they bundled her in. She did her best to ignore the assault on her senses as she searched for an end, a fold, a tuck, anything to tug at that would release her. She almost had to bury her face in the binding, but bit by bit, she worked out the structure of the knot and had to accept reality: it had been pulled so tight, it would have to be cut off. Or gnawed off. She took a moment to compose herself and tried to release some of the tension in her arms and shoulders, resulting from the exertion of the twists and strains of the last five minutes.

Susie took care of her teeth—a "perfect 32," her dentist had said. He wouldn't approve of Susie's next move. With a resigned sigh, she raised the binding to her mouth and started to chew. She had to fight the gag reflex as her teeth closed on the material and liquid oozed out. She spat the foul goo on the floor, not wanting to think what it might be, and went back to teasing out a thread, pulling on an edge, or biting through the fabric. The effort sapped her strength, and she had to stop after a minute. More spitting and more deep breaths. She would have killed for a drink of water, or anything palatable to rid her mouth of the taste. She could sense progress, and while her hands felt no looser, she knew she was more than halfway through the binding. She went back to work, determined to break free. She found herself making animal-like noises as she gnawed away, grunting with the effort and snorting through her nose. She was grateful there was nobody around to witness it. With a final snarl, Susie bit through the last bit of fabric, and the binding fell away. She let her hands drop to her sides. She spat the last of the liquid from her mouth and took several long, slow breaths to recover. After another minute, she could feel her pulse slowing. She massaged her wrists, clenched and unclenched her fists, and wriggled her fingers. Circulation returned.

Second part of the exercise complete.

She resisted the urge to stand and instead felt around her, her fingers seeking anything nearby she could either use or be wary of. Apart from dirt and dust—at least, she hoped that's all it was—she found nothing. She raised herself to her feet, and with one hand guiding her along the wall of the container, she searched for the pipe or tube she had touched with her foot earlier. She didn't have to move far; she almost tripped over it. When she reached for it, she knew immediately what she had found and allowed herself a moment of triumph. A scaffolding pole. About three feet in length, its heft left her no doubt what it was. She wielded it like a club, then like a sword, tried a few thrusts and parries before its weight forced her to place one end on the floor. Conscious there might be more objects lying around, she used the pole to probe ahead. It clanged when it hit more of its own kind, and Susie quickly realised the back of the container on the right was stacked with more poles. She blindly felt about, first with the pole, then dropped to her knees and advanced forward, exploring with her fingertips to see if she could find anything else she might be able to use. Her hands touched something softer—a sheet or canvas of some description. A tarp, she guessed, based on the feel and weight. She dropped the pole and picked up a fold of the tarp. She checked the edges and found it intact, though dirty and damp. It felt like the corners were reinforced with eyelets, though she had no way of knowing if there was anything she could use to fasten them with. She dragged it towards the door of the container, then crouched down to one side. She tried to map out the container in her head. Metal floor. Metal sides. No light. Two women, armed. How long until they came back?

A plan began to form.

***

Irina checked the time on the kitchen clock and peered through the window at the approaching dawn. A week after the shortest day, the sun had yet to show its face by 8:00 a.m., but a dull, pale blue light on the eastern horizon signified it wasn't too far away. She called to Ludmila to let her know she was going to check on their hostage and stepped outside.

The container had been sited beyond the old farm buildings, and she had to negotiate various implements and assorted machines as she made her way through the barn. The doors of the container faced west, and the area in front of them had been cleared of the debris that lay all around the disused dwelling. She reached the container, picked up a stone, and tapped on the door. She called out, "Hello," and waited for a response. Nothing came back.

She lifted the locking handle on the right-hand door and swung it towards her, rotating the locking catches at the top and bottom of the door. She heaved on the handle, and the door opened an inch. She called again, same negative result. For a moment, she wondered if the container was airtight and perhaps the woman inside had passed out or even died. She dismissed the thought. Even if the container was airtight, which she doubted, it was big enough for one person to survive for more than a few hours. She pulled the door open a little further and peered into the gloom. She hadn't brought a torch, and the meagre daylight did little to illuminate the inside of the container. She opened the door fully and stood back. She let her eyes grow accustomed to the light but could see nothing—no sign of anyone.

She noticed an old blue tarpaulin bundled haphazardly along one edge of the container and a few other objects at the back, but the interior appeared devoid of human occupation.

Puzzled but determined, she turned to open the left-hand door to allow more light in.

Lying full length on her stomach along the edge of the container with the tarpaulin spread over her, Susie watched through a tiny split in the fabric and waited until her jailer turned her back. She hoped her arms and legs hadn't gone to sleep while she'd been hidden, and steeled herself. She watched as the woman wrestled with the locking handle, her attention diverted. The noise of the rusty mechanism turning disguised Susie's movements, and she leapt to her feet, threw off the tarpaulin, and with the scaffolding pole held in both hands, swung at the woman.

The blow caught her in the small of her back and knocked her off her feet. She shrieked in pain, fell into the mud, and lay very still.

Susie wasted no time. She contemplated a second blow, but the woman appeared to be out cold, and Susie didn't want to commit murder. Besides, the effort of swinging the pole had been more than expected. She dropped it and ran.

She might have escaped the confines of the container, but she had no idea where she was or which way to go. She wanted to get away from the buildings, so she headed towards open ground. Fields surrounded the farm with one track leading towards a gap in a small woodland 200 yards away to the south. Susie stopped after 50 yards to assess her options. The farm track made the most sense; it had to lead to civilisation and possible help. Hedges and fences had been stripped away in pursuit of maximum yields and left no cover for escaping fugitives.

Skirting around the farm buildings, keeping as low to the ground as she could, Susie headed for the track, suddenly feeling very exposed. She had jogged about 80 yards, thinking she was in the clear, when she heard an engine start. Not a car, but something more agricultural. And more dangerous.

She risked a look back and saw the quad bike emerge from the barn. The woman on board wore combat fatigues and an expression of pure menace, hunched over the handlebars. She held the throttle wide open and closed the distance faster than Susie wanted to believe.

A shallow ditch ran down one side of the track, and Susie hoped it might act as some sort of obstacle to the quad bike. She left the track, jumped the ditch, and headed over the field. The stubble was hard going after the track, but Susie ploughed on, thankful she'd worn her boots.

The woman in control of the ATV hardly hesitated. She kept the throttle open and took the ditch at an angle, barely slowing in the process. Susie tried to run faster, and as her pursuer closed, she zigzagged from side to side. It made little difference. The machine caught her easily; she had nowhere to go. The woman could have run her over, but she cruised alongside, tracking Susie and edging closer all the time. Out of breath and exasperated, Susie stopped running. The woman stopped the quad bike but left the engine running. The pair stared at each other, 10 feet apart. The woman slowly pulled a handgun from inside her jacket and motioned for Susie to start walking back to the farm.

Susie glanced around. Standing in the middle of a field with a gun pointed at her, she had no choice and, deflated, trudged back the way she had come.

31

Tearing herself away from her children was never Alison Burton-Castle's intention. After a frantic drive through the early morning darkness to pick them up; After the undiluted joy of holding them again, going back into the office was never going to be a priority.

Jenni just wanted to shower and sleep. Noah, buzzed with excitement, sleep was the last thing on his mind. She agreed to take him with her to the office.

She rang ahead and by the time she arrived, her team were in place and putting their plans into operation.

Noah had been into the office with his Mum before, and many of the staff knew him. He basked in the cheers and applause that greeted his arrival. Despite the seriousness of the situation, Burton-Castle's staff were almost as relieved as she was, the children were safe and well.

Holly Holding was the first to greet Noah and his Mum. 'We're on it boss. As soon as you called we sent the emails with the new numbers.'

The Operations Director hugged Holding. 'You're a star Holly. Any feedback yet?'

'Not yet, but I'm pretty sure we'll be getting calls about the data cables.'

Burton-Castle couldn't resist giving her a knowing smile. 'That's no longer a problem. They found where all the stock went. It's being moved as we speak to a central hub. You can tell all the companies who need cables, to get in touch to find out where to get what they need.'

Holding looked stunned. 'You mean someone's been stockpiling?'

'Yup. The people who took Noah and Jenni bought up every metre of cable they could find. I guess they thought they'd make a killing selling it back when demand outstripped supply.

'Greedy bastards.' Said Holding.

'That's one way to describe them.' Burton-Castle gave a wry smile. 'They'll never see a penny now.' She took Holding's arm. 'Come on, we've got a busy day ahead of us.'

It looked like an interrogation room. A stark room, a single chair and bright lights. Susie recoiled when they dragged her into it. What were they going to do to her? Her mind raced. She had nothing to say, nothing to tell them they didn't already know.

Then she spotted the camera. Tripod mounted and aimed at the chair. Her stomach turned. Were they planning to film some sort of revenge beating, or simply torture her for their twisted enjoyment, or was this it? They wanted to film her execution.

She twisted and pulled, writhed and struggled, but after her earlier attempt to escape, they were taking no chances and had tied her hands behind her back and bound her ankles. She was reduced to an undignified kangaroo hop in order to move. The two women each held one of her arms, their fingers dug painfully into her flesh. They pulled her to the chair, forced her to sit, then looped a rope around her and secured it behind her back. She was pinned in place.

Rostyslav Kobzar entered the room. He had a malevolence about him that chilled Susie to the core. His dark soulless eyes examined her in the way a butcher might appraise a side of beef, working out where to start cutting. He came within a few feet of her and stopped. He folded his arms and exhaled loudly.

'So You're the one who has been causing all the problems?'

Susie ignored him. She refused to be intimidated and said nothing.

'I planned to get rid of you. You have cost me time and money and made me very angry.' His voice had a cold, vicious tone to it.

She'd been trained in interrogation techniques during her time as a Red Cap; sometimes as the interrogator and sometimes as the one being questioned. She wasn't going to meet his gaze, argue her case or even acknowledge him. She stared off to her right and focused on a spot on the wall.

He didn't appear to be concerned about her reaction. 'I have a better use for you. You are going to read a statement to camera. When you have done that, we will wait and see what happens. If our demands are met, you will be released. If however, our demands are not met, then I will have no choice but to have you eliminated.'

Susie didn't react. She heard what he said, processed it and understood. But she said nothing and did nothing more than stare at the wall.

Kobzar frowned at her. Nobody ignored him, especially when they were tied to a chair and being threatened. He beckoned Irina who still nursed a painful back. 'See if you can get her attention.'

Irina stepped into Susie's line of sight, a look of sadistic pleasure on her face. She leaned closer and placed one extended finger on the side of Susie's chin. She applied a little pressure, just enough to move Susie's head to the left. She drew her hand back, Susie's gaze switched to the finger and didn't see Irina's other hand. It whipped out of nowhere and slapped her across the cheek with a force that almost knocked her off the chair. Susie reeled from the blow and winced at the pain. Her cheek burned and her neck ached.

She remained silent and met Irina's gaze.

'You want more?' Irina raised her hand.

Kobzar put an arm out to restrain her. Like Irina, he leaned closer to Susie, his face just inches from hers. 'We can do this all day, or you can save yourself a lot of pain and read the statement. Your choice.' The menace in the voice left Susie in no doubt about his intentions.

She relented and broke her silence. 'What does the statement say?'

'Ah, she speaks.' Kobzar stood up straight and addressed Irina and Ludmila. 'We make progress.'

'I asked what the statement says. I didn't say I'd read it.' Susie's voice sounded defiant, despite the burning sensation in the side of her face.

'Oh, but you will.' Kobzar said. 'You can make it quick and painless, or slow and very, very painful. We've got all day and you're not going anywhere.' His hand disappeared into his jacket pocket and came out with a single sheet of paper. He held it out in front of Susie. 'All you have to do is look into that camera and read this. Sorry we don't have an autocue, you'll just have to do your best.'

Susie squinted at the statement. 'You'll have to hold it closer, I can't read it.'

Kobzar gave an exaggerated sigh and held the piece of paper a few inches closer. 'Is that better?' His voice dripped with sarcasm.

Susie leaned forward as best she could and read:

"My name is Susan Jones, I work for the Cyber Crime Unit. I have been investigating the ongoing breakdown of the online payment system.

I am being held hostage by an organisation determined to expose the Government's criminality and corruption. I have seen indisputable evidence that the UK Government caused this breakdown in a botched attempt to install software that would give them access to the private banking details of UK citizens.

The organisation now issues this ultimatum.

Unless the Prime Minister goes on national television and admits to this outrage and his part in it, an explosive charge will be detonated in London resulting in mass civilian casualties. I have also been told that unless this demand is met, I will be killed live on social media.

She stopped reading and looked up at Kobzar. 'Are you mad? This is bullshit. It's not true, you know it's not true, and you know the PM will never make such an admission.'

'Do I look like I care either way? He sneered at her. 'All we want is to see your Prime Minister grovel in front of the nation. After all the damage that's been done, he'll never survive.'

Susie's head tipped sideways as she tried to understand the man's motive. 'I get the feeling this is like some personal vendetta. What's he ever done to you to deserve such retribution?'

Kobzar gave a derisive snort. 'It is personal in a way. Remember the contract for the new 5G network?'

Susie nodded. 'What of it?'

'It was withdrawn at the last minute, it cost my client millions of dollars.'

Susie's face registered enlightenment. 'Aha. So that's who's behind this.'

'You've got it. Unfortunately for you, no-one will believe you, we've covered our tracks and left no traces. You might get a story out of it, but it'll remain one of those wonderful conspiracy theories.'

'And what if the PM doesn't go on TV?'

'If he refuses, he will have blood on his hands and the whole country will be baying for his head, especially after they see your pretty face quite literally, splashed, all over social media.

'And you seriously think you'll get away with this?' Susie forgot her burning cheek and the ache in her neck. She looked at Kobzar with incredulity.

'Of course. We're always one step ahead of you. Have you never wondered how these ladies knew you'd be in Starbucks? Has it never crossed your mind that we knew when Valley View was going to be raided and got our people out beforehand?'

This baffled Susie and she thought about it for a moment. 'So, you've turned someone.'

'Who says it's one person?' Kobzar almost grinned, his smile sent a chill through Susie.

Susie looked at Irina and Ludmila, they stood to one side, itching to cause her more pain. She looked back at Kobzar, he appeared to have all the time in the world. She knew she'd have to do what they wanted in the end. She just had to hope she could get out and raise the alarm before they could do whatever they were planning. 'All right. I'll make a deal with you.'

Kobzar looked surprised. 'You're in no position to make a deal.'

'I'm not asking for much, but if you're going to keep me here against my will, put me somewhere with a light, at least. I'm not an animal.'

'And if I don't?'

'Then I don't read your bullshit statement, you end up killing me and the PM doesn't humiliate himself on national TV. It's a small price to pay, to get what you want.' Susie stared at him; the ball was in his court.

Kobzar stared back at her. He didn't like bending to demands or looking weak in front of the two women. He could see the determination in Susie's eyes. He knew, she knew, he had to give in. 'Very well. Read the statement and we'll lock you in the attic. We might need you for a second video, so don't get any ideas about running off again. Do we have a deal?'

Susie's mouth twisted, she contemplated asking for more but settled for a minor victory. 'OK, set the camera going, I'll warn you now, I'm useless in front of a camera, so if I cock it up, you'll have to live with it.' If she had to do it, she'd make them work for it.

'No problem. One bit at a time, whatever it takes. It's not meant to be a Hollywood production. But don't take all day, I have to be in London tonight.'

Trent Bracewell's technicians worked feverishly. They had already stripped away the burned-out cables and under his watchful eye, had re-configured the modems with the new line IDs. They installed the new cables the moment the courier dropped them off. After working through the night, they completed the last connection by nine on Friday morning.

'Are we OK to go live?' Bracewell called from inside one of the server cabinets.

'Yep, go for it.'

He hit the master power switch and the boards lit up, modems beeped, and switches hummed.

Bracewell emerged, stepped back and watched the electrical activity as if expecting something to go wrong at any second. His hand poised over the switch just in case. 'You want to risk a test call?' He asked Jay, his chief technician.

Jay nodded and dialled in.

They held their breath, watched and waited. Bracewell rested two fingers on one of the data cables. 'So far, so good. No change in temp.'

'I'll try the rest.' Jay had a list of all the new numbers in front of him and proceeded to dial them, one at a time. The process took ten minutes.

Bracewell high-fived Jay and the other technicians. A broad smile lit up his face, despite the tiredness and the worry. 'Outstanding work guys, looks like we're back in business.'

Jay wiped his forehead with the back of his hand. 'Haven't pulled an all-nighter for a few years. Reckon I must be getting old, I'm bushed.'

'I think we all need some kip.' Bracewell said. 'The admin staff should be in by now, I think we can leave the place in their hands and go home. I'll drop an email to the people at Connectivity and tell them the good news. You guys get away and hope I don't call you any time soon.

He watched them leave, then trudged back to his office on weary legs.

Miles Wilson sat at the laptop in the farmhouse living room. He took the camera Ludmila handed to him and extracted the memory card. 'She did it then?'

Ludmila shrugged. 'You'll see.'

With the card inserted into the computer, he booted up DaVinci Resolve, the editing software he preferred, and loaded the video footage. It took him a moment to realise what he was looking at. 'Jesus.

How many takes did she have to do, this should only be thirty seconds or so. It goes on for half an hour.'

'Told you.' Ludmila walked away.

Wilson had a copy of the script he dragged the footage into the timeline editor and hit play. He watched Susie sit looking at the camera while the lights were adjusted. He heard Kobzar's voice off-camera, giving her a five-second countdown. She looked down slightly, Wilson guessed at the script, then started to read. It lasted a few seconds before Susie mumbled a few words and asked to start again. She repeated the process again and again and again. Each time a minor mistake, a line fluffed, a wrong word, or she simply paused for too long and apologised. He groaned. He would have to go through the video and cut over 29 minutes of video to be left with the thirty seconds they wanted. It was going to be fiddly and time-consuming.

True to his word and much to Susie's surprise, after they'd finished the video, Kobzar had her taken to an attic above a single-storey extension built onto the back of the farmhouse. It had a light but no windows and just a small door in one gable end, so low, even she had to duck down to avoid hitting her head. The pitched roof stretched up from the bare floorboards to a ridge high enough to let her stand, but little more. Both gable ends were exposed bricks and blocks of polystyrene insulation had been fitted between the roof trusses. It looked as if it had been used as a storeroom. A couple of large boxes of clothing and assorted household items littered the floor.

Susie could see no way out, but given it was already late afternoon, dark, and getting colder by the minute, she decided she needed warmth and something to sleep on. She hoped that once rested, she could come up with a way to get out and raise the alarm. A quick rummage through the boxes produced an old sleeping bag and three well-worn blankets. A further investigation revealed some old jackets and jumpers which she used as padding. By the time she had finished she'd managed to create a rudimentary bed. At least she wouldn't freeze. She positioned the bed close to one side of the attic and stuffed jumpers against the roof trusses to act as further insulation. Out of curiosity, she prised one of the polystyrene blocks out and poked at the roofing felt behind it. She noticed as she did so, one or two slates moved and it gave her an idea.

She looked around for something she could use to prise the slates apart and found a stash of discarded cutlery at the bottom of one of the boxes. She picked out a knife and fork and was about to see what she could do when she heard footsteps approaching.

After a hurried job of replacing the insulation and hiding the utensils, she lay back on her new bed and waited for the door to open. She heard a key in the lock and saw the handle turn. A voice called out. 'Step away from the door.' Five seconds later the door swung open and Susie saw both the women who'd captured her waiting on the far side of the door. One of them held a plate in one hand and a bottle of water in the other. The other woman held a pistol pointed directly at Susie. 'Stay where you are.' Said the one with the gun, while the other slid the plate towards Susie and rolled the water bottle after it. She said nothing. They closed the door behind them, locked it and retreated into the house.

Susie eyed the plate with suspicion. She was famished, having eaten nothing for almost 24 hours, but an inner voice cautioned her. Could they have laced whatever they had given her with poison or something to knock her out? She picked the plate up and examined what was on it. She groaned when she realised the thick hunks of white bread sandwiched a couple of slices of ham. She didn't eat meat. She hated being labelled a veggie, she just didn't like meat, never cooked it, never bought it and never ate it. Until times were desperate. And she figured her present predicament could be classified as desperate. She peered inside the sandwich, sniffed it and prodded it with a finger. It looked harmless enough. She felt her stomach rumble and gave in.

Five minutes later, she wished they had brought her another one. Her energy had returned and her determination to get out multiplied. She sat on the bed, removed the polystyrene, retrieved the knife and fork and started work.

The tiles nearest the floor became the focus of her efforts, partly because they were the easiest to reach and partly because they were the easiest to hide if anyone else checked up on her. She hacked at the roofing felt with the knife until she exposed three or four slates, then stuck the fork into the overlap and levered them apart. At least that was her plan. The extension must have been a recent addition and the roofers must have done a thorough job. The fork bent and the slates remained stubbornly in place. After five minutes of cursing, twisting and trying, Susie paused, aware that she was making enough noise to attract unwanted attention. She needed something with a bit more heft.

32

Nick and Tim arrived in the phone shop a little after 9.30 a.m. They'd both commented on how much quieter it had become, compared to a few days earlier. Nick was worried the shop might have been closed or even boarded up after the rioting, but it looked as normal as it ever did. The only difference being a sign on the door saying, "cash only".

Nick had already decided for the sake of speed, he just wanted a cheap, Pay-as-you-go smartphone, they'd discussed options on the way into town. Tim had brought cash knowing they'd be unable to use a card.

The transaction only took a few minutes and they were back in Tim's car by 9.45 a.m. Nick unboxed the phone, connected the charging cable to the USB socket and switched it on. 'Can't believe how much I've missed being out of touch.' He held the handset as if it contained the answer to all his worries.

'No surprise there mate. I've been trying to get in touch with you for the last 24 hours and couldn't understand why Susie wasn't returning my calls. You should have emailed earlier. Anna and I have been waiting for an update.'

Nick shook his head as he logged in to his account and waited for his details and contacts to upload. 'I'm sorry buddy, things kind of took off yesterday, it all happened so fast and we ended up out in the fields with no signal.'

'When did you last speak to Alex?'

Nick screwed his face up, the last few hours seemed like a bad dream. 'Must have been around 5.30 this morning.'

'Probably worth giving him a call. See if he's got any news and let him know your new number.'

Nick noted the number on the side of the box and called Hawke. It went to voicemail.

'He won't answer if he doesn't recognise the number.' Tim heard the automated message. 'Leave him a message or better still, text him and he'll get straight back to you. I know what he's like.'

Having done as Tim suggested, Nick said. 'I should give Alison a call, she'll be wanting to know what's going on.'

Tim nodded. 'You got her number?'

Nick looked blank for a moment and scrolled through the contact list on his new phone. 'I, er. No. I've never rung her and Susie would have no reason to pass on her number to me. Shit.'

'No worries. Alex will have it. He gets his ADC to make a note of that sort of thing.' Tim sounded reassuringly confident.

Nick stared at the phone and waited for it to burst into life. He didn't have to wait long before the default ringtone announced an incoming call from Tiger One.

'Nick, how are you doing?' Hawke asked before Nick had a chance to speak.

'I'm OK, got Tim with me. Just wanted to let you know I'm contactable and also find out if you've got any news?'

'Wish I did Nick. These people take travelling under the radar to a new level. We've tried every trick in the book, but they've gone to ground. We'll go on looking till we find Susie, nobody's capable of disappearing completely these days.'

'I appreciate that Alex. Tim and I are following up any leads we can think of and we'll let you know if we come up with anything. In the meantime, have you got Alison Burton-Castle's number? I'd like to speak to her and see how she's doing.'

'Sure. I'll get Mitchel to text it to you SAP.'

'Oh good God.' Tim burst out. He sat in the driver's seat scrolling through social media. 'I don't believe it.'

Nick turned to him. 'What is it?'

Tim continued to stare at the screen of his phone. A video was playing,

Nick heard Susie's voice. 'It's Susie.' His voice was hoarse with shock. He craned his neck to see Tim's screen.

'What's happened Nick?' Hawke's voice came over Nick's phone.

Nick didn't reply. He watched in open-mouthed horror as his wife read out a prepared statement to camera. She looked tired and defiant, the side of her face was red, her hair was a mess and her eyes were glazed. The video jumped every few seconds where it had been edited. The sound quality was poor but the message was chilling.

'Nick, can you hear me? What's going on?' Hawke's tone took on a more worried tone.

Tim took Nick's phone off him and replied. 'Alex, it's Tim. I've come across a video on Instagram. It's Susie, she's reading out a statement from the people we're after. It's already had over five thousand views. If you go online and look what's trending you won't be able to miss it.'

Nick tore his eyes away from the screen. 'Alex it's Nick, we have to find these guys. They're threatening to kill her if the PM doesn't do as they say.'

Hawke took a moment before he replied. 'OK guys, I'm not got to pussyfoot. This takes things to a whole new level. It might be best if you came down here. I don't want to rely on phone calls back and forth and if you're at the nerve centre you'll know first-hand what's going on and we can move quicker when we have to.'

Nick took little persuasion. 'Thanks Alex. I think I'd go spare left on my own. I'll get Tim to drop me back home and come down on the bike.'

Tim interrupted. 'Don't be a bloody fool Nick. Your leg will never cope with an hour bent at right angles in these temperatures. I'll take you down there, it's no problem.'

Hawke shared Tim's view. 'He's right Nick, you're both welcome of course, you've seen the set-up here. There's somewhere to sleep, showers, food and probably what you need most, company.'

Nick could see the sense in his argument. 'Yeah, OK. You're probably right. If Tim's OK with it. I'm grateful to both of you.'

Tim said. 'I'll need to call in at my place, pick up some stuff and let Anna know what we're doing. We should be you in a few hours.'

'Great, I'll let you know if I get any news in the meantime.'

'We'll do the same. And thanks again Alex.' Nick ended the call and shut his eyes. 'What a bloody nightmare.'

The Bell Jet Ranger turned towards Tilbury and approached the heliport flying 250 feet above the murky estuary. The sole passenger looked out over the lights reflected in the waters of the Thames and relaxed her grip on the armrests, knowing the one-hour flight from Holland was almost over. She did not like flying at the best of times, but helicopters took her anxiety to a whole new level. She knew the rewards would be worth it and her determination to see the culmination of their plans, outweighed the stress she felt.

She sensed the aircraft slow and start to descend and noted they were no longer over water. She looked out and saw the brightly lit concrete landing pad looming closer. They hovered for a moment then gently dropped the last few feet, the helicopter's suspension soaking up the last of the movement. Lang Yazhu exhaled and unfastened her seat belt. The pilot politely asked her to remain seated until the rotor blades had come to a stop, but she was having none of it. She stood up and collected her bag and beckoned him to open the door. She knew a car would be waiting for her and she was in a hurry. The engine slowed then died, and by the time the pilot had unbuckled his safety harness and opened the door, the blades had come to rest.

Yazhu stepped down, grateful to be on dry land, and looked for her transport. She saw no car but spotted a bearded man standing next to the exit gate with his hand held in front of his chest in a self-conscious wave, as if he wanted her to notice him, but didn't want to attract anyone else's attention. She assumed it must be Kobzar and ignoring the protestations of the pilot, she headed for him.

'Where is the car?' She demanded as soon as she was close enough.

With a hint of a smile and a brief shake of his head, he replied. 'No car, we're going by river. I have a launch ready and waiting for us.' He pointed in the direction of the water and at mooring bollards on the edge of the dock.

She saw nothing. 'What are you pointing at?'

'The tide's out. You'll see, it's moored on the lower jetty. It's a comfortable boat.' Kobzar could see the doubt in Yazhu's face and added. 'It's quicker than going by car and the captain knows the river well. We'll be in the city in under an hour.'

It wasn't what they had agreed, but Yazhu could see the sense in it. She handed her bag to him and nodded in the direction he'd pointed. 'Come on then, let's go.'

The launch was every bit as comfortable as Kobzar had promised. A 30 foot motor cruiser, designed for exclusive corporate engagements and equipped with the amenities and luxuries its intended passengers would expect. Yazhu stepped into the plush cabin to be greeted by a young woman holding a tray with two champagne glasses on it. She dismissed the drinks without a word and took a seat in one of the cabin's armchairs.

Kobzar called up to the captain to let him know they were ready. The captain gave the order to cast off, the engine note changed and they made their way into the centre of the river. The boat rocked gently in the swell, the movement didn't bother Yazhu, as a Macau resident she was used to travelling by boat and felt much more comfortable than she did when flying. They picked up speed as they cleared the dock and motored upstream towards the city on the rising tide.

Kobzar came back into the cabin and sat opposite the woman he'd been dealing with for the last six months. He'd never met her in person, their only contact had been via video calls. He quickly realised she was as formidable in the flesh as she was online. 'Have you seen the video?' He asked tentatively.

'Of course. What's the latest figure for it?' She stared out the window as they passed the few other watercraft, mostly heading downstream for the open sea. At 11.00 p.m.

Kobzar checked his phone. 'Current views are over 1.5 million, it's trending better than expected.'

'Good, your people have done an excellent job. The quality of the video is not great, but it doesn't matter. Has there been any reaction yet?'

'Only people sharing it and re-tweeting it, nothing official. Not that we expected anything at this stage.'

'What about the media?' Yazhu turned away from the window and the view, her eyes swept the interior of the cabin before settling on Kobzar.

'Not that anyone's reported. We assume they are under strict orders not to report it. There are thousands of comments on different social media platforms, it's not as if nobody knows about it.' Kobzar felt any tension between them had dissipated slightly and he risked a little flattery. 'I think your wording of the statement was a masterstroke, all the public's anger will be directed at the Prime Minister and the more he denies it, the less people will believe him. Your plan is brilliant, he'll be gone within the week.'

If the compliment did anything to melt Yazhu's icy demeanour, it didn't show. She waved it away. 'Save your praise for afterwards.'

They passed under the M25 at Dartford and cruised towards Docklands and through the Thames barrier. They followed the river's sharp left meander past the giant dome of the O2 arena. The lights became brighter as they cleared the Isle of Dogs and Canary Wharf, Yazhu appeared fascinated by it all and rarely spoke. Kobzar's knowledge of the landmark buildings was strictly limited and he found himself unable to answer her most basic questions. By the time the launch slowed to a stop in the shadow of the London Eye, Yazhu had given up asking him anything and waited to be escorted off the boat and up to the apartment they had reserved a year in advance.

Miles Wilson made an early start and was on the M40 heading for London before 7:30 a.m. He had a mission and looked forward to doing something he was good at, rather than playing nursemaid or editing videos.

He'd left the two Russian agents with strict instructions to keep checking on the Jones woman. When he recognised their almost total indifference to him, he reminded them it was Kobzar who they would answer to if anything went wrong. It appeared to have some effect and they made the right noises in reply.

He'd packed all he needed into the back of the car and trusted everything else he had asked for would be waiting for him when he arrived. The man they had paid to deliver the bulky part of the deal, assured him his instructions had been carried out to the letter.

It concerned him that Harrison hadn't been in touch and he had to keep reminding himself about the mobile signal at Valley View. There had been nothing on the news about the rescue of the kids, but then, the media had virtually ignored most of the activity of the last week and certainly never mentioned that the whole payment processing system was being held to ransom and depended on two children being found.

As he approached the junction with the M25, his phone rang. He expected the call from Kobzar and tapped a button on the steering wheel to accept the call. 'Just coming into London now, be with you in thirty minutes.'

'Change of plan.' Kobzar said, his tone made it clear the matter wasn't up for discussion.

'That's OK. Nothing's in place yet. What's the score?'

'We need a diversion. We can't take any risks after they got those kids back.'

The news shocked Wilson. 'How do you know they got them back? Harrison said he'd release them later today.'

'You haven't heard?'

'Heard what?'

Kobzar paused as he considered how best to put it. 'I don't know the details, but the Connectivity woman picked the kids up yesterday morning and she's issued all the new line numbers. The payment system is working again.'

Wilson said nothing as he digested the implications of Kobzar's words. It meant whoever had raided Valley View had found the kids, which meant Harrison would have either been arrested or he'd have put up a fight. The thought made his blood run cold. If Harrison had chosen to fight a team of highly armed special forces soldiers, there could only be one outcome. 'Do you know what happened to my lad?' His voice was a mixture of trepidation and despair.

'Can't tell you any more.' Kobzar replied with a complete lack of concern. 'I'll text you the new location. When you get there, head for the underground garage. I'll be waiting.' The call clicked off.

The blast of a car horn shook Wilson out of the swirling emotion that engulfed him. He'd slowed to 40 mph and drifted across the motorway. He swerved into the slow lane and accelerated to keep up with the traffic. He wanted to know more. Worry and frustration filled his brain and he had to fight them to concentrate on the road and what he had been told to do.

Saturday 30 December

Susie woke to the sound of rusty hinges squeaking as the attic door opened. With no phone, no watch and no windows, she had no idea of the time. She couldn't believe how well she'd slept, her bed made of bits hadn't been the most comfortable, but she realised she'd been so tired she would have slept on bare floorboards if she had to. She'd been warm enough and hadn't heard any noises until the door opened. She propped herself up on one elbow and rubbed her eyes. Itchy contact lenses.

The woman Susie had learned was called Irina, entered. When she saw Susie lying in her bed, she felt safe to take a few steps into the room and put the tray she carried down on the floor. 'Breakfast.'

Susie noticed the look in the woman's eyes. The hostility appeared to have been replaced by something approaching curiosity. She didn't seem to be in such a hurry to leave and Susie noticed the other woman wasn't standing at the door with a gun. She didn't look to see what was on the tray but met Irina's gaze. 'Thank you.'

Irina gave a hint of a smile but said nothing.

Susie smiled back. 'Can I please use the loo, I'm bursting.'

The look on Irina's face turned to concern, she looked over her shoulder at the door as if checking no one was watching or listening. 'I'm not supposed to let you out of the room.'

'It's OK, I promise to behave, but I really need to go.'

Irina backed to the door and looked out. She produced a pistol she'd had tucked into the waistband of her jeans and used it to beckon Susie. 'This way, I'll be right behind you and I'll shoot if you try anything.'

Susie held her hands up. 'Don't worry. I'm not going to argue with that.' She nodded at the Makarov and stepped past Irina. She walked slowly, and surreptitiously looked for anything with the potential to aid her escape; a sharp object, something heavy, a possible lever to prise the roof tiles apart. 'What time is it?' she asked, partly to make conversation and partly because she wanted to know.

Irina, three steps behind, checked her watch. 'Eight fifteen.'

'Thanks.' Susie passed a window and looked out. 'Nice day.' She knew the comment was banal but wanted an excuse to stop and get a better idea of her surroundings.

Irina didn't comment. she kept her gun trained on Susie and urged her forward.

They reached the bathroom and Susie reached for the door handle. She turned to her captor for permission to enter.

The request received a sideways tip of the head. 'Don't lock the door.'

Three minutes later, a relieved Susie emerged. 'That's better, thank you.'

The return to the attic gave Susie another opportunity to weigh up her options and do whatever she could to build some degree of trust with Irina. As they approached the door she turned to her. 'Sorry about yesterday, are you OK.'

Irina looked surprised. 'I'm fine. You did what I would have done. I can't blame you for trying.' She watched Susie enter the room, closed the door behind her and locked it. Not another word.

Susie looked down at the breakfast tray. Toast. She hoped it wasn't a metaphor.

33

Breakfast at TIGER HQ met with Nick's wholehearted approval. the full English, complete with black pudding. It was enough to make him forget the anxiety he felt over Susie's situation, almost. He poured himself a second mug of coffee and joined Hawke and Tim in the operations room. They were examining the timeline he'd prepared the previous day. 'Does any of that make sense?'

'It's just what we need Nick, 'Hawke commented without looking up, 'Tim and I have just been saying we need to see where we can fill in some of the blanks or answer some of the questions you've marked.'

'Have you heard from the guys going through the wreckage of Warrenford?'

'I called Fire and Rescue ten minutes ago, they're getting the incident chief to call me back as soon as he gets the message.'

'Great. It's been niggling me for days. One of the guys there reminded me of someone, but I can't think who.'

Tim tapped another question mark on the timeline. 'You've written something here about Susie getting a call from Whitehall. What's that about?'

'Yeah. She'd called Whitehall on Saturday while I was in hospital. She left a message and someone called her back on Sunday. Whoever it was told her about this guy.' Nick pointed to his doodle of Matthews. 'Without her phone we have no way on knowing who called her, so we can't trace Matthews. He's a mystery man.'

Hawke lifted a hand, index finger extended in a knowing way. 'What network is Susie on?'

'She's on EE, why?'

'I can get them to give us her phone records for last Sunday, we'll be able to trace the number that called her, and also track down whoever she called immediately afterwards. If you give me her number, I'll get one of the team to get onto them now.'

Nick wrote Susie's number on a slip of paper and passed it to the analyst who appeared in response to Hawke's signal.

'Are we trusting that Alison's team are all above suspicion?' Tim asked his focus still on the timeline.

Nick and Hawke exchanged glances. 'No harm in checking.' Hawke signalled for another analyst to join them. 'Georgia, call Alison Burton-Castle at Connectivity, her number's on the status board, ask her for details of people who have access to the confidential line IDs. I think she said there were three of them. We'll need whatever they've got on file. When you get them, run a complete background check and let me know.'

Georgia gave a quick affirmative nod and left.

Nick watched her leave and had another thought. 'What happened to the woman at the cottage, the one who'd been looking after the kids?'

Hawke raised an eyebrow. 'Good thinking. Her name's Pia. We put her in a safe house until we've got time to question her properly, from initial reports it sounds like she's had a hell of a time. Been virtually kept prisoner there. I gather she was told she'd be deported if the authorities ever found out about her.'

'It might be worth getting her in and seeing if she can throw any light on where they might have taken Susie. It's doubtful, but, hey, what've we got to lose?'

Hawke switched his phone to speaker mode when the call came in. 'This is Hawke.'

'Ah, hello Commander, it's Captain Roberts, Sam Roberts, I'm the incident chief here at the Warrenford, site. I have been asked to call you as a matter of urgency.'

'Thanks Captain, just so you know, I've got you on speakerphone and I have Nick Cooper and Tim Spencer with me, they're both involved and have full clearance.'

'That's OK, what can I tell you?'

'We're trying to work out who might have planted the explosives and wanted to know if you've been able to identify any of the bodies?'

Roberts sighed. 'It's been one of the worst incidents I've ever attended, and the forensic guys have had a gruesome job of piecing together the remains.'

'I'm sure. I don't know how you guys can do what you do.'

'Thanks, but...' Roberts paused. 'Yeah, it can be a real shit job at times. I'm sure I don't need to tell you.'

Hawke didn't want to dwell. 'What did you discover after all their work?"

'Right. Sorry. We've identified six bodies, three females and three males. Without going into too much detail, there's not a lot left to identify them, but...'

Nick interrupted. 'Hang on, there should be seven.'

'What seven bodies?' Roberts sounded surprised.

Hawke looked at Nick. 'You sure?'

'Yeah, there was a young woman downstairs on the reception desk, I think Susie called her Yasmin. There were two more women in the control tower, then there were the two comms guys plus Millard and Commander Eddington. That's seven.'

'I don't dispute what you're saying, but we've only got six bodies here.' Captain Roberts confirmed.

Hawke took a deep breath. 'Is there any way you can put names to any of them?'

'Well, you said there were three women and we have three female bodies. What you're asking is which of the four men you mention isn't here. Correct?'

'Correct.' Nick answered before Hawke could say anything.

'It would help if you could describe the four men, we might be able to tell you which one's missing. Otherwise it'll have to wait until the coroner can do a more thorough investigation.'

Hawke let Nick continue. 'The two tech guys were late 20s early 30s, one of them was Asian heritage, the other was white, both had short hair. Millard was late 40s early 50s thick beard, long hair, white and a bit overweight. Commander Eddington was tall, mid 50s, white, and when we left he was wearing police uniform.' Nick looked at Hawke and saw him close his eyes and slowly shake his head at the mention of his old friend.

'Give me a moment.' Roberts said. A minute passed and they waited in silence. 'Right, I can confirm we have the two comms guys as you call them and Commander Eddington, but not the other one, sorry didn't catch his name.'

'Millard.' Nick spoke through clenched teeth. 'I've had a feeling about him.'

'What about him?' Hawke asked.

'His accent, broad Norfolk. Just the way he spoke, he reminded me of someone, but I can't think who.' Nick tapped the side of his head hoping to unlock the answer.

Roberts interrupted Nick's search for an answer. 'Can I leave that with you, I need to get on here.'

'Of course, Captain, thank you for your help.' Hawke ended the call and turned to Nick. 'If Millard was the one who set the explosives, he's probably ex-forces.'

'Makes sense.'

'In which case it should be easy to track him down.' He called one of his team over. 'Can you search for a Wade Millard, check Army records first, maybe engineers or bomb disposal.' The analyst did another bob of affirmation and left.

Nick turned to Tim, 'Are you going to say it, or shall I?'

Tim suppressed a grin. 'Just 'cos he's a fireman and his name's Sam. I wouldn't lower myself.'

Hawke had two of his team take Nick's timeline and re-create it on a three-metre whiteboard mounted on an adjustable stand. It brought the focus of their attention up to eye level and meant they didn't have to lean over the table and develop back strain in the process. He took a red marker pen and circled one of the seven faces depicted at the control tower. He wrote Millard's name beside one of them and circled it twice, with a little more force than strictly necessary.

He studied the board and didn't hear Nick approach and stand next to him. 'What's next?' Nick asked.

Hawke pointed at two question marks on the timeline. Who was Matthews and who gave out the line IDs. 'If we get answers to those two questions, we can make progress.' He called across the operations room to the analyst he'd asked to obtain Susie's phone record. 'Curtis, what's happening with EE?'

'They're emailing it over now Commander, I'll print it and bring it over in a minute.'

Tim joined Nick and Hawke at the whiteboard. 'I've just been talking your man over there.' He jerked his head in the direction of the analysts. 'The one you asked to search for Millard.'

'And?' Hawke said.

'And... nothing, nada, zip. Nobody of that name on any records. Well, that's not strictly true, there were three; one was dead, one was in his seventies and one was a teenager. I think it's safe to say our Mr Millard is a fake.'

'How the hell did Rob end up with him on his team? His vetting process is by the book, they'd have checked every detail about him, education, medical history, family background. You can't fake that level of detail.' Hawke looked mystified.

Tim nodded. 'You're right. You or I might not be able to fake it, but some people can. I'd be interested in the dead guy. When was he born? When did he die?'

Nick caught the gist of Tim's comment. 'You're talking about creating an identity using the details of someone who's dead but was born at roughly the right time?'

'You've got it, wasn't there a film where the assassin did something like that?'

'Day of the Jackal,' said Nick. 'Great film.'

'I remember it well, based on Frederick Forsyth's book.' Hawke added. 'Trouble is, that loophole's been closed now everything's on computer.

Tim considered this. 'He might have done enough not to flag up any worries, especially if they were pushed for people.

While Hawke processed the information, Curtis arrived with a single sheet of paper and handed it to him. 'There's only seven calls all day.'

Hawke passed the paper to Nick. 'Any of those jump out at you?'

Nick studied the numbers. 'There's an incoming call from a London number, that must have been Whitehall ringing her.'

Hawke called Curtis. 'Call the London number, the one ending 037, see who answers.'

Nick continued. 'The next mobile number I don't recognise, it has to be Matthews. She said she rang straight after getting the call from the MOD.'

Curtis heard the remark. 'You want me to call that number as well?'

'No.' Hawke paused and pinched his nose. 'Forget the London number. Get onto the network, see if that mobile is active. Let's see if we can locate him first, rather than let him know we're on to him.'

'Please let me be there when you find him.' Said Nick. 'I'd like to shake him warmly by the neck.'

Hawke rested a hand on Nick's shoulder. 'You'll get your chance after I've had a word with him.'

'I've got the results of the Level 4 background checks on the three people at Connectivity.' Georgia called from her workstation.

'Ah, great. Any red flags?'

'Sorry Commander, they all check out. 100% clean.'

'OK, so we can eliminate them.' Hawke took the red pen and crossed off each of the three graphics drawn on the whiteboard to indicate Alison Burton-Castle's trusted team. 'I don't know if that's good or bad. What are we left with?'

Tim had poured himself a mug of coffee, he rested against a desk and surveyed the whiteboard. 'Has anyone asked Alison if she's had any visitors to her office in the last few months?'

Nick and Hawke exchanged puzzled glances. 'What are you suggesting?'

'Just a thought. Does she sweep her office for listening devices or could someone have got to her laptop?'

Hawke understood Tim's thought process. 'It's worth checking, it wouldn't take long to download the data onto a thumb drive.'

Nick said. 'She told Susie her laptop has multiple layers of security, she said nobody could get into it without the right codes and it creates a record of everyone who goes into it.'

'But what if she was already logged in, and left the room, or got distracted?' Said a pensive Tim.

They were interrupted by an enthusiastic Curtis. 'I've got a location for the mobile number.'

Hawke turned towards the analyst. 'Excellent, where is it?'

Curtis savoured the moment. 'You're not going to believe this.'

34

Don't play silly buggers, Curtis.' Said Hawke. 'Just tell us.'

'It's the address you gave me for Mrs Burton-Castle.'

Hawke had to take a moment. 'Are you sure?'

'No doubt about it Commander, I've checked it twice, 23 Radmore Road, Oxford. It's active now.'

Nick stared open-mouthed at the whiteboard, he could see question marks fading and answers appearing. 'You know what this means, don't you.' He didn't turn to look at Tim and Hawke, he knew they were thinking the same thing.

'Are you suggesting Alison Burton-Castle is behind this?' Hawke asked

'I doubt it, she was sick with worry about her kids. But it looks like Mr Burton-Castle has an alias.'

'I need to speak to her right now.' Hawke reached for his phone.

Nick held a hand up. 'Hold on Alex. We don't want to spook him.'

Hawke said. 'Don't worry, I'm just ringing to see how she's doing.' He gave Nick a conspiratorial wink as he tapped Burton-Castle's number and switched the speaker on.

All three listened as the phone rang, once, twice, three times, then. 'Hello.'

'Hello Alison, it's Alex Hawke, I was calling to see how you're all doing.'

'Oh, Hi, thanks, the children are tired but otherwise seem remarkably OK, I don't think they were treated too badly. Noah thinks it was all a bit of excitement, Jenni was more bothered about not having a phone or a change of clothes. But, yeah, so far so good.'

'How about you and Mr Burton-Castle?'

'You mean Don?'

'Yes.'

'Oh, sorry, he's not Mr Burton-Castle, he's Donald Matthews. My husband died in an accident five years ago. Don and I have been together for couple of years, we're not married.'

Hawke was momentarily silent. He saw the look on Nick and Tim's faces, they looked as shocked as he felt. He chose his words carefully. 'I understand Alison, my mistake. Has he recovered from his injuries?'

'Huh. Between you and me, I think he was milking it for all it was worth. Anything for a little sympathy and attention. But he's OK thanks. He's in his study, spends half his life in there, tells me it's confidential government business.'

'I see. And how are you? You've been through hell these last few days. I gather you got the new numbers out yesterday.'

'I suspect it'll catch up with me eventually, but I'm good at the moment. It looks like the payment companies are all online again, so hopefully all the chaos should subside.'

Hawke thanked her and ended the call. He shook his head slowly while looking at the whiteboard. 'We need Mr Donald Matthews brought in for questioning, I think he has a lot to tell us.'

Nick took the red pen and stepped up to the whiteboard. He stabbed it on Matthews name and circled it three times, then drew lines connecting him to the questions they'd written at the bottom of the board. 'That bastard dropped Susie in it, he must have got the data off Alison's laptop and he must have tipped off the people in the cottage. Alison would no doubt have told him in all innocence.' He paused as another thought hit him. 'And he must have been party to the kids being abducted. What a fucking devious shit.'

'It explains all that.' Hawke jutted his chin at the whiteboard. 'But we're still in the dark about Millard, maybe Mr Matthews can help us with that.'

Tim added. 'He may even be able to tell us where Susie is.'

The idea of that brightened Nick's mood.

***

Hawke decided against telling Alison Burton-Castle they were about to bring Matthews in for questioning. He asked the local police to keep it as low-key as possible and not give him the chance to make any phone calls. He also warned them Matthews presented a flight risk but advised against cuffing him or cautioning him. He was helping with enquiries and not being arrested.

Two hours after the pick-up had been ordered Matthews arrived, escorted by two uniformed officers. Hawke chose to use one of the offices instead of the interview room, he arranged two chairs facing each other and had one of the technical team set up a couple of concealed cameras to enable Nick and Tim to observe.

'What is this all about? Don't you know who I am?' Matthews blustered, indignation written all over his face.

'Please take a seat Mr Matthews, I'm Commander Hawke. We've asked you here to help us with an ongoing situation.'

'Asked?' Matthews scoffed. 'I don't remember being given any choice. Those men wouldn't let me talk to my wife and they took my phone from me before bundling me into their car and driving here at a ridiculous speed without a word.'

Hawke remained unruffled. 'I'm sorry you've been inconvenienced, but we believe you may be in possession of certain facts.'

'Do you indeed? And what gives you the authority to drag a senior civil servant out of their house on a Saturday afternoon without explanation, without allowing me to call my solicitor or telling anyone where I'm going?' Matthews folded his arms and glared at Hawke.

'All in good time, Mr Matthews. If you'll allow me to explain.'

'You can start by explaining what this place is. It's obviously not a police station and you're not in uniform.'

'You've been brought to the headquarters of a covert government organisation. I can assure you we have the authority to bring in whoever we want to question. You haven't been arrested but we trust that as a senior civil servant you will be willing to cooperate.'

Matthews huffed and appeared to accept Hawke's explanation, albeit reluctantly. 'Very well. What do you want to know?'

Hawke picked up a buff-coloured folder from the small coffee table between them. He opened it and studied the first page as if reading it for the first time. 'A woman named Susan Jones called you at 10.47 a.m. last Sunday, and you called her back ten minutes later. Can you tell me about those calls?'

Nick and Tim watched the feed from the hidden camera showing a close-up of Matthew's face. They saw his eyes dart left and right while he tried to look affronted.

'You must be mistaken. I've never heard of the woman.'

'Not even when your wife, I mean Mrs Burton-Castle, mentioned her to you?'

'I deal with a lot of people in my job, you can't possibly expect me to remember them all.'

'I mentioned her to you when I spoke to you while you were lying in bed, injured.' Hawke emphasised the word lying.

'Possibly, but I'd been assaulted, I wasn't very receptive.

'You called Susan Jones a second time last Sunday and asked her to drive to a Starbucks restaurant. Do you deny doing that?'

'Of course I deny it, I don't know what you're talking about.'

Hawke produced the mobile phone the police had taken from Matthews when they picked him up. 'This is your phone, correct?'

'I've never seen if before.' Matthews barely looked at the device, his eyes flitted around the room and settled on nothing.

'It was on your desk, in your study when the police came to your house.' Hawke held the phone in front of Matthew's face. 'If it's not yours, whose is it?'

Matthews appeared to have some sort of internal conflict going on inside his head. He stared at the phone, then at Hawke, then at the paper in Hawke's hand. Finally, he said. 'I may have spoken to her but I can't remember the details.'

'So, you can confirm this is your phone? Hawke rephrased his previous question.

'I suppose it must be, I get given a new phone now and then at work.'

'We know that. The phone issued to you was found smashed when you were assaulted.'

This stumped Matthews and he seemed to suddenly deflate. 'I, I can explain.' he stammered.

Nick nudged Tim without taking his eyes off the monitor. 'He's cracked him.'

Hawke continued the pressure. 'Can you also tell us who you called between the two calls you made to Ms Jones? And, before you say anything, I should tell you we've traced the location of that phone.'

At this Matthews slumped forward and dropped his head into his hands.

***

Once Matthews had accepted defeat, Hawke took him back through the timeline and drew more details out of him. He confessed to downloading the data off Alison Burton-Castle's laptop when she left it open and left the room. He admitted to handing the thumb drive to a Russian who had been blackmailing him.

Hawke pressed him. 'You're only a victim of blackmail if you've done something wrong. What did you do?'

Matthews couldn't look him in the eye, he stared at the ground and in a voice barely above a whisper said. 'Last year, I was on a trade mission in Macau, I'd gone back to my hotel and went to the bar for a drink. A girl, no, a young woman, very pretty, joined me, asked me to buy her a drink, and...Do I need to go into details?'

'And they filmed the whole thing.' Hawke finished. 'A classic honey trap.'

Matthews nodded slowly. 'They pulled me aside the next day and showed me the video.'

Who's "they"?'

Matthews shrugged. 'I don't know, a couple of local heavies.'

'What did they say?'

'They didn't. They just showed me the video and left. I never heard another thing about it for two or three weeks. Then I got a call from the Russian.' Matthews shuddered at the memory.

Hawke checked his notes. 'This was Rostyslav Kobzar?'

Matthews nodded again.

'And he knew your partner was the Operations Director at Connectivity?'

'He knew everything. He knew about Alison, he knew her routine. He promised me if I gave him the data he wanted, the video would be deleted.'

'And you believed him?' Hawke tried not to sound incredulous but failed.

'I know, I am such an idiot. I knew if that video got out, my relationship would be over, probably my job as well. I thought I had no choice and obviously I had no idea of the damage he could do with the data.'

'You must have known you'd be locked up if you were caught?'

'I didn't think I'd be caught.' Matthews said simply.

'So, after that, Mr Kobzar had you in his pocket,' Hawke continued. 'You told him about Jones, you sent her to Starbucks, you feigned being assaulted and you warned him about the planned rescue of Alison's children?'

Matthew said nothing, he sat with his head in his hands and snivelled.

Hawke stood up and gave Matthews a pitying look. 'I'll give you five minutes to pull yourself together. Then I want to talk to you about Kobzar, he's in the wind and we want to find him.'

Nick and Tim watched Hawke leave and turned to greet him a few seconds later as he entered the room they had sat in for the last ninety minutes.

Hawke fell back into a spare chair. 'If I live to be a hundred and fifty, I'll never understand how stupid some people are.'

'We never thought he break so quickly.' said Nick.

'Nor did I at first. He's weak, as well as stupid.'

Tim asked. 'What did Alison say when you called her?'

Hawke couldn't help a little smirk. 'It was just as well I called after they'd picked him up. She'd have killed him if she'd got her hands on him, she never wants to see him again. She had some very unladylike words for him.'

Tim drove through the dark on their way back up the M40, Nick sat in the passenger seat and mulled over what they had learned from Matthews. 'If we believe what he said, he's never met Millard or whoever he is.'

'You're right; I don't think he'd even heard of him. He seemed more worried about the guy he called Kobzar, the Russian.'

'It makes sense. Susie said those two women spoke with an accent she thought could be Russian, he sounds like the man in charge.'

Tim turned off the motorway and followed the A34 towards Yarnton. 'He's just the local man, the enforcer. Someone's giving him orders; there's no way he could have organised the virus. This has been planned for months if not years.'

Nick sat in silence for a couple of minutes as they sped South. 'You know I said I had a feeling about Millard?'

'You have mentioned it once or twice.'

'Sorry, I know you've never seen him, but when I think about him, I'm pretty sure he's someone you know.'

'Are you thinking back to Afghanistan?'

'Could be. Certainly army. I want to look at some old photos when we get back, can you hang on and see if any of them ring any bells?'

'Mate, I'll do anything that helps. I'll let Anna know; she's making supper.'

It took another ten minutes to get to Nick's house and five more for Nick to rummage through his collection of old photo albums and emerge with the ones he wanted. 'These are my second tour. There's some group shots and I'm sure you're in these.' He put the album on the breakfast bar, and the pair flipped through the pages.

Nick found a magnifying glass and scanned the images in more detail. 'Not sure what I'm looking for, but I'll know when I see it.'

Tim shook his head slowly as they searched. 'It's one hell of a record, mate; I can't believe it was over 12 years ago.'

'Hmm, I know. It's a bit sad, really. I hardly ever print anything these days, only if clients ask. It's all digital now. I miss the real thing.'

'There's nobody here jumping out at me,' said Tim as they reached the last page of the album, 'maybe your imagination is playing tricks on you.'

Nick frowned. 'Have another look with this.' He handed Tim the magnifying glass. 'I'll go and see if there's another album.' He left the kitchen and returned two minutes later with a cardboard box. 'This has a got a bunch of prints I didn't think were worth putting in an album. They're a bit of a mishmash, but I can't think where else to look.'

They pushed the album to one side, spread the prints out and quickly sorted them into piles, army and non-army. They leafed through the army ones: lots of group prints, some random, some of specialist units or teams, a few individuals, some posed, some candid. Nick examined each one and passed it to Tim, who peered at it more closely. Nick picked up one group shot and paused a little longer. He'd photographed a large group of about twenty, all in desert fatigues, most standing side by side, doing their best to look mean and moody. Four of the men squatted at the front. Tim was pictured in the middle of the group. 'Who's this young man?' Nick tapped Tim's image.

'Jeez. We thought we were the real deal back then. Thought we were invincible.' Tim ran his finger from left to right along the row and tried to remember who was who. He stopped when he reached a figure two from the end on the right. 'What's he doing there?'

Nick glanced at the face Tim had singled out. 'The older guy? Who is he?'

'Wilson. Bloody Lieutenant Wilson.' Tim's jaw clenched, his eyes narrowed.

'What about him?'

'He was bomb disposal, supposed to disarm any IEDs we detected.'

'Shit,' Nick snatched the print and the magnifying glass from Tim and studied the face in more detail, 'it was his fuck up that resulted in you getting blown up.'

'And two of my guys coming home in coffins.' Tim glared at the print.

Nick said nothing. He looked at Wilson's image, and enlightenment spread across his face. 'That's him.'

'I know, I've just told you.'

'No, that's Millard. Millard is Wilson. That's the face that's been bugging me. I remember now he had a broad Norfolk accent and those hooded eyes.'

'Are you sure?'

'Hundred per cent. He was dishonourably discharged when they discovered he was under the influence on duty. He was held responsible for your injuries and the death of your two men. I never forget a face, well, hardly ever. The beard and glasses had me fooled, but I knew there was something about him that reminded me of someone. Well spotted mate.'

Tim gave a slow shake of his head. 'Thanks, but that's one face I never wanted to see again.'

'That's probably why the print never made it into an album.'

'We need to call Alex and get him to trace him.' Tim pushed the print away.

'Can you remember his first name?' Nick reached for his phone. 'I'll ring Alex now.'

'Sadly I can, it's Miles, Miles bloody Wilson.'

35

By ten in the evening, Susie had managed three more trips to the bathroom since her first visit. She was convinced Irina must have assumed she had a bladder issue of some description but had been too polite to say anything. Every time she made the trip, she went out of her way to be the model prisoner and attempted a little small talk to break the ice. She'd learned about Stockholm Syndrome and acted the part of the hostage seeking to bond with her captor.

She had seen what she wanted on the first trip, every subsequent trip was designed to generate the impression that she could be trusted and didn't need to be followed at gunpoint. The ploy appeared to be working on the last trip, Irina had unlocked the attic door, stood aside and waited for Susie to do what she had to do. When she returned, Susie thanked her for her patience and thanked her again for bringing her something warm to eat earlier in the evening. Irina's reply was brief and noncommittal, but the ice maiden thawed. Susie had the object she'd picked up hidden inside her jacket and waited for the door to close before she brought it out and examined it thoroughly.

She'd seen the window's broken latch bar on her first visit to the bathroom and knew it would be perfect to lever the slates apart. She knew there was little chance it would be missed, but just in case, she decided to wait until late in the day before she took it. The bar itself was solid, but the bracket holding it in place had rusted through and the bar snapped off in her hand without making a sound.

Susie listened to Irina's footsteps as she walked away from the door and waited until she was certain she would be undisturbed until the following morning when she'd be back with more toast and find her gone.

The latch bar was every bit as effective as Susie hoped, and within two minutes, she'd been able to work one tile free. She lifted it into the attic and stashed it beneath her bed. She'd only need to remove four or five to make enough room to squeeze through. But she didn't want to get out until she was sure the two women were asleep. She waited.

Unlike Donald Matthew, Pia Cavell entered Hawke's office with enthusiasm. She took a seat and looked relieved to be there. The female officer who had accompanied her to the TIGER HQ, brought her a cup of coffee and a plate of Hobnobs, then waited outside.

Hawke had been briefed on what she had already told the team that had been looking after her in the safe house. He wanted to assure her she was safe and kept introductions informal and friendly. He sympathised with her for the trauma she had endured over the previous two years and told her she would never have to go back to that place.

He wanted to know more about Harrison and the other people who had arrived with the two children.

'What was Harrison's second name?' He asked conversationally.

'Thurlow.' She spelled it out for Hawke. 'But he changed it.'

Hawke looked confused. 'What did he change it to?'

'No, he changed it to Thurlow.'

'Ah. Do you know what it was before he changed it?'

'Wilson.' She said proudly. 'He didn't tell me, but when his dad arrived, I knew that's what it was.'

'His dad was called Wilson?'

'Yes, Miles Wilson.'

Hawke remained poker-faced. The revelation confirmed what Nick had rung to tell him before Pia arrived. He wanted to celebrate this news with a fist pump or a muted shout but restrained himself. 'That's great, thank you.'

He went on to get details of the two women who had arrived with the Burton-Castle children. Pia knew their first names, didn't know their surnames, but gave him a description of them both. The descriptions were good enough for the facial recognition software to produce a reasonable facsimile that might help to identify them.

She knew nothing about where Miles Wilson and the two women had gone after they escaped through the tunnel. She told Hawke she'd heard them mention a farm, but they never said where it was or what it was called.

The last three tiles only took two minutes to remove. Susie added them to the one under her bed, then replaced the polystyrene block to stop the cold air blowing in. She had to take a wild guess at the time and lay quietly, listening for any signs of life in the farmhouse.

Silence.

The previous morning, when Irina had brought her toast and she'd visited the bathroom, it was daylight, and she realised the hole she had created would face East towards the sunrise. She planned to get out when there was just enough light to see where was going, but well before the sun peeked over the horizon. She trusted breakfast would arrive at the same time and unless they changed their routine, she'd be able to get clear of the place before they realised she was missing.

Impatience nagged at her. The need to escape fought with the worry of getting re-captured. After her efforts in building Irina's trust, Susie knew that if she was caught again, she'd get no sympathy, no matter how much they said they needed her for another video.

With a final look around the attic, she made her mind up and decided it was now or never. Not wanting any light to be seen from outside, and to make it harder for them to see when they came looking for her, she stood on tiptoes and removed the single light bulb in the centre of the attic.

Plunged into darkness and going by feel alone, Susie knelt and removed the polystyrene block. Cold air rushed in. She'd stuffed the sleeping bag with clothes and blankets in an attempt to disguise her absence and hopefully buy her another few seconds. She climbed over the bed, stuck her head through the hold and peered out. A faint light on the eastern horizon confirmed she'd waited long enough. The edge of the roof extended a mere couple of feet below her, and beyond that, a dark void. She'd have to climb to the ridge and hope the other side presented a better opportunity to get down to the ground.

She wriggled and twisted to get her shoulders through the hole, then had to drag her legs through while she hung on to the roof. The tiles were slippery, and she lay across them, reached back into the hole and pulled the polystyrene block back into place as best she could. She paused for a couple of seconds and listened for any indication of movement.

Satisfied, she started to inch her way to the ridge. Her boots gave her no purchase and she had to cling to the tiles with bare hands, stretch out on her belly, and slither up the slope, caterpillar like, one tile at a time. It took her more than three minutes before she pulled herself to the top and sat aside the ridge. The curved ridge tiles weren't just wet, they were icy and without gloves, her hands felt frozen. She rubbed them together and tucked them under her armpits while she recovered from her climb.

There was just enough light to make out the end of the ridge furthest from the house. She pushed and pulled herself along it until she could look down and see if there was a way off the roof that wouldn't raise the alarm or result in a broken leg.

She made out the roof of a small extension built onto the gable end of the building and judged it to be about eight feet below her. It would have to do. She managed a controlled slide down the western side of the roof until she reached the gutter. It brought the roof of the extension to with a couple of feet. She dropped down onto it without making a sound, then lowered herself off its side, before she let go and fell the last couple of feet to the ground.

Crouching in the dark, Susie listened again, and again she heard no signs of life. In the pre-dawn light, she managed to get her bearings and worked out where she was in relation to the other building she'd seen when she escaped from the shipping container almost 48 hours earlier.

She kept to the edges of the buildings until she reached the one she was after, an open-sided barn used as an implement store. With fingers crossed, she stepped cautiously towards the back and found what she was looking for. She breathed a sigh of relief when she found the ignition key was still in place. Ludmila hadn't removed it after escorting her back to the farm and she just hoped she hadn't gone back to retrieve it later.

Susie said a quiet thanks to the spirits of sloppy security.

The quad bike had been parked facing into the barn and she had to pull it out backwards, careful to avoid hitting anything that would make a noise. Tempted to start the engine and just go-for-it, she resisted, and wanted to get as far as she could from the farmhouse, as she knew how noisy the machine was. It was heavy to push and twice she lost her footing and almost ended up face down in the mud, but she cleared the barn and headed towards the track where Ludmila had caught her.

Once on the track, the quad was easier to push, and Susie speeded up to a gentle jog. She glanced back over her shoulder, half expecting lights to come on and someone to emerge from the house, but it remained quiet, the only noise, the rumble of the knobbly tyres, the whirring of the gearbox and her laboured breathing.

Ahead of her, she could see where the track entered the woodland, another fifty yards to go. She tried to go faster, but despite her fitness, her reserves of strength had been sapped by cold and tiredness and were close to zero. She offered up a silent prayer to the mechanical gods that the engine would start when she turned the key.

Out of the corner of her eye, she saw a light. She kept jogging but risked another peek behind her. A single light shone in one of the upstairs bedroom windows of the farmhouse. It spurred her on, and with a last gasp effort she reached the shelter of the woods. She slowed to a walk, then stopped. The exertion had warmed her, she was out of breath, but couldn't rest.

Instrument lights came on when she turned the key. She jumped onboard and hit the starter button. The engine coughed and missed. She held her thumb on the button and kept the starter spinning. It coughed again, fired once, missed, then roared into life. In the silence of the woods, the noise was deafening, it would wake every living thing for miles around. She held the clutch in, stamped on the gear lever, thumbed the throttle and released the clutch. The machine took off. Front wheels left the ground for a second, before Susie threw herself forward and hung on, head down, eyes squinting against the freezing air.

The little woodland was only a hundred yards deep and she emerged onto a paved road. She stopped and looked back at the track, saw a sign "Upper Marsh Farm", and made a mental note for future reference. She had to decide, left or right, which was the quickest way to find help. There was no way of knowing. Being left-handed and seeing the light in the sky on her left, she pointed the quad bike in that direction and sped off.

Within a minute her lack of gloves, helmet or any basic protection from the elements, took its toll. She wanted to go faster but she felt exposed, vulnerable and frozen to the bone. The early morning winter air whistled through her clothing and numbed her fingers, toes and face. She didn't dare slow down and feared looking behind in case someone was pursuing her. The bike had no mirrors, so she squinted against the thirty mile an hour blast and kept going. After another five minutes, her eyes were streaming and her face was numb, she started to wonder if she should have turned right instead of left when she got to the end of the farm track. Should she turn around or go on? The fear of meeting someone coming in the opposite direction made the decision for her, she crouched as low as she could and pressed on. There had to be a village, a hamlet or just a single house somewhere.

With her speed down to less than 20 mph, and her eyesight failing, she almost missed the sign announcing the village of Carsden. She slowed to a crawl, turned a corner and went up a short incline to bring her to the centre of what she imagined was a picture postcard village in daylight, complete with duckpond, church, pub and convenience store. At sunrise in the middle of Winter, it looked deserted. The store devoid of life, and not even an early morning dog walker in sight.

She spotted a phone box and killed the quad bike's engine. She staggered off the machine, every joint and every limb protesting after being frozen in place for the last ten minutes. A few stretches and some quick on-the-spot jogging, restored a little circulation and she stumbled forwards, longing to speak to Nick. She'd reached the door to the box, before two things stopped her in her tracks. The first was the sudden realisation that Nick didn't have his phone anymore. No problem, she could ring Anna and get a message to him. The second thing was a little more final. The phone box no longer had a phone, it had been converted into a community book exchange. Susie shook her head as reality hit home. Who the hell uses a public phone box these days.

Her teeth were chattering, and she could no longer feel her fingers. She doubted she could hold a mobile phone, let along press the right numbers. She rubbed her eyes with the back of her hands and stared at the store. Somebody had to be awake. She tried to jog towards the store but found her legs didn't want to play that game and approached the door at as brisk a walk as she could manage.

She heard movement inside and banged on the door.

'We don't open 'til Nine.' A male voice called from inside.

'I nnnee hel..' Susie discovered her jaw, like her legs, didn't want to cooperate. She worked the muscles around her mouth for a moment and tried again. 'I need help.' This time it came out as something more intelligible. She banged on the door again for emphasis.

'Hang on.'

She heard footsteps and the rattle of keys. The lock turned and the door opened to reveal an elderly man, wearing pyjamas, dressing gown and slippers. He peered at Susie through a pair of filthy spectacles.

'Good grief, you look frozen, what's happened to you?' Despite the stubble on his chin, the thinning silver hair and the ruddy complexion, he had a kind face. He looked concerned and stood aside to usher Susie inside.

She stepped into the warmth and wanted to hug the old man. 'Sorry to bother you, but I need to make a phone call, I don't have a phone and the phone box,' She pointed over her shoulder. 'isn't a phone box. It's a real emergency. Can you help?'

The man smiled. 'Of course, come and sit down, I don't have a mobile phone, but you can use my wife's.' He led Susie into the back of the store where a gas stove radiated heat and a couple of chairs were arranged beside it. 'I'll go and get it for you, the kettle's just boiled, I'll make you a nice cup of tea while you use the phone.'

Susie could have kissed him.

36

Anna stirred scrambled eggs while Tim laid the table. It might have been New Year's Eve, but it was Sunday and it had become something of a habit to have a cooked breakfast on Sundays. They weren't normally up before nine in the morning, but Coco the new puppy had other ideas and neither of them were complaining.

When Anna's phone rang, Tim saw the screen light up before she heard the ringtone. The caller's number showed, but neither of them recognised it.

'Can you get it.' Anna peered at the device without touching it. 'It's no one I know.'

Tim tapped the screen to accept the call and switched the speaker on. 'Hello.' He said, warily.

'Tim, it's Susie.' A breathless voice announced.

Anna almost dropped the wooden spoon she had in her hand; Tim picked the phone off the worktop. 'Susie, are you OK?'

'Yeah, I'm fine; cold, hungry, tired and filthy dirty, but otherwise, I'm fit as a fiddle.'

Anna called out. 'We've been worried sick about you.'

'Where the hell are you?' Tim asked. 'Have you rung Nick; he's going out of his mind.'

'No, his phone got destroyed at Warrenford, Anna's is the only number I could remember.'

Tim looked at the handset and frowned. 'Your name didn't come up when you rang.'

Susie gave a brief laugh. 'That's 'cos my phone was taken off me. My new best friend, Gerald, has let me borrow his wife's phone to call yo u.'

'Who's Gerald?'

'I'll introduce you later. I'm in a village called Carsden, Gerald runs the local shop, he's been looking after me.'

'Where's Carsden?'

'Haven't got a clue, it'll be on a map. Is there any chance you could get in touch with Nick and let him know I'm OK and where I am. And can you ask him to come and get me in the Volvo.'

'Of course we can. Only one teeny tiny problem.'

'Tell me. He's OK isn't he?' Asked a worried Susie.

'Oh, nothing like that. It's just that you've got the keys for the Volvo. It's still sitting the field where you left it.'

'Doh. Never thought about that.' She paused for a moment; they could hear her rummage in her pockets. 'Ah. It's here, it's a single key. They must have missed it when they took everything off me.'

'Don't worry about it now love.' Anna, called. 'We'll go and pick him up and then come and get you.'

'You sure?'

'Absolutely.'

'Can I ask you another favour?'

'Ask away.' Said Anna.

'When you get to our place, can you nip up to my room and get me some fresh clothes. I've been wearing the same stuff for the last three days and...well, you know what I like.'

'Say no more.' Said Tim. 'Can we call you back on Gerald's phone if we need directions?'

They heard muted conversation for a few seconds, then. 'Yeah, Gerald says that's fine, and, thanks guys, see you soon.' The line clicked off.

'The scrambled eggs might have to wait, love.' Tim hugged Anna; and a wave of relief washed over them both. 'I'll ring Nick and Alex, if you find where Carsden is.

Lang Yazhu stood at the picture window and looked across the Thames at the Houses of Parliament. The building epitomised everything she hated about the country, arrogance, superiority, prejudice and outdated class values. As she sipped her green tea, she relished anticipating what was to come.

When she heard Kobzar's phone, she turned and saw him emerge from the bathroom, towel in hand, dabbing his face post-shave. He hurried, partly in response to the ringtone and partly because of the disapproving look on Yazhu's face. He gave the screen a cursory glance before accepting the call. 'I told you not to call me unless it was urgent.' He kept his voice low.

He held the phone close to his ear, not wanting Yazhu to hear the other side of the call. He became aware of the colour draining from his face and his pulse racing. If the woman hadn't been in the room with him, he would have screamed and shouted. He managed a restrained. 'I see. Hang on, the signal's rubbish. I'll go outside and see if it's any better.

He slid open the patio doors, stepped onto the balcony and closed the door behind him. The woman might hear him raise his voice, but she wouldn't be able to hear what he had to say if he managed to stay in control and not lose his temper. 'When did you find out?'

He listened, fist clenched, knuckles white.

'And you just call me now?'

He saw Yazhu on the other side of the glass. She gave him a curious look. He gave her a nod and hoped his demeanour conveyed that of a man in control of the situation. He turned his back to her and remained silent as his question was answered.

'Shit.' He continued to hold the phone to his ear but said nothing and gathered his thoughts. 'Yes, I know you have no transport. If that woman was still there, you wouldn't need transport. We needed her for the next video.' He watched a water taxi burble under Westminster Bridge and disappear, and a tourist sightseeing barge emerge going upstream. He had to keep a lid on developments and not give any indication to Yazhu that anything was wrong. He looked over his shoulder and saw the woman studying him. He acted the part of someone receiving a positive situation report. 'OK, sit tight, I'll have someone come and pick you up.' He ended the call and went back i nside.

'That all looked very serious. Is anything wrong?' Yazhu's intense stare bore into him.

'It's the woman we caught the other night, the one we used for the video. She's being difficult, nothing we can't handle.'

'I hope so.' There's been nothing in the media about the Prime Minister responding to the statement. 'We need her to pressure him to confess. I want him gone.' Her mouth twisted in anger.

'He'll be gone soon. Give me a minute, I'm going to get Wilson to record the second video now.' Kobzar retreated to the balcony to issue new orders.

•••••

Hawke wasted no time.

He acted as soon as Tim ended the call. 'Mitchel, get onto SU6. I want two assault teams ready to go the second we have a location. They can use their helicopters this time and tell them they can expect armed resistance.'

Mitchel nodded, picked up his phone and made the call.

With the knowledge that Susie was out of danger, Hawke gave the go signal to the tactical unit known as AT10. He had them standing by to raid Kobzar's nightclub. They'd been keeping it under surveillance for the last 12 hours since Pia mentioned Wilson talking about him. He called the unit leader. 'Go in hot, and search for anything that might give us a clue about their intentions.'

He grabbed his ballistic vest and slipped it on while he waited for Mitchel to finish passing on his instructions. He headed for the door and beckoned his ADC. 'With me. We're going back up the M40. Your driving skills are required. I need to organise tactical support.' He paused momentarily and called one of the team. 'Inform Thames Valley what we're doing. I don't want them getting their knickers in a twist if one of their guys sees us.'

•••••

Two minutes later, the big black Discovery left the TIGER HQ with its discreet grill-mounted blue lights flashing and its engine roaring. Hawke braced himself as Mitchel hurled the big vehicle through the three roundabouts that lead onto the slip road. By the time they joined the main carriageway, they'd already topped 100 mph. Hawke deployed the two-tone sirens and the less-than-discreet blue lights built into the wing mirrors and aerodynamic roof bars. The combined effect ensured any vehicles in the fast lane jumped out of their way as if they'd been hit with a cattle prod.

He sat with his head down and consulted notes on a clipboard and the screen of his phone. He occasionally looked up but appeared to regard their blistering pace as normal and had every faith in Mitchel's ability as a trained high-speed pursuit driver.

As they hurtled through the Stokenchuch cutting, Hawke's phone buzzed. He recognised the number and tapped a button on the side of his headset to accept the call. 'Tiger One.'

'Commander, it's AT10, we've cleared the nightclub and checked the offices. Nothing to report, nobody here, no resistance.'

'Good work Sargeant, get the forensic team in and keep them covered in case anyone returns.'

'Copy that.' The call ended.

Hawke returned to his clipboard and made a note, then called Tim. 'You got to Susie yet?'

'We're two miles away, I'll get her to call you as soon as we pick her up.'

Susie sat at the back of the Carsden village store and kept warm by the stove. She witnessed a regular stream of locals calling in for their Sunday papers, random essentials and a quick chat with Gerald. She watched the clock on the wall as it ticked slowly toward 10.00 a.m. Whenever she heard the tinkling bell to announce a new arrival, she craned her neck in the hope of seeing a face she knew. The feeling in her fingers and toes had returned and she could see properly again after cleaning her contact lenses with some solution Gerald found for her.

As much as she wanted to borrow the phone again, she knew Nick, Tim and Anna would be going as fast as they could to get to her. She forced herself to be patient. Two young girls entered the store, Gerald appeared to know them and asked after their parents. Susie guessed they had been bribed with a little cash to run an errand and she watched as they chose bars of chocolate bars and packets of sugary chews. Her stomach rumbled.

Apart from distracting her, the young shoppers had left the door ajar, so the bell didn't tinkle when Nick walked in. The first she knew was when he tapped her on the shoulder, she jumped in surprise, turned and saw him standing next to her. She leapt to her feet and threw her arms around his neck. 'Oh, my darling man. Am I pleased to see you.'

Nick held her tight and buried his face in her hair. He said nothing for several moments and simply hugged her as if he never wanted to let her go.

Susie lifted her face to look at him. 'Are you all right babe?' She swore she could see his eyes watering.

Nick released her and sniffed. 'Never better, just got something in my eye.'

'You big old softy.' Susie kissed him and squeezed his hand.

They were interrupted by Gerald. 'This must be Nick.' He held his hand out.

Susie introduced him. 'This is Gerald, he's the kind man who's been looking after me and let me use his phone.'

'My wife's phone.' Gerald corrected.

Nick shook his hand, then couldn't stop himself from hugging the man. 'Can't thank you enough, Gerald.'

'You're very welcome.' Gerald looked mildly embarrassed. 'I think your wife needs a hot bath and roaring fire; she was frozen when she knocked on the door.'

Nick put an arm around Susie's shoulders. 'Don't worry I'll take good care of her.'

'Thank you again, Gerald.' Susie gave him a kiss on the cheek and led Nick out of the store. Tim and Anna were waiting in the car, engine running, warm air blowing. Susie and Nick jumped in the back. 'You guys are the best.' Susie leaned forward and kissed them both.

Anna looked at Susie, concerned. 'We've been so worried about you. You look like you've been through hell.'

Susie caught her reflection in the rear-view mirror. She grimaced. 'Yeah, not great, but could have been worse. Sorry about the smell.'

'Minor detail.' Said Tim. 'Don't worry about it. Hawke's waiting for me to call him. Can you remember where they were holding you? He's got two assault teams ready to go.'

'Upper Marsh Farm.' Susie said. 'At least that's what the sign said at the end of the lane. It must be four or five miles in that direction.' She waved a hand at the road out of the village.

'How the hell did you get here?' Nick frowned, still holding her hand.

Susie nodded at the quad bike she'd left beside the phone box. ' They let me use that.'

'How kind.' Nick gave her a rueful smile.

Tim was already on the phone with Hawke and passed on the information Susie had given him. He paused and turned to Susie. 'He wants to know who's in the place.' He held the phone up to catch Susie's reply.

'I'm pretty sure it's just the two women who captured me, the same two that chased me in the car. They're both armed.'

Hawke acknowledged the extra details. 'OK, they're on their way to the farm now.'

The Augusta Wildcat skimmed over the treetops of the Woodland, hovered momentarily, then settled 100 yards from the farmhouse. Two SU6 soldiers jumped out of each side and ran at a crouch towards the building. The four men paused at the garden's edge behind a low stone wall. They kept their weapons trained on the house. 'Spectre One in position.' Matt spoke quietly, his throat mic picking up every sound.

The second helicopter appeared behind the farmhouse, moving slowly forward 50 feet above the ground. 'Spectre Five in position, rear exits covered.'

Hawke stood outside his command vehicle, leaned his elbows on the bonnet and peered at the farmhouse through binoculars. They had parked halfway along the woodland track, close enough to see what was happening but far enough away to be out of danger. 'Tiger One to all Spectre, be advised, two hostiles, both female, both armed. You're cleared for lethal force if necessary, arrest preferred.'

'Copy Tiger One, will arrest if possible.'

Hawke checked the area around the farmhouse, no one else in sight. 'Go, go, go.'

The four men in front of the farmhouse sprinted forward, two to the left, two to the right. The front elevation was picture book; door in the centre with a storm porch, windows either side with two windows on the first floor. Each pair paused at a front corner and checked for movement. Confirmed clear, the pairs split, one man remained at each corner to cover the sides of the building, the other two advanced to the middle and met up at the front door. Matt, callsign Spectre One, pulled a limpet charge from a pocket on his body armour and fixed it to the door. He armed the device, and then he and the other soldier, Spectre two, flattened themselves against the wall of the house on either side of the storm porch. The charge had been designed to effect entry by destroying locks. It directed its explosive force in one direction and when Matt hit the red button on his controller, the muted *crump* was the only audible evidence of its activation. That, a brief flash and a cloud of grey smoke, followed by the sound of wood crumbling. Before the smoke cleared, Spectres One and Two kicked what remained of the door to one side and rushed into the house.

While the two men entered the house from the front, the remaining four men in the second helicopter rappelled to the ground and fanned out to cover the doors and windows at the back.

Within thirty seconds Hawke heard Matt report. 'Spectre One, ground floor clear, checking first floor.'

He didn't reply, he knew when to get the airways clear. He studied the farmhouse through his binos and flinched when he saw a flash, then a split second later, heard the sound of a single shot. He waited, not wanting to distract a man in a firefight. Three seconds later three more shots rang out in quick succession. Not the rapid fire of the MP9's Unit 6 used, but three single shots fired by a pistol.

Matt's voice came over the radio, calm and matter-of-fact. 'Two hostiles located in upstairs room. Give me a minute, I'm going to try and talk some sense into them.' Hawke raised an eyebrow at the non-military parlance and the unusual radio etiquette.

He jumped back in the Discovery. 'I think we can move, sounds like they've got it under control.'

Mitchel drove out of the woodland and approached the house. He parked next to the ruined front door. Hawke called to the two soldiers who'd remained at the front corners of the house. 'Sweep the outbuildings and let me know what you find. I'll be inside.' He tapped his headset again and alerted the four men at the back of the house to look out for the other two. Before going into the house, he called Tim. 'Location secure Tim, you guys can drive in. Just stay in the car until we've neutralised the two women.'

As he ended the call, he heard the unmistakable *brrrrrp* of an MP5. After a few seconds, Matt reported in. 'Took a little persuasion to get them to throw the towel in. One of them's injured the other saw sense. Both now disarmed and cuffed.'

Hawke stepped into the house; he wanted answers.

37

The two Russian women were both handcuffed and sat on chairs in the farmhouse kitchen. Irina gazed morosely at the floor, Ludmila looked defiant, her right forearm bandaged. Susie arrived and noted one of the SU6 men stood at one side of the kitchen keeping watch, while Hawke spread paperwork over the table.

She smiled at the two women. 'Hello ladies, nice to see you again.'

Irina didn't look up. Ludmila simply sneered.

Hawke looked up. 'Well, good to see you. Haven't lost your fighting spirit then?'

'Morning Alex, how's it looking?'

'Hard to say, nothing here makes much sense. I was hoping we might find one or two clues. Did you pick anything up when you were here?'

'I don't how much sense you can make of it, but they had me locked in a room above here.' She pointed to the ceiling. 'If they were in here, I could make out the odd word, but if it was these two,' she tipped her head in the direction of her former captors, 'they spoke in Russian, and I didn't understand a word.'

Ludmila spat out several words Susie assumed must have been a Russian insult.

'There was one English voice I heard, a broad Norfolk accent, I'd swear I'd heard it before.'

Nick arrived in the kitchen and caught the end of Susie's remark. 'That was your friend and mine, Wade Millard, or Miles Wilson to give him his proper name.'

Susie did a double take. 'Shit. You mean?'

'Yeah, he was the one who planted the explosives in the control tower. He's working for them.'

Susie was about to ask more questions, but Hawke held up a hand. 'We can go into more detail later, right now I'm more concerned about the threat they made you read out.'

Susie shook her head. 'Bloody hell, you've seen that?'

Nick gave a rueful smile. 'Sweetheart, the whole bloody country's seen it, your face is all over social media.'

Hawke interrupted. 'When you heard Wilson talking, can you remember him saying anything specific?'

Susie squinted at the ceiling. 'Not a lot, I heard him say something about the city and he mentioned detonators. At least that's what it sounded like. He was talking to a Russian man, the one who made me read the statement.'

'He's called Kobzar, Rostyslav Kobzar. He had a night club in the West End, we raided it this morning. No sign of him.'

Susie nodded. 'Nasty piece of work. From what I could tell he was instructing Millard, Wilson, whatever he's called.'

Nick butted in. 'Tim knows him, he's ex-army bomb disposal, bit of an explosives expert.'

'Makes sense, the Russian was banging on about damage and casualties, he kept telling Wilson how important it was.'

Hawke listened and frowned. 'But no mention of a target?'

'Nothing specific. When he said the city, I'm guessing he meant The City, the square mile, the financial district.' Susie shrugged. 'Ask these two; they speak English, they must know something.' She turned to Irina and Ludmila, who sat listening impassively to every word.

Hawke looked at his prisoners. He didn't approve of beating information out of people, and he assumed they would have been trained to resist interrogation. He could use a little psychology though. He called two of the Unit 6 men into the kitchen and walked behind Ludmila. 'Take this one outside and lock her in the shipping container they put Susie in.'

With her hands cuffed in front of her, Ludmila could only curse as the soldiers grabbed an arm each and led her out of the house.

Hawke turned to Irina. 'Now, if you want to cooperate and tell me what you know, I'm authorised to offer you political asylum. Or, if you don't want to help us, I can have you sent back to Russia, and if you're lucky, you might spend the rest of your life in a gulag. It's more likely you'll be shot for failing your mission.' He folded his arms, stared at her and said nothing more.

Susie added to the pressure. 'Irina, think about it. You're young, you're skilled, you've got a future, but not if you go back to Russia. You've been sent on a suicide mission. Do yourself a favour and help us. You could save lives, maybe hundreds of lives.'

Irina looked up at them both for the first time. 'I don't know anything. I just follow orders.'

'You will know more than you realise.' Hawke turned the chair Ludmila had just vacated and sat facing Irina. 'We know about Matthews and he's under arrest. We want to know more about Miles Wilson, where is he now?'

Irina attempted a defiant look but failed. She glanced left and right as if checking she couldn't be overheard. 'How do I know you won't put me in prison?'

'You don't. But it's up to you. Whatever happens, your career in Mother Russia is over. You can have a life in this country, or face the consequences with your employers.' Hawke remained stony-faced, his eyes locked on hers.

'Colonel Kobzar told us he was sending someone to pick us up.' Irina's voice had a bitter tone.

Hawke looked around theatrically. 'Looks like he lied to you. Once he knew Susie had escaped, he had no more use for you. He threw you under the bus, as they say.'

Despair wrapped itself around Irina. A cornered animal has three options: flight, fight or freeze. Irina only had one; she froze. Her resilience fell away, and she sat motionless as the reality of her situation sunk in.

Susie tried again. 'Irina, please. Did you hear Colonel Kobzar and Wilson talk about what they were planning to do? The statement threatened mass casualties, are they going to explode a bomb?'

Irina gave a defeated nod. 'They didn't say where. I heard them talk about a tower, but they didn't say which one.'

Hawke lowered his voice and encouraged her. 'That's very helpful Irina, thank you. Did they say when they were going to explode the bomb?'

This was met with a more positive nod. 'Tonight.'

'Think very hard Irina, can you remember them mentioning the name of the tower? The Walkie-Talkie, The Shard, The Cheesegrater, The Gherkin, The Nat-West Tower, One Canada Square?'

Irina looked at Hawke as if he was speaking in tongues. She shook her head. 'Nothing like that, I would have remembered one of those names.'

Susie looked thoughtful. 'What about the Telecoms Tower?'

Hawke gave Susie a sideways look and pursed his lips. 'Not really in The City.'

'Maybe not, but if all the chaos of the last week had been about telephone lines, it would make it the obvious target.'

Irina looked from Susie to Hawke and back, then shrugged. 'I don't know.'

Hawke stood and called Mitchel. 'Get onto the Met, and have them instigate a search of all the landmark towers in the City. Tell them it's urgent and they're looking for a large device. They'll kick up a hell of a fuss, but say it's a direct order from me.' He paused and studied Susie for a moment. 'And tell them to include the Telecoms Tower in their s earch.'

Mitchel went out to the command vehicle and Susie asked Hawke. 'What about Ludmila, should we get her in here?'

Hawke shook his head. 'I got the distinct impression that one would be a harder nut to crack. She's lucky she only got grazed when she decided to open fire against this lot. They'll interrogate her thoroughly when they get her processed.'

'Have they found anything in the outbuildings? I never stopped to look when I took the quad bike.'

'Just the usual farm stuff: animal feed, bags of fertiliser, bags of cement, fuel cans, toolboxes, used machinery. Nothing that gives us any clues.' Hawke gathered up the paperwork on the kitchen table. 'We need to get down to London and coordinate the search. These guys can hold on here until uniform arrives to secure the place. What are you doing for transport?'

Susie looked at Nick who shrugged. 'We're in Tim's hands, the Volvo's putting down roots in a field.'

'Can we go and get it? I've got the key.' Susie pulled the object in question from a jacket pocket and held it up in front of her face.

'I'll have to let you to sort that out between you. I need to get going.'

'What about me?' Irina had remained sat on the chair, listening to the conversation without saying a word.

Hawke gave her an appraising look. 'When the police get here, you'll be taken into custody initially and fully de-briefed. Depending on how things go today, we'll decide how best to use you.' He called the Unit 6 man who'd been keeping watch over the prisoners. 'You can take the cuffs off her, but don't let her out of your sight.' He turned and left the kitchen.

Susie joined Nick. 'Fancy another trip to London then?'

Nick put his mug down and hugged her. 'I can see you're keen. But don't you want to get cleaned up and have something to eat before heading off again?'

Susie stepped back and looked down at her mud-encrusted clothes. 'Yeah, guess so. Maybe something to eat first, then a quick shower and some clean clothes.'

'Come on then, can you remember where you parked the Volvo?'

Susie tapped her forehead. 'I'm sure I'll remember.'

***

Hawke paced the floor of the TIGER ops room with his phone pressed to his ear as reports came in from the teams searching the towers. By 3.30 p.m. they had all proved negative so far and only 4 buildings were left to be given the all-clear. Some of the taller buildings had proved time-consuming and gaining access to them had been a challenge. The tenants on some of the floors claimed their security put them above suspicion and tried to block the teams from entering. A shortage of sniffer dogs, trained to detect explosives, also slowed the process. As each negative report came in, Hawke grew increasingly frustrated.

They had identified every landmark tower in the city and marked them on a map, displayed on one of the giant monitors. With each report, a line was drawn through the building's name and the search team moved on to the next tower. All the obvious and most well known had been cleared, it only left some of the more obscure buildings. Hawke was ready to dismiss them as they wouldn't have the spectacular appeal he assumed Kobzar wanted, but he felt he couldn't take the risk.

When Susie and Nick arrived in the ops room, he saw them and beckoned them over and noticed Susie's refreshed appearance. 'You're looking a little better than the last time I saw you.'

Susie smiled. 'Never underestimate the effects of food, a hot shower and some clean clothes. How's the search going?'

Hawke shook his head. 'Nothing yet, not even a hint.'

'Have they searched the Telecoms Tower yet?' Susie asked as she peeled off her jacket.

''They've just gone in, it's one of the last and it took a while to get clearance.'

Nick asked. 'Any more news about Wilson? He's got to be wherever they're planning to detonate their bomb.'

'We thought the same, but at the moment he's in the wind. We don't know if he's heard about his son. If he finds out he's in hospital he might be tempted to visit him.'

'Is there anything else we can do, I'm not good at sitting around waiting?' Susie said as she scanned the wall of monitors.

'If you want to do a little digging, there's a box over there with all the stuff they found in the nightclub run by Kobzar. We went through it briefly, but a fresh pair of eyes might find something relevant.'

Susie spotted the bankers box on a desk at the back of the ops room. She went over to it and lifted the lift. 'Is this all there is?'

'Every last scrap of paper, including the scrap paper out of the bin. He's obviously not the sort who puts much in writing.'

Nick joined Susie, and the pair tipped the contents of the box onto the desk and started to sort through it. 'It's mainly just receipts and delivery notes.' Susie said, as she examined the first few bits of paper she picked up.

'That's what we thought.' Hawke called over to her. 'We hoped there might to something relating to where he is now. Irina said he had a place in London, but we couldn't find anything with an address on it .'

Susie sat down at the desk and picked through the paperwork. Nick pulled out anything that had been crumpled and thrown away and flattened it out, while Susie took each item, examined it quickly and put it into one of two piles: possibles and rejects. The rejects pile grew rapidly as she discounted one piece of paper after another. Nick kept feeding her with fresh material and within five minutes every item had been accounted for.

They pushed the reject pile to one side and went through the possibles pile with a more critical eye. She picked up a delivery note from an office furniture company and her finger caught on something stuck to the back of it. She hadn't noticed it on first inspection but realised it was a pay-and-display parking ticket held in place by the sticker used to fasten it to the windscreen. She pulled it free of the delivery note and held it under the desk light. It showed the location, date and time. 'Whereabouts in London is Cleveland Street?' She called out, in the hope one of the analysts would know.

'It's off Euston Road, goes towards Oxford Street.' Came the reply.

The information didn't help her, so she pulled her iPad out and opened the Map application, she typed in the street name and gave a little fist pump as the page loaded.

'What's special about Cleveland Street?' Asked Hawke.

'Well according to this, someone, Kobzar maybe, parked there two days ago. And it just happens to be the address for the Telecoms Tower.'

Hawke responded immediately and came over to examine the ticket. 'Well spotted. How did we miss that? Hang on. If you're right and it is the target, I need to warn the team going in there.'

'Are they Sappers?' Susie asked.

Hawke hesitated a moment, as he grasped the meaning of Susie's question.

'Bomb disposal.' Susie clarified.

'Ah yes, sorry. No, they're armed police, they know nothing about explosives.'

'If it is the target, bomb disposal needs to get there ASAP.' Susie spoke without taking her eyes off her map.'

Hawke called to Mitchel. 'Get bomb disposal over to the Telecoms Tower, there's a team at Canary Wharf on standby.'

Mitchel responded with a thumbs-up, his phone already in his hand.

Hawke's phone buzzed. He checked the incoming number, accepted the call and listened. 'Thank you Commander, we got there just before you rang. Get your guys out of there and evacuate the area. Bomb disposal are on their way.' He ended the call and tipped his head in Susie's direction. 'You were right. They've discovered a device in the main cable room. God knows how they got in there. Security in that place is next level.'

Susie gave a little head-shake. 'I just hope those guys get there in time. Is there any way we can monitor their progress?' She nodded at the wall of monitors. 'Can you patch into the CCTV at the tower?'

'I think that's possible.' He attracted the attention of one of the team and repeated Susie's question.

The technician looked doubtful. 'I'll need to call someone at the tower, we can patch in if they let us, but it's a private network, we can't just snoop.'

'That sounds like a no to me.' Hawke said. 'Especially as I just asked them to evacuate the area.'

'Not to worry, we'll have audio?' She looked at Hawke for confirmation.

He gave a brief nod. 'And live feed from their body cams.'

38

The live feed from the body cams of the three Explosives and Ordnance Disposal Team lit up three of the giant screens in the TIGER ops room. They showed the main entrance to the Telecoms Tower and jiggled around as the men walked towards the door.

Hawke had donned a headset to enable him to communicate hands-free with the team and had his technician feed the audio through speakers so that Susie, Nick and the rest of his team could follow their progress.

The explosives had been identified on the fourth floor and as their trusty robot had never mastered stair-climbing, they had to proceed on foot. For three minutes nobody spoke as the sappers slowly climbed the stairs, hampered by the bulky padding they wore. The sound system amplified the sound of their laboured breathing.

Susie tore her eyes from the screens and saw the rest of the TIGER team fixated on the live video. The tension in the room reflected the apprehension they all felt and the admiration they had for the men's bravery. She saw some of the team holding crossed fingers or faces frozen in fear and awe.

The silence broke when the team leader spoke. 'Entering the cable room now.'

They watched the feed from camera one as the door opened to reveal multiple rows of racking, each comprised of dozens of data units, stacked one above the other with multi-coloured bundles of wires and cables connecting them to the master feed on the floor above. They heard soft footsteps as the team leader advanced. The second and third members of the team joined the first and the camera feeds gave those in the room a wide-angle view of the room.

The second team member spoke urgently but quietly. 'It's there, where the ARU said it was, on the floor to your right.' His camera picked up what he'd seen. The edge of a rough shape poked out from the base of one of the racks. The shape looked to be a box about two inches high and six inches wide. Its shape was difficult to determine; it had been wrapped in what looked like a black bin liner and taped with black insulation tape. It had two wires, one red and one blue, protruding on one edge.

The other two cameras focused on the object from different angles and the watchers in the ops room held their breath.

The team leader removed his body cam, lay down and held the camera in his hand at floor level to get a better image of the device. He used a torch to inspect it in more detail. A single red LED flashed at the back of the box.

'Can't see a timer or an aerial.'

The camera showed a gloved hand reach forward and touch the device, then reach further back to feel around its hidden side.

'It doesn't appear to be connected to anything.'

The hand moved and reached down the other side of the box, following the two wires into the darkness.

'I don't believe it.'

The other two cameras showed the team leader lying flat with his arm stretched under the racking. He pulled back with the two wires in his hand.

'They're not connected to anything.' He turned towards the other two and held the wires for their cameras to pick up. 'Pass me the stethoscope, I need to check out this box before we do anything else.'

The stethoscope looked very different to the sort hung around doctors' necks; a single round disc two inches in diameter similar to a miniature loudspeaker with a single wire attached. The watchers could see the team leader plug the other end of the wire into his coms pack, then place the disc on the upper surface of the box.

Silence fell over the ops room again, as they watched him move the listening device over the suspect package. After an agonising minute, he stood up and picked the box up in one hand. He flipped the box over in his hand and held it up for the other cameras to see.

'It's a dummy. Nothing in it but the flashing light.' To prove his point, he pulled the insulation tape away and ripped off the plastic cover to reveal a cardboard box. He tore the lid of the box open to expose a tiny mechanism taped to the inside, with the flashing LED stuck through the side.

He removed his helmet and the padded collar around his neck and faced the cameras of his two colleagues. 'Someone wanted to waste our time.'

In the ops room, a dozen people exhaled simultaneously.

'Good work Lieutenant, you had us all about to turn blue.' Hawke spoke for all the assembled watchers. 'Just sorry you've had a wasted trip.

'Don't apologise Commander, it looks genuine. Those guys did the right thing to call us in.' He reconnected his body cam to his chest harness and the team in the ops rooms could see the other two sappers remove their protective gear. 'We'll do a visual check of the rest of the building. The ARU reported nothing else, but a second look won't do any harm. Unless of course you need us at another location.'

'Thank you Lieutenant. Please remain on standby. I'll let you know if any of the other teams report in. We believe there is only one threat so if what you've found is it, then their intention must have been maximum disruption.'

The third member of the team, pulled the door open to leave the cable room and all those watching in the ops room heard a click as he stepped out onto the central stairwell of the tower. Nobody saw what he had touched or what he'd activated, they only saw a blinding flash and a deafening explosion. All three screens turned black, and a graphic appeared – Signal Lost – The audio signal buzzed for a moment then went ominously quiet.

For several seconds everyone in the room stood and stared at the screens unable to comprehend what they had witnessed. Hawke shook himself and spoke into his headset microphone. 'Lieutenant, we've lost signal, can you hear me?'

No reply.

Hawke repeated the message and met the same response. He looked around the room. Some of his team couldn't tear their eyes away from the blank screens. Others turned to look at him as if he could explain and help them understand. He closed his eyes and lowered his head, shaking it slowly as the reality and the tragedy hit him.

Susie stood next to him and placed her hand gently on his arm. 'Alex, we need to get medics to them.'

He tipped his head to the side and opened his eyes. 'I know. You're right. It's...' He took a deep breath which seemed to revive him. He stood up straight, squared his shoulders and turned to Mitchel. 'You heard what she said. There's a medical team waiting behind the cordon.'

Mitchel nodded, spoke urgently into his headset mic and listened for confirmation. 'They're on their way Commander.'

Hawke thanked him and turned to the rest of his team. 'Let's hope it's not as bad as it looks. We can't let it stop what we're doing. Keep in touch with the rest of the search teams.'

Susie tapped Hawke on the arm again and indicated they needed to talk out of earshot of the rest of the team. They moved to a corner of the ops room.

'What is it?' Hawke asked.

'I have a horrible feeling about this.'

Hawke frowned at her. 'We all do.'

No. not this.' she indicated the three black screens. 'I think this was a smokescreen, a diversion.'

'You think there's another device?'

Susie nodded. 'Even if the Telecoms Tower was the target, it would never result in mass casualties. It would do all sorts of damage to telecoms in London but there's not a lot of people in its vicinity.'

Hawke considered this. 'I see what you're thinking, but we've searched every other tower and you could apply the same argument to most of them. This time on a Sunday night, there's no one around.'

Susie reacted to his words with sudden alarm. Her eyes popped, her mouth fell open and she took an involuntary step backwards. She held one finger up. 'We're forgetting one vital thing. This isn't any old Sunday night, is it?'

'Oh sweet Jesus. The fireworks.' Hawke clasped his hands to his head.

'They led us up the garden path with their talk of towers in The City and we've overlooked the blindingly obvious.'

Hawke appeared to snap into another gear and called across to Mitchel. 'Find out if they've searched Big Ben, if they haven't, tell them to drop everything else and do it urgently. This is top priority.' he turned to Susie. 'I hope we're not too late, there'll be thousands on the embankment already.'

Susie followed him as he returned to the centre of the ops room. 'What can I do to help?'

'Just give me a minute.' Hawke started issuing directives to his team. They had practised for emergency scenarios on multiple occasions and fell seamlessly into predetermined roles. Each team member had their own list of contacts with detailed instructions about who to call and what to say.

Susie watched, impressed. She knew to keep out of his way and could see why the man had risen to the top. He remained calm, didn't shout and trusted every individual to do their job. He let them get on with it but responded quickly if asked to make a decision or offer a solution. It was a masterclass.

The minute he'd asked for stretched to five and once satisfied, he turned to Susie. 'There's part of me hopes you're right and we know what we're dealing with but there's another part of me hopes you're wrong and we don't have the nightmare of trying to evacuate anything up to a hundred thousand revellers from the banks of the Thames.'

'But if I'm wrong, where else can we look?'

'That's the trouble, it would have to be somewhere else in the area if mass casualties is their objective.'

Mitchel stood a few feet from Hawke and turned to him the moment he ended a call. 'That was Commander Lewis; she says they've searched Big Ben and it's clear.'

Susie slumped. 'Bloody Hell. What do we do now?'

***

'We need to speak to Irina; she's not telling us everything.' Hawke said to Susie. 'if it's not Big Ben then we need to press her.'

'Where is she now?'

'Uniform took her away, they're holding her at a facility in Wembley. We'll have to go and see her, there'll be too much red tape getting her brought here.' Hawke reached for a jacket he'd left draped over the back of a chair. 'You'd better come with me. You and her have got history, you might have more success getting something out of her than I have.'

'No problem. What about Nick?' Susie glanced across to see Nick engrossed in a conversation with one of the technical team.

Hawke followed her gaze. 'I doubt he'd let you out of his sight. He'd better come with us, there's not much he can do here.'

At the mention of his name, Nick looked up and could see Hawke was getting ready to leave. 'Are we off again?' He addressed the question to Susie and Hawke.

'Yeah, we're going to have another word with Irina and you're coming with us.'

Hawke stopped as he passed Curtis, the analyst was just ending a call and looked ashen faced. 'Any news from the Telecoms Tower?'

Curtis shook his head. 'Sorry Commander. It looks bad, two of the guys never made it and the third is seriously injured. I spoke to their CO. He said initial reports indicate it was a small device but they were so close to it they never stood a chance. The dummy they found was just there so they'd drop their guard. He suspects they hit a pressure switch on the way out and that activated the explosion.'

Hawke dropped his head. 'Oh God, those poor guys. Find out where the injured man has been taken and will you and tell the CO I'll call him later.'

Curtis nodded.

Susie spoke quietly. 'If only I hadn't mentioned the place.'

'If you hadn't someone else would have done. Whoever planted that device knew exactly what they were doing.' Hawke took a deep breath and inclined his head towards the exit. 'And I think we know who that person is. We have to stop him.' he headed for the door.

***

Forty-five minutes later they arrived at the heavily guarded facility not far from Wembley Stadium. Despite Hawke's rank and reputation, they all had to undergo the usual security procedure and it took another fifteen minutes before Susie was sat at a table in a private visitors room, awaiting the arrival of Irina. Hawke and Nick watched in an adjoining room via a live video feed.

Irina was escorted into the room by a female officer who appeared to treat her with surprising care. Irina looked relaxed and alert, Susie noted she wasn't handcuffed. They must trust her.

The escort left the room and Susie smiled at the woman who had been her captor 24 hours earlier. 'How are you Irina?'

She made eye contact with Susie, studied her for a moment then spoke. 'I am good. Why are you here?'

'I need to ask you some questions.'

'I have already answered questions. I told the army man what I knew.'

'That's been very helpful but we think you might know more, something you may think isn't important but it might help us.'

Irina shrugged. 'Like what?'

'You said you heard Colonel Kobzar talk about towers?'

Irina nodded.

'We've searched all the towers we could think of but haven't found anything. Are you sure he didn't mention any names?'

'The army man said some names. I hadn't heard any of them.'

'Irina. If we can't find where they are planning to detonate their bomb, thousands of people will die. Do you want to be responsible for that or do you want to prevent it happening?'

Irina looked as if she'd been backed into a corner. 'I don't want people to die, but I don't know. The Colonel may have mentioned a name but I can't remember what it was.'

They were interrupted by a knock on the door and the female officer returned with a tray with two mugs of coffee and a plate of biscuits. She placed them on the table and turned to Susie. 'Your boss thought you'd appreciate these.'

'Thank you,' Susie twisted to read the officer's name badge. 'Elizabeth.'

'You're welcome.'

Irina watched the officer leave. 'What did you call her?'

'Elizabeth, that's her name.' Susie picked up her mug and took a sip.

'Elizabeth.' Irina repeated as if trying out the word for the first time. She looked at Susie with a sudden intensity. I' think that was the word the Colonel used, the Elizabeth Tower.'

Susie almost choked on her coffee. 'Oh my God, Irina. Are you sure?'

Irina nodded to herself and repeated the word over and over. 'Yes, that's what he said, I remember. Does it help?'

Susie turned and faced the cameras, knowing Hawke and Nick would be watching. 'It is Big Ben. Big Ben is the name of the bell, the building's proper name is the Elizabeth Tower.'

***

The crowds grew by the minute. On the Victoria embankment, Westminster Bridge and the surrounding areas on both sides of the river, a sea of humanity bustled along shoulder to shoulder and revelled in the entertainment building up to the main event at midnight. After the disruption of the last few days, the mood was one of celebration and freedom, spirits ran high.

By 9:30 p.m. with almost 100,000 tickets sold and people paying up to £50 for the best vantage points, it was shaping up to be one of the UK's biggest event crowds of the year.

Extra tube trains had been laid on and every available police officer had been drafted in to supplement the private security arranged by The Mayor of London. Every street in the area had been closed to vehicles since early afternoon and barriers prevented pedestrians from spreading too far from the carefully controlled routes to the designated viewing areas.

Hawke had been involved in the planning stages of the event and he knew the problems they would face when they reached central London. He asked Mitchel his ADC and regular driver to remain at TIGER HQ and feed him live updates. As he wanted to make phone calls on the move, he asked Susie to take the wheel of the command vehicle. He'd checked her service record and heard stories about her ability from Nick and Tim and he had every confidence she was up to the job.

They left the Wembley facility at speed, blue lights flashing and two-tone siren blaring. In her previous life in the Royal Military Police, Susie had been assigned close-quarter protection duties, a role requiring extensive driver training in pursuit and evasion. Driving with blues and twos was nothing new, but she relished the opportunity to carve through traffic and ignore speed limits. Hawke, strapped into the passenger seat, made phone call after phone call.

He spoke again to Commander Lewis at the Met. 'I know you've reported it clear, but we have confirmation the Elizabeth Tower is the target. Please have your team check it again.'

Susie caught the sound of a raised voice at the other end but the noise of the siren drowned out the protest. When he ended the call and without taking her eyes off the road, she asked. 'How close can we get?'

Hawke looked up from his notepad; they were barrelling along the A40 at 80mph and passing Shepherd's Bush. He made a quick assessment. 'Turn off the Westway in a minute and go down through Paddington. We'll just have to hope we can get through the crowds.'

39

Two armed police officers in Hi-Viz jackets patrolled the entrance to the Elizabeth Tower. They had been advised that another inspection had been ordered and when a team of four arrived, they checked their IDs, unlocked the door and showed them the way to the staircase. Twenty minutes later the team returned to ground level, out of breath after negotiating the 334 steps. They reported nothing suspicious in the belfry, just a dozen or so bags of cement and plaster for the ongoing restoration work.

The police officers locked the door to the staircase and resumed their vigil in the hidden walkway below the bustling crowds. They could hear the excited chatter and the music from a live band, but could see no further than the end of the shuttering.

They were surprised to see another police officer appear out of the darkness at the Westminster Bridge end of the shuttering. He looked a little overweight, his uniform was a snug fit and he carried a black holdall in his left hand. He approached them with a resigned look and a waist-level casual wave. 'Looks like we're the only ones who are going to miss out on all the fun.'

The two officers exchanged glances. They weren't expecting anyone to join them or relive them. 'Hi, what's happening? Who sent you?'

The new arrival tapped the radio mic velcroed below the left shoulder of his jacket. 'I got a call from Lambeth nick, they told me to come over here and give you guys some extra support, they're worried about reports of a bomb threat. I'm Terry by the way.'

'Hi Terry, I'm Dave, this is Mario. Yeah, we know about the bomb threat. They just sent another team over to search the place. They found nothing, must be a false alarm.'

'Have they been and gone?' Terry made the remark sound casual but looked up and down the walkway as if checking for something.

Mario looked irritated. 'Like I said, they found nothing, they left a few minutes before you got here.'

'Sorry,' Terry turned away from the other two and lowered his holdall the ground. 'must be going deaf in my old age.'

Dave nodded at the holdall. 'What's in the bag?'

Terry didn't answer. He kept his back to them, unzipped the holdall and reached inside. 'Sorry about this.' He stood up and spun around to face them with a suppressed Makarov in his hand.

Taken by surprise, Dave and Mario started to swing their MP5s towards Terry but they were too slow by half a second. Terry fired twice, two head shots at close range, he couldn't miss. Both officers were dead before they hit the ground. Terry searched the bodies for the keys he wanted then peeled off the restricting jacket, took off the helmet and picked up the holdall. Miles Wilson then opened the door to the staircase and started to climb the stairs to the belfry. The booming music from the street above drowned the sound of the shots, nobody heard a thing.

Susie rounded Marble Arch and accelerated down Park Lane; the big Discovery's engine roared as the rev counter spun towards the red line. The traffic parted at the sight and sound of her approach and she sped towards Hyde Park Corner at over 90 mph.

Nick sat in the back behind her and hung onto the door handles to avoid being thrown about as Susie braked hard, turned left towards Piccadilly then right around the Wellington Arch then sharp left onto Constitution Hill. 'Bloody Hell babe, I'd forgotten what you're like when you get the bit between your teeth.'

Hawke hung onto the grab handle above the door. 'You're doing great, don't go down the Mall, it's too busy, go around the Victoria Memorial then it's a left straight down to Big Ben.'

Susie followed his instructions and the tyres howled as she swung around the Wedding Cake, then aimed the command vehicle at Westminster. Within 100 yards she had to stand on the brakes. The crowd heading for the embankment filled the road ahead of her, walking shoulder to shoulder as if it were a pedestrian precinct. Hawke hit a secondary siren and it woop-wooped above the incessant scream of the two-tone.

People glanced over their shoulders at the noise but appeared to think they had right of way. Susie was down to little more than walking pace. The Discovery inched through the crowd as people reluctantly stepped to one side. Her frustration grew. 'For fuck's sake,' she muttered, 'get out of the bloody way.' She added to the cacophony of noise by banging on the horn. It had little effect. 'Time?' she called.

'It's 23:37,' said Hawke, 'just keep this up.'

Susie shook her head. 'It's no good, we're never going to get through this lot in time.'

'We don't have much choice.'

'Yes we do. We have to warn them. You'll have to take it from here Alex, I can run there quicker than this.' With that, she stopped the car, put the transmission in park, unclipped her seatbelt and jumped out before Hawke or Nick realised what she was doing.

Her adrenalin was already pumping and she was straight into her stride. She never heard Nick calling after her or Hawke cursing her. When she'd changed earlier, she'd put on a pair of lightweight boots that were almost as good as running shoes. She charged through the crowd, nipping between gaps and weaving between groups and individuals. She could see the Elizabeth Tower half a mile ahead and knew she could cover the distance in three minutes.

She ignored the protests from those she brushed past a little too close for comfort and pressed on. The crowd grew as she neared Parliament Square and she had to get more aggressive to barge her way past. Shouts of 'hoy,' and 'excuse me' were ignored as she sought out the gate in the railings that gave access to the walkway. She almost missed it. A small sign stated "strictly no admission". Susie had read the operating procedures and knew to lift the gate by half an inch to release the catch and swing the gate towards her.

The passing crowd barely noticed as she closed the gate behind her and descended five steps to the walkway. Still breathing hard from her run, she kept going then slowed as she reached the doorway to the Tower and saw the two police officers lying where they'd been shot.

She rushed forward and knelt between them. She glanced about in case whoever had shot them was still in the area, but could see nobody. She didn't need to check for signs of life, their injuries made it unnecessary. She needed to let Hawke know and realised in her haste to jump out the car she didn't have a phone. She reached for one of the officer's radios and pressed the transmit button. 'Anyone there?'

The was a moment's delay. 'Who is this?'

'My name's Susan Jones, I'm with the Tactical Emergency Group. I'm at the base of the Elizabeth Tower, two officers are down, both dead, badge numbers 5537 and 4328. Contact Commander Hawke at TIGER, and get back up and bomb disposal here now.' She dropped the radio and picked up one of their guns, checked the 15 round magazine was full then ejected the magazine from the other officer's weapon and stuffed it into the waistband of her jeans. She stood up and looked at the door leading to the staircase, it was ajar.

She came to warn them and she'd failed. She assumed whoever had killed them was either on their way up to the belfry or already there and she shuddered at the thought of what they might be doing. She hefted the Heckler and Koch MP5, she knew the popular sub machine gun inside out having carried one in her army days. If she had to fight it out, there was no other weapon she'd rather have. Her eyes came to rest on the two officers and she felt driven to avenge them. It had to be Wilson. He was already responsible for the murder of the Cyber Crime team at Warrenford and she assumed he was behind the explosive device that killed two of the bomb disposal team at the Telecoms Tower. He must know he'd spend the rest of his life in prison. With nothing to live for, he'd have no qualms about going out in style.

Susie scanned up and down the walkway. How long could she wait for backup? She thought Hawke would have got through the traffic or the message would have reached another armed unit. There was nobody in sight. Every passing second brought the prospect of a devastating explosion and the deaths of thousands of innocent people that much closer.

She had to act.

She poked her head through the doorway leading to the stairs and listened. The music and the hubbub on the street drowned any possibility of hearing footsteps. Peering up the inside of the tower gave her no more clues. She guessed Wilson wouldn't be expecting anyone to follow him. She started climbing.

Keeping close to the wall on her left, she held the machine gun at the ready, aiming up as the staircase wound its way around the four walls of the tower. She didn't rush, she didn't want to trip, but she climbed as fast as she dared, round and round, up and up. She passed doors off the staircase leading to offices or storerooms and narrow stained glass windows giving glimpses of the streetlights below. She ignored them and pushed herself harder, all the while, the yawning void on her right. Her fitness gave her the stamina to keep going, she could race up a staircase when she had to but she didn't want to arrive out of breath and unable to hold the gun steady.

She hadn't counted how many steps she had climbed but eventually reached a landing with a door leading off to the clock room. She didn't imagine Wilson's target would be the clock mechanism, so she continued to climb the remaining 42 steps to bring her to the belfry. She slowed as she neared the entrance and got her breathing under control, sucking in the cold night air as quietly as she could. She took one last glance down the centre of the staircase to see if anyone else was on their way up to help her.

She was on her own.

Wilson was nowhere to be seen. The noise from the street 300 feet below had faded but was still enough to disguise the sound of her footfall or his movements. Susie inched forward, the stock of the MP5 pressed against her shoulder her eyes scanned ahead through the weapon's sights. She'd passed down one side of the five-foot high plinth positioned below the giant bell of Big Ben. It loomed over her and when she caught a flash of movement out of the corner of her eye, she ducked down and peeked around the corner.

A man she didn't recognise bent over a stack of three cement bags with his back to her. Nick had told her that Wade Millard had reverted to his original name of Miles Wilson, but neither of them knew he had changed his appearance. She expected to find an overweight man with unkempt hair and a wild beard. The man she saw didn't have a beard and his hair was cut short to the point of being non-existent. She couldn't see his face, but from what she could see, he didn't wear glasses. She retreated behind the plinth suddenly unsure who she was up against.

Big Ben hung in the centre of the belfry with a quarter bell in each of the corners. Keeping low, Susie backtracked around three sides of the plinth to approach the man from the other direction. She passed two more stacks of cement bags, both with wires leading out of them. It made her wary. She stopped and repeated her previous manoeuvre to see the man's face. This time she had to look around a corner to her right, making it impossible to bring the gun to bear. She risked a quick peek, exposing as little of the left side of her face as she could. She snapped back after a split second. The man was looking down, but she had no doubt it was Wilson, the hooded eyes gave him away.

With her back to the plinth, Susie calmed her breathing as best she could. She listened again for anyone coming up the stairs to help her but could hear nothing. A glance at her watch told her she only had six minutes until midnight. She had no reason to believe midnight was the chosen time for Wilson to detonate his device, but somehow it made sense and the idea had taken hold in her head. She moved the fire selector on the side of the gun from fully automatic to two-shot bursts and took another deep breath. She had done plenty of combat simulations in training. She had been deployed in tense situations ready to use a loaded weapon if required. But she had never fired at another human being with lethal intent. The implications of what she was about to do weighed on her. If Wilson was about to trigger a device that would cause untold death and injury, she had no choice. There was also the small matter of her own self-preservation.

Susie reached into a jacket pocket for something she could use to distract Wilson. All she could find was a couple of one-pound coins, they would have to do. She lobbed them between two of the quarter bells where they clanged on the iron framework of the belfry. The noise was minimal but it was enough. Wilson jerked his head up and glanced towards the outer edge of the tower. Susie stood up and stepped forward with the gun held tight into her shoulder, her cheek pressed against the stock and the sights levelled on Wilson's chest.

'Don't move.'

Wilson jumped in surprise then froze momentarily when he saw the gun aimed at him. 'What the fuck?' He dropped the wires he held in each hand and dived for the pistol he'd left lying on one of the cement bags.

'Don't.' Susie shouted.

Wilson paid no attention to the warning; his right hand reached the barrel but he fumbled his attempt to spin it around to grab the pistol grip.

Susie aimed for his hand and pulled the trigger. The sound of the two shots echoed off the bells and two ejected brass cases pinged off the metalwork. Both bullets hit Wilson in the wrist, millimetres apart. He screamed as his arm was blown sideways and blood poured from where his shattered radius bone protruded through his skin. He fell to his knees holding his right arm to his chest with his left arm supporting it.

Within seconds Susie could see the effects of shock taking hold, his face drained of colour, the pain overwhelming him, his breath coming in short gasps. As much as she didn't care about his suffering, she needed him lucid enough to disarm his explosive device. She took a couple of paces towards him and picked up the Makarov pistol which she stuffed into the waistband of her jeans alongside the spare magazine.

'How do I disarm this?' She nodded at the wiring and what she assumed must be a timing device or switch.

'Fuck you.' Wilson spat. Sweat poured down his face.

Susie was in no mood for gentle persuasion. She used the stock of the MP5 as a club and jabbed Wilson's injured wrist. His screams would have been heard at street level.

Susie held the weapon ready to jab him again. 'Tell me, or I'll grind your wrist into a pulp you miserable traitorous bastard.'

Wilson raised his head to look Susie in the eye. 'Do your worst, we're both going to die any minute now and I don't care anymore.' He spoke through gritted teeth.

Susie kicked him in the shoulder and he fell sideways clutching his arm as blood pooled around him. She picked up the wires he'd dropped and followed them back to the timer where they were joined by three other wires she assumed must be from the other bags of cement, she now realised that the explosives had been hidden inside the bags where the cement would disguise the scent from the sniffer dogs. With all the restoration work in progress, nobody would have given them a second look.

She examined the timer unsure what would happen if she simply pulled the wires out. The small yellow box had a single switch and two small LEDs, one of them glowed red. She assumed it meant the device was armed. She had no way of knowing if hitting the switch would disarm the device or send a signal to the detonators and send her and countless others to an early grave.

Another glance at her watch told her she had less than two minutes to do something.

Wilson whimpered on the floor, she swore he was laughing between gasps for air and failed attempts to push himself back to a sitting position.

She heard a shout that made her jump. It came from the staircase and sounded like someone calling her name.

'In the belfry, hurry.' Susie shouted back, not caring if the voices were friend or foe.

Wilson heard the noise too and somehow managed to pull himself upright. With his left hand he stretched for the timer. Susie, distracted by the shout from the stairs, caught the movement out of the corner of her eye and smashed the machine gun across his arm. He fell back again cursed her and passed out.

Two men appeared at the entrance to the belfry. They both appeared out of breath from the climb but rushed to where Susie beckoned them. 'Please tell me you guys are bomb disposal.'

They both nodded.

'I don't know what to do.' She pointed to the timing device and the wires leading away from it.

The men wore the protective clothing Susie had seen on the camera feeds from the Telecoms Tower. She stepped to one side as they bent over the timer, they conferred in low voices then one of them turned to Susie. 'Don't touch the switch, we have to pull the detonators out of all the bags of cement. He demonstrated and took hold of the nearest wire that disappeared into one of the bags of cement. He gently pulled six inches of wire then a silver tube emerged about four inches long and half an inch in diameter. 'Get around that way to the other bags and do the same thing, I'll do these and Mick'll do the others. Be as quick as you can, but treat the detonators gently.'

His last words were almost drowned out as the Westminster Chimes began.

Susie rushed left, Mick went right. She copied his actions and made safe the pile of three cement bags. All the while the four bells rang out as if she needed any extra pressure. She returned to the first guy at the same time as Mick appeared from the other direction holding two sets of three detonators. The quarter bells had stopped and they heard the crowd counting down. They turned to see Big Ben's hammer lift a fraction before it struck. She looked at her watch, the digital readout flicked from 23:59.59 to 00:00.00. The timer clicked and both LEDs flashed red.

40

Monday 1 January

As she heard the Westminster Chimes preceding the main event, Lang Yazhu stepped onto the balcony to witness the culmination of her plan. Rostyslav Kobzar stood alongside her. They both held a glass of champagne.

As the chime of the last quarter bell faded, the noise was replaced by thousands of voices counting down the last few seconds to midnight.

Yazhu tensed as the countdown reached 3, 2, 1, and gasped as the sky lit up. She stared at the Elizabeth Tower as fireworks exploded all around it and the bongs of Big Ben rang out to welcome in the New Year. The Tower stood resolutely intact. She expected to see the walls of the belfry explode outwards and the top of the tower to collapse in what she hoped would be a fitting metaphor for the British Empire. There was no explosion, no flash, not even a spark to be seen.

She continued to stare, uncomprehending, waiting for something to happen, convinced there must be some mistake. The twelfth and final bong sounded, and her eyes remained glued to a point just above the illuminated clock face at the top of the tower. The spectacular display of fireworks, lasers and drones was lost on her. She was oblivious to the music.

Kobzar's focus switched from the Elizabeth Tower to the woman next to him. He could see the muscles in her jaw pulsing. He could see a year's planning coming to nothing. He could see the repercussions that would come his way if he didn't act.

He pulled his phone from an inside jacket pocket and called Wilson. It rang and rang. He waited for the voicemail to cut in, growing increasingly concerned with each ring. Wilson should have armed his device and been out of the tower by now. He'd proved his system worked when he destroyed the control tower at Warrenford, and he had assured Kobzar that his timing device was fail-safe and as a backup, he had a remote trigger. So why didn't he answer his phone?

The voicemail cut in eventually. 'What's going on? Why has nothing happened?' Call me back.' He ended the call.

Yazhu turned to him, her eyes narrowed, her chin jutted, and she flung her glass of champagne at the wall. It shattered into a thousand tiny shards, some of which bounced off and hit Kobzar. 'You told me your man was an expert.' She pointed a long bony finger at the Elizabeth Tower. 'Look. Look. It's still standing; your man has failed. You've failed.' She looked around for something else to throw at him, her fists clenched. She stepped towards him, grabbed his champagne glass and smashed it across his face.

Kobzar jumped back and held a hand to his cheek. A trickle of blood oozed between his fingers. 'You...' He stopped himself from going further, however much he wanted to fight back or tell her what he thought of her. He turned and went back into the apartment to get something to soak up the blood. He still had his phone in his other hand and reacted with surprise when it rang. He assumed it was Wilson and answered without looking at the screen. 'Where are you? What the fuck are you doing?'

The reply turned his blood to ice. 'We are coming for you.'

Kobzar dropped the handset as if it were red hot.

Susie covered her ears with her hands as the hammer fell on the giant bell just three feet from where she stood. The noise vibrated through her whole body and she had to wait until the last chime faded before she could hear or speak. The two bomb disposal men appeared unconcerned about the noise. They checked the detonators and removed all the connecting wires before declaring the area safe.

Wilson lay unconscious and crumpled on the floor as blood continued to seep from his wrist. She didn't want to be responsible for him bleeding out, so, with the help of Mick, the second of the bomb disposal officers, she pulled him straight, removed his sweatshirt and wrapped it around his wrist. She then raised his arm and fastened a sleeve of the sweatshirt around part of the metal framework to keep his arm elevated. It was as much as she was prepared to do.

She heard footsteps at the entrance to the belfry. She stood up and turned to see a breathless Commander Hawke approaching.

'You're a bloody fool, Ms Jones, but it looks like you did the right thing.' He looked as if he was about to hug her, but propriety asserted itself just in time.

'Sorry to run off and leave you. We were never going to get here in time if I'd stayed in the car.' Susie looked suitably chastened.

Hawke opened his mouth to speak but was interrupted by the sound of a phone ringing. Neither of them recognised the ringtone, but they quickly identified it as coming from Wilson and retrieved the handset from his back pocket. Hawke looked at the screen, the caller ID was simply RK. He had no doubt who it was and let it ring until the voicemail cut in. They both listened to Kobzar's message and waited until he finished before they spoke.

'I need to trace that. Did you hear the fireworks in the background, he can't be far away.' Hawke pulled his own phone out, spoke to one of his team and gave them Kobzar's number.

Considering the noise of the show in full swing in the sky outside, Susie was amazed Hawke could hear anything at the other end. She was even more amazed when the response to his request came back within thirty seconds.

Hawke spoke quickly and ordered an armed response unit to the address.

Then he rang the number.

He waited for Kobzar to answer and said in his most chilling voice. 'We are coming for you.' He ended the call and looked at Susie. 'He's on the other side of the river. The handset has been traced to the Lambeth Apartments.'

'He's either going to fight it out or he'll make a run for it.'

'Depends if he's on his own or not. He won't get far, all the roads around are closed to traffic.'

Susie looked hopefully at the doorway to the staircase. 'Where's Nick?'

'He's in the Command Vehicle. I had to leave it on the side of the road and Nick didn't think his leg was up to climbing up here.'

'Makes sense, but I guess he's mad at me?'

'Oh yes,' Hawke smiled, 'but I think he'll forgive you when he hears what you've done.'

'At least he gets to see the fireworks for free.'

Hawke looked down at Wilson. 'We'd better get some medics up here for this one. If he thinks he can escape justice by dying, he can think again.' He called TIGER HQ and issued more instructions.

The two bomb disposal men continued their work in extracting the explosives from inside the bags of cement and Susie and Hawke started the descent of the staircase.

By the time they reached ground level, Susie was relieved to find the two armed officers Wilson had killed had been taken away. She hoped they would receive the recognition they deserved. She still carried the MP5 she'd taken from one of them and had a spare magazine and Wilson's Makarov pistol tucked into her waistband. 'Who can I give these to?' She asked Hawke as they jogged by to his Discovery.

'There's a gun safe in the back of the car. Stick them in there and I'll get someone to return them to the Met when we get a minute.'

They arrived at the Command Vehicle, its blue lights still pulsing. Nick saw them coming and jumped out of the passenger seat and held his arms wide for Susie. 'Come here you.'

She handed the machine gun to Hawke and hugged Nick. 'Sorry babe, just had to do it.'

Nick wrapped his arms around her. 'One of these days you're going to give me heart failure.'

Hawke jumped behind the wheel. 'Come on you two. We're not done yet.' He started the engine and waited while Susie and Nick climbed aboard. He donned his headset and pressed buttons on the communications system. He waited a second then started speaking. 'Sit-rep?' He waited while whoever he'd called brought him up to speed. 'OK, let me know when you find him. And, just a thought, check the river.' He ended the call and switched the two-tone siren on. 'We can't go over Westminster Bridge, we'll have to go along to Lambeth Bridge and meet up with armed response on the other side.' He swung the Discovery in a tight U-turn and weaved through the pedestrians into Parliament Square.

•••••

Kobzar grabbed Yazhu by the arm. He'd never had any cause to touch her before and couldn't believe how frail she felt. 'We have to get out of here, they know where we are.' He ignored the lifts and led her to the staircase at the rear of the building.

'Where are you taking me.' Yazhu protested.

'We can get out the same way we came here.' He pushed open the door to the staircase and briefly checked the stairwell was clear. 'Hurry, they'll be coming in the front, we need to get clear of the place before they get here.' He half dragged, half carried Yazhu down 11 flights of stairs then shoved the emergency exit door release bolt and headed onto the path that ran along the Albert Embankment.

Their launch was moored alongside the Lambeth Pier. As all the sightseeing boats and water taxis were out on the river giving wealthy clients an expensive view of the fireworks, it was easy for them to approach and climb down to the craft without attracting any unwanted attention.

Kobzar had instructed the boat's owner/driver to stay ready to take them back downriver to Tilbury. The driver assumed they would be watching the fireworks and hadn't expected them so soon. He'd been paid £1,000 in cash to bypass the usual rules of the river with the promise of another £1,000 if he got his passengers to Tilbury without incident. He wouldn't have such easy money again and didn't want to upset them. He jumped when he heard Kobzar and Yazhu drop onto the launch and rushed to the wheelhouse to start the engine.

'Get a bloody move on.' Kobzar shouted at him, while he led Yazhu to what the driver referred to as the saloon. At least it was warm and sheltered them from the elements. As Kobzar settled his paymaster into her seat, he looked up at Lambeth Bridge and saw blue lights speeding towards them.

He was aware there was no one else on board and called up to the driver. 'I'll cast off, just go when I say so.' He shimmied along the walkway on the side of the boat to the bow and unfastened the mooring rope. The launch faced upstream, and the current started to push the bow away from the pier. Kobzar retraced his steps to the stern, repeated the process with the mooring rope, and then shouted. 'Go. Fast as you can.' He grabbed for the side of the cabin as the propellor churned the water behind the boat and it headed towards the centre of the river, the driver bringing it around to face downstream.

Kobzar stood at the back of the launch and watched multiple blue lights come to a stop on the bridge and figures emerge from the vehicles. There was nothing he could do about them. He joined the driver in the wheelhouse. 'Is this as fast as this thing will go?'

The driver appeared insulted to have his pride and joy referred to as a *thing*. He kept his eyes on the river ahead and steered towards Westminster Bridge and the arch designated for downstream traffic. 'If I go any faster, I'll stand out and the river police will be after me.'

'Break the rules. If you want your bonus, give it max gas.' Kobzar reached in front of the driver and pushed the throttle lever forward. The engine note deepened and the rear of the launch sunk an inch or two as the propellor spun a little faster. The driver tried to pull the lever back, but Kobzar kept his hand on it and scowled at him.

***

Hawke rested his elbows on the parapet of Lambeth Bridge and looked through his binoculars. He focused on the vessel they had seen pull away from Lambeth Pier and head downstream. 'It has to be Kobzar; by the look of it, there's also a woman in the boat's cabin.'

Susie and Nick joined him, and Susie squinted as she followed the boats' progress under Westminster Bridge. 'Can you get the river police to stop them?'

'I think we can do a little better than that.' Hawke returned to the Discovery, donned his headset, and pressed buttons on the communications console. 'Tiger One to River Raptor.'

Susie could only hear one side of the conversation and walked closer to Hawke to find out who he was talking to. Nick joined her and leaned in close. He spoke quietly, 'He's calling up aerial support.'

Susie nodded but didn't comment; she listened as Hawke spoke into the boom mic and gave instructions. He ended the call with, 'Tiger One out.' and turned to Nick. 'You're right; they're the tactical air support unit based at Battersea. They've been on standby in case of trouble.'

'Are they going to stop them?' Susie waved her hand in the vague direction of the river.

Hawke looked upriver towards the London heliport, his face grim. 'They'll stand off until they're clear of the show and the crowds. They work with the river police and won't go in hot unless Kobzar thinks he can outrun the police launch, and he'll have a job, that thing can shift.'

As he spoke, they saw the navigation lights of a helicopter rise from behind the twin chimneys of Battersea Power Station. It turned towards them and gained height. They could hear it above the noise of the show and saw it bank away from the river to avoid the drone display and the mass of humanity on either side of the Thames.

Hawke watched the helicopter disappear from view. 'They'll cut out the bend in the river and pick them up at Greenwich. No point in creating too much excitement with an audience of thousands watching. They'd think someone was filming a scene for the next James Bond film.

Susie looked downcast. 'Can we get to Greenwich? I'd like to see him brought in.'

Nick gave a resigned shake of his head. 'Not had enough excitement for one day?'

Hawke gave a wry smile. 'Sorry, Nick, I'm with Susie on this one. Besides, I need to make sure he's properly processed. Come on, jump in.'

The driver navigated a path through the waterborne spectators, and after another five minutes when they passed under Tower Bridge, the river traffic thinned out. Kobzar wanted to go faster, but the driver insisted they were going as fast as the launch could go.

Kobzar peered through the windscreen at the river ahead. The launch was making good progress, and so far, he'd seen no indication of the river police. He looked behind at the receding lights of the fireworks reflected in the boat's wake. He dared to think he might get to Tilbury and get out of the UK without having to contend with the British police.

He knew from their trip upriver that the journey could take over an hour, but this time they were going faster, and there were fewer boats on the water.

The roof of the cabin prevented him from looking up at the night sky.

Despite the crowds leaving the fireworks, Hawke, Susie and Nick raced 6 miles through South London with blue lights flashing and siren blaring to arrive at Greenwich Pier 15 minutes after leaving Lambeth Bridge. Local police were waiting for them in force, a police RIB waited in the water and the tactical support helicopter hovered overhead.

A uniformed officer wearing a Hi-Viz jacket approached the Discovery as they pulled to a stop under the shadow of the Cutty Sark. He waited until Hawke opened his door then introduced himself. 'Commander Hawke, I'm Inspector Cale.' He looked as if he was uncertain whether or not to salute, but Hawke saved him the trouble and shook his hand.

'Good to meet you Inspector, have you been patched into the chase boat radio?'

Cale nodded. 'They've just called in, approaching Millwall South Dock now, about 200 yards behind the target. lights off, awaiting your command.'

Hawke returned his headset to the command vehicle and indicated the pier where three marked police cars were parked. 'Can I use your radio Inspector?'

'Of course.' Cale led the way and called ahead for one of his men to call the police launch.

Hawke took the mic offered to him. 'Tiger One to chase boat, you're clear to intercept the target.'

Susie and Nick had followed Hawke to the edge of the pier, they looked upriver and saw the piercing spotlight of the police boat stab through the darkness and pick out the launch it had been following since it passed under Blackfriars Bridge.

Hawke noted the spotlight with a satisfied look and spoke into the mic again. 'Tiger One to River Raptor, your target is lit. If they don't pull over before they get to the pier, you are authorised to open fire.'

'River Raptor to Tiger One, copy.'

The helicopter swooped over the river and switched on its powerful searchlight to pick out the target which maintained its cruise down the centre of the river. The helicopter took up position over the speeding police launch as it closed quickly on the target. The combined effect of the two pursuers' lights bathed the motor launch in artificial daylight.

The police launch caught its prey and pulled alongside.

Inside the launch, Kobzar became hysterical, he pushed the driver to one side and grabbed the wheel. He steered violently away from the police launch and pushed the throttle lever in an effort to extract more speed. He kept the boat turning through 180 degrees and it leaned at an angle it had never been designed for. It hit its own wake and lurched and bounced. The motions catapulted Lang Yazhu across the floor of the saloon and threw the driver from the wheelhouse.

The police launch had been designed for such manoeuvres and could turn tighter. Within seconds it was alongside again. A voice over the loud hailer ordered Kobzar to heave to. He had no intention of giving up and spun the wheel again, trying for another 180-degree turn. This time the police launch was ready for him and turned quicker, crossing behind him and coming alongside as he fought for control. While Kobzar kept his boat turning, the pilot of the police launch let his boat drift wide to collide with him. The impact jarred Kobzar from the wheel, he fell against the wall of the wheelhouse and lay dazed while the wheel spun back to the straight-ahead position and the boat, still at full throttle, headed directly for Greenwich Pier.

The pilot of the police launch saw what was about to happen and used his boat to nudge Kobzar's boat away from the Pier and towards the mudflats 100 yards further downstream.

It only took a few seconds for the boat to cover the distance and with the engine screaming it ran into the mud, slowed to a stop and tipped to one side

Kobzar dragged himself to his feet with difficulty and looked out the window of the cabin. He saw six armed police jogging towards him along the Thames footpath. He had nowhere to go. He glanced into the saloon and saw Lang Yazhu lying in a corner. She wasn't moving. The owner of the boat picked himself off the floor and switched the engine off.

In the silence that followed, Kobzar heard a shout. 'Armed police, come out with your hands above your head.'

41

Tuesday 2 January

Nick sat on the edge of the bed and gave Susie a gentle shake. 'Wake up sleepy head, you're in the news.'

Susie opened her eyes and blinked against the light. 'What time is it?'

'Almost eleven, you've been out like a light.'

Susie sat up and took the mug of coffee he'd brought her. 'What did you say about the news?'

'Check it out.' He nodded to the phone on her bedside cabinet.

Susie grabbed the handset and opened the BBC news app. She scrolled down for a moment, then stopped and read the headline. 'Special Forces Prevent Catastrophe.' She read on in silence and then looked up at Nick. 'It doesn't mention me anywhere.'

Nick nodded. 'They never mention people by name, but it refers to you, *"a female member of the team located the explosive device and called the bomb squad."*

Susie pulled a face. 'Huh, why let facts get in the way of a good story?'

'If they named you, you'd be hounded by the press and you'd have a target on your back the bad guys would be aiming at.'

'I suppose so. Does it mention anything about Kobzar and the woman in the boat with him?' Susie skimmed the article looking for any more details. 'What a surprise, nothing at all, just a few third-hand facts.'

Nick sympathised and waited until she'd finished reading, before he added. 'Hawke rang earlier. I told him you were still asleep and he said he'd call back when you were awake. He said he'd update us both together rather than telling me and me forgetting something when I told you.'

This appeared to galvanise Susie and she threw off the covers. 'Give me ten minutes to get showered and dressed and we can ring him from the kitchen.'

Nick took Susie's empty coffee mug. 'I'll go and set up the laptop. Just to warn you, he wants a video call.'

Susie groaned. 'Great. I'll have to smarten myself up a bit I suppose.'

***

Susie walked into the kitchen fifteen minutes later wearing a dark blue polo-neck jumper and jeans. Her hair was still wet from the shower and she tied it in a loose ponytail.

Nick sat at the breakfast bar facing the laptop. 'There's more coffee in the pot if you want it.'

'Thanks love, I'll wait until we've talked to Alex.'

At the mention of his name the laptop buzzed with an incoming video call. Nick clicked to accept it and Hawke's face filled the screen with a thumbnail image of Nick in the top left-hand corner. Susie squeezed in beside him. 'Morning Alex.'

They exchanged brief pleasantries, Hawke asked after them both and then adopted a more serious demeanour. 'I'm sure you've both seen the news?'

Susie and Nick nodded in unison.

'We tried to keep a lid on it, but you know what the press are like, they've cobbled together a story from what little they found out. At least we kept your name out of it.'

'Thanks for that.' Susie said, 'What can you tell us?'

'Kobzar's being held under the terrorism act, from what I've heard he's not saying much other than claiming it'll cause an International incident if he's not released.' Hawke rolled his eyes.

Susie leaned in. 'Have you discovered anything about the woman in the boat with him?'

Hawke nodded. 'She was called Lang Yazhu, CEO of a global telecoms business in Macau, called...' He looked down to consult a note. 'Guangsu. It's mandarin for lightspeed.'

Nick frowned. 'Should that mean anything to us?'

'No reason why it should, but a couple of years ago, they tendered for the UK 5G contract, spent a fortune on the bid and got turned down. According to the spooks at Victoria Cross, she took it badly and swore revenge.'

Susie picked up on Hawke's comment. 'You said *"was called"*, does that mean she's dead?'

Hawke nodded slowly. 'According to the medics, she was very frail and they think she was thrown about in the boat when Kobzar tried to escape. She broke her neck, it was enough to kill her.'

Susie shook her head. 'Bloody hell, it did look pretty bumpy from what we could see, but I never realised it was that bad.'

'And that's not all. I'm afraid our friend Miles Wilson didn't make it either. Despite your first aid efforts, he lost too much blood.'

Susie gasped and held her hand to her mouth. 'Oh my God. Does that mean I'm responsible?'

Hawke held a hand up. 'There will be an enquiry, of course. But considering what he was about to do, I think you will be exonerated.'

Nick put an arm around Susie's shoulders. 'Exonerated? She should get a bloody medal.'

'I agree. Don't dwell on it now. You did the right thing. In fact you did the only thing you could have done.'

Susie's face fell and she said nothing.

'On a brighter note,' Hawke attempted to raise her spirits. 'The immigration officials have interviewed Pia and discovered all her documents are in order and she has nothing to worry about. She's not going to be deported, in fact, as a result of what she's been through, she wants to retrain as a Counsellor'

'What about the boyfriend who kept her prisoner?' Nick asked.

'Yes. A very unpleasant young man.' Hawke's face was a mask of disdain. 'They operated on him but the bullet severed his spine. He'll never walk again. I wouldn't wish that on anyone but given the way he treated his girlfriend I might make an exception.'

Susie looked up and nodded. 'Rough justice eh?'

Hawke took a deep breath as if turning a page in the conversation. 'Which brings me to the last thing I wanted to talk to you both about.'

Susie and Nick exchanged glances.

'I've been asked to stay on at the Tactical Intelligence Group for another year.'

'That's great Alex, congratulations.' Susie said.

'Thanks, but what I wanted to know was if you would be interested in joining the team. I know you were embedded with Rob's unit at Warrenford, but you've proved to me you've got skills I could use.'

Susie was taken aback. 'Err, wow, thanks Alex. That's a bolt out of the blue. What role are you thinking?'

Hawke spread his hands. 'Up to you. You've seen the operation, you've met most of the team, you know what we do. Have a think about it and let me know in a day or two.'

A broad smile spread across Susie's face. 'I will. An offer like that doesn't come along very often. I'll call you before the end of the week.'

THE END

Many thanks

Setting out to write a book takes a degree of commitment and once started requires constant motivation, inspiration and perspiration. Getting the the end involves the support of family, friends and experts in their field who are prepared to take the time to make suggestions, point out plot holes and give honest feedback. To all those I am forever grateful and appreciate their patience.

The Author

Duncan Robb has loved thrillers for more years than he cares to admit or remember. Like many readers the idea of writing a novel swirled around in his head for many years before putting pen to paper in the early 00's. Before that Duncan's writing had been non-fiction where as General Secretary of the British Triathlon Association back in the 1980's he'd produced a monthly newsletter that led to the creation of 220 The Triathlon Magazine, still going strong almost 40 years later.

While still taking part in the occasional triathlon, Duncan moved into the events industry where as a full time photographer, he focused (no pun intended) on the conferences and exhibition market. His experiences proved a fruitful source of inspiration for his first book – Sharp Focus – and the creation of Susie Jones, former Royal Military Police turned investigative journalist and passionate triathlete.

Duncan lives in rural Derbyshire with his wife Frances, they have six children and at the last count, nine grandchildren.

If you would like to be kept up to date with news about forthcoming books, please visit the website: duncanrobbauthor.com

Also by

Sharp Focus – Susie Jones Investigates – Book One – available here

Susie Jones, investigative journalist, passionate triathlete and former Red Cap, discovers an illegal operation to distribute dangerous and unlicensed diet pills.

Her determination to expose those behind the campaign puts her life on the line and she finds herself up against a rogue chemist, a corrupt politician and ruthless criminals who'll stop at nothing to prevent her getting to the truth.□

As Susie digs deeper she unearths an even greater threat and is faced with a tense race across international boundaries to prevent a sinister attack with personal consequences.

The first book in the **Susie Jones Investigates** series - shortlisted for the 2022 Lindisfarne Prize for Crime and Thriller fiction.

Joint Force – How Susie & Nick first met – a free short story available here

It all started here. A chance encounter, a mutual goal and a bond created.

Printed in Great Britain
by Amazon

56203157R00205